New York Times **bestselling author**
Kerrelyn Sparks's novels are:

"An absolute delight!"
> —Lynsay Sands, *USA Today* bestselling author

"Full of vulnerability and tenderness . . . rich romance."
> —*Publishers Weekly*

"Mixed paranormal romance with humor . . . Sparks clearly
has a style all her own, one that readers love."
> —*USA Today*'s Happily Ever After blog

"Infuse[d] with deliciously sharp wit . . . wickedly fun."
> —*Booklist*

"Stellar . . . excellent storytelling."   —*RT Book Reviews*

Also by
Kerrelyn Sparks

SO I MARRIED A SORCERER
HOW TO TAME A BEAST IN SEVEN DAYS

Eight Simple Rules for Dating a Dragon

Kerrelyn Sparks

St. Martin's Paperbacks

EIGHT SIMPLE RULES FOR DATING A DRAGON

Copyright © 2018 by Kerrelyn Sparks.

All rights reserved.

For information address St. Martin's Press, 175 Fifth Avenue, New York, NY 10010.

ISBN: 978-1-250-10825-8

Our books may be purchased in bulk for promotional, educational, or business use. Please contact your local bookseller or the Macmillan Corporate and Premium Sales Department at 1-800-221-7945, ext. 5442, or by e-mail at MacmillanSpecialMarkets@macmillan.com.

Printed in the United States of America

St. Martin's Paperbacks edition / April 2018

St. Martin's Paperbacks are published by St. Martin's Press, 175 Fifth Avenue, New York, NY 10010.

10 9 8 7 6 5 4 3 2 1

For my own adopted sisters—
MJ Selle, Vicky Yelton, and Sandy Weider,
Bestest best friends, critique partners,
quality control experts,
And all around wonder women.
Consider yourselves Embraced.

Acknowledgments

❧

With the completion of another longer-than-usual book, I am once again relieved and grateful that my publisher, St. Martin's Press, never hesitates to allow me all the room I need in order to tell a story. My sincere thanks to everyone at St. Martin's, including Jennifer Enderlin, Brant, Alexandra, Marissa, Brittani, Jordan, the art department, the lovely ladies at Heroes and Heartbreakers, and everyone else working behind the scenes to make my books shine. A special thank-you to my new editor, Monique Patterson, for loving this series and for so graciously taking me on.

I am always grateful to my dear friend and literary agent, Michelle Grajkowski of Three Seas, for continuing to watch over me. My critique partners/best friends are listed in the dedication, for they are always there for me with encouragement, love, and even tough love, whenever I need a swift kick in the pants. My husband and children are a never-ending supply of love and support. Special thanks go to my husband/best friend/tax man/road manager, who keeps me laughing and is always on the lookout for Brody in whichever form he may have adopted.

And finally, I owe a huge debt of gratitude to my readers

and booksellers/librarians for Embracing the new series. To me, you are also Embraced, because lending your support to an author is your awesome power. Thanks to you, the magical world of Aerthlan can continue to flourish.

Eight Simple Rules for Dating a Dragon

AERTHLAN

Rupert's
Island

Great Western Ocean

Lourdon

Isle of Mist

Isle of Moon

Convent of the
Two Moons

Ebton

Ebport

Danport

Ronsmouth

Ron

Isle of Secrets

N

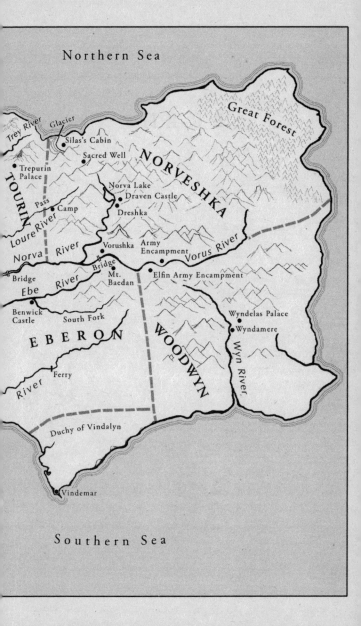

Prologue

❧

In another time on another world called Aerthlan, there are five kingdoms. Four of the kingdoms extend across a vast continent. For centuries, these countries have been ravaged by war.

The fifth kingdom consists of two islands in the Great Western Ocean. These are the Isles of Moon and Mist. The island people worship the twin moons in the night sky. Several villages exist on the Isle of Moon, but there is only one inhabitant on the small Isle of Mist—the Seer.

Twice a year, the two moons eclipse or, as the people call it, embrace. Any child born when the moons embrace will be gifted with a magical power. These children are called the Embraced, and traditionally, the kings on the mainland have sought to kill them. Some of the Embraced infants are sent secretly to the Isle of Moon, where they will be safe.

For as long as anyone can remember, the Seer repeated his dire prediction of war, destruction, and despair. But not anymore. Now he claims a wave of change is sweeping across Aerthlan, a change that will bring peace to a world that has known violence for too long. And that change is happening because of five young women from the fifth kingdom.

The women were hidden away as infants on the Isle of Moon, and there, they grew up as sisters. The oldest, Luciana, now rules over Eberon with her husband, King Leofric. Brigitta reigns over Tourin with her husband, King Ulfrid, also known as the infamous pirate Rupert.

Three sisters remain: Gwennore, Sorcha, and Maeve. They know nothing of their families. Nothing of their past.

They only know they are Embraced.

Chapter One

❦

Gwennore was ready to scream.

But if she did, others might hear and foil her escape. What could she do but continue her climb up the hillside, even though she felt as if she were falling into a dark pit.

She was a storm on the verge of breaking. An overfilled wineskin about to burst. A sizzling pot threatening to boil over. *Luna and Lessa, help me*, she sent up in fervent prayer to the twin moon goddesses.

Maybe she should learn to curse like her sister Sorcha. But the ever-rational part of Gwennore's brain reminded her that it was more sensible to do what she always did. Remain calm. Eviana was beside her, and it would be a shame to expose an innocent child to foul language. The little girl was only three years old. Today.

"Gwennie?" Eviana tugged on her hand. "What's wong?"

Gwennore forced a smile. "Nothing. Everything is perfectly fine."

Eviana scrunched up her little nose with a dubious look.

The child was far too insightful, Gwennore thought,

even though it was one of the things she loved about the little girl. "Shall we rest a moment to catch our breath?" When Eviana nodded, Gwennore glanced down the hill at the encampment along the Norva River.

Tonight was the Spring Embrace, when the two moons would align in the sky, and that meant a number of Gwennore's family and friends would be celebrating their birthdays. Her oldest adopted sister, Luciana, now the queen of Eberon, would be twenty-three, and her twins, Eric and Eviana, were turning three. Sorcha, just six months younger than Gwennore, would be twenty-one. The king of Tourin was turning twenty-nine. Ulfrid was his real name, but his wife, Brigitta, still preferred to call him Rupert.

And there were even more reasons to celebrate. Brigitta and Ulfrid had brought their little boy, Reynfrid, for everyone to see. The general of the Tourinian army, Stefan Landers, and his wife, Lady Fallyn, had traveled with them. Gwennore had been delighted to see the former nun again and meet her adorable two-year-old daughter. And more babies were on the way, since Luciana, Brigitta, and Fallyn were all expecting.

With so much to be thankful for, Luciana and Brigitta had teamed up to plan a huge party on the banks of the Norva River, which served as the border for their two countries. On the northern side of the river, in the country of Tourin, there had to be at least fifty tents set up.

On the southern bank of the Norva, the Eberoni had erected even more tents. On both sides of the river, meat was being roasted over large pits, and food was being prepared. People bustled back and forth over the bridge, a comforting reminder of the peaceful and relaxed relationship between the two countries. After all, the two queens, Luciana and Brigitta, considered themselves sisters.

Unfortunately, those same two women were competing

with each other to see who could arrange marriages for the three remaining sisters. It was ridiculous. Gwennore was happy for Luciana and Brigitta, truly she was, but just because they were happily married, that didn't mean it could happen for her.

For the last few years, Gwennore's level of frustration had been slowly escalating. How could she tell her older sisters that they were wasting their time and money giving her beautiful gowns? The noblemen at the Eberoni and Tourinian courts wanted nothing to do with her. No matter how well she was dressed, she was still an elf.

She doubted her sisters would ever understand, for they had always considered her as one of them. The five young women had grown up at the convent, surrounded by love, so it had come as a hard blow when Gwennore had realized that people on the mainland saw her differently. All the love and acceptance to which she was accustomed was gone. To the people of Eberon and Tourin, she didn't belong.

With her white-blond hair, lavender-blue eyes, and pointed ears, it was obvious she hailed from the elfin kingdom of Woodwyn. But for some unknown reason, the elves there had rejected Gwennore and sent her as a babe to the Isle of Moon. She had no memory of Woodwyn and no recollection of ever meeting another elf. What little she knew about them and their language had been learned in the convent when she'd transcribed a few of their books. She felt sure she would never fit in there.

Just as she could never feel at home in the countries of Eberon or Tourin. The only place she had felt truly comfortable was the convent on the Isle of Moon.

But that had changed after Luciana had given birth. Gwennore had found two sanctuaries at Ebton Palace—the vast library where she could hide in a curtained-off window seat and escape with a good book, and the nursery, where there was no need to hide or escape. There, she was free to be herself.

The twins had grown up with Gwennore, loving her just as her adopted sisters had at the convent. It was Eviana, though, with whom Gwennore felt a special bond. From the moment the little girl was born, Gwennore had been drawn to her. She loved her with a maternal fierceness that gave her enough joy that she remained at the palace in spite of the prejudice she encountered from other courtiers.

The main problem, as far as she could see, was that no one understood the elves. They attacked Eberon to the west and Norveshka to the north, streaming across the borders to kill and maim, then retreating without bothering to claim any plunder or land. Since they didn't seem to want anything, other than the pleasure of killing a few people, they had a reputation of being coldhearted and vicious.

So what man in his right mind would want to marry Gwennore? The fact that she'd been raised in a convent to abhor violence didn't seem to matter. Nor the fact that she prided herself on her ability to remain calm and rational. She was intelligent enough to converse in all four mainland languages, yet she was still regarded as some sort of violent creature that might go on a killing spree at the drop of a hat.

A month ago, Luciana had planned an elaborate ball at Ebton Palace. Noblemen had flocked around Sorcha and Maeve, as well they should, since they were both beautiful young women. Usually at these events, the only men willing to dance with Gwennore were Luciana's friends Brody and the newly promoted Colonel Nevis Harden. But Nevis was usually away with the army, and

Brody was a shifter, who could take human form for only two hours a day. Gwennore and her younger sisters had been shocked when Luciana had revealed the truth about Brody, but now Gwennore was accustomed to seeing him in his usual guise as a furry black-and-white dog.

At this particular ball, Luciana had invited two young earls, with the hope that they would fall for her sisters. The two earls had found Gwennore, half hidden behind a column, and after looking her over, they had smirked and talked to each other as if she weren't there.

"Maybe she's part fox," one had muttered. "Could be why she has those pointed ears."

The second earl nodded. "I wonder if she's hiding a tail beneath her skirts."

The first one snorted. "Who on Aerthlan would be willing to find out?"

"Maybe the Seer would have a go at her," his companion replied. "I hear the old man is blind. And he's lived alone for decades. He must be desperate."

The first earl snickered as he looked Gwennore over once again. "No one could be that desperate."

Gwennore's cheeks had flared hot. "Leave me be, or I'll tell the king and queen how rude ye are."

They had looked worried for a few seconds before the first one lifted his chin in defiance. "The king needs the support of us nobles. He doesn't need the likes of you." And with that, the two had sauntered off to enjoy the ball.

"Shall I clobber them for you?" Brody whispered as he came around the column.

He had heard. Gwennore's face burned even hotter. Of course he had heard. As a spy, Brody was accustomed to eavesdropping on private conversations.

"Come on, let me punch them," Brody growled. "They deserve it."

Gwennore shook her head. "Luciana has worked too hard to make this ball a success. I don't want to ruin it with a brawl."

Brody frowned. "She needs to know that she's matchmaking with a pair of assholes."

"I'll warn Sorcha and Maeve," Gwennore whispered. "That will be enough. I don't want to cause any more political problems for Luciana and Leo." They were still having enough trouble with a traitorous group of disgruntled priests led by Lord Morris.

Brody scowled at the two earls. "As soon as I shift, I'm going to bite them." He gave Gwennore a wry look. "And no one can stop me, because I'm a naughty doggy who never passed obedience training."

That had made her smile.

"That's more like it." Brody smiled back as he leaned against the column. "Did you want to dance again?"

"Ye've already done yer duty with me and Sorcha. Ye should dance with Maeve now."

His smile turned into a grimace. "No. Hell, no. Not as long as she persists in calling me Julia."

Gwennore's laugh abruptly ended when she spotted one of the earls talking to Maeve. "Oh, dear."

A growl sounded low in Brody's throat.

"Are ye planning to shift now?" Gwennore whispered.

"Considering it," Brody muttered. "I can either stay human and insist she dance with me, or become a dog and bite the bastard."

"Or ye could become a dog and dance with two left feet," Gwennore teased him.

Brody snorted. "I can do that while still human." He strode toward the earl and Maeve, and Gwennore had waited to make sure her youngest sister was safe before escaping back to the nursery.

But now that she was here on the Norva River, there

was no library or nursery where she could hide. Her hope of enjoying the celebration surrounded by only family and friends was gone, for Luciana and Brigitta had both invited a number of single noblemen. And just a few minutes ago, the infamous two earls had shown up.

"I can't stand it anymore," Gwennore whispered as tears filled her eyes. If she had to endure one more man eyeing her like she was some sort of loathsome insect, she might explode like a screeching demon from hell.

The only solution to her problem, as far as she could tell, would be to return to the Convent of the Two Moons. Mother Ginessa and the nuns would welcome her. She would be loved there. But then she would have to go for months without seeing her adopted sisters or this little girl she loved so much.

"I can't stand, too." Eviana lifted her chubby arms in the air, her signal that she wanted to be held.

With a smile, Gwennore picked her up. With the little girl's arms wrapped around her neck, she closed her eyes to keep the tears from flowing. This was why she stayed.

But as much as she cherished moments like this that made her heart swell with love, she was always aware of an underlying twinge of heartache. For she had no doubt that this was as close as she would ever get to motherhood.

How could she give this up? No, she would stay at Ebton Palace to be with the twins. And when Luciana gave birth in three months, Gwennore would be there to help with the newborn. Twenty months ago, she'd gone to Lourdon to help Brigitta with her baby boy.

This was her life. Always the helpful one, moving silently like a ghost through the shadows of the royal palace and only coming to life in the nursery. Or her own imagination. For she still dreamed of a world where she could shine. It would be a beautiful world, filled with wonder and excitement. And a tall and handsome stranger would love her for who she was.

"When do we see the fwowers?"

Eviana's question pulled her back to the real world. A world where she was using a flower-picking expedition to evade scornful glances and crude insults.

Gwennore sighed. Why waste her time wishing for the impossible? This was reality, and she should accept it and make the most of it. "We'll see the flowers soon. There's a whole field of them on top of the hill."

She shifted the little girl onto her left hip, then held up her long silk skirt with her right hand to climb the last remaining steps. "I spotted them from the carriage window when we were arriving yesterday."

"I can give some to Mama?"

Gwennore nodded. "She'll think it's the best birthday present ever."

Eviana grinned. "Ewic won't have fwowers for her."

"Maybe we should pick some for him, too."

Eviana scrunched up her little nose. "He poked me."

"Did ye tell him to stop?"

She shook her head. "I poked him back."

Gwennore snorted. "Do ye have a present for yer brother? 'Tis his birthday, too, ye know."

Eviana bit her lip while she considered, and the movement made her look so much like her mother that Gwennore smiled. The little girl had her mother's black curly hair, but her green eyes had come from her father.

"I don't think Ewic wants fwowers," Eviana mumbled.

"Ye make a good point," Gwennore said. "We'll have to find something more suitable for a boy. Maybe a walking stick from the forest or a pretty rock from the riverbank."

"A *big* wock!" Eviana stretched her arms wide.

"All right." Gwennore took a deep breath as she

reached the top of the hill. The winter snow had melted over a month ago, and now the afternoon sun shone on a carpet of bright-green grass dotted with flowers of yellow, orange, and purple. "Well, what do ye think?"

Eviana gasped. "It's bootiful!" She squirmed to be let down, then rushed about plucking flowers.

Gwennore watched her for a moment, then glanced back toward the encampment by the river. Kegs of beer and wine had already been opened, and the sound of laughter blew toward her on a breeze. She spotted the two kings, Leofric and Ulfrid, trying to teach their sons, Eric and Reynfrid, how to skip stones across the river. Her adopted sisters were busy overseeing the cooking. Luciana spotted her with Eviana and waved.

Gwennore waved back, then settled on a grassy spot to watch the little girl. A shadow moved across the ground, and she glanced up at the cloudless sky. A large bird was flying high overhead.

Her eyes narrowed. An extremely large bird. Was it Brody in eagle form, watching over them? She looked down at the camp and spotted Brody as a dog, following the two nasty earls and nipping at their heels.

She glanced back at the bird, but it was too far away and the sun was too bright for her to see clearly. Surely it couldn't be the Chameleon. No one knew the mysterious shifter's real name or what he even looked like, but since he apparently had the ability to change into any animal or human, Brody had dubbed him the Chameleon.

After causing so much trouble three years ago, the villainous Chameleon had disappeared. Brody had searched high and low for him to no avail.

"Look, Gwennie!" Eviana ran toward her with a big bunch of flowers in her hands. "Awen't they pwetty?"

"Oh, they're lovely!" Gwennore pulled the blue ribbon from the end of her braided ponytail and used it to tie the bouquet together. "There. Perfect. I think ye should pick some flowers for Aunt Sorcha. 'Tis her birthday, too."

"All wight!" Eviana bounced away.

Gwennore lifted her face to the warm sun, closed her eyes, and took a deep breath. Life was good, she reminded herself. Two of her sisters had become queens, and now the countries of Eberon and Tourin were at peace. The Seer had predicted even more peace, so Mother Ginessa had finally relented and allowed Gwennore and her younger sisters to leave the Isle of Moon and live on the mainland. The other two countries, Norveshka and Woodwyn, still caused trouble every now and then, but they seemed far away now.

A screech echoed in the distance, and she opened her eyes. That hadn't sounded like an eagle. Whatever it was, way up high in the sky, it seemed to be circling. An ominous feeling crept under her skin, and suddenly she recalled the way Luciana had looked last night when Maeve had suggested they play the Game of Stones.

"We're all together again," Maeve had said when Brigitta had joined them. "We should bring out the Telling Stones, so ye can predict our futures."

Luciana had grown pale. "I'm too weary from travel. Perhaps another time."

Gwennore hadn't missed the worried glance Luciana had exchanged with Brigitta. They'd looked the same way almost three years ago when Luciana had selected a handful of Telling Stones to predict Gwennore's future. Luciana had completely avoided playing the game since then, and Gwennore couldn't help but feel that her oldest sister had seen something that had frightened her.

Green, brown, and the number three. Those were the pebbles Luciana had picked for Gwennore. To Maeve and Sorcha, the interpretation had been obvious. The colors signified the country of Woodwyn, since the elfin flag pictured a tall green tree growing from brown earth.

But Luciana was the one with the gift of foresight, and she had declined to agree with them. She'd also failed to explain the number three, even though Sorcha had claimed it meant Gwennore would meet a tall and handsome stranger in three months.

That hadn't happened, of course. Not that Gwennore had expected it. With her rational mind, she preferred to believe that people were responsible for making their own future. Still, she had to wonder what the three meant.

Three. Today Eric and Eviana were turning three. Gwennore glanced at the camp as the feeling of foreboding grew more intense. Was whatever Luciana feared going to happen today?

"Gwennie!" Eviana wrenched her out of her thoughts by shoving a plant in her face. "Look at the funny fwower."

"Oh, I know this." Gwennore set aside Luciana's bouquet of flowers to take the new plant. Instead of flower petals, it was topped with a sphere of white fluff. "'Tis called a puffball. We grow them at the convent, because we can use the leaves to make medicine."

Eviana wrinkled her nose as she studied it. "I've never seen one before."

"That's because the gardeners at Ebton Palace consider it a weed and pull it out."

"Why?" Eviana pushed out her bottom lip. "Why is it bad? I think it's pwetty."

Gwennore sighed, feeling a sudden kinship to the plant that wasn't welcome in most gardens. "There's a saying that if ye make a wish afore blowing on the puffball, then yer wish will come true."

"Weally?" Eviana's eyes lit up.

Gwennore nodded. As she gazed at the ball of white

fluff, she thought about wishing for that magical world where the tall and handsome stranger was waiting for her. But what were the chances of that actually happening? It made more sense to wish for something that could possibly come true. A long and happy life for Eviana and Eric.

"I'm weady!" the little girl announced.

"Me, too!" Gwennore took a big breath and started to gently blow.

Eviana huffed and puffed, spitting more than blowing, then giggled as white florets detached from the flower head and floated away on a breeze. "We did it!" She danced about. "Guess what I wished for!"

"Ye shouldn't say, or it won't come—"

"I wished you not be sad."

Gwennore stiffened. Good goddesses, was she so obvious that even a three-year-old could tell? "Ye think I'm sad?"

Eviana nodded. "'Cause we get pwesents, and you don't. But I'll give you some fwowers, too."

Gwennore smiled. "That's very sweet of you, but ye needn't worry. My birthday will happen in the fall at the Autumn Embrace. I have the same birthday as yer papa. And Brigitta, Maeve, and Brody."

"Weally?"

"Yes. Really."

Eviana clapped her hands together. "Then we can have another party?"

Gwennore nodded. "Now let's get some flowers for Sorcha, so we can head back to camp."

"All wight!" Eviana skipped away, stopping every now and then to pluck a flower.

A large shadow swept over them, and Gwennore glanced up. *Good goddesses!* Her heart lurched.

Dragon.

She scrambled to her feet. What was a Norveshki

dragon doing here? Was that what had been circling them? Why would it be interested in her? *Not me.* Icy-cold terror crept into Gwennore's bones, freezing her for a few seconds. *Eviana.* Dragons were known for kidnapping small children.

With a shriek, the dragon swooshed down. Fire burst from its mouth and hit the ground, creating a wall of fire between the hill and the encampment. Heavenly goddesses, it was cutting them off!

"Eviana!" Gwennore dashed toward the little girl. She would grab her and run for the nearby forest. There, the larger trees could shelter them from the dragon's view.

Eviana's eyes grew wide with terror, and the flowers tumbled from her hand. She turned and ran. Away from the forest.

"Nay!" Gwennore struggled to catch up with her.

The dragon swooped down.

Gwennore heard the beating of its wings and its breath huffing just above her head. She reached out a hand to grab Eviana, but the dragon shoved her with its powerful back legs, flattening her facedown on the ground. She barely caught her breath before she saw the talons of the dragon's forelegs curl around Eviana.

With a squeal, the little girl squirmed.

"Eviana!" Gwennore scooted forward on her elbows while the dragon hovered a few inches above her. She seized its talons and attempted to pull them back. But they only tightened, digging into Eviana's skin till beads of blood blossomed on the girl's white dress.

"Stop it!" Gwennore cried. "Ye're hurting her!"

Whoosh, whoosh. The air around them stirred as the dragon beat its long, black wings.

It was going to take off! Gwennore frantically yanked at its talons, but it enveloped the little girl in its forelegs and pulled her tight against its smooth chest.

A bolt of lightning struck the ground just as the dragon rose in the air. Leo was attacking. The ground beneath Gwennore trembled from the impact, and a booming noise deafened her ears.

The dragon rose high enough for her to gain her footing. A sudden blast of wind shoved the dragon to the side, causing it to collide with her and knock her back down. That had to be Brigitta's husband, using his wind power to attack.

As the dragon struggled to regain its equilibrium, she scrambled to her feet and grasped one of the creature's forelegs to try to keep it from flying away. If the two kings succeeded in frightening the dragon enough that it released Eviana, she would fall, and it would be dangerous for her to fall more than a few feet.

A second lightning strike ripped past them, then another one, dangerously close to the dragon's head. The air sizzled with energy, buzzing in Gwennore's ears.

With a screech, the dragon shot up into the air. Gwennore gasped as she was pulled off the ground. Her arms strained, and panic threatened to overwhelm her. Should she let go? *No!* She couldn't leave Eviana alone.

Higher and higher, the dragon rose. The people below grew smaller, their screams more distant. The Norva River was now a blue ribbon, winding through a miniature forest. Luna and Lessa help her! If she lost her grip, she would plummet to her death.

Another bolt of lightning streaked past them, and she cringed. Poor Leo! He had to be frantic, but what could he do? If he hit the dragon directly, the shock would kill his daughter. And if Ulfrid used his wind power to make the dragon crash into the ground, Eviana would die.

"Gwennie," Eviana whimpered.

"I'm here!" Gwennore's arms burned. How long would

her strength last? How long could she hold on with this fierce grip before her hands began to cramp?

Don't think about it. She hissed in a breath between clenched teeth. She had no choice. Letting go would mean death. Letting go would leave Eviana unprotected. "I won't leave you."

A squawk sounded in the distance, and she spotted an eagle following them. Brody. *Thank you.* She wasn't alone.

But could she hold on all the way to Norveshka? If only there was a way to reason—

Of course! If the dragons worked for the Norveshki army, then that meant they were able to follow orders. They had to understand the Norveshki language.

"Can you hear me?" she yelled in Norveshki. "You must return us immediately!"

No answer, but then how could a dragon reply?

She raised her voice. "You have kidnapped a princess! She's the daughter of the king and queen of Eberon and the niece of the queen of Tourin. Those countries will declare war on Norveshka! They will attack you!"

The dragon made an angry huffing noise.

"Return us now!" Gwennore screamed. "Return us or hundreds of Norveshki will die. Take us back now!"

Do as she says, brother.

Gwennore flinched as a deep male voice reverberated in her head. Who—what was that?

No, another male voice answered.

She gasped. There were voices in her head? And they were arguing? Goddesses help her, she had to be losing her mind. She twisted in the air, looking around.

Another dragon! It was coming from Norveshka and flying straight toward them.

Is it true what the woman says? the deeper voice asked. *Have you taken a princess?*

The queen needs a princess, the other one replied.

She was hearing the dragons, Gwennore realized with a shock. The voices were speaking Norveshki, and there was no one else around, other than Brody, who was far behind.

This is a mistake, brother. You must return the child, the deeper voice insisted.

That had to be the newcomer. "He's right!" Gwennore yelled. "It's a terrible mistake. Take us back now!"

Silence.

Was it just her imagination, or had she felt the muscles in the dragon's foreleg flinch? The dragon that was carrying her and Eviana had grown tense.

She heard us, he hissed. *The damned elf can hear us!*

Stay calm, the newcomer urged him.

No! The dragon shot straight up into the sky.

Gwennore cried out, struggling to keep her grip. The wind buffeted against her, threatening to tear her loose. Good goddesses, the dragon was trying to kill her!

"Gwennie," Eviana whimpered.

"I'm here!" Tears stung Gwennore's eyes as the ache in her shoulders and hands became more agonizing.

The dragon went into a series of rolls.

As Gwennore was tossed about, one of her hands slipped loose. *No! Luna and Lessa, help me!* The dragon used his back legs to kick her loose.

Down, down, she was falling. *Dear goddesses, am I going to die?* The wind rushed past her ears, mingling with the little girl's screams. *Eviana. I wanted to protect you.*

Something dark blocked her vision, then *bam!* She struck something so hard, it knocked the breath out of her.

Stunned, she was unable to think for a moment. Then, with a rush, her mind raced. She was still alive. Black, leathery legs held her suspended in the air.

The other dragon had caught her. He'd saved her life. *Thank the goddesses!*

But why? Why would a dragon save her? What did he want with her? She lifted her gaze to his smooth gray chest, then higher to his long neck, covered with black scales. His head was frightening. Black horns sprouted from the thick, knotted ridge across his brow. His long snout ended with flaring nostrils, and his jaw looked strong enough to crush bones.

Whoosh, whoosh. The air around her billowed as the dragon beat his leathery wings and rose higher in the sky. Where was he taking her? What if he decided to drop her? She wrapped her arms around his foreleg.

Be still. He bent his long neck, angling his head downward so he could study her with gleaming gold eyes.

I have you.

Chapter Two

❧

Gwennore did grow still. The way the dragon was staring at her was so fierce, she wondered if he could stop his prey from escaping by simply locking his sights on him.

Power. Strength. Those qualities were to be expected with a ferocious creature like this, but she sensed more than that. A high level of intelligence. And a feeling that he saw more than she wanted him to.

Once again, she was being examined as if she were a strange species of insect. Earlier, she had decided to unleash her rage on the next male who did that, but her tirade would have to wait. It would be foolish to verbally assault a fire-breathing dragon. Especially one that could kill her by simply dropping her.

Are you all right?

The dragon's voice slipped into her mind like a lullaby. How could he look so strong, yet sound so gentle?

Were you harmed in any way?

She shook her head.

How is it you are able to hear me? Do other elves have this ability?

"I-I don't know." Was that why he had saved her life?

Because he was curious about a strange ability she possessed? Did that mean he would have let her die if she couldn't hear him? Did he believe that was the only thing that made her worthy of being saved?

Dammit. She allowed herself to curse. Why not, when she was in the middle of a nightmare, completely at the mercy of a frightful dragon? She glanced back at him and discovered he was still staring at her. Blast him.

"You should watch where you are going," she fussed at him. "You could run into a tree. Or a mountain."

As the dragon looked away, she had a bizarre feeling that he was amused. *Stop imagining things.* If she was going to survive and protect Eviana, she needed to face reality.

It seemed fairly certain that they were on their way to Norveshka. The first dragon was still holding Eviana in his clutches. Her dragon—she didn't know what else to call him, but he was definitely not hers—seemed to be focused now on catching up with the first.

While her dragon increased his speed, strong winds buffeted against her, causing her ears to ache. Her hair unraveled from its braid, and tendrils whisked across her face. Cold air shot through her thin silk gown, chilling her to the bone. So cold. How high were they?

She ventured a look down. Good goddesses! She squeezed her arms around her dragon's foreleg. They were so high, the trees appeared no bigger than ants. *Don't look down!*

She quickly shifted her gaze to the first dragon and wondered how Eviana was doing. Was she freezing to death? Would she be traumatized for the rest of her life?

And how was Brody? She leaned to one side then the other, trying to catch a glimpse of him in eagle form, but the dragon's chest was too wide for a clear view.

Stop squirming. The shifter is still behind us.

Her breath caught. The dragon knew about Brody? "He's a friend. Please do not hurt him."

The dragon made no reply, but snorted a puff of hot air from his nostrils.

She'd annoyed him. Not a smart thing to do when he could drop her. She cleared her throat. "I suppose I should thank you."

I suppose you should.

His wry tone pricked at her. Did he think her manners were lacking? That was rich when dragons went around kidnapping small children.

Another puff of hot air. *And I should apologize for my brother's actions. I will make sure the child is safely returned.*

"Thank you!" Praise the goddesses! She could only hope and pray that this dragon would be trustworthy. So far, he seemed somewhat civilized. She'd always thought of dragons as frightening, destructive creatures that burned down villages and terrorized the innocent. And the rumors about them were even more horrendous. Some people claimed the dragons stole children so they could feast on them.

The dragon's talons suddenly flinched.

She winced as the sharp points dug into her skin. "Too tight!"

Sorry. His talons retracted a bit. *Crosswind.*

The wind seemed the same to her. A terrible thought jumped into her mind. Had he heard what she was thinking? She was hearing him, so what if it worked both ways? Oh, dear goddesses, no!

Her heart raced. Nay, it couldn't be true. That would be too horrendous! But wait. If the dragon only knew Norveshki, all she had to do was keep thinking in Eberoni. That would keep her thoughts private, wouldn't it?

But how could she tell for sure? Maybe she should mentally call him a rude name, like *filthy bastard*, to see if he reacted. No, bad idea. If she made him angry, he might drop her. *Oh, no! What if he understood all that?*

She tightened her grip on his foreleg. *Stop thinking about him!*

Once again she sensed amusement. Dammit. There was no way she could stop herself from thinking. And she had to stay mentally alert if she was going to protect Eviana.

Your name is Gwennie?

He must have heard Eviana screaming her name. "My name is Gwennore and the little girl is Eviana."

Gwennore.

A shiver ran along her skin. A dragon shouldn't have such an appealing voice. She winced. Had he heard that?

She glanced toward his head. She'd been wrong, thinking all his scales were black. When the sun shone on him, his scales glistened an iridescent purple and green.

It reminded her of a black pearl she'd once found in an oyster shell. She'd thought it was so beautiful she'd kept it in her small treasure box, along with a few gifts her sisters had given her. Dear goddesses, would she ever see them again?

You will, she promised herself. For she had to make sure Eviana was returned to her parents. Would this dragon keep his word and help her? If he didn't, how on Aerthlan would she manage to get Eviana home?

Anxiety threatened to consume her, so she tried to calm herself by mentally picturing her small treasure box and the gifts inside: an embroidered handkerchief from Luciana, a short story from Brigitta, a pretty shell from Maeve, and a small drawing of her from Sorcha.

The dragon's talons suddenly tightened, jerking her

back to the grim reality around her. She eyed the creature warily. Did she dare trust him?

Brigitta had told her sisters about her encounter with dragons, and she'd called them magnificent. She claimed that they had helped her husband take back his throne.

But what about all the children who had been kidnapped? Were some dragons bad and others good? Was this a good one? Gwennore had to hope so. Her and Eviana's lives might depend on it. "Do you have a name?"

Yes.

She waited, but there was nothing more, only that same feeling of amusement she kept getting. Was he playing with her? Blast him. "If you won't tell me, I'll be forced to name you myself."

Oh, I'm afraid.

"You should be. I could name you . . . Puff."

He snorted, and more hot air escaped his nostrils.

"Was that a huff?" She smiled to herself. "Or a puff?"

I could drop you.

She squeezed his leg, pressing her face against the leathery skin. It was surprisingly soft.

But I won't.

Oh, he was definitely playing with her. She was tempted to hit him. "Tell me, Puff. Why did you bother to save me if you won't even introduce yourself to me?"

I took pity on the trees. Your fall would have torn off some branches.

She slapped his leg. "That's not funny."

Did you just hit me? After I saved you?

She winced. "It was a friendly pat. Did I mention how grateful I am that you rescued me? It would be a shame to harm any of the trees, don't you think?"

A low grumbling sound reverberated through her mind. Was that a dragon chuckle? It had a very pleasant and soothing effect, even though she ought to be peeved that he found her so entertaining.

I could take you back to your friends, but I'm assuming you wish to remain with the little girl.

"That is correct. I must stay with Eviana."

There was a moment of silence before he replied, *She is not your child. Why did you risk your life for her?*

"Her mother, Luciana, is like a sister to me." Gwennore didn't want to mention that Eviana was probably as close as she would ever have to a daughter of her own. But then an alarming thought struck her. If she hadn't run away to avoid those two nasty earls, if she hadn't taken Eviana with her, then the little girl wouldn't be in so much danger right now.

Tears stung her eyes. "This is my fault."

No. It is my brother who took her.

"I gave him the opportunity." Dammit, she should have been stronger. She should have slapped those earls and stood up for herself. By acting like a victim, she'd allowed herself to become one. And poor Eviana was paying the price for it.

Guilt wrenched at her heart. How could she let strangers insult her and strip away her humanity? They didn't know who she really was. But she should know her own worth. Her sisters knew her worth. Even Eviana knew.

She blinked away her tears. "I will not leave Eviana's side. I will do whatever I must to protect her."

There was a pause that stretched out for so long, she thought the dragon had forgotten about her. But then, a soft whisper wafted across her mind, so gentle she wasn't sure she'd actually heard it.

Loyal and brave. The dragon's forelegs curled around her like arms, drawing her close to his smooth gray chest.

"What are you doing?" She found her cheek pressed against the soft leather of his chest.

Keeping you warm. His voice was once again loud and clear. *You were cold.*

She did feel warmer and more . . . safe. With a glimmer of reassurance, she realized Eviana was being held like this, too, so she should be surviving the trip without freezing.

But how strange that a dragon not only had saved her life, but was concerned for her comfort. And how tempting it was to use her special power to find out more about him.

As one of the Embraced, Gwennore had been born with an ability that was close to a perfect fit for her. With her ever-rational and inquisitive mind, she liked to figure out problems and fix them. Using her gift, she could touch a person and then determine if they were healthy, and if not, she could see in her mind's eye what the problem was.

But it was not quite a perfect gift, because knowing what a problem was didn't mean she automatically knew how to fix it. Luckily for Gwennore, there had been a nun at the convent, Sister Colleen, who was renowned for her knowledge of the healing arts. Sister Colleen had spent many hours teaching Gwennore, so she could put her gift to good use.

There were certain areas of a human body that would give Gwennore the best reading of a person's health. She could press her fingers on the neck beneath an ear, or place her palm against a brow, or the method she favored the most—wrapping her hand around a wrist and pressing her fingertips against the pulse.

Would her gift work on a dragon? She was eager to know. Closing her eyes, she pressed the palm of her hand against his chest. The warmth of his skin melded with her hand and soon, she could feel beyond the skin to the rushing of blood through his body and the steady beat of his heart. It was a powerful beat, much stronger than she'd ever felt from a human.

What are you doing?

She jerked her hand back as her eyes flew open. "Nothing." Had he felt her reading him?

You should rest for now. We have a long way to go.

"As you wish." She burrowed her hands into the folds of her skirt and rested her cheek against his warm skin.

After a while, she lost all sense of time. Her world closed in till it was only her, cradled in a soft leathery cocoon, resting against the comforting warmth of the dragon's chest and hearing the steady beat of his wings.

When everything around her suddenly turned white, she realized they were traveling through a cloud. She held out a hand, and the cool, white vapor sifted through her splayed fingers. *Amazing.* She smiled to herself. She was inside a cloud!

Fluffy wisps blew past her, feathering her cheeks as the dragon descended, then suddenly they were surrounded by a beautiful, clear blue. She ventured a look down and wasn't frightened this time, for she was being held so close.

The view was stunning. Mountain peaks blanketed with snow. Mountainsides thick with forest. Wide valleys of green pastures. Bursts of color from clumps of wild-flowers. Rivers rushing and foaming, flooded with snow-melt. Every now and then, a deadly spot of scorched earth where hot steam ascended from geysers and cones of white ash.

Norveshka. A land of extremes. Where the highest mountains on Aerthlan stood sentinel over the deepest valleys. Where cool green meadows collided with patches of hot, barren crust. Where people lived among dragons.

Fascinated, Gwennore watched the land pass by beneath her. The dragon swooped down, giving her a view of a lovely waterfall crowned with a rainbow. Down in the valley, a young boy was herding goats. He glanced up and waved. Farther along the valley, she spotted a village. Brown log cabins were topped with green grassy roofs. Window boxes overflowed with bright-red flowers. Several people looked up and waved.

"They have no fear of you."

Why would they? We protect them.

"But why do you kidnap children?"

She heard something like a hiss. *I don't.*

"Why did your brother take Eviana?"

There was a long pause. *It's . . . complicated.*

"I have time."

We're close to Dreshka now.

She recalled the geography she'd learned at the convent. The village of Dreshka spanned the Norva River, only a mile south of Norva Lake. "That is the capital?"

Yes. Most probably, my brother will deposit the child in the garden at Draven Castle. It has a flat space that is large enough for us to land. I will leave you there—

"Leave? But you said you would return us."

As soon as it can be arranged. Trust me.

Could she really trust a dragon?

He tilted to the left, heading north to follow a rushing river as it cut through a deep canyon. After a while, the canyon opened up to a wide valley. White, fluffy sheep dotted the green meadows, along with wildflowers of purple and yellow. In the distance, she saw Draven Castle perched on a mountain.

It was magnificent. White limestone gleamed in the afternoon sun. The numerous towers and turrets were topped with differently shaped spires of greenish copper.

As they drew closer, Gwennore spotted the village that straddled the river. *Dreshka.* The community looked idyllic with all the grassy roofs and window boxes overflowing with flowers. A few stone bridges arched over the Norva River.

The castle presided over the village, its thick walls rising from the gray granite of the nearby mountain. The dragon veered to the right, headed to the south side of the castle. She spotted a long flat lawn, surrounded by flower beds and fruit trees.

As they approached, she saw the first dragon set Eviana on the grass then fly off, slowly gaining altitude so he could clear the nearby forest. Eviana remained huddled on the ground, her white dress stirring slightly in the breeze caused by the beating of the dragon's wings.

I will drop you close to her.

"Thank you." Gwennore felt a twinge of reluctance to part with her dragon. For the time being, he was the only ally she had in Norveshka. "Will I see you again?"

He glided down toward the lawn. *I'll send the general to you.*

"General? Will he take us back to Eberon?"

The dragon's forelegs opened, and she rolled forward, falling a foot onto the ground.

"Umph." She lifted herself up on her elbows in time to see him soar past her. "Puff . . ."

I am never far away. He circled around the castle, disappearing from her view. *Gwennore.* His last word floated through her mind like a soft whisper.

She slowly rose to her feet. Eviana was some twenty yards away, not moving.

"Eviana!" She ran to the little girl, who raised her head and blinked sleepily.

Had the poor child fainted out of fear? Tears crowded Gwennore's eyes as she fell to her knees and gathered the girl into her arms. "Eviana, sweetheart . . ."

"Gwennie!" Eviana wrapped her arms around Gwennore's neck. "I thought you . . ." She let out a wail as a shudder racked her small body. "I thought you were gone."

"Nay, sweetie." Gwennore held her tight, rubbing her back. The acrid scent of urine reached her nostrils. At some point during the flight, the child had wet herself. "I won't leave you. I promise. And I'll get ye back home."

"I want my mama!"

"I know." Tears ran down Gwennore's cheeks, as once again she felt responsible for the terror this child had endured. "Are ye injured in any way?" She rested her palm on Eviana's brow to get a reading.

Heartbeat was fast. Respiration too quick and shallow. No broken bones. Four small puncture wounds where the dragon's talons had pierced the skin. Those would need to be washed and treated. The little girl would also need clean clothes, a hot meal, and a safe place to rest.

Shouts from within the castle drew Gwennore's attention away from the little girl, and she spotted two soldiers watching her from the battlements. One motioned for her to approach the southern gate.

She rose to her feet, casting a wary look at the closed gate. It looked forbidding with its thick wooden walls studded with iron points and painted with a black swirling design. Above it, the Norveshki flag flapped in the breeze. The bottom half of the flag was three stripes in red, gold, and blue. On the top half, a red dragon flew across the blue background. Why a red dragon, she wondered, when they were actually more green and purple. But the golden dragon eye on the flag was correct. Puff's eyes had definitely been gold.

With a loud creak, the southern gate slowly opened.

Gwennore steeled her nerves as she helped Eviana to her feet. "Come with me."

"I wanna go home."

"We will soon." Gwennore smiled, even though her heart was pounding with trepidation.

A dozen armed guards strode toward them. Black leather boots and breeches, blue tunics emblazoned with a red dragon. At least their swords were sheathed. She hoped that meant they would be treated as guests and not prisoners.

Even so, they were definitely eyeing her with suspicion. It couldn't be helped, she supposed, since Norveshka was currently at war with Woodwyn. But the way they were inspecting her like an insect made her wish once again she could unleash her frustration and give the offenders a verbal lashing.

Not now, she reminded herself. But soon.

She pasted a friendly smile on her face and spoke to the guards in Norveshki. "How do you do? I am Gwennore, and this is Eviana, the daughter of King Leofric of Eberon."

One of the guards bowed his head. "I am Karlan, captain of the royal guard. Come this way." He motioned toward the gate.

Gwennore noticed the other guards had surrounded them. "As you wish." She took Eviana's hand and led her forward.

"I can't undesand," Eviana whined.

"They're speaking the Norveshki language," Gwennore explained in Eberoni. "They invited us inside."

"But I wanna go home."

"We'll be fine. Don't worry." Gwennore squeezed the girl's hand, then switched to Norveshki to address the captain. "You must know that we were brought here by a pair of dragons. Against our will, I might add. But I am sure we can work together to remedy the mistake before any—"

"No mistake," Karlan said as he led them through the gate.

Gwennore swallowed hard. *Remain calm.*

They entered a large square courtyard. The castle loomed up on all four sides, three stories high, with towers in each corner topped with curiously shaped green copper spires. Along the battlements, Gwennore spotted numerous carved statues of green marble that gleamed in the late-afternoon sun. Narrowing her eyes, she realized the statues were all dragons, their long bodies undulating like snakes and their mouths wide open as if they meant to swallow their prey in one hideous gulp. Even the green copper gutters had downspouts that were designed to look like dragons.

The ground was paved with stones, mostly smooth, though she spotted some odd carvings etched in here and there. Swirls and symbols, similar to the ones that were painted on the gate.

She winced as the gate banged shut behind them. "Mayhap I was not clear, Captain. This little girl is the Eberoni princess. Her father will not—"

"The queen requested a princess."

Gwennore's mouth fell open. "Are you saying your queen ordered this kidnapping?"

With an annoyed look, Karlan motioned to a group of women entering the courtyard from the southeastern tower. "Queen Freya is coming. Be careful what you say to her."

"But we need to clear this up as soon as possible." Gwennore turned toward the approaching women.

There were five of them in all, one leading the pack with four following behind. The one in front had to be Freya, queen of Norveshka. She held her head high, and the way her dark-red hair was braided and piled on top of her head added a few inches to her impressive height. Her gown was bright red, while the others wore duller shades of red and burgundy. Her heavy necklace was studded with multiple large rubies, while the other ladies had only one small ruby displayed on black velvet ribbons around their necks.

"So many rubies," Gwennore whispered. Even the queen's hairpin was sparkling with rubies.

"It's Rubeday," Karlan muttered.

Gwennore had always thought it odd that the Norveshki had named their days after gemstones. Ametheday, Diamonday, Emeralday, Garneday, Opalday, Rubeday, and Sapphirday. "You mean the Norveshki dress with the jewels of each day?"

"Only the royal family and those who are currently in their favor. It is a sign of their power." Karlan lowered his voice. "Watch your tongue."

Was the queen difficult to get along with? As Queen Freya drew closer, Gwennore could see streaks of gray in her hair and worry lines across her brow and around her mouth. Anxiety, plus insomnia from the looks of the dark circles beneath the queen's eyes. That would be enough to make anyone grumpy.

Karlan and the other guards bowed, so Gwennore followed their example and curtsied.

The queen ignored them as her gaze shifted to Eviana. Then her face lit up with a smile that made her look ten years younger. "My baby!" She leaned over, extending her arms to the side as if she expected the little girl to run into her embrace.

With a frightened whimper, Eviana wrapped her arms around Gwennore's legs.

"Oh, my!" Queen Freya pressed a hand to her chest as she straightened. "Isn't she beautiful?"

"Yes, Your Majesty," several of her ladies-in-waiting murmured.

Gwennore cleared her throat. "Your Majesty, may I present Eviana, the daughter of Queen Luci—"

"Eviana?" Queen Freya looked confused for a moment, then nodded with a smile. "Yes, of course. That is what I named her. I chose a lovely name, didn't I?"

"Yes, Your Majesty," another of her ladies answered.

Gwennore gave the ladies-in-waiting a wary look. Why were they agreeing? "I beg your pardon, Your Majesty, but Eviana was named by her mother, Queen Luciana of Eber—"

"Liar!" Anger flashed in the queen's eyes. "The child is mine. I was in labor all yesterday and last night."

"This little girl is three years—"

"I would know my own baby!" the queen interrupted Gwennore. "She is mine. Is she not, Captain?"

Karlan nodded. "Yes, Your Majesty."

Gwennore shot him an astonished look, and he turned away, avoiding her gaze. She glanced at the ladies-in-waiting, but they, too, refused to look at her.

"She looks just like her father, King Petras." Freya smiled at Eviana. "She has his black hair and green eyes."

"Her father is King Leofric—"

"You lie!" Freya glared at her. When she waved a hand imperiously, the sun glistened off her ruby rings. "Who is this elfin woman?"

"Her name is Gwennore, Your Majesty," Karlan replied.

Freya narrowed her eyes. "Why is she here? Has she come from Woodwyn to steal my baby?"

"Your Majesty, I would never harm Eviana." Gwennore held the girl close. At first, she'd thought the queen was merely deceitful, but now she had a terrible feeling that the queen actually believed Eviana was hers.

Gwennore glanced at the others, but they all looked away, their faces shuttered with embarrassment and guilt. *Good goddesses.* The truth struck her hard.

The queen was mad. And all these people knew it.

"Give her to me!" Freya made a grab at Eviana's arm, and the little girl screamed.

"You're frightening her." Gwennore stopped the queen by grasping her around the wrist. The contact immediately triggered her gift, and she gasped at how quickly she was bombarded with information. Never had her gift reacted this strongly. But then, never had she touched someone this ill.

Sickness permeated the queen's entire body. How she even managed to stand was a miracle.

Freya tried to yank her hand away, but Gwennore tightened her grip and concentrated. The queen's mind and body were deteriorating, but why? She was so close to seeing the cause.

"Let go of me!" Freya screamed.

Poison. "Your Majesty, I can help—"

"How dare you touch me!" Freya wrenched her hand away and stumbled, nearly losing her balance. "Arrest her!"

"Your Majesty." Gwennore reached out to steady her. "I can help you. I'm a—"

"You're an assassin!" Freya slapped her hand away. "You came here to kill me and my baby! Arrest her!"

Karlan and one of his guards grabbed Gwennore. Eviana wailed, clinging to her skirt.

"Please, Your Majesty," Gwennore pleaded. She knew the queen didn't care about her, but surely, she cared for the child she believed was hers. "This is frightening Eviana. Let me take her someplace quiet so she can rest."

"You are going to the dungeon," Freya announced. "And then tomorrow, I will decide whether you live or die."

Gwennore's heart lurched. Good goddesses, how could she escape this? She couldn't reason with a woman who was mad. She looked around frantically. All the gates were shut and guarded. And Eberon was so far away.

Could the dragon help her? *Puff, can you hear me? I'm in trouble!*

"Take her away!" Freya waved her hand.

"Yes, Your Majesty." Karlan tugged at Gwennore, and she stumbled. Eviana clung to her, crying.

Gwennore struggled to breathe as panic threatened to swallow her whole. This couldn't be happening. It was a nightmare, and she needed to wake up. *Now.*

"Release her." A deep, compelling voice echoed across the courtyard.

Immediately the guards let go. Gwennore fell to her knees as she pulled Eviana close. *Am I waking up now? Will we be back in the nursery at Ebton Palace? Please let it be so. Then Eviana would have no memory of today.*

Karlan came to attention, tapping a fist against his chest. Each of the guards did the same.

The queen turned toward the northwestern tower. Her ladies-in-waiting gave a collective sigh.

Thump, thump, thump. The sound of booted feet echoed across the courtyard.

Gwennore rose shakily to her feet to face the new-comers. The late-afternoon sun shone into the courtyard at an angle, casting much of the western portion in shadow, so she couldn't see the men clearly.

There were three of them, tall with long-legged strides. The one in front had set the pace, and the two flanking him had matched it, so all three sets of boots rang out in unison.

Thump, thump, thump, thump. They walked—no, stalked—toward her, for their strides were powerful and determined. While they were in shadow, she could only see that they were dressed alike. Army uniforms, per-haps, since Karlan and his guards were still standing at attention.

As the first man stepped into the sunlight, the ladies-

in-waiting gave another collective sigh. And Gwennore's
heart stilled in her chest.

He was beautiful. His hair, black and wavy, ended
at his shoulders. Incredibly broad shoulders. The cut of
his jaw, the sharpness of his cheekbones, the smooth
breadth of his brow, pale against the dark slashes of his
eyebrows—it all added up to make a remarkably handsome man. And his eyes, a brilliant green, were looking
at her.

With a jerk, she pulled her gaze away so she wouldn't
be caught gawking at him. The other two men were visible
now. Not quite as handsome, but their looks and uniforms
were similar. Brown leather boots and breeches. Leather
breastplates over dark-green shirts. Their green capes
billowed behind them as they crossed the courtyard.

Her gaze drifted back to the one who was watching her.
He was more than beautiful. There was an aura of power
about him. He must be the general that Puff had said
would come, for he looked capable of controlling an
entire army. Even the fiercest of dragons would obey his
command.

Goddesses help her, she no longer wanted this to be a
dream. For even with all the danger around her, she
wanted this man to be real. She wanted him to be the tall
and handsome stranger that the Telling Stones foretold.

Three. The numbered stone could refer to the three
men. Or Eviana turning three. And the colored stones—
with a small shock she realized they were the same as his
uniform.

Green and brown.

Chapter Three

❦

As the three men came to a stop, Gwennore noted that the ladies-in-waiting were curtsying, so she did, too.

Karlan bowed. "My lord general."

"At ease," the gorgeous man in the middle said.

Freya rushed to his side. "Silas, you arrived just in time. I've discovered an assassin." She pointed at Gwennore. "You should arrest her!"

Gwennore popped up from her curtsy, ready to defend herself. But before she could say anything, the general had enveloped the queen's hand in his own and turned her away.

"Your Majesty." He flashed a smile that caused a few of the ladies to stumble as they rose from their curtsies. "I came as quickly as I could after hearing the news. May I congratulate you on the birth of your daughter?"

"Why, yes." Freya blushed. "Thank you. I was in labor a dreadfully long time, you know."

"Yes, so I hear." He patted her hand. "But thank the Light, you and the babe are doing remarkably well."

What nonsense was this? The gorgeous general was acting like the others—playing along with the queen's delusion. Gwennore drew in a deep breath to voice her objection, but the general shot her a warning look with his sharp green eyes.

When she lifted her eyebrows as if to question him, he inclined his head ever so slightly. *He's asking me to trust him.* It was as clear as if he had spoken. For a moment she wondered if she was experiencing a mental connection with him like she had with Puff.

Don't jump to conclusions, she chided herself. She was only hoping for a connection because he was the most handsome man she'd ever met.

Something flared in his eyes, a spark of gold in the emerald green, and her knees grew weak. Good goddesses, was she about to swoon like these other silly women? She needed to be stronger than this.

"Thank you, Silas," Freya said, drawing his attention back to her. "Doesn't the baby look just like her father?"

"Yes, indeed." The general glanced at Eviana, who was still clinging to Gwennore's legs. "And to mark the occasion, I have brought you a gift." He motioned to Gwennore. "A nanny. As you can see, the princess has already developed a special fondness for her."

Freya gasped. "You brought the elf here?"

"Of course." He gave Gwennore a wry look as if he was daring her to contradict him. "She's a noblewoman I captured some time ago in battle, but since then, she's learned our language and proven herself quite useful."

So General Gorgeous had no problem spinning lies or manipulating a madwoman. Gwennore snorted. But since she was in danger of being imprisoned and even executed, she was not in any position to reject his solution.

Even so, she wondered if she could actually trust him. As the general of the Norveshki army, wouldn't he see her as an enemy?

"We dare not trust an elf," Freya muttered. "She could be a spy. Or an assassin."

"We *can* trust her," the general insisted. "Lady Gwennore cares deeply for the princess. Enough to risk her life for her."

Gwennore's heart lurched into a fast pace. He knew her name? And what she'd done? Puff must have told him everything that had happened. That meant General Gorgeous could hear dragon voices, too. It made sense, she figured, since his job would require him to communicate with dragons. But did that mean he had ordered the first dragon to kidnap Eviana? Or perhaps, he had ordered Puff to try to stop the kidnapping. Which side was he on?

"But elves are such violent creatures," Freya whined.

"They are fierce warriors, that is true," the general agreed. "That is why Lady Gwennore will make an excellent nanny. No one will protect your daughter as well as she."

"Well . . ." Freya looked confused. Her hands fluttered around her chest, causing the rubies to sparkle in the afternoon sun. "I suppose we can give her a try."

"Excellent." He turned toward Karlan. "You and your men may return to your posts."

Gwennore exhaled with relief. She wasn't going to the dungeon. And as the official nanny, she could remain close to Eviana.

"And remember." The general stepped closer to Karlan and added softly, "Lady Gwennore is my guest. She will be treated with respect."

"Yes, my lord." Karlan motioned for his men to follow him back to the main gatehouse.

With Gwennore's superior hearing, she'd heard the general's whisper. He had to be on her side. For one thing, he kept referring to her as a lady. The status of noblewoman would shield her from any physical abuse during her stay here in Draven Castle.

So, most probably, she had two allies in Norveshka—

Puff and General Gorgeous. She could only hope they would both prove to be trustworthy and honorable.

The general turned to the nearest lady-in-waiting. "Your name, please?"

The woman stumbled back a step. "O-Olenka, my lord general."

"Lady Olenka, would you please escort Lady Gwennore and the princess to the nursery? And make sure they are well taken care of."

"Yes, yes, of course, my lord general." Olenka nodded, then curtsied again.

"I'll drop by to check on you later." The general shot a pointed look at Gwennore. "Till then."

Gwennore inclined her head, understanding he intended to have a talk with her. That was fine. She needed to talk to him, too.

"Oh, everything will be perfect, my lord general! You can trust me." Olenka motioned for Gwennore to follow her. "Come along now."

Gwennore lifted Eviana in her arms and walked toward Lady Olenka. As she passed the queen, she bowed her head. "Good day, Your Majesty."

Freya narrowed her eyes. "If anything happens to my daughter, I'll have your head. I will not lose another child!"

Another child? How many had the queen lost? "I will protect her with my life," Gwennore told her, then followed Lady Olenka toward the northwestern tower.

As she neared the general's two companions, she noted there was a slight difference in their uniforms. One had three brass stars embedded in his leather breastplate, while the other had two. Did that mean they were officers? The general had four stars on his breastplate.

These men were handsome like the general—tall, muscular, long dark hair. No doubt they knew how to make a few ladies swoon. She blinked in surprise when they both smiled at her.

The general cleared his throat. "Aleksi, see if His Majesty is available. I need to speak to him."

The one with two stars nodded. "Yes, my lord."

"And Dimitri." The general addressed the other officer. "You will go to the nursery and stand guard."

Dimitri stiffened. "The *nursery*?"

"You've been promoted to chief babysitter." Aleksi smirked, then winced when Dimitri elbowed him in the ribs.

"Aye, and he'll be damned good at it." The general waved at the two men. "Go."

Even though the general's voice was brusque, Gwennore didn't miss the twinkle of amusement in his eyes. The two men saluted him, giving him wry looks. As Aleksi strode toward the northern wing, Dimitri headed toward the northwestern tower with Lady Olenka and Gwennore.

"By the Light, my heart is still pounding," Olenka whispered as they neared a large double door. She glanced back at the general and sighed dramatically. "Did you hear him? He called me by my name."

Gwennore snorted. "What else would he call you?" With her superior hearing, she caught the rest of the general's conversation with the queen.

"Your Majesty." He tucked her hand under his arm. "You must be exhausted. Please allow me to escort you back to your suite, so you can rest."

"That is very kind of you, Silas." The queen went meekly along with him while the other ladies-in-waiting followed. "I fear I'm not feeling quite myself these days."

"Yes, I gathered that," the general said, and the melancholy tone of his voice pricked at Gwennore's heart. He did feel sorry for the queen after all.

"This way." Olenka opened the door to enter the square-shaped tower. "Quickly now!"

Gwennore looked around as she stepped into the foyer. It was rather plain with a stone-paved floor and unadorned wooden paneling along the walls. The only furniture was a wooden table topped with seven pillar candles. The candles were marked with the hours of the day, and the lit one had burned down to early evening. The large, circular tray the candles sat on was decorated with seven jewels around the perimeter. A small metal arrow pointed toward the ruby. For Rubeday, she realized.

"Look," she whispered in Eberoni to the little girl in her arms. "'Tis a weekly clock."

Eviana turned her head to look. "It's pwetty. Gwennie, when are we going home?"

"Soon, sweetie." *I hope.*

"I don't like it here. I can't undesand anybody." Eviana wrinkled her nose. "And my clothes are wet."

Gwennore brushed back the little girl's hair. "We'll find something else for ye to wear. And give ye a bath. And have something to eat, all right?"

Eviana nodded.

"Will you please stop dawdling?" Olenka fussed in Norveshki as she rushed up the stairs. "We must hurry! The general will be checking on us soon, and we mustn't disappoint him."

Gwennore suppressed an urge to roll her eyes. Instead, she muttered in Eberoni, "Does he cause the sun to rise in the morning?"

Dimitri choked back a laugh.

Gwennore winced. Apparently, the officer had understood her. "Sorry."

He stepped closer and said in Eberoni, "The nursery is on the top floor. Shall I carry the child for you?"

Eviana tightened her grip around Gwennore's neck and buried her face against her shoulder.

Gwennore smiled. "I appreciate the offer, but I think I'll have to keep her with me."

Dimitri nodded, then switched to Norveshki. "I'm sure it's been a difficult day for you both."

Olenka stopped on the first landing of the stairs and glared down at them. "What's taking you so long?"

"We're coming." Gwennore started up the stairs, slowly since she was carrying Eviana. She winced as the little girl's wet clothes soaked into her bodice.

"I have to make sure everything's perfect." Olenka frowned as she smoothed her hands over the skirt of her burgundy gown. "If we hurry, I might have time to change clothes. But should I wear something bright and bold?" She struck a dramatic pose. "Or something more soft and sedate." She folded her hands primly together.

Gwennore groaned inwardly. "I think the gown you're wearing is perfectly lovely."

Olenka sneered at her. "What would an elf know about anything?" She turned to Dimitri, who was trudging up the stairs. "Tell me, Colonel. What sort of woman does the general prefer?"

He gave her a wry look. "One with good manners."

"Ah." Olenka waved a dismissive hand. "Well, I have that covered."

When Dimitri snorted, Gwennore bit her lip to keep from smiling.

Olenka brushed back a red curl from her brow. "If only I had washed my hair this morning!"

Gwennore sighed as she reached the landing. "There are more important things to fret about." Like how traumatized Eviana would be. Or how soon she could get the child back home.

Olenka nodded. "You're right. I should be thinking

about what I'm going to say to him." She gathered up her skirt and started up the next flight of stairs. "I need to be intriguing. Perhaps a little mysterious."

"Why?" Gwennore followed her. "Is the general the only man left alive on all of Aerthlan?"

"What?" Olenka glanced back her, looking thoroughly offended. "He's the most handsome man on Aerthlan!"

Gwennore shrugged. "He's tolerable, I suppose, but I've seen better."

When Dimitri choked back a laugh, Gwennore winced. No doubt he would tell General Gorgeous what she'd said.

"*Better?*" Olenka huffed. "Who could be more handsome than General Dravenko?"

So that was his name? Gwennore paused at the next landing to catch her breath, then kept climbing. "The kings of Eberon and Tourin are both exceptionally handsome."

Olenka snorted. "How could someone like you ever meet royalty?"

Gwennore gritted her teeth. "Someone like me has two sisters who are queens. Luciana and Brigitta."

Olenka sputtered. "You-you're their—how can you be their sister? Aren't you from Woodwyn?"

"No, I grew up with four adopted sisters in a convent on the Isle of Moon," Gwennore explained.

Dimitri's eyes narrowed. "What are their names?"

"Luciana, Brigitta, Sorcha, and—" Gwennore stopped when both Olenka and Dimitri stiffened with astonishment. "Do you know Sorcha? We always suspected she was from Norveshka because of her red hair."

"Wha-what was your name again?" Olenka asked.

"Gwennore."

"Oh, my dear Lady Gwennore." Olenka took her by the arm. "Let me help you up the stairs. Is there anything I can do to make your stay more comfortable?"

Gwennore glanced at Dimitri, who looked thoroughly amused. "Eviana will need some clean clothes, a hot bath, and a hot meal."

"Of course." Olenka eyed the little girl curiously. "So is she really the Eberoni princess?"

Gwennore nodded. "She's the daughter of King Leofric and Queen Luciana."

Dimitri winced. "No wonder I'm standing guard. We can't let anything happen to this child."

Gwennore scoffed. "Something already has. She was abducted by a dragon. And if she isn't returned soon, both Eberon and Tourin will be attacking your country."

Dimitri nodded. "I understand. But you needn't worry. General Dravenko will take care of it."

"And we'll take good care of you both," Olenka insisted. "You'll tell the general how nice I was, right?"

Gwennore swallowed her frustration as she continued to climb stairs. As far as she could tell, the lady-in-waiting was being nice only because she wanted to score points with General Gorgeous. "If you knew Eviana wasn't Queen Freya's child, why did you play along? I could have ended up in a dungeon. And poor Eviana may be traumatized for life."

Olenka hung her head. "I am sorry about that. It just seems better to never upset Her Majesty."

"Or you could end up in a dungeon?" Gwennore asked wryly, and Olenka winced. "How many children has the queen lost? Was it her grief that caused her to fall into madness?"

With a gasp, Olenka jerked to a stop. "Hush!" She quickly looked around. "You must never speak of that."

"Why?" Gwennore paused on a step. "How can you help the queen if you don't acknowledge her illness?"

With a hiss, Olenka pressed a finger against her mouth.

Then she leaned closer and whispered, "There is no help for it. And we are forbidden to speak of it."

Gwennore thought back to the moment when she'd held the queen's wrist. *Poison.* She was fairly sure of it.

"Come, we're almost there." Olenka hurried up the last of the stairs. When she spotted a maid, she called her over. "We need your help making the nursery ready."

"Yes, my lady." The maid curtsied. "I'll bring some wood for a fire." As she dashed away, Olenka strode over to the double doors and flung them open.

When Gwennore entered the large room, Olenka motioned to a door on the far side of the nursery. "The dressing room is over there. I'll start a bath for the princess and find something for her to wear."

"Thank you." Gwennore set Eviana on her feet, although the little girl still clung to her skirt.

"If the general comes, be sure to tell him how helpful I am," Olenka added.

Gwennore sighed. "Would you prefer that I tell him you wish to be courted?"

Olenka gasped. "No, don't say that!" She waved her hands frantically. "Please! I only want to show my loyalty. Nothing more."

"All right," Gwennore agreed, even though she was totally confused.

"Thank you!" Olenka dashed across the room as if she was desperate to escape. She burst into the dressing room and slammed the door.

"Was it something I said?" Gwennore muttered in Eberoni.

Dimitri nodded. "Yes, actually. She and the other courtiers only want to be close to those in power. It makes them feel powerful. But the court ladies would never risk marriage with the general." He frowned. "Or Aleksi. Or me."

"Why not? I would think any woman would be honored to marry you."

Dimitri gave her a wry smile. Just as he opened his mouth to respond, the dressing room door flung open, and Olenka jumped out, eyeing Gwennore with suspicion.

"Is it true what General Dravenko said?" she asked. "That he captured you some time ago in battle?"

Gwennore winced. She couldn't very well say that the general had lied.

"He captured you, but never returned you?" Olenka's eyes grew wide as she pressed a hand to her chest. "I should have realized it before. This is so dramatic! The general has taken an enemy elfin woman to his bed!"

Gwennore flinched. "*What?*"

"That's why he's coming here to check on us. He's worried about you." Olenka pointed at her. "He wants to protect his lover."

"No!"

"And that's why you frightened me with that offer of courtship. It was a warning for me to stay away from him."

"That's not it," Gwennore insisted.

Olenka nodded with a knowing gleam in her eyes. "I can understand how you might be threatened by someone as beautiful as I am. No doubt you see me as serious competition, but I assure you, I only wish to be helpful."

"I do appreciate your help, but please don't—"

"No wonder you acted like he wasn't all that handsome." Olenka smirked. "It's how you keep people from suspecting the truth. Obviously, you're not accustomed to dealing with someone as perceptive as I." She waved a hand in the air. "But don't worry. I won't say a word. Even though it's gloriously dramatic!" She jumped into the dressing room and banged the door shut.

Gwennore gawked at the closed door for a moment,

then turned toward Dimitri. "Please tell me she's the only one who will jump to that ridiculous conclusion."

Dimitri shifted his weight, then winced. "I'll be outside, standing guard." He closed the doors as he left.

Gwennore stared into space for a moment. A few minutes ago, she'd been relieved that the general was protecting her and Eviana. But she hadn't realized what it might look like to others. Goddesses help her. She needed to go home as soon as possible.

"Gwennie, look!" Eviana's excited voice shook her out of her thoughts. The little girl caught her hand and dragged her toward one side of the room.

Half a dozen windows lined the long wall, allowing the sun to pour in and brighten the room. Between the windows, cushioned window seats looked warm and inviting. Beneath the windows and seats, shelves held a huge assortment of books and toys.

Dimitri opened the door to let the maid in. She set a basket of kindling and logs by the hearth, then whisked off a white sheet that was protecting more toys from dust.

Eviana's eyes lit up at the sight of a wooden cradle filled with dolls, a red-painted wagon, a toy pram, and a rocking horse. "Can I play with these?"

"I believe so." Gwennore looked around the long, rectangular room. It had to take up most of the western wing.

Opposite the wall of windows, there was another long wall with a fireplace in the middle. On each side, there were several beds, still covered with dust sheets. The center of the room was empty, leaving plenty of room for children to run about.

The maid pulled off another white sheet that was covering a comfy armchair in front of the fireplace. As she folded it, she cast a few curious glances at Gwennore.

Smiling, Gwennore introduced herself and Eviana.

"May I help?" She removed a sheet from a second armchair.

The maid blushed. "Y-you don't have to do any work, my lady." She set her folded sheet on the small table between the two armchairs, then rushed over to the nearest bed to pull off another dust sheet.

"I don't mind. I like to keep busy." Gwennore folded her sheet. "May I ask your name?"

"Nissa." The maid's blush turned a brighter pink. "I-I've never met an elf before."

"I've never met a Nissa before. It's a lovely name."

Nissa smiled shyly as she folded up the sheet. The bed she had uncovered was definitely for a child. It was short and low to the ground with a railing around the edge. A blue quilt on top was embroidered with red dragons.

Gwennore set her folded sheet on top of the stack Nissa was making. "Is that a little boy's bed?"

Nissa nodded as she added her folded sheet to the stack. "Prince Tyrus slept there."

Gwennore ran her fingers along the railing of the prince's bed. The quilt looked freshly laundered. "This room has been kept clean."

"Yes." When Nissa pulled off another dust cloth, a crib was revealed. "We have orders to clean the room every fortnight. In case there's a new . . ." She glanced over at Eviana, then quickly folded up the sheet.

"What happened to Prince Tyrus?" Gwennore asked. "Did he outgrow the nursery?"

Nissa winced. "No." She hurried over to another bed and tugged at the dust sheet.

An ominous feeling slithered down Gwennore's spine. She glanced at the empty crib and the bed once used by a prince. Then she noticed the headboards. Symbols and swirling designs had been carved into the wood, much like the ones she'd noted earlier in the courtyard and on the gate. "What happened to the prince?"

A pained expression crossed Nissa's face before she looked away. "He's . . . gone. He was almost two."

Gwennore's ominous feeling crept into her bones. "And the crib? Was it used by the prince, or was there another . . . ?"

"Another boy." Nissa drew in shaky breath. "He lived only six weeks."

Gwennore swallowed hard. As she watched Nissa uncover another bed, she realized this one had a white quilt embroidered with pink and lavender flowers. At the head of the bed, pillows were trimmed with ruffles and white lace.

"Oh, that's pwetty." Eviana skipped toward the bed with a doll in her arms. "Can I sleep there?"

"It does look like a bed for a princess, doesn't it?" Gwennore answered in Eberoni, then switched to Norveshki to address the maid. "Was there a little girl?"

Nissa glanced at Eviana, then looked away, her eyes glimmering with tears. "Anya was the queen's firstborn child. She lived to be three."

Gwennore drew Eviana close to her. "The queen lost three children?"

A tear rolled down Nissa's cheek as she folded up the last dust sheet. "She had two miscarriages as well."

Gwennore's heart wrenched. Five children! That would be enough to drive anyone to the brink of madness. "I'm so sorry."

As Nissa deposited the last sheet on the stack, Gwennore noticed there were more swirls carved into the white headboard of Princess Anya's bed. "What do the carvings mean?"

Nissa turned pale. "Oh, it-it's nothing." She grabbed

hold of a ball-shaped bead hanging from a leather thong around her neck. The wooden bead had been painted gold to represent the sun god called the Light.

Gwennore had noticed that many of the Enlightened in Eberon and Tourin wore similar pendants around their neck, although the necklaces worn by nobles were usually made of gold. It was normal for them to touch their sun pendants whenever they were upset or felt the urge to pray.

"The carvings must have some sort of meaning," Gwennore persisted. "I saw the same design on the gate and on the paving stones in the courtyard."

Nissa winced. "Those are runes. For protection. But you needn't worry about them."

"Protection against what?"

"It is forbidden to speak of it." Nissa dashed toward the dressing room. "I'll see if the child's bath is ready."

"Wait!" Gwennore followed her. "It is my job to protect Eviana. If there is some sort of danger here, I must know about it."

Nissa paused for a moment, frowning, then shook her head. "I mustn't speak of it. There's no reason for you to worry. I don't think it can affect you or the little girl. It only harms those who marry into one of the three clans."

Marry? Gwennore glanced at the closed doors where Dimitri was standing guard outside. "Is this related to the reason why no woman would want to marry the general or his companions?"

Nissa winced. "No one wants to end up like the queen."

Gwennore gave her an incredulous look. "How could that possibly happen? I am sorry for Her Majesty's misfortune and madness, but those things cannot be contagious."

"The king's mother went mad, too," Nissa whispered. "And now some are saying that the king may be afflicted as well."

Gwennore stepped closer. "What is happening here?"

Nissa shook her head. "Please don't ask me about it. It is forbidden to speak of the curse." With a gasp, she slapped a hand across her mouth.

"A *curse*?"

"Don't say it!" Nissa looked around frantically.

The dressing room door flew open and Olenka stood there, her face pale and stricken. "Did someone mention the Curse of the Three Clans?"

Nissa flinched, then clasped her sun pendant in her fist. "May the Light protect us."

"Is that what it's called?" Gwennore asked. "The Curse of the Three Clans?"

Olenka huffed. "Well, you didn't hear it from me!" She glared at the maid.

"Please forgive me!" Nissa fell to her knees.

"What's wong?" Eviana ran over with a frightened look.

"Nothing," Gwennore assured her in Eberoni. "We-we're just trying to decide which bed ye should rest in."

"Oh." Eviana pointed at the princess bed. "I want the pwetty one."

"Of course." Gwennore switched to Norveshki and helped Nissa to her feet. "Please don't worry. I have no intention of telling anyone."

"Thank you, my lady," Nissa whispered.

"You won't tell the general on us?" Olenka asked.

"Of course not." As far as Gwennore was concerned, it was all nonsense. How on Aerthlan could a curse cause madness or children to die? The very notion was ridiculous!

And yet, as she looked at the empty beds, she had to wonder what could cause such tragic misfortune. The queen's madness could certainly be attributed to the overwhelming grief of losing five children. But what about the reading Gwennore had done when she'd grabbed the queen's wrist? Could poison be behind the queen's madness?

Gwennore's skin chilled when an even more horrid thought popped into her mind. What if poison had caused the deaths of all these children?

Her gaze shifted to the runes sketched above each bed. Had a dark curse dug its claws into Draven Castle? Or was something else going on, something just as sinister but caused by humans?

She pulled Eviana close. Whatever was going on here, she didn't know, but she sensed one thing for sure.

It was evil.

Chapter Four

General Silas Dravenko was ready to slam a fist through a wall. He paced back in forth in the queen's sitting room, frustration dogging his every step.

It had been six months since his last visit to Draven Castle, and in that time, the queen's condition had grown considerably worse. She now believed the children she had kidnapped were actually her own. And no one dared tell her the truth. Everyone was too afraid of inciting her wrath.

Too terrified of a damned curse.

He halted, his hands clenched. How could a dragon's dying words from five hundred years ago still be causing so much turmoil? By the Light, he was sick to death of this wretched curse! It hung over his country like an ominous black cloud that no one dared look at. Instead, his countrymen huddled in its shadow, bent over with fear, too superstitious to even speak of it.

Silas smacked a fist into the palm of his other hand. He'd never wanted to believe in the curse. Never wanted to accept all the pain that it had allegedly caused. Never wanted to surrender to a destiny of doom and despair that everyone claimed was impossible to change.

Dammit! Was he the only one who believed there had to be a logical explanation for everything? Two years ago, he'd launched an investigation into all the problems supposedly caused by the curse. He'd insisted that all the queen's food and drink be tested before she consumed it.

Some of the courtiers had openly mocked him for denying what everyone else accepted as truth. Others had warned him that if he continued to behave in a paranoid manner, then everyone would believe that he, too, was succumbing to the curse and going crazy.

He snorted. It was crazier to actually believe in the damned curse. Unfortunately, he'd been forced to postpone his investigation when the elves attacked a Norveshki village close to the border. The king had immediately declared war against Woodwyn, and Silas had had no choice but to march the army to the southern border. For the last two years, he'd been busy protecting the country.

Thankfully, there were no recent problems with the other two countries that bordered Norveshka. Both Eberon and Tourin had new kings who wanted peace.

With a groan, Silas began to pace once again. That peace had been obliterated the second Queen Freya had ordered the kidnapping of the Eberoni princess. How could the king have gone along with it? Was Petras losing his mind, too?

Don't even think that.

Silas had been at his camp close to the Woodwyn border when a carrier pigeon had brought the news from his spy here in the castle. His attempt to stop the fiasco hadn't been quick enough. No doubt, King Leofric and King Ulfrid were already assembling their armies. They would demand the return of not only the princess, but also the elfin woman Gwennore, since apparently, she'd grown up with Luciana and Brigitta.

And Sorcha. The thought of her brought Silas's steps to a halt. When he returned Gwennore and the little girl, would he be able to see Sorcha?

She won't remember you, he thought with a sigh. She'd been only a few months old when she'd been sent away. He could hardly remember her himself, but he'd wondered about her often over the years. Had she grown up well? Was she happy? Was she courageous and smart? *Like Gwennore.*

The frustration in his heart eased. The elfin woman obviously felt a great amount of love toward Luciana's child. So chances were good that she felt the same way toward her adopted sisters, including Sorcha. He smiled at the thought of his sister growing up with the loving support of good friends. At least something in this world had gone right.

But how strange that the only comfort he'd found today had been caused by an elf. His smile faded.

How had she been able to hear the dragons? As far as he knew, no dragon had ever had a mental conversation with an elf. There were only a few Norveshki men who could communicate with the creatures, and they were all descended from the Three Cursed Clans.

Why was she different? And why was she so damned beautiful? Crap, where had that thought come from?

He'd met plenty of elfin warriors over the years. Hell, he'd killed more of them than he cared to remember. But Gwennore was the only female elf he'd ever seen. By their standards, she might be quite ordinary.

He snorted. Who was he kidding? Her skin was a luminous white that reminded him of the sun glistening off freshly fallen snow. Her eyes were the color of wild bluebells that carpeted the forests in early spring. Her hair was as white as a cloud on a summer day. If there were such a thing as an angel, she would look just like—

Elf, he reminded himself. She was a damned elf, not an angel.

The first time he'd encountered an elfin army on the field, he'd been fifteen years old, and he'd laughed at the sight of them. How could men who were pretty even fight?

But a few seconds into battle, he'd realized his mistake. A minute into battle and he had struggled to stay alive. Their graceful moves were carefully crafted for the sole purpose of delivering death. Their elegant features masked a vicious determination. And their calm demeanor was merely a camouflage for their impassioned courage.

Apparently, an elfin woman could be just as courageous and determined. And even more graceful and beautiful.

The door creaked open, and he turned to greet Lady Margosha as she entered, carrying a tray.

The lady-in-waiting glanced at the closed bedchamber door. "How is Her Majesty?"

"Better, I believe. Two of her ladies are with her." Silas leaned into the hallway to make sure it was empty, then closed the door. Lowering his voice, he whispered, "Thank you for sending the warning."

Lady Margosha winced. "A little too late."

"Still appreciated, though." He had been relying on Margosha for years now, even though he hated the risk she took whenever she dispatched a carrier pigeon to him.

His conscience pricked at him again when he noticed there was more gray than red in her hair. The older woman could have retired to a nice cottage in the village, but instead, she had volunteered to wait on the queen, claiming that the younger ladies would benefit from her years of experience. Her true reason, though, had been a secret agreement with Silas to serve as his spy.

He cleared his throat. "You don't have to do this anymore if you don't want—"

"I know that," she whispered. "But our country is suffering, and this is the only way I know to help. If anyone can save us, I believe it is you."

Her confidence in him was humbling. "I'll try my best." He relieved her of the heavy tray and plunked it on a nearby table.

She patted him on the shoulder. "You were always a good boy."

He snorted. As his former governess, Margosha had usually called him a naughty boy. "I didn't realize the queen had gotten this much worse."

Margosha glanced at the closed bedchamber door. "It only became apparent the last few days. I kept hoping I was just imagining it, but . . ." Her eyes filled with tears. "How can I watch this happen again?"

Silas felt his gut clench. Margosha had served his mother for years, helplessly watching as she had slowly descended into madness. He'd been six years old that spring when his mother had leaped off a bridge and been swept away by the Norva River, thunderous and swollen with snowmelt.

"It won't happen again," he whispered. "We won't let it."

Margosha blinked back tears. "I hope you're right."

He took her hand and squeezed it. After his mother's death, she'd become his governess and had helped him survive the grief. "Remember what you always told me. Never give up. Even when it seems that everyone else has."

She nodded with a sad smile.

He glanced at the tray. A pot of tea and a small plate of bread and cheese. "Are you still having all her food tasted?"

"I've been tasting everything myself." She gave him a wry look. "And as far as I can tell, I'm still sane."

"Are you sure?" He smiled when she swatted his arm.

"You were always a naughty boy," she grumbled.

"That sounds more familiar."

She huffed, but her eyes twinkled with humor.

His smile faded. "I can't believe Petras did this. Doesn't he realize Eberon and Tourin will declare war on us? I must return the princess and the elfin woman as soon as possible."

Margosha nodded. "I agree."

"If you don't mind, could you send some clothes to the woman? She arrived with nothing."

"I'll send a few things." Margosha gave him a curious look. "How did she come here with the princess? Is she not from Woodwyn?"

"She's the adopted sister of Queen Luciana of Eberon and Queen Brigitta of Tourin. And she grew up with Sorcha."

"Oh, my." Margosha's eyes widened. "I'll be sure to send some lovely things then. But how did she manage to arrive with the child?"

"She hitched a ride on a dragon."

Margosha's mouth fell open. "That was extremely brave of her."

Silas nodded. Loyal and brave. The two qualities he admired the most.

"Well." Margosha picked up the tray. "I should take this in before the tea grows cold. And don't worry. With any luck, Her Majesty will forget what she did today. And if not . . ."

"We'll deal with it," Silas told her.

"Yes." Margosha knocked on the bedchamber door, then went inside.

As Silas left the queen's suite, he told himself once again that whatever happened, he would deal with it. No stupid curse would destroy his country.

He headed to the king's offices on the ground floor of the northern wing and found Aleksi standing outside the door, leaning against the wall as he frowned at his boots.

"What's wrong?" Silas asked.

Aleksi jumped to attention and saluted. "His Majesty is not here."

"What?" Silas eyed the closed doors. He knew for a fact that Petras had been here earlier. "The offices are empty?"

"Lord Romak is in the outer office," Aleksi muttered. "He said he could fit you in for an appointment next Opal—"

"An appointment?" Silas growled.

"Next Opalday—"

"That's six days from now. Eberon and Tourin will attack before then."

Aleksi winced. "Then it's true? The little girl is the Eberoni princess?"

"Yes." While his friend muttered a curse, Silas opened the door and strode inside.

The outer office was small and sparsely furnished with a wide desk on one side and a line of plain, wooden chairs along the opposite wall. It was a cold, comfortless room that offered no warmth of a fireplace or sideboard stocked with wine for those who waited for an audience with the king. With no windows, and with walls covered in wooden paneling, it was also a dark room, relieved only by a weekly candle clock on the table in the corner and the brass candelabra sitting on Lord Romak's desk.

Silas had never cared for Romak. Like so many courtiers, he flattered and weaseled his way into being close to those in power. When the king's old secretary had died eight months ago, Romak had somehow produced a paper from the old secretary recommending Romak for the position.

King Petras had gone along with it out of love for the old secretary who had served him faithfully for so many years. But after only three months, Romak had been awarded a title and land, becoming Lord Romak. His rapid ascent to power had made Silas suspicious, but he'd been too busy battling Woodwyn to return to Draven Castle. His letters from Petras had seemed normal, so he'd been more concerned with the mental state of the queen.

"My lord general." Romak jumped to his feet and bowed.

"My lord." Silas inclined his head, watching the older man carefully.

Although Romak's hair was silver at the temples, most of his hair was black, which indicated he was a descendant from one of the Three Cursed Clans. That was not uncommon, though, Silas reminded himself. The three clans traced their beginnings back five hundred years, so there were numerous descendants.

A few descendants, like Aleksi, Dimitri, and himself, could communicate with dragons and with one another telepathically. Could Romak? Silas tried to read the man's thoughts, but caught nothing. That left two possibilities: Romak either possessed no mental powers, or had erected an excellent shield.

Silas gave him a test. *What are you up to, you little weasel?*

Romak gave no indication that he'd heard as he scurried around the desk, still bent over in a subservient position. "What an unexpected pleasure, my lord. Shall I have a servant bring you some refreshment?"

Silas shook his head. "I'm here to see His Majesty."

"I'm afraid he's not in right now, but I'll gladly set an appoint—"

"Since when do I need an appointment?"

Romak waved a dismissive hand as he smiled in an ingratiating manner. "I mean no offense, my lord. This is simply the best way to assure that—"

"Are you determining who is allowed to see the king?"

Romak's smile froze, and his eyes glinted with irritation that was so quickly suppressed that Silas wasn't sure he'd seen it. Romak folded his thin hands over his waist and bowed low. "I am merely trying to fulfill my duties to the best of my ability."

Silas noted the multiple rings the secretary was wearing, each one set with a large gemstone. Was the weasel selling access to the king? "Where is His Majesty?"

Romak circled back around his desk. "I believe he went to the Sacred Well. He goes there quite often these days."

"Why?" Silas noted the way Romak's lips tightened. The weasel didn't like all these questions.

"It seems to give His Majesty some comfort and peace of mind in these trying times."

Silas tensed inside. The Petras he knew had never been overly religious. Why was he behaving like this now? "As soon as His Majesty returns, he must agree to send the Eberoni princess back home. If he doesn't, Eberon and Tourin will declare war on us."

Romak straightened a stack of papers. "We are aware of the situation."

"And doing nothing."

Romak's fingers clenched like claws around the papers. "We will take care of the matter."

"You mean His Majesty will."

Romak's beady eyes seethed with anger. "Of course. I know the extent of my duties. Do you? Why are you not with the army where you belong?"

Silas scoffed. "I don't have to explain my actions to a secretary. I'll speak to His Majesty when he arrives."

"I suggest you leave Draven Castle, or His Majesty will wonder why you have abandoned your post in these perilous times."

Was the weasel planning to make him look like a disobedient subject who shirked his duty? Silas stepped closer to the desk. "Why are you so eager for me to leave? Are you afraid of what I might discover here?"

Romak smirked. "Paranoia. I see the madness is spreading."

Silas's hands curled into fists. As much as he wanted to plant one in Romak's face, he resisted. For even though he suspected Romak was up to no good, he couldn't make accusations without proof. And if he acted too impulsively, people would, indeed, wonder if he was losing his mind. "I will see His Majesty as soon as he returns."

"Yes, my lord general." Romak bowed.

Silas strode from the room.

"Well?" Aleksi asked.

"I should have returned months ago," Silas muttered as he stalked down the hallway.

Aleksi walked beside him. "Why isn't the king here?"

"Good question." Silas couldn't understand why Petras had run off to the Sacred Well. There was nothing there but a hot spring bubbling up in the middle of an underground cavern. "Tell Karlan to alert me the minute His Majesty returns. And make arrangements for a boat so we can take our guests downriver to Eberon. We'll leave at dawn."

Aleksi's eyes widened. "We're taking the child back? Without the king's approval?"

"If we wait, Norveshka could end up at war with three countries. Petras will understand."

"If he doesn't, you could be charged with treason."

"The risk will be mine alone. You're simply following orders."

Aleksi huffed. "You think I'm worried about myself? I've faced death with you too many times to chicken out now."

"I know." Silas clapped him on the shoulder. "Go on, then."

Aleksi sprinted down the hallway to Karlan's office.

With a sigh, Silas headed for the courtyard. This wouldn't be the first time he'd had to risk the king's wrath. But it was his sworn duty to protect the country, even when the danger came from the king or queen.

As Silas stepped into the courtyard, his gaze fell on the runes etched into the stone pavement. Protection from the damned curse. He snorted. Fighting superstition with more superstition. Since the so-called curse had persisted for five hundred years, it should be obvious by now that the runes were absolutely worthless. But that had been the only solution his ancestors could come up with.

Why did no one seek a more rational explanation? If the queen was being poisoned, then a human was behind it. Romak? Perhaps, but Silas knew from experience that things were never as simple as they seemed.

Even though he much preferred being with his troops than a gaggle of overdressed, fawning courtiers, he would have to spend some time here. Something rotten was going on at Draven Castle, and he needed to get to the bottom of it.

His gaze wandered to the top floor of the western wing, where the nursery was located. He'd better make sure the princess was faring well. And her fearless nanny.

As he crossed the courtyard, a mental picture of Gwennore flitted across his mind, and he smiled. She was nothing like the vain and self-serving courtiers who inhabited the castle. There was an aura of honesty and goodness about her that was refreshing, a sense of loyalty and courage that was admirable. Not to mention she was damned beautiful.

But how strange that he was looking forward to seeing an elf again.

Chapter Five

❧

"I like the toys here." Eviana splashed about in the tub in the dressing room. "But I wanna go home."

"Me, too." Gwennore soaped up the little girl, who was playing with an assortment of painted, wooden toys that bobbed on the surface of the warm water.

"Look, a big fish!" Eviana picked up one that was painted blue.

"That's a whale." Gwennore touched a sleek black toy. "And this one is a seal." *Like Maeve.*

How she missed her sisters! For as long as Gwennore could remember, she'd never spent a night separated from all four of them.

Tonight, when the full moons embraced, her youngest sister, Maeve, would shift into a seal. She'd been doing it every month at the full moon for almost three years now. Gwennore could still remember the first time, that summer night on the Isle of Moon.

Poor Maeve had been so frightened. Brody had warned them what to expect, so Gwennore and Sorcha had accompanied their youngest sister to the nearby beach. Love and encouragement had been all they could offer, for poor Maeve had been forced to endure the pain on her own.

Luckily, once she'd entered the water, she'd found another seal there, eager to swim and play with her. Ever since then, Maeve had looked forward to her monthly romp in the ocean. She claimed the shifting didn't hurt at all now.

Gwennore figured her little sister would have to make do with the Norva River this time. And most likely, there would be no other seals to keep her company.

It had to be a miserable night there at the camp. No doubt, the party had been canceled, and the two kings were mobilizing their armies. Luciana had to be scared to death.

Tears threatened to fall, but Gwennore blinked them away. She couldn't afford to be weak now. For Eviana's sake, she needed to remain strong and confident.

"Are you done?" Olenka rushed into the dressing room. "Nissa has brought some food."

Eviana clutched at Gwennore's arm. "What's wong?"

"Everything's fine," Gwennore assured her in Eberoni. The poor child was so easily frightened now. "'Tis time for ye to eat, so let's get ye dressed." She lifted the little girl from the tub and winced as pain shot across her back.

"Are you hurt?" Olenka handed her a white linen towel and a child's nightgown from the nearby cabinet.

"My back is a little sore."

Olenka *tsk*ed. "You shouldn't have carried the child up all those stairs."

Gwennore nodded, even though she suspected her aches and pains were the result of her body slamming into Puff's forelegs. As she dried off Eviana, she spotted the small punctures where the dragon's talons had pierced the little girl's skin. "I'll need an ointment for these."

"Of course. I'll send the maid for it." Olenka hurried out the door.

Gwennore slipped the nightgown over Eviana's head, combed out her hair, then led her back into the nursery.

"Come and eat." Olenka motioned to the small table set with bread, cheese, fruit, and pastries.

Eviana took a bite from an apple tart and grinned. "This is yummy!"

A knock sounded at the door, then Dimitri opened it to let another servant in. She bobbed an awkward curtsy, since her arms were burdened with a huge stack of clothes.

"Begging your pardon. Lady Margosha sent these for . . ." The servant gulped at the sight of Gwennore. "For . . . you."

Gwennore groaned inwardly. Once again she was being regarded with horror.

Olenka's mouth fell open. "Those are the most beautiful gowns from our storeroom!"

The servant nodded. "Lady Margosha gave them to me. She said the general ordered it."

"Oh, really?" Olenka aimed a smirk at Gwennore. "With the way he's behaving, everyone's going to figure out that he's your lover."

The servant gasped and dropped half of the clothes while Dimitri muttered a curse and shut the door.

"It's not true!" Gwennore cried.

"Careful with those!" Olenka snatched the fallen clothes up and dumped them on top of the servant's load. "By the Light, there must be enough here to last a week."

Another shot of alarm skittered through Gwennore. She couldn't remain here with Eviana for a week! Didn't the general understand that they needed to return to Eberon as soon as possible? "I must see the general right away. It's urgent."

Olenka snorted. "I bet you're not the only one feeling *urgent*." She motioned for Gwennore and the servant to follow her. "Fortunately, there's a bedchamber close by."

Gwennore gritted her teeth. Could this day get any worse? After making sure Eviana was happily eating, she followed Olenka and the servant through the dressing room to a bedchamber.

"This is the nanny's room." Olenka whisked the dust cover off a wide, four-poster bed. "Put the clothing here."

While the servant arranged everything on top of a blue linen bedspread, Gwennore looked around the room. A comfy armchair, draped with a dust cover, rested close to the hearth. Next to the chair, there was a table and candlestick. Two small tables flanked the bed. The room was bright, thanks to several windows that faced west, where the sun was moving toward the horizon.

"Quickly, now," Olenka told her. "You should change before your lover arrives."

"He's not—" With a frustrated groan, Gwennore glanced down at her bedraggled gown, stained with urine. No matter what ridiculous things people might think, she still needed to talk to the general right away. "I'd like to wash up first."

"Of course." Olenka frowned at her own gown. "I have a water stain on my skirt from drawing the bath. I should change, too." She dashed through the dressing room, calling back, "I'll return shortly!"

The servant curtsied and started to leave.

"Wait." Gwennore gave her an apologetic smile. "Could you help me with these laces?" She turned sideways, motioning to her back.

The servant inched toward her slowly as if she were a poisonous snake ready to strike.

"I'm not going to hurt you. What's your name?"

"K-Kendra, my lady."

"I'm Gwennore." She lifted her loose and tangled hair out of the way. Goddesses help her, it might take an hour to get a comb through the disheveled mess.

Kendra fumbled with the laces for a few minutes, then gasped. "I didn't know elves were spotted green and blue!"

"Green and . . . ?" Gwennore winced. "Those must be bruises. I took a hard fall earlier."

"Oh. Well. You're all done now."

"Thank you." Gwennore turned to face her. "Could you mind the princess while I bathe?"

"Yes, my lady." The servant dashed from the room as if she were escaping the threat of imminent death.

Gwennore groaned. The next time someone acted as if she were a frightful creature, she really would vent her rage.

She removed her soiled gown, selected a clean shift from the new clothes on the bed, then went back to the dressing room. She'd noticed before that there were pipes along the wall. When she turned a spigot, cool water splashed into the tub. *Amazing.* She would have to ask how this was accomplished, so Luciana could replicate it at Ebton Palace.

After washing and putting on a clean shift, she peeked into the nursery to make sure Eviana was all right. Nissa was back, and Kendra had left.

Gwennore returned to the nanny's bedchamber and selected a blue silk gown. When she slipped it over her head, her back twinged once again.

A shadow moved across the room, and she glanced at the windows. A large eagle was flying back and forth.

"Brody!" She ran to the windows and nearly tripped on the hem of her gown. Without the laces done, the gown was dragging on the floor and in danger of falling off.

Pinning the bodice against her chest with one hand, she used her other hand to unlatch the window and push it open. The eagle flew inside and landed on the floor.

As Brody's form began to shimmer, she realized he would be naked once he shifted. Quickly, she pulled the dust cover off the armchair and tossed it on top of him. He flailed about underneath it, then emerged.

At the sight of his bare shoulders, she turned her back to him. Then, with a silent groan, she realized the back of her gown was open.

"Gwennie, are you all right? Where's Eviana?"

She glanced back to find him standing with the white sheet wrapped around his waist. "Eviana is next door in the nursery. Please let Luciana know that we're perfectly fine, and we'll return as soon as possible."

Brody scowled. "You're not fine. I saw the bruises on your back. What the hell did they do to you?"

"Nothing. The bruises happened when I fell through the air and crashed into Puff."

"Puff?"

"He's the dragon who caught me."

Brody stepped toward her, an incredulous look on his face. "One of those wretched dragons abducted you, and you named him *Puff*?"

"He didn't abduct me. He saved my life!"

"He brought you here against your will."

"No, I asked him to. I needed to stay with Eviana. And Puff promised he would help me get her back home."

"Wait." Brody held up a hand. "The dragon *promised*?"

Gwennore nodded. "I can hear them. And communicate with them."

Brody's eyes widened. "How? I can't do that."

"I don't know how, but Puff said he would help. And I think the general will, too."

"General Dravenko?"

"Ye know him?" Gwennore glanced at the door to the dressing room, which was still open just a crack. "He should be here any minute now."

Brody nodded. "I'll talk to him. I've dealt with him before."

"Oh, good." She stepped closer. "Before he comes, I need to tell you something. Ye know about my gift, right?"

"Aye."

Gwennore lowered her voice. "I touched the queen's hand. And she's mad."

"Angry?"

"No. Crazy. She's lost five children. And I think she's the one who ordered the kidnapping. She believes Eviana is her daughter who passed away."

Brody grimaced. "That is crazy."

"I know." Gwennore adjusted her hold on her bodice to keep her gown from falling off. "And there's more."

"You want me to tie off those laces?"

"Ye don't mind?"

"No." He motioned for her to turn. "You were saying?"

"I detected something when I touched the queen's hand." Gwennore stumbled back when he tugged sharply at her laces.

"Hold on to the bedpost," he grumbled.

She grabbed on. "I believe the queen is being poisoned."

"What?"

Gwennore glanced back at him. "I might be able to use my gift to help her."

Brody snorted. "She's the reason you and Eviana were kidnapped. Why on Aerthlan would you want to help her?"

Why, indeed? Gwennore wondered. The most sensible thing for her to do was to leave this place as soon as possible and make sure Eviana was safely returned home.

But ye were born with a special gift, she argued with herself. Wasn't she supposed to use it? If she could help the queen recover, then the woman might stop kidnapping children. Then no more children and parents would be traumatized.

Green and brown, the colors of the Norveshki army. The number three for Eviana's third birthday. Gwennore swallowed hard. Had the Telling Stones predicted that she would come to this place? Was she meant to be here?

When Silas reached the nursery, he found his colonel and best friend scowling as he leaned against the closed doors.

"Something wrong?" Silas asked.

Dimitri sighed. "Why did you do it?"

"Do what?"

"Tell everyone you captured her in battle."

"Lady Gwennore?"

"Who else?" Dimitri grumbled.

Silas shrugged. "She was about to be arrested as an assassin. I needed to vouch for her character, so I made it sound like I'd known her for a while and trusted her."

Dimitri snorted. "Well, you definitely succeeded."

"Is there a point to this?"

"Some people think you're bedding her."

Silas flinched. "*What?* How did they—"

"You said she was your captive and she'd proven herself useful."

Silas gave him an incredulous look. "There must be a hundred ways to be useful that have nothing to do with—" An image flitted through his mind of Gwennore, her arms and legs wrapped around him, her naked body pressed against him. *Damn.* She was breathtaking. And he—

"Are you drooling?"

Silas wiped his chin, then realized his friend had been joking.

While Dimitri snickered, Silas raised a fist, threatening to punch him. "When I said useful, I meant her intelligence and fluency in several languages."

"Right."

"Sod off." Silas pushed him aside so he could access the nursery door.

"She said the little girl is the Eberoni princess. Does the king realize the mess he's—"

"He's not here."

"But I saw him—"

"I know, but he left again. I don't know why." Silas noted the worried glint in his friend's eyes. No doubt Dimitri was wondering if Petras was also succumbing to insanity. "Don't even think it."

"He has put our country in danger."

"I'm going to fix it."

Dimitri winced. "You've had to fix things before. And he's not always grateful—"

"I know the risk. But no matter what, we are returning the princess and Lady Gwennore tomorrow. It is the only way to avoid war with Eberon and Tourin."

Dimitri nodded. "You're right."

Silas reached for the doorknob. "I'll tell Lady Gwennore to be ready before dawn."

"Oh." Dimitri grabbed his arm to stop him. "I should tell you. She grew up with Sorcha."

"I know."

Dimitri huffed. "Is there anything you don't know?" His eyes took on a mischievous glint. "Actually, I did hear something rather shocking from Lady Olenka, but you probably—"

"What?"

"According to her, you're the most handsome man on Aerthlan."

Silas scoffed. "If you learn something *important*, let me know." He reached for the doorknob once again.

"So I guess you're not interested in Lady Gwennore's response."

Silas hesitated. Had she agreed? He caught Dimitri smirking at him. *Bastard.*

Dimitri grinned. "I heard that."

"I let you hear it."

With a snort, Dimitri crossed his arms and leaned against the wall. "So you don't want to know what she said?"

"Don't need to. I can read her mind too well."

"Oh, right." Dimitri's mouth twitched. "Then you must have heard her call you General Gorgeous."

Silas hissed in a breath, then pointed a finger in his friend's face. "Stop invading her mind."

"Why not? You are."

"I can't help it," Silas grumbled. "She's practically shouting at us."

"I know," Dimitri agreed. "It's so strange. Why are we hearing her?"

"I don't know. If we didn't have our shields up, she could probably read our minds, too. She can hear the dragons."

"Crap."

"Precisely. If any other elves have that ability, imagine the havoc they could cause during battle." Silas frowned. "I need to talk to her."

Dimitri nodded. "At least you'll know if she's lying or not, since you can read her mind."

That was true, although Silas found it very distracting when she called him General Gorgeous. It kept reminding him that she was absolutely beautiful. The image of her naked in his bed flitted through his mind once again, and he shoved it aside. "It's not right for us to invade her privacy. I'll have to tell her how to erect a mental shield."

"You can't do that without admitting that you've been hearing her." Dimitri grinned. "General Gorgeous."

"Smart-ass." Silas entered the nursery to the sound of his friend's chuckling. As he approached the little girl by the hearth, he noted she was happily eating with a servant watching over her. Where was Gwennore?

His gaze wandered about the room, not finding her. Memories of his childhood rushed at him, slowing his steps to a halt. How long had it been? Almost twenty years since he'd lived in this room. He'd been sent far away at the age of seven to avoid the so-called curse.

The servant spotted him and curtsied. Then the little girl noticed him, and her eyes grew wide with fear.

Silas smiled at her and said in Eberoni, "Don't worry. I'm a friend. I know your aunt Brigitta and her husband, King Ulfrid. And I've met Brody several times."

The little girl bit her lip, then softly replied, "I wanna go home, please."

Guilt pricked at him. How many kidnappings had occurred over the last few years that he'd been unable to stop? He squatted in front of the little girl so she wouldn't have to look up at him. "Your name is Eviana, right?"

When she nodded, he continued, "The sun will be setting soon, so it's too late to take you home today. But I will take you tomorrow morning. Can you be brave and spend one night here?"

She frowned, jutting out her bottom lip. "I'll miss the party then. It's my buffday. Ewic's, too. And my mama's."

Tonight the two moons were eclipsing, so that meant Eviana and her twin brother were Embraced. Silas had heard the rumor before from his spy at the Eberoni court. He'd also heard that all five of the adopted sisters were Embraced. What kind of gift had his sister, Sorcha, grown up with? And Lady Gwennore—what was her gift? "Is it Gwennore's birthday, too? I know it must be Sorcha's."

Eviana's eyes widened with surprise. "You know Aunt Sowcha?" When he nodded, she smiled. "It is her buffday. And King Ulfwid's. That's why they're having a big party." Her smile faded. "I'm gonna miss it."

"I'm sure they'll wait for you to get back. They won't want to celebrate without you."

"Weally?"

Silas smiled. "Really." He straightened and addressed the servant in Norveshki. "It's the child's birthday today. Could you run to the kitchen and tell them I want a cake sent here tonight? And some party food."

"Yes, my lord." The servant dashed from the room.

Eviana's lip trembled. "Is something wrong?"

"No, she'll be right back. Do you know where Lady Gwennore is?"

The little girl pointed toward the dressing room.

He refilled her cup with more apple juice. "I need to talk to Gwennore. Will you be all right here?"

She nodded. "I want to play with the dollies."

"Excellent plan." He headed toward the dressing room.

The door was cracked open, and he peeked inside. Empty. Gwennore had to be in the adjoining bedchamber. Just the thought of a bed made her naked image creep into his thoughts once again. *Dammit, stop that.* He slipped into the dressing room and froze when he heard a man's voice.

What the hell? Gwennore was with a man in the bedchamber? Silas eased closer to the door.

"Hold on to the bedpost," the man ordered.

What? Silas peered through the narrow opening of the door and spotted her at the foot of the bed with a man partially hidden behind her. With her gown loose and her hair disheveled, she looked like she'd just enjoyed a rough tussle in bed. *Dammit. Stop thinking about her that way.* But who the hell was this man?

"I believe the queen is being poisoned," Gwennore said softly in Eberoni.

"*What?*" the man responded in the same language.

Silas's breath caught. Did Gwennore believe, like him, that there was a logical reason for the queen's illness?

"I might be able to use my gift to help her," Gwennore continued.

Silas grew tense. Could she really help the queen? What was this gift she had? And who was this man she talking to? He eased the door open wider and his heart lurched. *Dammit!* The man was naked with a sheet tied around his waist.

A surge of anger blasted through Silas, but then the man shoved his shaggy black hair back from his brow, and Silas recognized him. Brody, shifter and spy for King Leofric.

Of course. Silas noted the open window. Gwennore must have let Brody in while he was in eagle form, and then he'd shifted. That explained why he was wearing a sheet.

"She's the reason you and Eviana were kidnapped," Brody grumbled, referring to the queen. "Why on Aerthlan would you want to help her?"

Gwennore stood still, her hands clasped around the bedpost as her mind raced with one thought after another.

Yes! Silas smiled to himself as he listened in. At last, he'd found someone who thought the same way he did.

After a few moments, she said, "If I can help the queen, she might stop having children kidnapped."

"But if she's being poisoned, something dangerous is going on," Brody argued. "You shouldn't get involved."

She frowned. "But shouldn't I use my gift—"

Silas barged into the room. "Can you really help?"

Gwennore gasped. Startled by his sudden entrance, she let go of the bedpost just as Brody gave her laces a sharp tug. She stumbled back against the shifter, but when he caught her, she trampled on the edge of his sheet, accidentally pulling it off his waist.

"Shit!" Brody dropped to the floor, scrambling to cover himself with the sheet.

"Ack!" Gwennore slapped a hand over her eyes. "I didn't see anything!" She lurched forward, but her foot caught on the hem of her gown and she fell forward onto her knees. She caught herself, her hands planted on the floor.

It had all happened so fast, Silas was caught off guard and started to laugh. But then he noticed how Gwennore's white-blond hair had swept forward, the ends trailing on the floor. When she shoved her hair back, her back arched and his mouth dropped open. *Holy Light.* This was how she would look in a moment of wild passion.

With her gown askew, her breasts were nearly spilling out of the bodice. He stared at her, entranced, and by the Light, he wanted to touch her. He wanted to cup her breasts in his palms, tug the bodice down till he could see her nipples, see them tighten into sweet little buds. Then he would tease them. Taste them.

Not again! Her thoughts screeched into his head, and his gaze jerked up to her face.

He's staring at me so fiercely! He wants to squash me like a bug! Anger blazed in her eyes as she scrambled to her feet. "I am not an insect!"

Silas flinched. How could she think—

"Don't ye dare give me that horrified look! I'm a woman and I have the exact same female parts as every other woman on the planet!"

Damn. Silas gulped. It would be hard from now on not to think about her female parts. Or his own parts that were reacting. "I assure you, I will never forget."

"Sheesh, Gwennie," Brody muttered.

Heat flared in her cheeks, and she glanced frantically around the room. *Dear goddesses, what have I done? Should I crawl under the bed? How can this day keep getting worse?*

"My lady." Silas stepped toward her. He wanted to tell

her she was beautiful, but he suspected she wouldn't believe him right now. With her cheeks inflamed with embarrassment, she was refusing to even look at him. "Could you excuse us for a moment? I need to talk to Brody."

"Of course!" She dashed from the room.

Silas winced at the sound of the door slamming. "I didn't mean to upset her."

Brody snorted as he rose to his feet. "You should have thought of that before you had your dragons kidnap her and Eviana."

"The dragon that kidnapped Eviana is not under my command."

"Whose command, then?" Brody tied the sheet at his waist.

Silas sighed. It wouldn't help matters if he admitted that the king and queen of Norveshka were responsible for the abduction of the Eberoni princess. "A mistake was made."

Brody scoffed. "You could say that again."

"I want peace with Eberon and Tourin. And I will offer my sincere apologies to King Leofric when I deliver his daughter safely to him tomorrow."

"You can do that?"

"Yes." Silas nodded. "I'll bring the princess and Gwennore down the Norva River by barge. We'll leave at dawn, and by noon, we should be at Vorushka, close to the border. If Leofric can meet us there—"

"I'll make sure he does," Brody replied. "Before I go, I should verify that Eviana is all right."

"Of course." Silas motioned for the shifter to follow him through the door to the dressing room.

Silas pushed open the door to the nursery. The servant was back, and the little girl was pushing a small pram around the room, loaded down with a dozen dolls. Gwennore's gown was properly laced up now, and she was sitting by the fire, trying to tame her beautiful hair with a brush.

Brody watched silently for a while, then retreated to the bedchamber. "I'll trust you to take good care of them."

"You have my word." Silas joined him. "What is this gift Gwennore was talking about?"

Brody gave him a wary look. "I don't think it's any of your business."

"She seemed to think she could help us."

"That's not happening. Whatever is going on here, it sounds dangerous. I don't want her involved."

A twinge of annoyance shot through Silas. "Do you care about her that much?"

"She's a good friend. And a good person. I've seen her get hurt too much. I don't—"

"Who's been hurting her?" Silas growled, and when the shifter looked surprised, he paused, wondering why he had reacted so strongly.

Brody tilted his head, watching him carefully. "She's been enduring some prejudice at the Eberoni and Tourinian courts. Snide remarks and rude stares from other courtiers."

"And you let the assholes get away with it? What kind of friend are you?"

Brody scoffed. "I've offered my help, but she always refuses. She doesn't want to cause any strife between her sisters and their subjects. I've never seen her lose her temper before. That is, until she encountered you."

Silas stiffened. "I wasn't being snide or rude."

"You were staring at her."

"Because she's—" Silas stopped himself.

Brody's eyebrows lifted as he waited.

Silas motioned toward the open window. "Didn't you need to go?"

Brody snorted. "Fine. See you tomorrow." He pulled off the sheet, shifted into an eagle, and flew out the window.

As Silas headed back to the nursery, his heart began to thud in his chest. It was time for a long talk with Gwennore.

Chapter Six

❧

Gwennore winced as she accidentally ripped out a few more strands of hair. How could this day keep getting worse? After promising herself that she would vent her rage with glorious indignation, she'd finally done it. In the worst way possible.

I have the exact same female parts as every other woman on the planet!

With a groan, she dropped the hairbrush on the table next to her chair. Of all the stupid things to say!

She glanced over at Eviana, who was babbling to the dolls, happily bestowing names on each of them. After everything the child had been through today, she was still able to find joy. *I should be resilient like that*, Gwennore thought. *And most of all, I need to be strong.*

After all, it was her weakness, her reluctance to stand up for herself that had set up the scenario resulting in Eviana's kidnapping. So, instead of being embarrassed, she ought to feel relieved. And proud. She had, at last, released her anger and defended herself.

But why had she picked General Dravenko to be on the receiving end of her rant? He was, most probably, her best hope for getting Eviana home, so he was the last person on Aerthlan she should have yelled at. What a foolish mistake for someone who prided herself on always being reasonable and intelligent.

Why him, of all people? Had she finally reached her limit where anyone would have set her off?

She shook her head. There was a growing suspicion in her mind, one she was trying to ignore, but what if she'd lost control with the gorgeous general because his gawking stare had hurt her feelings more than the others?

With a sigh, she leaned over and rested her face in her hands. He could definitely be considered the Most Handsome Man on the Planet, what with the way his leather breeches clung to his long muscular legs and the way his shirt and leather breastplate accentuated his broad chest and shoulders. She suspected he was even taller than Leo and Rupert, and the way he walked with those long legs had nearly caused every woman in the castle to faint. Including Gwennore.

Some might say his jawline was too sharp and his gaze too intense, but she thought it suited the aura of power that emanated from him. And there was passion—she could sense it in the glittering green of his eyes and his wide, expressive mouth. Power and passion—he embodied them both, and she found herself acutely aware of him in a way she'd never felt before with any other man.

From the first moment she'd seen him, she had hoped he could be her tall and handsome stranger as foretold by the Telling Stones. But the sad truth was something she couldn't avoid. She was an elf, Norveshka's worst enemy. It was no wonder the general had looked at her like she was a bug. And now, after her ridiculous rant, he probably thought she was a fool.

How could she ever face him again?

"My lady? Are you all right?"

It's him! She kept her head buried in her hands and felt

the sudden rush of heat radiating from her cheeks. Why was the man's voice so smooth and appealing? It reminded her of the dragon, but with Puff, she'd felt a degree of comfort. This man had her on edge.

Would he go away if she ignored him? *If I make a snoring sound, will he think I'm asleep?*

"Lady Gwennore," he said softly in Norveshki. "Are you awake?"

There was no help for it. She would have to talk to the man for Eviana's sake. Straightening up, she feigned a yawn. "I was just resting." She ventured a quick glance at him and noted his mouth curled up and his eyes twinkling with humor.

Great. He thought she was amusing. It was better, though, than being regarded with horror. Puff had found her amusing, too, but the embarrassment was easier to take from a dragon than a gorgeous man. *Puff, can you still hear me? Please come back and take Eviana and me home. If anyone can save us, it's you.*

The general's smile faded. "We need to talk."

"All right." She eased to her feet and winced as a shot of pain crossed her back.

"Are you injured?" he asked.

I'm a wreck. My back is killing me, and I'm so mortified I want to crawl into a hole. "I'm fine."

"No, you're not." General Dravenko frowned at her. "Did the dragon hurt you?"

"I'm a little sore, that's all. It happened when Puff caught me, but I'm sure he never intended me any harm."

The general muttered a curse, then turned to Nissa. "Heat up some water, so you can make some hot compresses."

"Yes, my lord." Nissa ran into the dressing room.

"It was an accident," Gwennore insisted. "Puff won't be in trouble, will he?"

"Would you stop calling him Puff? He's a war dragon, for Light's sake."

"Then he works for you, right?" Gwennore asked. "Pray, please don't punish him. I would have fallen to my death if he hadn't caught me. If anything, he deserves an award."

The general's eyes narrowed. "You're quick to come to his defense."

"Of course. He saved my life. I shall always be grateful to him. And he was really very sweet and gentle. He held me so carefully—"

"I saved you, too." General Dravenko gave her an annoyed look. "You would have spent the night in the dungeon if I hadn't—"

"That's not nearly as terrifying as a plummet to my death."

"Would you like to go to the dungeon, then? It can be arranged."

"Are you threatening me?"

He gritted his teeth. "No. I'm trying to protect you. And I can do it better than a damned dragon."

She snorted. Who was he kidding? His manner of protection was a disaster. Everyone in the castle was going to believe they were lovers.

He hissed in a breath, drawing her attention back to his face.

Blast him. It should be a crime to have both a gorgeous body and a beautiful face. But she wouldn't let him intimidate her. After all, she needed his help. "I appreciate your protection."

He gave her a dubious look that made her wonder how much he could see through her.

She cleared her throat. "I suppose I should thank you."

"I suppose you should."

She blinked. That sounded familiar somehow. Hadn't her conversation with Puff gone much the same way?

"We need to talk." His brusque words interrupted her thoughts as he started toward the bedchamber. "Come with me."

She huffed. Didn't he realize what it would look like if they were alone in a bedchamber? *Oh, wait.* Brody was still there. If the general tried anything unseemly, Brody could shift into a dog and bite him. Hopefully, on his gorgeous rump.

The general halted with a jerk, then glanced back at her. She quickly looked away, so he wouldn't know that she'd been watching his buttocks while he walked.

"Are you coming?" he asked softly.

"Excuse me." The maid suddenly emerged from the dressing room with a large copper kettle of water, and he stepped aside to let her pass.

"Thank you," General Dravenko told the maid, then looked at Gwennore and beckoned with his hand. "Come."

Gwennore's heart fluttered as he strode into the dressing room. The way the man moved was lethal, like a wildcat prowling through the forest.

She glanced over at Nissa and found her standing nearby, gawking at the open door that the general had just passed through. The kettle tipped in her hands, allowing water to drip from the spout onto her slippers, and she didn't even notice.

Gwennore groaned inwardly. "Could you watch Eviana for me? I need a moment with the general."

Nissa sighed dreamily. "Don't we all?"

Gwennore's cheeks grew warm. "I'm going to talk to him for a few minutes. That's all."

Nissa broke free from her trance. "Yes, my lady." She bobbed a curtsy. "Begging your pardon, my lady."

Gwennore started toward the dressing room, then hesitated as she passed by the servant. "Does the general . . . talk to a great number of women?"

Nissa shook her head. "I don't believe so. He's from one of the Three Cursed Clans, and that frightens most women away."

Gwennore recalled how Olenka had reacted to the prospect of a courtship with the general. "Why? Are they afraid they'll go insane like the queen?"

Nissa winced. "Please don't speak of it anymore. It is forbidden."

"Why? What could happen to you?"

Nissa grew pale as she glanced around the room. "People disappear."

"What?"

The maid scurried toward the hearth to hang the kettle on a hook over the fire. She obviously didn't want to talk, and Gwennore didn't want to frighten the poor girl with more questions. Still, she found herself extremely curious about this so-called curse. It couldn't be real, yet something sinister was going on here.

Brody would tell her it was none of her business. Or that pursuing the matter could put her in danger. He had a point, she thought as she strode through the dressing room. She needed to keep her priorities straight.

First and foremost, she had to convince General Gorgeous to return Eviana to her parents. It shouldn't be hard, since Brody would be there to help her. She closed the bedchamber door behind her, then strode into the room.

Brody was gone.

She glanced around once again. General Dravenko was across the room, his back to her as he gazed out an open window. "Brody left? Without saying good-bye?"

The general turned to face her, and she was struck with the realization that she was alone with him in a bedchamber.

She stepped back. "We shouldn't be here."

"We need privacy to discuss some important matters." He motioned toward the open window. "Brody was in a hurry to let Eviana's parents know that she's fine."

"They will not feel at ease until they have her back."

"I understand." General Dravenko closed the window. "And I fully realize the damage that has been done. As soon as I learned what was happening, I tried to stop it—"

"You sent Puff?"

"Yes. I am sorry he arrived too late. And I apologize for the pain and suffering—"

"It wasn't your fault." Gwennore waved a dismissive hand. "But you can rectify matters by returning Eviana and me as quickly as possible."

The general opened his mouth to respond, then hesitated. "There are several other things I'd like to discuss first."

She lifted her chin. "After you agree to send us back, I will feel comfortable discussing those things with you."

His eyes glinted with amusement. "Are you negotiating with me?"

"I'm protecting Eviana the best I can."

"She is safe here. You have my word."

"But that's the problem. She shouldn't be here. She should be with her parents, don't you agree?"

His mouth twitched. "Leofric should hire you to be his chief counsel."

Her heart skipped a beat. That was perhaps the most flattering thing she'd ever heard. She remained in a daze till she realized he had moved toward her. Only the bed was between them now.

She retreated another step.

"I have a question for you." He tilted his head, watching her carefully. "How are you able to hear the dragons?"

That again? She shrugged. "I don't know."

"Do any other elves have the ability?"

"I don't know. Am I being interrogated?"

He bit his lip as if he was trying not to smile. "Is this where I say something like . . ." He glanced down at the bed, then slanted a pointed look at her. "I have ways to make you talk."

Her eyes widened. Was he threatening to torture her? But then, why had he looked at the bed?

He cleared his throat as if he was trying not laugh. "I'll ask again. Do you know of any other elves who can hear the dragons?"

"I don't know any other elves."

"You were born in Woodwyn, right?"

"I was, but they sent me away when I was two months old. I don't know why."

"You don't know who your parents are?"

"Does any of this matter?" She glared at him. "After I return to Eberon, I won't be here to listen to your precious dragons. Puff will never have to speak to me again."

The general's expression turned serious. With his jaw set and his eyes taking on a fierce gleam, she was reminded once again that he was a powerful warrior.

"It matters a great deal," he said softly. "We are at war with Woodwyn. I need to know what the elves are capable of."

She groaned inwardly. She'd been right. The general saw her as an enemy. "I don't know anything."

"What is your gift?"

She winced. How much had he heard of her conversation with Brody? "You shouldn't eavesdrop on people's private—"

"I know you're Embraced," the general said, ignoring her objection. "So what is your gift? How can you help the queen?"

She shrugged. "The queen's health is not my concern."

He strode around the foot of the bed. "You said yourself that if you helped the queen, she might stop kidnapping children. Then no child would have to go through what Eviana did today."

Gwennore grew tense. The man was definitely a warrior. He knew exactly where to strike for the most effect.

"You also said the queen was being poisoned." He came to a stop beside her. "I've always suspected the same thing, but I had no way of proving it. Can you help me figure out what's going on here?"

Now he was appealing to her curiosity. She shook her head. "Brody thinks it would be too dangerous, and I have to agree. I just learned from the maid that people disappear if they talk about the curse."

"What?" His eyebrows rose.

"That's what Nissa told me. And I have no reason to doubt her. Her fear is real."

Frowning, he folded his arms across his broad chest. "I'll investigate the matter. But meanwhile, you would be working with me, so you would be safe. I can protect you."

"I don't think your method of protection is very helpful." She waved a hand at the bed. "Everyone thinks that we're . . ."

"Lovers?"

Her heart lurched. Why did his voice have to sound so alluring? A glint of gold in his pupils caught her by surprise, but when she blinked, they were back to a brilliant emerald green. Had she just imagined it?

"Gwennore—"

"We shouldn't be alone." She turned toward the door.

"Why not? Are you afraid I'll seduce you?"

With a huff, she whirled around to face him. "As if you could."

His mouth curled up. "Is that a challenge?"

"No!"

"You can't leave now." He moved close to her. "People will think I lasted only a few minutes."

The scoundrel! She slapped his shoulder.

He grinned. "Did you just hit me? After I saved you?"

She opened her mouth to reply, then paused as a memory flitted through her mind. Hadn't Puff said the exact same thing? How odd . . .

"What is your gift?" The general interrupted her thoughts.

She'd been warned all her life that being Embraced was a death sentence on the mainland, so she hesitated to answer.

"I won't let any harm come to you. You have my word."

She supposed that was true. After all, if he wanted her help, he would have to keep her alive. "I can sense if a person is healthy or not, and if not, I can usually determine the cause."

His eyebrows lifted. "You're a healer?"

She winced. "I wouldn't say that. Just because I can tell what sort of illness a person has, it doesn't mean I can actually cure him. We have an excellent healer at the convent, and she taught me a great deal about medicinal herbs and concoctions, but there are still things that are beyond me. I cannot guarantee that I would be able to help the queen."

"You're being honest. Thank you."

She snorted. Had he expected her to lie?

He gave her a wry look. "How could you tell she's being poisoned?"

"I sensed it when I did a reading on her. She's not just mentally ill. Physically, she's . . . wasting away. I'm sorry."

With a frown, he nodded. "How do you do a reading?"

"I touch a person, then somehow I . . . connect." She shrugged. "It's a gift. I don't know how to explain it."

"Show me." He spread his hands to either side.

She blinked. "You?"

"Yes." His eyes twinkled with humor. "Where would you like to touch me?"

She scoffed. "There's no need to. I can tell by looking at you that you're perfectly healthy."

"Touch me. I want see how you . . . connect."

Her cheeks grew warm.

With his hands still extended to the side, he crooked his fingers. "I'm waiting."

She ignored him, folding her arms across her chest. "There are several spots that can give me a good reading. A person's wrist, forehead, or the neck below the ear."

"Go ahead, then." He smiled. "Lady's choice."

Her heart fluttered. The man's smile was a weapon, and he knew how to use it. She reached out to grab his left wrist with her right hand.

She pressed her fingers against him, and instantly she felt his pulse. Stronger than she had expected. She closed her eyes to concentrate, letting her senses join the rush of his blood as it coursed through his veins and arteries.

Her breath caught. His heart was larger than normal. But it appeared quite healthy, thumping with a steady beat.

She reached past his heart, venturing up his chest and neck. There seemed to be some sort of wall blocking his brain. That was odd.

She moved down his body, swooping over his toned muscles. There was an abrasion on his left arm—no, more like a tattoo. Interesting. A few battle wounds had healed nicely. He would be the type to recover quickly.

The warmth of good health radiated from his entire body, but an extra amount of heat seemed to be concentrated in one area. His groin.

With a flinch, she released him.

"Something wrong?"

She shook her head as she stepped back. "You've had a few minor wounds, but they've healed well."

"Where?"

Was he testing her? The scoundrel. "A cut on your right shoulder and another below the ribs on the left."

His brows lifted as if he was impressed. "I stubbed my toe this morning. Can you tell me which foot?"

How could she admit that she hadn't gone past his groin? "Actually, I did detect a problem. Before it reaches a point where it's too debilitating, I recommend you eat more fruits and vegetables."

He frowned. "What is it?"

"Constipation."

He snorted. "My ass."

"Exactly."

His mouth twitched. "Let's make a bargain. Agree to help me, and I'll return Eviana tomorrow."

Gwennore's heart took a small leap. "Tomorrow?"

"Yes." He nodded. "I could take her by boat down the Norva River to the Eberoni border. She could be back with her parents by noon."

Praise the goddesses! "I need to go with her."

He shook his head. "If you agree to the bargain, you'll have to stay here."

"But she'll be too frightened to travel without me. She's been traumatized enough!"

After a moment, he sighed. "All right. I'll make allowances as long as you agree to the bargain."

"I can't guarantee that I'll be useful."

"Do you think our problems here have been caused by a curse?"

She shook her head. "No."

"Do you think there must be a reasonable explanation?"

"Of course."

"Then you're already useful. With your gift of healing and your intelligence, I believe you can help. And I can't tell you what a relief it is to find someone who actually thinks the same as I. Most people around here won't even talk about the damned curse."

She winced. "They're afraid they'll disappear."

"You won't disappear. Not when you're with me. So do we have a deal? After we return Eviana, you'll come back with me."

She hesitated. As much as she wanted to accept the bargain for Eviana's sake, she also had to look out for herself. "I'll have to insist on a time limit. I'll remain here no longer than two weeks."

He arched a brow. "Two months."

"One month."

"Deal. Now we have to seal it with a kiss."

"What?"

With a grin, he extended a hand. "I was joking."

She scoffed. For a man living under a curse, he seemed rather jovial about it. But in a way, she found that appealing. He was refusing to accept the curse or cower in fear.

She glanced at his hand. Could she really do this?

What choice did she have? She needed to get Eviana home. And to be honest with herself, there were other reasons that made her want to agree. She was curious about the so-called curse. And even more intrigued by the thought that she might be able to break it.

She glanced at the general, and his eyebrows lifted with a questioning look as he waited. Good goddesses, how could she work with this gorgeous scoundrel of a man? Tentatively, she placed her hand in his. "I agree."

He gripped her hand firmly. "Partner."

She pulled her hand away as warmth rushed to her face. "If I am to live here for a month, I expect you to let everyone know that we are not . . . involved in any way."

"We will be involved. We'll be working together. And since it is forbidden to speak of the curse, we'll have to keep our investigation secret. The easiest way for us to spend time together with no one suspecting is to let them think we're lovers."

"I don't want people thinking that!"

His mouth curled up. "Too late."

She huffed. "Aren't you offended by the idea? People will think you're sleeping with the enemy."

"They'll think I have excellent taste."

"What? Haven't you seen how people look at me?"

"No. I'm too busy staring at you, myself. Do you really not know how beautiful you are?"

Her mouth dropped open.

He leaned closer to peer into her mouth. "Even your teeth look good."

"Stop that!" She stepped back. The scoundrel was playing with her. She couldn't believe half of what he said.

He gave her an exasperated look. "Can you have Eviana ready to leave before dawn?"

"Yes."

"Good. I'll see you tomorrow then." He opened the door and strode through the dressing room into the nursery.

Gwennore followed him and discovered that Olenka had returned. She was wearing an elaborate pink ball gown and long white gloves. Her wrists were encircled with numerous sparkling bracelets. A gleaming ruby necklace matched the tiara perched on top of her perfectly coiffed hair.

She sank into a deep curtsy. "My lord. I hope you are pleased with the great care I have given your guests."

He nodded as he passed by. "Yes, thank you."

Olenka jumped up and scurried after him. "Is there anything else I can do? Shall I arrange for a private room for you and . . ." She glanced back at Gwennore.

"No!" Gwennore winced. She hadn't meant to shout.

The general's eyes danced with mischief. "It will be difficult to spend a night away from my darling Gwennie, but she should remain here with the child tonight."

Gwennore hissed in a breath. *Blast him.*

A knock sounded on the door, then Dimitri opened it and let several servants enter. They were carrying trays filled with food and a cake topped with three candles.

A birthday cake? Gwennore dashed toward Eviana. "Look! There's a cake for you."

Eviana squealed with delight.

The general smiled as he spoke to the little girl in Eberoni. "Happy birthday. I wish I had something new to give you, but if you like, you may take three of the toys here with you when you go home tomorrow."

Eviana bounced on her feet, clapping her hands.

Gwennore gave the general a shy smile. "Thank you."

He winked at her.

Her smile turned into a glare.

With a chuckle, he strode from the room. Dimitri gave him a wry look, then closed the door after the servants left.

"Isn't he dreamy?" Olenka pressed her hands to her chest.

"I know." Nissa filled a plate for Eviana. "He had me go to the kitchen to order the cake and food." She glanced at Gwennore. "Would you like some, my lady?"

Gwennore shook her head. She was too tense right now to think of food. She'd just struck a bargain to work with the general, and she still didn't know what to make of him. Was he a hero or a scoundrel? Either way, he made her heart flutter and her knees grow weak.

No doubt, he could protect her physically. But what about her feelings? If she wasn't very careful, she could lose her heart.

Chapter Seven

❧

Late that night, Aleksi knocked on Silas's bedchamber door to let him know that the king had returned.

"Is everything set for tomorrow morning?" Silas asked his friend as they strode down the hallway.

Aleksi nodded. "I rented a barge. And I'll have our horses saddled and ready in the courtyard at dawn."

"Excellent." Silas glanced around to make sure no one was in sight. Luckily, it looked like everyone in the southern wing had already retired for the night. Even so, he lowered his voice to a whisper. "Lady Gwennore will be returning here with us."

"Really? Why?"

"I believe she can help me investigate the so-called curse. Our work will be secret, though, so not a word to anyone other than Dimitri."

Aleksi gave him an incredulous look. "You're going to trust an elf with our problems?"

"She has no ties to Woodwyn."

"How can you be sure of that?"

"I know about her past. She grew up on the Isle of Moon with the queens Luciana and Brigitta—"

"She might tell them about the curse," Aleksi grumbled.

"If we get rid of the curse, it'll no longer matter." Silas waved a dismissive hand. "Don't worry about Gwennore. I can read her thoughts, so I know she's trustworthy."

With a dubious look, Aleksi glanced away.

"What?" Silas asked.

"I can hear her, too. She keeps calling you General Gorgeous."

Silas snorted. "What does that have to with anything?"

"You might not be seeing things clearly if you're enjoying her flattery."

"I see very clearly. Sometimes, I think I'm the only one around here who does. Or I did. Gwennore actually thinks like me, so we'll make a good team."

Aleksi grimaced.

"*What?*" Silas's voice grew louder with exasperation.

"You have me, Dimitri and Lady Margosha helping you," Aleksi mumbled. "I don't know why you need anyone else."

Silas slanted an amused look at his young captain. Since their other friend, Dimitri, was only a few months younger than Silas, the two of them had grown up as sparring partners. Aleksi, however, was five years younger and had followed the two older boys around like a puppy. Even now, he tended to get grumpy if he felt he was being overlooked.

After delivering a light punch to Aleksi's shoulder, Silas explained, "Gwennore has a special gift no one else has. With her help, we could finally make some progress."

Aleksi sighed. "The curse has been going on for five hundred years. It's probably impossible—"

"Don't say that." Silas pointed at his friend as they slowed to a stop. "You see? That's why I need her. While everyone else is wallowing in fear of the curse, Gwennore refuses to believe in it. And I know she's brave. She proved that today."

Aleksi gave him a sheepish look. "I know the rumor can't be true, since you just met her, but you should know that people are saying the two of you are lovers."

Silas shrugged. "It'll make a convenient excuse to explain why we're spending time together."

"Then you don't mind that people are saying you're sleeping with the enemy? I heard some of the courtiers are wagering how long it will take before the elf stabs you to death in your sleep. The most popular bet has her killing you three nights from now."

Silas gritted his teeth. "If you hear anyone making a disparaging remark about her, tell him he will be receiving a visit from me."

Aleksi's eyes widened. "Dimitri's right. You're attracted to her."

Silas looked away. There was no point in denying it. Not when he kept envisioning the woman in his bed. He resumed his walk toward the stairwell. "She's an intelligent, brave, and beautiful woman. But it doesn't matter. Nothing will come of it."

"She calls you General Gorgeous. Doesn't that mean she's attracted to you, too?"

Silas shook his head, then smiled as he recalled her physical assessment of him. Constipation. "She thinks I'm full of shit."

Aleksi snorted. "You're right. She *is* intelligent."

Silas cuffed him on the shoulder once again. "She'll be here for only a month. Then she's going back to her sisters where she belongs." *To live with my sister, Sorcha.*

"We'll have to hope she's not too clever," Aleksi mumbled. "If she figures out too much . . ."

Silas winced. His young friend was right. If Gwennore uncovered Norveshka's biggest secret, she would never be allowed to return to her sisters, especially when two of those sisters were the queens of potentially dangerous countries.

He reached the top of the stairs and spotted the king trudging up the steps, followed by two of his personal guard. Behind them, the secretary, Lord Romak, shot Silas an annoyed look.

"Aleksi," he whispered. "When I talk to His Majesty, make sure Romak isn't close enough to hear us."

"Understood," Aleksi replied.

While they waited at the top of the stairs, Silas took the opportunity to observe his older brother. In the last two years, the king's black hair had acquired some gray at the temples. New wrinkles on his brow and dark circles beneath his eyes made him look both tired and stressed.

Silas grew tense, recalling the rumors that Petras might also be succumbing to madness. It couldn't be true, though. He refused to believe it, just like he refused to believe in the curse.

"Your Majesty." Silas bowed as the king reached the landing.

Petras regarded him with an expression that was both affectionate and annoyed. "Come with me." He glanced back at Romak. "You may retire for the evening."

A hint of anger flickered over the secretary's face before he pasted a smile on his face and bowed. "Your Majesty is most gracious."

While Silas accompanied Petras down the hallway, he glanced back to make sure Aleksi was herding the secretary down the stairs. Then he leaned in close and whispered, "I don't trust Romak. You should get rid of him."

Petras shook his head. "He hasn't done anything to give me cause."

"That you know of. Have you noticed the number of rings he's wearing? Are you paying him that well?"

Petras's mouth thinned with irritation. "I am aware of what's going on around me. I've asked Karlan to keep an eye on Romak. We haven't found him taking any bribes or dipping into the royal treasury."

"Then where is his wealth coming from?"

"I'll figure it out." Petras heaved a sigh as he opened the door to his private sitting room. "This is the way it is here. The courtiers are constantly jockeying for more wealth and power. The only one I can really trust is Karlan."

"And me." Silas entered the dark room, lit only by a fire in the hearth. "I will always have your back."

"I know that." Petras closed the door, leaving his two guards in the hallway. "But frankly, you're not supposed to be here. Romak has been trying to convince me that you've abandoned your post for the sole purpose of interfering with my business."

"The damned weasel."

"He has a point." Petras lit a long stick of kindling in the fireplace, then used it to light the candles on the mantel. "You are interfering."

Silas scoffed. "How could I not? Do I have to tell you the danger you put the country in today?"

With an angry flick of his wrist, Petras tossed the stick into the fire. "Do I have to tell you the danger of going against my wishes?"

Silas gave him an exasperated look. "Do you seriously want a war with Eberon and Tourin? You put me in charge of protecting our country, and that's what I'm doing. We can't afford to fight three countries at once. Our army is depleted enough."

Petras added another log to the fire. "We have plenty of money. Hire more soldiers."

"From where?" Silas gritted his teeth. "We've already

taken women into the army. Do you want to risk the children next?"

Petras straightened with a worried look. "Surely, it's not that bad."

"It *is* bad," Silas ground out. "We've been officially at war with Woodwyn for two years now. Unofficially, we have a long history of skirmishes with all of our neighbors. We can't afford to lose any more people. That's why we need peace with Eberon and Tourin. And to do that, I have to return the princess tomorrow."

Petras hissed in a breath. "The queen requested a princess."

"Dammit." Silas walked away a few steps while he attempted to tamp down his frustration. "Taking the girl was wrong, Petras. You can't traumatize children and families like that."

"You think I don't know that?" Petras yelled. "But what am I supposed to do when my wife is crying every day and threatening to throw herself off the highest tower? I have to give her a reason to live! I'm losing her, Silas!"

A pain ripped through Silas when he realized how much his brother and sister-in-law were suffering. "It'll get better. I'll do whatever I can to help her."

"You don't live here." Petras's eyes glistened with tears. "You haven't had to watch her slip further away every day. Or witness her mind slowly deteriorating. I'm afraid she'll end up killing herself like our mother did."

"Petras." Silas pulled his brother into an embrace. "Don't worry. I'll fix things. Somehow."

With a scoff, Petras took him by the shoulders and moved him back. "*You* will fix things? Do you have any idea how it makes me feel to have a younger brother who thinks he has to clean up after me?"

"I don't mean it that way."

"But that's what you're doing." Petras squeezed his shoulders in a tight grip. "Are you going to defy me by returning the girl tomorrow?"

Silas swallowed hard. "By the Light, brother. Don't ever doubt my loyalty."

Petras regarded him sadly. "Are you returning her?"

"What choice do I have? It's the only way to avoid war."

"Since when is a general afraid of war?"

Silas snorted. "It's not fear. It's honesty. I'm facing the facts, Petras. Our country is dying from within."

"Don't say that!" Petras shoved him back.

"It's true." Silas took a deep breath. "Our first priority has to be saving ourselves. So I strongly urge you to end the war with Woodwyn."

"No."

"There is no point to it, Petras. Nothing is ever gained, and any loss of life becomes more of a disaster for our country. We should send an envoy to negotiate."

"Absolutely not." Petras shook his head. "The last time we sent an envoy, he never came back. The damned elves must have killed him."

Silas sighed. That had been Dimitri's uncle. "Lord Tolenko went over twenty years ago. It's time for us to try again."

Petras turned to gaze at the fire.

Silas cleared his throat. "When I return the princess tomorrow, I might get to see Sorcha."

Petras glanced back. "Sorcha?"

"She grew up with a group of adopted sisters on the Isle of Moon. The elfin woman who came with the princess is one of the sisters. And the current queens of Eberon and Tourin are also sisters. So there's a good chance Sorcha will be with Queen Luciana when I return the daughter."

Petras remained quiet for a while as if lost in thought. "Then she's had a good life?"

"I believe so."

Petras frowned. "Don't bring her back here. She needs to stay away from the curse."

Silas sighed. If he and Gwennore could do away with the so-called curse, it might be safe for Sorcha to finally return to her real family.

Petras turned back to gaze into the fire. "All of our problems go back to the curse."

Or people's belief in the so-called curse, Silas thought.

"For more than four centuries, it affected only a few members of the royal family, but in the last two generations, it has become so much worse." Petras sighed. "The entire population is suffering now."

"We can't be sure the curse is responsible for—"

"Of course it is! We lost two of our siblings and our mother. I've lost five children and I'm in danger of losing my wife. This damned curse must come to an end." Petras slanted a wary look at him. "I found a way to get rid of it."

"What?" Silas stepped closer. "How?"

Petras turned back toward the fire, and the light flickered over his face, causing eerie shadows. "It's a secret." A small smile lingered on his mouth. "After five hundred years, we will finally be free."

"How?"

Petras's eyes gleamed with excitement. "If I tell you, you must keep it secret."

Silas leaned close. "You have my word."

Petras lowered his voice to a whisper. "It's Fafnir."

"Faf—" Silas straightened with a jerk. "From the Ancient Ones? He was killed five hundred years ago."

"He's still alive," Petras insisted. "You know the Ancient Ones could live for hundreds of years."

"That may be true, but they're all dead now."

"Fafnir survived." Petras's eyes glittered in the flickering firelight. "And since he's all alone, he wants to make peace with us. He said he would take away the curse. I only have to do what he tells me to."

A sliver of apprehension crept down Silas's spine. "What is he telling you to do?"

Petras looked back at the fire, his mouth shut.

Silas grew more tense. "How often do you talk to him?"

"Several times a week. I've been meeting him at the Sacred Well."

"For how long?"

Petras shrugged. "Just over a year."

"And now you tell me?" Silas frowned. "So he suddenly appeared about a year ago? After he was gone for five hundred years?"

"Are you doubting me?"

"Not you." While Silas believed it was possible that his brother was talking to a dragon, he had to wonder if it was actually Fafnir. Any dragon could say he was an Ancient One and try to use that status to manipulate the king.

"Fafnir is real," Petras grumbled. "He was injured in the final battle, so he went into hibernation for a long time to recover."

Five hundred years? Silas drew in a deep breath. "I need to meet this Fafnir."

Petras shook his head. "He doesn't want anyone else to know about him. There would be some who would want to kill him. So not a word to anyone, understand? Fafnir is our best chance of getting rid of the curse."

"What if the curse isn't real? And he's just using—"

"Stop it!" Petras gave him an incredulous look. "How can you even say that? How many loved ones do you have to lose before you accept the truth?"

Silas gritted his teeth. Just because the pain was real, it didn't mean the curse was, too. "What exactly is this Fafnir telling you to do?"

"He wants to defeat Woodwyn."

Silas scoffed. "Why? What would he gain from it? And how would that get rid of the so-called curse?"

"He also wants to take over Tourin."

"*What?* No, absolutely not."

Petras gave him a stern look. "You work for me, Silas. Don't forget that."

Silas walked away a few steps with his mind reeling. A war on two different fronts? Three fronts, most probably, because the minute he attacked Tourin, Eberon would enter the war as Tourin's ally. This would be disastrous for Norveshka. A terrible suspicion crept into his thoughts. What if this dragon, whoever he might be, was using the king to destroy the country?

"I'll get rid of the curse," Petras insisted. "And then Freya will get well, and we'll have more children. Our fellow countrymen will be able to have more children. Norveshka will be healed once and for all."

"I want that, too, but—"

"Then don't argue with me. When Fafnir tells us what to do, we must do as he says. And then he will lift the curse that the Ancient Ones put on us."

Silas swallowed hard. He and Gwennore would have to work quickly to prove the curse wasn't real. He also needed to see if people were disappearing like Gwennore had said. And he needed to investigate this dragon who was giving orders to the king. "Before I agree to follow orders from Fafnir, I must speak to him."

"Impossible. He will talk only to me."

The sliver of apprehension slithered down Silas's spine once again. "Are you the only one who has seen Fafnir?"

When Petras nodded, Silas hissed in a shaky breath.

He only had his brother's word that this Fafnir was real. What were the chances that an Ancient One had survived five hundred years in secret?

Silas glanced at the king and silently cringed at the wild, unfocused gleam in his eyes.

Dammit to hell. Was Petras going mad, too?

Gwennore winced. Now her rump was as sore as her back. And her arms were tired from supporting Eviana.

It was the next morning and they'd been traveling for about half an hour on horseback, following the Norva River. She had learned how to ride during her stay at Ebton Palace, but she wasn't accustomed to trips as long as this.

The night before had been difficult. Eviana had missed her mother so much that she'd started crying. Gwennore had let the little girl share her bed in the nanny's room, but they'd only slept about an hour before Nissa had arrived before dawn to help them get ready to leave. The servant had laundered their clothes from the day before and given them a pillowcase to store the three dolls Eviana had selected as her birthday present.

When they had arrived in the courtyard, the general had offered to carry Eviana on his horse, but Gwennore had thought it best to keep the girl with her. After all, the Norva River was close by, so it should be a short ride to the boat.

"The river here is too rocky and shallow for a boat," the general had explained. "We'll have to ride for a while." When he reached for Eviana, the little girl had latched onto Gwennore, refusing to let go.

"She's a little grumpy from lack of sleep," Gwennore had admitted. "I had better hold her for a while."

General Dravenko had frowned. "Fine. But when you get tired, let me know."

Before they had even finished passing through the

small hamlet of Dreshka, Eviana had fallen fast asleep. At first, Gwennore had thoroughly enjoyed the journey, for she'd never seen a Norveshki village close up before. And once they had journeyed into the nearby countryside, a glorious sunrise had revealed some of the most beautiful scenery she'd ever seen. Forested hillsides and rocky cliffs flanked the winding river, and the air was cool and scented with the crisp fragrance of evergreens.

For a moment she thought she heard the whisper of voices in the distance. Puff? She glanced up at the sky but couldn't spot any dragons.

It was a shame Puff couldn't return her and Eviana. Flying with him was certainly more pleasant than riding a long distance on horseback. Now that they were half an hour into the trip, her rump was starting to ache, along with her arms that were supporting the weight of the girl's drooping body.

To take her mind off her discomfort, she decided to study General Dravenko, who was riding in front of her. He was wearing a different uniform today. It was still green and brown, but his breeches were made of cool linen instead of leather. A definite improvement, she thought, recalling the reading she'd taken on him the day before. The man had trouble with too much heat. *Good goddesses, don't think about his groin.*

She lifted her gaze to his head. His shoulder-length black hair stirred in the breeze that wafted through the valley. It was thick and wavy, the ends curling. Would it be as soft as it looked? *Don't think about touching him.*

There was a sheathed sword on his back. It looked long and heavy, and she wondered if its weight ever bothered him. Probably not. His shoulders were so broad. His back so strong. He was a man accustomed to carrying the burden of leadership. Intelligent, strong, and too handsome for his own good. *Don't think about that.*

How was she going to work with him? Especially when the scoundrel was going to let everyone think they were lovers.

He turned his head to the side, and she stifled a sigh at the sight of his gorgeous profile. *Stop thinking about him.*

Unfortunately, without him to distract her, all she could think about was her aching arms. How could a three-year-old be so heavy?

He moved his horse to the edge of the path and halted. Glancing back, he motioned for her to approach.

She reined her horse to a stop beside him. "Is something wrong?" She raised her voice over the sound of the rushing river.

He maneuvered his horse closer till his leg brushed against hers.

Her heart pounded as he edged even closer, his thigh now pressed against hers. "What are you doing?"

"Shh. You'll wake her up." His voice was so low, she could barely hear him. "I'll take her."

"I'm fine."

"No, you're not."

She snorted. The man shouldn't assume he knew how she felt. Even if he was right.

"We'll be entering a canyon soon, and the path will become steep and narrow. Let me take her. For safety's sake." He reached for the child.

As the back of his hand grazed against Gwennore's ribs, she sucked in a breath. A fluttering feeling started in her stomach and inched up to her chest.

Silently, she watched as he settled the sleeping girl on his lap. The fluttering feeling crept into her heart, and she inhaled, suddenly realizing that she'd been holding her breath. This man was affecting her too much. But how amazing that a warrior like him could also be so gentle. He would make a wonderful father.

His gaze lifted to her eyes, and her heart grew still. Time seemed to stretch out as she lost herself in the glittering green of his eyes. Suddenly, somehow, it felt like she'd known this man more than a day. She'd always known him. She'd been born knowing him. She'd only been waiting for him to make his appearance.

A glint of gold flickered in his eyes, then he blinked and looked away. His chest expanded as he took a deep breath, and Gwennore also looked away, suddenly feeling embarrassed. What on Aerthlan had come over her?

Behind them, Aleksi cleared his throat.

"We should be going," General Dravenko said quietly as he urged his horse to take the lead.

They rode for another half an hour, then the trail led them into a narrow canyon that the river had carved through a mountain. The sound of rushing water became so loud that it drowned out all other noises. The light dimmed as the increasing shade cast them into a cool and eerie twilight. They were forced to go in single file, the general taking the lead and the young captain, Aleksi, riding behind Gwennore. After seeing them off, Dimitri had stayed behind at Draven Castle. She assumed he was exhausted after guarding the nursery all night.

Just thinking about exhaustion made Gwennore yawn. Her rump was aching something fierce now, along with her back. And the sight of General Dravenko in front of her wasn't helping. Why was he affecting her so much? Was he the tall and handsome stranger promised by the Telling Stones?

She shook her head. She shouldn't give any credit to a silly game. It was no more real than the so-called curse she was going to investigate.

Eventually they came around a bend, leaving the canyon behind and emerging into bright sunshine. Gwennore's breath caught at the beautiful sight before her. The path headed downhill, weaving its way back and forth until it reached a wide valley. The river beside them spilled over a cliff in a spectacular waterfall, then grew wider and tamer as it meandered through the valley.

From their lookout point, Gwennore could see a village nestled close to the river, along with several boats and barges tied off at the long pier.

Soon they were approaching the village, and people wandered into the main street to gawk at the visitors. They seemed to recognize the general, Gwennore thought, for many of the older men saluted him and older women bobbed small curtsies. He called out to some of them by name.

She looked curiously about. The homes were small but tidy. The kitchen gardens green and well tended. Long-haired cattle and fluffy white sheep grazed in nearby fields. Freshly baked bread scented the air and reminded her that she'd missed breakfast and hardly eaten any dinner the night before.

As they passed through the village, she saw more of the people. Odd, but it seemed like everyone was elderly. Only a few were middle-aged. She glanced around again. No young adults or children? Perhaps they preferred to live in the bigger towns like Vorushka.

With her thoughts elsewhere, she was slow to hear the hushed whispers emanating from the villagers.

Is that an elfin woman? Why is General Dravenko traveling with her?

Is the little girl his? Is she his love child?

Has he been sleeping with an elf?

Oh, no! The general would never do anything that horrible!

When they reached the pier, the general stopped his horse and turned in his saddle to address the crowd. "Good people, I would like to introduce you to Lady

Gwennore, whom I regard as a trusted ally and friend. I expect you to honor her with the same trust and respect that you hold for me as your Lord Protector."

"Yes, my lord." The words rumbled reluctantly through the small crowd.

They were still eyeing her with suspicion, but Gwennore couldn't blame them for that. Some of them might have lost family members in the war against Woodwyn.

"Lady Gwennore has been visiting us with the young Eberoni princess here," General Dravenko continued. "We're returning the little girl to her parents today in Eberon. I would appreciate any blankets you could spare to make the princess more comfortable."

The villagers scurried off to their homes, and soon they had made a comfortable pallet on the floor of the barge. On a table close by, they left several baskets full of food.

After making sure Eviana was sleeping soundly on the pallet, Gwennore sat at the table with Aleksi to enjoy a late breakfast. Meanwhile, the general was overseeing the crewmen as they readied the barge for departure.

Thanks to the river's steady current, the barge began to move smoothly downriver. Gwennore leaned back in her chair, enjoying a thick slice of buttered bread while watching the lovely scenery.

Once again, she thought she heard the murmur of whispered voices coming to her on a breeze. The sound seemed to be coming from the forests, though, and not the sky.

"Do you hear anything?" she asked Aleksi.

With his mouth full of food, he nodded and motioned to the general and crewmen talking at the back of the barge.

"No, it's coming from—" A shadow fell over the table, and she glanced up and spotted a dragon far overhead. "Look!" She pointed at it. Perhaps it was a dragon voice she'd been hearing, after all. *Puff, is that you?*

Aleksi snorted, then refilled his cup with cider.

She frowned. Why wasn't the dragon answering her? "Isn't that Puff?"

Aleksi shook his head. "It's another one."

Hello? Gwennore attempted to contact him, but still no reply. She sighed. "He's not as friendly as Puff."

Aleksi's eyes twinkled with humor. "You seem to like the one you call Puff."

"Of course. He saved my life." She motioned to the new dragon. "Why is he circling overhead like that?"

"Orders from the general. The dragon is watching over us to make sure the princess remains safe."

"Are you expecting some sort of danger?"

"No, no." Aleksi offered her the jug of apple cider. "It's just a precaution."

She refilled her cup. "Then where is Puff? He told me he wouldn't be far away."

"Well, he isn't too far away." Aleksi glanced over at the general, who was talking to the helmsman. "General Dravenko told me you're going to return with us."

Gwennore scoffed. "I didn't have any choice, since I was desperate to get Eviana back home as soon as possible."

Aleksi tilted his head. "You didn't have a choice?"

"No. I agreed, so the general would agree to return Eviana today."

"But he was already planning—" Aleksi bit his lip. "Want some more bread?" He passed her the basket.

Gwennore narrowed her eyes. "What were you saying?"

"Nothing." Aleksi jumped to his feet. "I should see if the general is hungry."

"Wait." Gwennore rose to her feet. "Was he already planning to return Eviana?"

"I—I don't know everything he's up to." Aleksi winced. "Obviously."

"When did you rent this barge?" Gwennore demanded. "Before or after he made the bargain with me?"

Aleksi grimaced. "I've already said too much."

She drew in a sharp breath. Had the general tricked her into agreeing to the bargain? She'd already seen how easily he had lied to the queen. Had he deceived her, too? Had he used her own desperation against her?

With her heart pounding, she clenched her fists. How dare he manipulate her like this! She turned toward him, ready to unleash her anger, then stopped with a jerk.

Somehow he already knew. He must have overheard their conversation, for he was watching her with a stricken look.

She scoffed. He might as well admit his guilt, for it was written clearly on his face.

Chapter Eight

❦

Dammit. She was so damned quick at figuring things out, Silas thought. Hearing Gwennore's thoughts over the last few seconds had been like witnessing a shipwreck. And now she was pissed.

But once again, she'd proven how clever and discerning she was. He strode toward her. "We need to talk."

Her lovely lavender-blue eyes flared hot with anger. "I have nothing to say to you."

"Then you will keep your end of the bargain?"

She gritted her teeth. "It was not a bargain. It was an act of coercion and deception. You should be ashamed."

Silas shot Aleksi an annoyed look for not keeping his mouth shut, then turned back to Gwennore. "We still need to talk."

"Mayhap you need to talk, but I have nothing to say." She crossed her arms and looked away.

Her odd manner of speech threw him for a second, but he ignored it. "Look. We're going to be stuck together on this barge for the next three hours. Are you going to pretend that I don't exist?"

She studied her fingernails without responding.

"I'll take that as a yes," he muttered. "But wouldn't you like to vent your anger? I do deserve it, after all."

She snorted.

At least she was listening. "So for the next two and a half hours, I will allow you to berate me."

"*Allow* me? As if I need your permission. I'll yell at you whenever I please. And for as long as I want."

His mouth twitched. This was more like it.

"Don't you dare smirk at me." She glowered at him. "I am not entertaining."

She was delightful. He bit his lip to keep from smiling. "How about I let you throw me overboard?"

"Can you swim?"

"Yes."

She shrugged. "Then it's hardly worth my trouble."

He stifled another grin. "I'll promise to be wet and miserable for the rest of the trip. If I dry out too much, I'll jump back in."

With a huff, she planted her hands on her hips. "This is all a jest to you, isn't it? You tricked me!"

"Come." He took her by the arm to lead her toward the side railing where they could be alone. When she jerked her arm free, he added, "I'm just trying to put some distance between us and the child, so you don't wake her up when you start screeching at me."

"*Screeching?*" Her voice rose, then she winced and gave him an annoyed look. "For your information, I don't screech. I am not the sort to lose control."

He gave her a wry look, since he could recall her losing it the day before. Her hair had been loose and wild, unlike today's neat and tidy braid. She'd looked magnificent— so much so, that a wicked part of him wanted to push her until she lost control again.

"Come on." He stepped toward the railing while he

smiled at her. "Aren't you curious why I'm so desperate to have you return with me?"

She glanced away, her cheeks turning pink. *Blast him. I am curious, and the scoundrel knows it. I should slap the smile off his handsome face.*

Silas took a deep breath. Her reactions to him were affecting him too strongly, making his heart race and his groin tighten. If he didn't teach her soon to close off her mind, he might lose control, himself, and take her to bed. *Fool*, he berated himself. He would need to seduce her more slowly than that. First, he would kiss her. A gentle kiss, then a more passionate one. *Dammit, what are you thinking?*

Thank the Light she couldn't hear his thoughts. But hell, she was going to be livid once she learned that Aleksi, Dimitri, and he could hear her.

He bowed his head. "Please accept my apology. I am truly sorry."

She scoffed. "Am I supposed to believe that? You've spent the last few minutes joking about the situation."

"That was my attempt to be so charming that you would forget about being angry." When she gave him an incredulous look, he winced. "Apparently, you are immune to my charms."

I wish. She eyed him warily. "You lied to the queen, telling her that you'd captured me in battle months ago."

"I needed to vouch for your character in order to save you from a night in the dungeon. I could have never convinced Freya that you were harmless if I'd admitted that I had just met you yesterday."

That actually makes sense. She frowned. "But you still lied, and because of that, everyone thinks that we're . . ."

He waited, but she seemed unable to finish the sentence. "Lovers," he said gently and felt his pulse speed up when her cheeks blushed a pretty pink.

She waved a dismissive hand. "The truth remains that on more than one occasion, you have proven yourself a deceitful scoundrel—"

"Now I object. *Scoundrel* is a bit much."

"Then you admit to being deceitful?"

"Yes." He nodded. "And I apologize for it. If I were truly a scoundrel, I would feel no remorse." He motioned for her to join him by the railing.

She wandered slowly toward him. "I'm not sure you truly are remorseful. But it hardly matters, since I have decided to remain with my sisters."

"You're reneging on our agreement?"

"Why shouldn't I when I was coerced?" With a frown, she watched the shoreline as they floated down the river. "Besides, the problems here are not really my concern."

"Shouldn't you feel some sort of moral obligation to help me? After all, you're a healer—"

"I have no medicine with me."

"The physician at Draven Castle should have some."

She winced. "Given the condition of your queen, I don't think you should trust that physician or any of his concoctions."

Silas nodded. "An excellent point. I have an army physician who is trustworthy. I'll send for her."

Gwennore looked away as she gripped the railing. "Then you don't need me. That other woman can help you."

Was she jealous? "Annika doesn't have the gift that you have. And I don't think she's as discerning as you are. You were very quick to figure out my deception."

She snorted. "You're complimenting me on that?"

"I'll do whatever it takes to get you to stay. I need you."

Scoundrel. "You could probably figure out who's poisoning the queen without me."

He sighed. "We're dealing with more than the queen's madness. She's had no surviving children."

"Is there no heir to the throne?"

He shrugged. "There is one. But you're not understanding how devastating our problems are." He lowered his voice. "Unfortunately, those problems are state secrets that I dare not reveal. That is why I resorted to trickery. I can't tell you how bad it really is unless you agree to stay so we can fix everything."

A glint of alarm flickered in her eyes. "Then don't tell me. There's no guarantee I can fix anything."

"I know that, but the problems are health-related, so your gift could be exactly what I need." He leaned closer. "I will tell you this much. I did plan to return Eviana today, no matter what. The last thing I want is war with Eberon or Tourin. I don't want war with Woodwyn, either, but I haven't convinced the king to end it yet."

Her eyes narrowed as she studied him closely. "You're a general who doesn't want war?"

"I want peace and prosperity. Gwennore, I'm trying to save my people. Please help me."

She shook her head. "I belong with my family."

"Then consider me family."

She scoffed.

"I'm serious." This was his last card to play, so he had to hope it worked. "Sorcha is my sister."

Gwennore's mouth dropped open. "What?"

"I have a brother eight years older than me. There was another brother and a sister between us, but they both died, and my mother thought it was because of the curse. When Sorcha was born, Mother feared for her life, so she sent her to the Isle of Moon, where she would be safe. I haven't seen her since she was about six weeks old."

Gwennore bit her lip. *He doesn't look like Sorcha.*

"She took after our mother, while I look more like my

father. She had the biggest green eyes and the softest red hair. Could scream loud enough that the whole castle could hear her." Silas smiled. "I'm hoping to see her today."

"You probably will."

"Gwennore—"

She lifted a hand to stop him. "I believe you're sincere, but I want to go back to my sisters. I'm sorry." She bowed her head, then strode toward the pallet where Eviana was sleeping.

Dammit. Silas gripped the railing. He wouldn't give up on Gwennore. And even if he was forced to work without her, he wouldn't give up. His brother was in trouble. And his country was dying.

Gwennore settled on the pallet next to Eviana. Exhausted both physically and emotionally, she stretched out beside the little girl and closed her eyes against the bright sun overhead. But the image of General Dravenko still appeared in her mind, and his expression of despair and disappointment needled her already frazzled nerves.

Why should she care if she had disappointed him? He was the one who had deceived her.

But he was desperate. It was obvious just by looking at his eyes. Something was terribly wrong in Norveshka, and his secrecy made her even more curious. Blast him.

It's not your problem, she argued with herself.

Or was it? Growing up at the convent, she'd heard over and over that there had to be a reason why she and her sisters were Embraced. According to Mother Ginessa, whenever the two moon goddesses, Luna and Lessa, aligned in the night sky, it was so they could bless certain children with special powers, and those gifts were supposed to be used to make the world a better place. This was a chance for her to do that.

But Brody was right that it could be dangerous. And she hadn't forgotten Nissa's warning about people disappearing. The most sensible thing for her to do was to return to the safety of her sisters.

Or was that the cowardly thing to do? With a sigh, she sat up. Beside her, Eviana stirred and opened her eyes.

"Gwennie?" She blinked sleepily at her, then looked around. "Where are we?"

"On a boat, headed for Eberon and yer parents."

"Weally?" Eviana sat up and reached for the pillow-case filled with her three new dolls. "I can't wait to show Mama my new babies."

Gwennore brushed back the little girl's curls. "She's going to be so happy to see you. Are ye hungry?"

"Yes!" Eviana jumped to her feet, the dolls forgotten.

Gwennore sat her down at the table and poured a cup of apple cider. "Here."

While the little girl drank, Gwennore prepared a plate of buttered bread, cold ham, cheese, and sliced apples.

"So you're not staying with us, after all?" Aleksi asked in Norveshki as he poured himself a drink.

Gwennore glanced over at General Dravenko, who was standing alone at the bow of the barge. "No," she whispered. "I can't work with a dishonest man."

Aleksi grimaced. "I wouldn't call him dishonest. He said he would return the girl and he's kept his word."

"He deceived me." Gwennore set the plate of food in front of Eviana.

"I've known Silas since I was two years old. He's an honorable man."

With a snort, Gwennore looked away.

"I'm serious." Aleksi lowered his voice. "Silas risked his neck, arguing with His Majesty for an hour before he finally got permission to return the girl."

Gwennore turned back to the young officer. "He argued with the king?"

"Yes. The king relented, but he's still angry at Silas for interfering in his business."

"So the king wanted to keep her?" Gwennore motioned toward the little girl, who was busily eating. "Why?"

Aleksi sighed. "He's afraid his wife will commit suicide if he doesn't give her a reason to live."

Gwennore swallowed hard. "Then the Norveshki king and queen are both behind the kidnapping of children."

Aleksi winced. "Please don't repeat that to anyone in Eberon or Tourin. Silas wants peace with those countries. And he's trying to stop the kidnappings."

A sudden thought caused a chill to run down Gwennore's back. "What happened to the other abducted children? Did they disappear? Why aren't they still in the nursery?"

"I wondered about that, too." Aleksi frowned. "I asked a servant about it, and she said that once the kidnapped children grow past the age of the royal children who died, the queen realizes they're not hers and rejects them. But there are so many couples in Norveshka who can't have children that the kidnapped ones are quickly adopted. They end up in loving—"

"What do you mean? Couples who can't have children?"

Aleksi's eyes widened with alarm. "Dammit, I keep saying too much." He cast a worried glance toward General Dravenko. "Forget what I said."

Gwennore thought back to how she'd noticed the lack of children in the last village. Was this one of the state secrets that the general had referred to? "What is going on here?"

Aleksi winced. "Look, if you're truly grateful that the

general is returning you and the girl, then please don't tell anyone about our problems. All right?"

Gwennore nodded. "I won't say a word."

Aleksi heaved a sigh of relief. "Thank you." He scurried off toward the back of the barge.

Gwennore glanced at General Dravenko and noted that he was scowling at Aleksi. The general's gaze suddenly shifted to Gwennore, and the intensity of his glittering green eyes made her breath hitch.

No. She turned away to tend to Eviana. If returning to her sisters was the cowardly thing to do, then so be it. Being a coward was the best way to keep from getting hurt.

If he'd deceived her once, he could do it again. And the more she became attracted to the scoundrel, the more his deceptions would rip at her heart.

But he had stood up to the king in order to save Eviana. He had kept his word that he would send her back.

Was he an honorable man or a scoundrel?

He needed her. And knowing that made Gwennore's heart soften. At last, someone who thought she was special, who thought she was intelligent, who saw her true worth.

With a groan, she lowered her head, resting her brow in the palm of her hand. She didn't know what to do.

Gwennore noted that the sun was high in the sky when they arrived in the town of Vorushka, situated close to the Eberoni border where the Vorus River fed into the Norva. As soon as the barge docked at the pier, the mayor of Vorushka and a group of men descended on them, demanding to know why the Eberoni army had made camp across the border.

"They come in peace," General Dravenko assured the mayor. "We have the Eberoni princess with us." He motioned to Eviana, who was clinging to Gwennore's skirt. "As soon as we return her to her family, the army will leave."

Eager to be rid of an encroaching army, the mayor quickly provided the general and his company with horses and a fancy open carriage for the princess and Gwennore. As they rode through town, she looked curiously about. Once again, the townspeople came out of their homes and businesses to gawk at the general, the elfin woman, and the Eberoni princess. And once again, Gwennore noted that there were very few children.

Were the children dying, or was the problem one of infertility? How could she help with something like that? The general thought too highly of her.

How strange was that? After a few years of being unappreciated, she was astounded that someone would think that much of her. It was appealing, she had to admit. But should she be willing to endanger herself just because she was curious and flattered?

When they came to a stop close to the one bridge that spanned the Vorus River, she spotted the Eberoni and Tourinian flags marking the encampment on the southern bank.

"Ready to go home?" General Dravenko asked in Eberoni as he opened the carriage door.

"Yes!" Eviana jumped at him, wrapping her arms around his neck. "Thank you!"

With a smile, he stepped back, still holding the little girl. Gwennore's chest tightened. After today, she might never see him again.

She gathered up the pillowcase containing the birthday dolls, then descended from the carriage, ignoring the general's outstretched hand. For a small part of her was afraid that if she took his hand, she would not let go.

He set the little girl on her feet. "You're the bravest

child I've ever met. Not many children take a ride with a dragon."

She lifted her chin. "Ewic never has."

The general smiled. "Let's get you back home."

Gwennore took Eviana's hand and followed the general toward the bridge. There was an excited bounce in the child's step, and Gwennore thanked the goddesses that the little girl had come through this ordeal so well.

As they stepped onto the bridge, she spotted a small troop of armed guards escorting the kings of Eberon and Tourin, along with Brody and her sisters. With a grin, she waved at them.

"Gwennore! Eviana!" The squeals of her sisters carried toward her, and soon, her sisters were running toward her.

"Mama!" Eviana pulled loose from Gwennore and dashed across the bridge.

"Careful." Gwennore chased after her, the end of the pillowcase clenched in one fist.

They all collided with happy cries and hugs.

"My baby." Luciana picked up her daughter and held her tight. With tears running down her cheeks, she turned to Gwennore. "Bless you. I can't thank you enough—" Her voice broke with a sob.

Gwennore wrapped her arms around Luciana and her daughter. "I'm so sorry."

"Sorry?" Sorcha asked as she joined the group embrace. "Why would ye be? Ye risked yer life!"

"I shouldn't have taken Eviana away from the camp," Gwennore confessed.

Brigitta sniffed as she hugged them all. "It's not yer fault a dragon took her."

"Aye." Maeve latched on to Gwennore from the back. "We were so frightened for the both of you."

"Are you all right?" Luciana set her daughter on her

feet and looked her over. "You weren't injured in any way?"

"I'm fine," Eviana declared. "The nice man bwought me back. And last night, he gave me a buffday cake and a—" Her eyes widened as she glanced around. "Where is my pwesent?"

"Here." Gwennore handed her the pillowcase.

"I have new dollies!" Eviana grinned.

"How lovely." Luciana glanced at Gwennore. "Nice man?"

"General Dravenko." Gwennore glanced toward the bridge. The general had stopped midway across the bridge, and Brody and the kings, Leo and Ulfrid, were greeting him.

Ulfrid, formerly the pirate Rupert, shook the general's hand and gave him a fond slap on the back. Brody shook his hand next. Leo stood to the side, since it was dangerous for anyone to touch him. But the general didn't hesitate to shake Leo's gloved hand.

"He is nice," Brigitta said. "Rupert and I met him when we were in Norveshka. He helped us take back the throne."

"I should thank him for returning Eviana." Luciana regarded him curiously. "Perhaps we should invite him to the celebration tonight. What do you think, Gwennore?"

She glanced at the bridge. The general had turned toward them, and his gaze met hers for a few sizzling seconds.

"Gwennie?" Sorcha nudged her. "Is something wrong?"

"I—" Gwennore looked at Sorcha, then the general. His gaze had switched to Sorcha, and his eyes glistened with tears. He started toward them, accompanied by Brody and the two kings. "I have to tell you something."

Sorcha scoffed. "Don't tell me ye fell for the man."

Heat rushed to Gwennore's face. "Don't say that. They're coming this way."

"She's just teasing you," Maeve said. "We know ye only met him yesterday. Although he is somewhat good looking."

Somewhat? "Are ye blind?" Gwennore muttered.

"His looks are not important," Luciana declared. "What we need is his assurance that no child will ever endure what Eviana did. The kidnapping of children has to stop."

"I agree," Brigitta said. "I think Rupert should send an envoy back with the general to make sure our country's children will be safe."

Luciana nodded. "We should send an envoy, too."

Gwennore swallowed hard. This should be her job. She could help more than any envoy.

She glanced at the general as he approached, and once again, she had the feeling that she had been waiting for him her entire life. Even so, the unknown was frightening. The unknown was exciting.

His gaze met hers once again, and her heart squeezed. The unknown was hers for the taking. "I will go with him."

"What?" Brigitta asked.

Gwennore's heart thudded in her chest. The general had come to an abrupt halt, his gaze intense as he stared at her. "He asked me to help him."

"What kind of help?" Luciana asked.

"He needs my gift as a healer. I can't give you any details, but if I'm successful, the kidnappings will stop."

Her sisters looked at one another.

"Didn't the Telling Stones foretell she would be in the land of dragons?" Brigitta whispered.

Luciana winced. "But I sensed danger. I'm not sure you'll be safe there, Gwennie."

"I'll be fine." Gwennore drew in a shaky breath. "General Dravenko has promised to protect me. He considers us family."

Sorcha snorted. "How is that? I've never met him afore."

"Ye have." Gwennore took Sorcha's hand. "When ye were a wee babe."

"What?" Sorcha's eyes widened.

Gwennore squeezed her hand as the four men approached. "The general is yer brother."

Chapter Nine

Sorcha stiffened and eyed the general with suspicion.

She's not pleased, Gwennore thought as she released her sister's hand. Over the past few years, she had learned that it was rare for any moment to be perfectly happy. There was always a catch. How could Sorcha be happy that she had family when that family had apparently rejected her?

Happy endings were hard to come by. Luciana and Brigitta had become the rulers of Eberon and Tourin, along with their husbands, but they still had problems. The Eberoni former chief counsel and head priest, Lord Morris, was secretly gathering a group of disgruntled priests and nobles from both countries.

Morris had received a huge amount of gold from the former Tourinian king, Gunther, and he was using it to buy spies and create havoc. He and his followers wanted to return to the good old days where the Embraced were hunted down and killed, and everyone worshipped the Light under the guidance of priests who held the power of life and death over their flock. Of course, the best way for Morris to achieve such a goal was to make himself king and head of the Church of Enlightenment.

And he wasn't the only one causing problems. The Chameleon had come close to taking over Eberon and Tourin before disappearing in the form of an eagle.

On a personal level, Gwennore wished that all her loved ones could be perfectly happy, but it didn't seem possible. Her heart wrenched as she watched Leo crouch down in front of his daughter. It was so obvious that the poor man wanted to hug Eviana, but he didn't dare when his touch could harm or even kill. All he could do was smile through his tears and ask her if she was all right.

He wasn't the only man with glistening eyes. General Dravenko blinked away tears as spoke to his sister in the Eberoni language. "Sorcha, I have always hoped I would see you again."

She ignored him and turned to Gwennore. "Are ye sure I'm related to this man? He doesn't even look like me."

"He looks like his father, while ye resemble yer mother," Gwennore replied.

Sorcha frowned. "How can ye know that? Have ye met my parents?"

Gwennore shook her head. "I don't believe . . ."

"They have passed on to the Realm of the Heavens," General Dravenko said softly.

With a wince, Sorcha turned away. "Why should I believe any of this?" When she gave Gwennore an entreating look, her eyes glimmered with moisture. "Do ye trust him?"

"Well, I . . ." Gwennore glanced at the general. He had already proven himself capable of deception and trickery.

He gave her a wry look before turning to Sorcha. "I brought you something." He reached into his pocket and withdrew a velvet pouch. "This belonged to our mother. She would have wanted you to have it."

Sorcha opened it and pulled out an ornate ring with an oval sapphire surrounded by diamonds. "Oh, my."

Her sisters crowded around her for a better view.

"It's magnificent," Luciana murmured.

"It must be worth a fortune." Sorcha eyed the general once again. "I don't suppose ye would give this to me if I wasn't yer sister?"

His mouth curled up. "True."

She fit the ring on her finger. "Am I from a noble family then?"

He shrugged. "You could say that."

She gave him a dubious look. "If ye're so rich and powerful, why do ye need Gwennore's help?"

"I believe her special gift will help us," he explained. "I will not let any harm come to her."

Sorcha removed the ring and dropped it back into the velvet pouch. "How can I be sure ye won't abandon her? After all, ye abandoned me."

He winced. "You were not abandoned. You were sent away so you would be safe."

She scoffed. "Why should I believe that? Ye still live in Norveshka. Was no one worried about yer safety?"

"I was sent away," he said quietly. "About a year after you were. I went to a remote area far to the north."

Sorcha's eyes widened. "We were both rejected? Why?"

"Not rejected." He shook his head. "At that time, a plague was sweeping through the country of Norveshka. Most adults survived, but many children died, including a brother and sister of ours. After you were born, Mother was afraid she would lose you, too, so she sent you to the Isle of Moon. She was trying to save you."

"But she never asked me to return," Sorcha protested. "She never contacted me."

"She died a few days after you left," he murmured.

Sorcha stiffened. "Fr-from the plague?"

He shook his head. "She drowned in the Norva River."

When Sorcha glanced toward the river, he added, "North of here, by the town of Dreshka. Father died ten years ago."

Sorcha's shoulders slumped. "I see."

He was being careful not to mention anything about the so-called curse, Gwennore realized.

"I am hoping it will be safe for you to visit soon," he added.

"Is it safe for Gwennore now?" Luciana asked.

"I will protect her. You have my word."

"You had better, my lord general." Sorcha grabbed on to Gwennore. "If anything happens to my sister, I'm coming after you."

The general smiled. "Spoken like a true Norveshki. Please, call me Silas."

Sorcha lifted her chin. "I will after you safely return my sister."

He nodded, then turned to Gwennore. "We need to go now so we can be back before nightfall."

A thrill of excitement shot through Gwennore. She was really doing this!

"We will trust you to take care of her then," Luciana told him. "And I thank you for returning my daughter."

"My pleasure, Your Majesty." He bowed his head.

"We are counting on you." Brigitta extended a hand, and when he took it, she inhaled sharply, closing her eyes.

"Brigitta." Gwennore caught her sister as she stumbled back. Her special gift must have been triggered by the general's touch.

"Are you all right, Your Majesty?" he asked.

"Yes." Brigitta drew in a deep breath.

"We need to say good-bye." Luciana pulled Gwennore and her sisters aside. "Are you sure you want to do this?"

Gwennore nodded. "I agreed to only one month. And if I am successful, no more children will be kidnapped."

"Please be careful," Brigitta whispered. "When I touched the general, I came close to passing out."

Gwennore winced. "That bad?"

Brigitta nodded. "He is a man of many secrets."

Gwennore's heart pounded as the barge floated away from Vorushka. What adventures were waiting for her at Draven Castle? Now that they had to go upriver, the crew was hard at work on the oars and poles. The only ones not working were herself and the general.

He motioned for her to join him at the table. "We should make our plans."

"All right," she responded in Norveshki as she took a seat. "Where did Aleksi go?"

"I sent him to the army camp to fetch Annika and some medical supplies. They should arrive tomorrow."

"I see." She poured herself a cup of apple cider, but the pitcher ran out after a few drops.

"Not to worry." He rummaged in a nearby basket and pulled out another pitcher. "We still have wine." He poured two cups full.

She took a taste and winced at how strong it was.

He sat in the chair beside her and scooted up close.

She stiffened. "What are you . . . ?"

"I don't want us to be overheard," he whispered. "Everything we discuss from now on must be kept secret."

"Then we should speak Eberoni."

He shook his head. "These men trade with the Eberoni. They know the language."

"Oh." She gasped when he took her hand.

"They'll think we're having a romantic moment." He lifted her hand to his mouth and kissed her knuckles.

"Stop that." She pulled her hand from his grasp.

"Ah." His eyes twinkled with humor. "Now they'll think we're having a lovers' quarrel."

Warmth flooded her cheeks. "Is this a jest to you?"

"No. No one will dare harm you if they believe you are special to me. That is the best way for me to protect you."

"I understand that, but it doesn't mean you can touch me without my permission."

"Would you give me permission?"

She started to say no, but the entreating look on his handsome face gave her pause. Good goddesses, this man was far too appealing. She took a bracing sip of wine.

He rested an arm on the back of her chair. "You'll need to call me Silas."

"But I hardly know—"

"And I'll call you Gwen. Or Gwennie. Is there an endearment you prefer?"

"Excuse me?"

"Sweetheart? Snookums?" His mouth curled up. "Bunnykins?"

She grimaced. "Are you serious?"

"I guess *bunnykins* was too much."

She slapped his shoulder.

"I love it when you play rough, snookums."

"Stop it." Her mouth twitched. The man was outrageous.

He grinned. "That's better. We have to seem comfortable together, or no one will believe we're lovers."

She snorted. "Then I'll be sure to slap you whenever I feel like it."

"Excellent." He scooted even closer and lowered his voice. "How do you think the queen is being poisoned?"

His close proximity made her pulse race, but thank the goddesses, they were finally talking business. "The easiest way would be through her food or drink."

"That's what I thought. So for the past year, one of the queen's ladies-in-waiting, Margosha, has been secretly testing everything the queen eats or drinks. So far, she's encountered no effect."

Gwennore winced. "She does it voluntarily? That could be dangerous."

"I know, but Margosha is determined to help me. She served my mother for years, then she was my governess for a year after Mother died."

"Oh." Gwennore recalled how he had mentioned his mother drowning in the Norva River. "How old were you when your mother passed away?"

"Six." He turned his head to gaze at the passing shoreline. "That was a horrible year. I lost a brother and a sister. Then Sorcha was sent away. And then Mother . . ." He closed his eyes briefly.

What a terrible thing for a child to endure, Gwennore thought. Was he lonesome growing up? And why would a man have such pretty eyelashes? When he opened his eyes to look at her, her breath hitched. "I'm sorry about your mother."

"It wasn't an accident," he whispered. "I'm not sure if she was overcome with grief or in the grip of madness, but she threw herself off the bridge in Dreshka."

Gwennore gasped.

"I tried to be enough for her. Enough of a reason for her to live . . ."

Gwennore clasped his hand. "You mustn't blame yourself. You were only a child."

He squeezed her hand with his own. "The following summer, when I was seven, the plague swept through the country again. The physicians claimed that the disease became more dangerous in warmer temperatures, so I was sent far to the north where it is always cold."

How sad, Gwennore thought. *He must have been lonely.*

His mouth curled up. "It wasn't that bad. The castle is

owned by Aleksi's father, Lord Marenko. He was a former general, so he trained Dimitri, Aleksi, and myself."

"That was when you became close friends?"

He nodded. "You can count on them. And Lady Margosha. She'll help us however she can."

"I see." Gwennore withdrew her hand and took another sip of wine. "Are you sure she's tested everything the queen eats or drinks?"

"Yes. I don't think the problem could be as simple as the water supply, or everyone in Draven Castle and the village of Dreshka would be crazy."

"True." She sipped more wine while she considered. "It has to be something that only the queen comes in contact with. Mayhap the poison is embedded in something she wears, such as her clothes."

"*Mayhap*? I heard you say that before. Where did you learn Norveshki?"

She frowned. "Is there something amiss with my use of your language?"

"Your grammar is perfect. You have a bit of an accent, but I like it. Very much."

She drank more wine, trying to ignore how flattered she was. "I learned all four mainland languages in the Convent of the Two Moons where I grew up. The sisters there are famous for transcribing and illustrating books."

"I know. I have a few of them."

"Really?" She smiled at him. "I learned Norveshki by transcribing *Torushki's Bedtime Tales of a Mountain Troll*."

"Are you kidding? That has to be about five hundred pages long."

"Four hundred and eighty-six pages, to be precise, including the illustrations. And I transcribed it twice. By the time I finished, I was fairly fluent in the language."

He winced. "That book is four hundred years old."

"I know." She shuddered. "I kept imagining four hundred years of sweet young children having nightmares. Why on Aerthlan do the Norveshki tell their children such frightful tales right before bedtime?"

"They are cautionary tales to warn children not to wander off into the forest. A great deal of our country is covered with vast forests, where it is easy to get lost. And there are bears, wolves, and wildcats—"

"Pray, tell me the mountain trolls do not actually exist. I had a few nightmares myself when I was doing the illustrations."

His mouth twitched. "*Pray*? You do realize you were working on a book that is four hundred years old."

"Yes, I know. But we receive more orders for it than any other Norveshki book. It is a classic."

He gave her a pointed look. "Four hundred years old."

Her eyes narrowed. "Are you telling me my manner of speech is archaic?"

"No." He grinned. "I'm saying you're a classic."

Warmth invaded her cheeks, but she wasn't sure if she was embarrassed or flattered. "I shall endeavor to update my speech to more modern usage."

"You don't need to change, Gwennore. I like you the way you are."

More heat rushed to her face, and she gulped down more wine. "You needn't flatter me to ensure my cooperation. I realize you consider my kind the enemy—"

"You're not from Woodwyn. You're my sister's adopted sister. And you're clever, brave, and beautiful." When she started to object, he raised a hand. "I know you don't want to believe it. Brody told me you've been encountering prejudice, but you shouldn't listen to a few ignorant fools who are afraid of you."

She swallowed hard. "You think they're afraid?"

He nodded.

"And you're not?"

"No. You're one of a kind. That might frighten some, but I find you intriguing. And incredibly beautiful."

She turned away, her heart thundering in her ears. Good goddesses, how could she spend a month with this man? Was he being honest with her, or was he still trying to manipulate her? He'd promised to protect her, but who would protect her heart?

She glanced up at the sky. *Puff, are you still there? If I need to run away, would you take me?*

The dragon from before was still there, circling overhead and not answering her.

"Where is Puff?" she asked softly.

The general sighed, then took a drink of wine. "He's busy at the moment."

"He said he would never be far away."

A look of annoyance crossed the general's face. "I thought we were talking about us. Why are you thinking about the dragon all of a sudden?"

"Why shouldn't I? He saved my life." She eased her nerves by concentrating on cutting an apple into slices. "I could be wrong, but I think he likes me."

With a snort, the general stole one of her apples slices, then bit into it. "Maybe you should date him then."

"*Date*?" It was a term she wasn't familiar with.

"It's a modern Norveshki word for 'courtship.'" He tossed the rest of the apple slice into his mouth.

She scoffed. "I couldn't possibly be courted by a dragon. We're not even the same species."

"But you think he likes you," the general muttered. "And you seem more than a bit obsessed with him."

"Don't be silly." She slapped his hand away when he tried to steal another slice of apple. "I'm merely grateful that he saved my life. And I consider him an important ally in case I find myself in trouble."

The general arched an eyebrow at her. "I said I would protect you."

She shrugged. "Puff can do things that you could never do."

He gritted his teeth. "I can do things that Puff could never do."

"Can you fly?"

He leaned close. "I can take you places he never can."

Her skin pebbled with gooseflesh. "There is no need for you to compete with him. I have no intention of dating a dragon. Or anyone else, for that matter."

The general swept a lock of hair away from her brow and tucked it behind her ear. "The first rule for dating a dragon is that whenever he takes you for a ride, you hold on tight and never let go."

She swallowed hard. Somehow, she had a strange feeling he was referring to himself. She turned away and gulped down the rest of her wine. *Don't fall for him, don't fall for him.*

He hissed in a breath. "I can't take it anymore."

She gave him a wary look. "Excuse me?"

"Gwen, you know how I can communicate with the dragons. Dimitri and Aleksi can, too. There are only a few Norveshki men who can, and we're all descended from the Three Cursed Clans."

She blinked. "There are no women with the ability? I mean, other than me?"

"None that I have ever heard of. Now perhaps you will understand how unusual you are."

"I—I don't know why I can do it. Mayhap—I mean, perhaps you should tell me more about the curse."

He waved a dismissive hand. "It's not real, so there's no need."

"But there might be something in the mythology of it that will give us a clue as to how to be rid of it."

"Forget the damned curse," he growled. "I'm trying to explain something to you. You're not going to like it, but I can't continue like this. It's not fair to you."

A sliver of apprehension stole over her. "What is it?"

"Since Dimitri, Aleksi, and I can communicate with the dragons, we can also talk to one another with our minds. But we don't like the idea of anyone invading our thoughts, so we have learned how to erect mental shields."

She nodded, recalling the wall she'd encountered when she'd done a reading on him.

"I'm telling you this so you can learn how to build a shield. You don't have one, Gwen."

She stiffened. "How—how would you know that?"

He winced. "I'm sorry, but I've been hearing your thoughts."

Chapter Ten

❧

Silas groaned inwardly at the horrified look on Gwen-nore's face. Dammit, he hated revealing this to her. But it was better to be honest with her, so she could learn to protect her privacy. And if he had to listen to any more of her struggle against her attraction to him, he couldn't guarantee he would behave himself.

"You—you've been hearing *everything*?" Her voice rose.

"Shh, not so loud." He looked at the oarsmen, who were stealing glances.

She slapped a hand over her mouth, then leaned over and moaned. *Good goddesses, no! He must have heard me calling him General Gorgeous. And he heard all the times I—dammit, he can hear me now!*

"It's nothing to concerned about," he whispered. "So I found out early in our relationship that you're attracted to me—no big deal."

She shot him an incredulous look. *No big deal?*

"That's why I made it clear that I'm attracted to you, too. So we would be even."

"We will never be even," she ground out. "Not when I can't hear you. I can't believe you . . ." She lowered her head into her hands and groaned. *I'm so embarrassed.*

Mortified. Where can I crawl into a hole? Should I throw myself off the barge and swim ashore? We're not that far from Eberon. I could be there before nightfall.

"Gwen, relax."

She glowered at him. "How can I relax when you've been invading my privacy? How dare you!"

"I didn't do it on purpose. Your mind is so open, it's like you're shouting at me."

"You want to hear *shouting*?" Her voice rose again.

"Gwen." He touched her shoulder.

"Don't touch me." She jumped to her feet and stumbled a second before grabbing on to the table. *Goodness, I drank too much.* He reached out to steady her, but she slapped his hand away. "Don't. And stop invading my mind!"

"I never wanted to." He stood and leaned toward her to whisper. "Surely you agree that it's better for me to tell you now than to let the situation continue as it is."

"You should have been honest from the beginning." *Holy goddesses, have I been a fool? Brigitta warned me he has a great deal of secrets. And I know he's capable of deception. The scoundrel.*

"If I was truly a scoundrel, I would have never told you the truth."

He heard me! "What else are you not telling me?"

"I'll tell you everything you'll need to know in order to help me."

Her eyes narrowed. "That means you plan to keep some things secret."

He winced. "I will be as honest as I possibly can."

"That's not very reassuring."

"It should be. If I do keep something secret, it's because it would be dangerous for you to know."

But that only makes me more curious. She looked away.

He groaned inwardly. If she found out the biggest secret of Norveshka, she would not be allowed to leave. And then she would really resent him. He would have to make sure she stayed focused on the health problems. It was her curiosity about the dragons that was dangerous.

"I'm not sure I can trust you," she muttered.

"I realize that. But I will do my best to protect you. First we need to protect your privacy." He stepped closer. "Let me show you how to build a shield."

"Leave me alone!" She backed away. "I want to be alone for a while." She rushed to the side of the barge and grasped the railing. *Dear goddesses, what have I gotten myself into?*

With a sigh, Silas sat down and refilled his cup. This hadn't gone well. But he would have to be a fool to think it could have gone any other way.

Don't think about him. He'll hear you, Gwennore admonished herself. *Wait—so what if he does? Then he'll know what you really think. That he's a rotten scoundrel. A low-down, dirty rat of a stinking bastard!*

Behind her, she heard a cough as he choked on his wine, and she smiled to herself.

Taking a deep breath, she attempted to calm her nerves. One month. That was all she had promised the filthy bastard. She would concentrate on figuring out how the queen was being poisoned. And she'd work with the women he had mentioned—Lady Margosha and the army physician, Annika. For the most part, she would completely ignore the sorry, rotten bastard. She'd pretend that he didn't even exist.

He cleared his throat behind her.

A wicked temptation to take revenge popped into her mind. Did she dare? Why not? He deserved it.

She closed her eyes and envisioned herself sauntering

up to him and shoving her discarded chair out of the way. Then, ever so slowly, she would lift up her skirt till she could straddle his legs and settle in his lap. Then she would stroke her fingers down his cheek, and when his green eyes glittered with heated desire, she would pull her hand back and slap him silly.

"Not funny," he growled.

She glanced back, affecting an innocent look. "Is something wrong?"

When he stared back at her, her heart stuttered in her chest. Goodness, the gleam in his eyes was even hotter than she'd imagined. She turned back to gaze at the shoreline. Two could get burned playing that game.

Don't think about him. She concentrated on the shoreline and the hillside covered with thick forest. Behind the hill, there were peaks of mountains covered with snow. Such a breathtakingly beautiful country.

The scent of pine and spruce trees wafted toward her on a cool, fresh breeze. So many trees. No wonder there were tales to warn children not to wander off. But were the mountain trolls real? The illustrations in *Torushki's Bedtime Tales of a Mountain Troll* had shown them as short, swarthy-looking creatures with long, bushy hair and beards, bulbous noses, pointed teeth, and bare feet. They dressed in dirty furs and never bathed.

They probably stank as bad as the bastard sitting behind her.

He sighed loud enough that she could hear.

Don't think about him. So did the mountain trolls truly exist? She focused on the view in front of her and strained her ears. As an elf, she'd always had better hearing than her sisters. There was the lapping of waves against the barge and the rhythmic swooshing sound of oars, but she listened beyond that.

Once again she heard a whispering sound, murmurs

carried to her over a soft breeze. She glanced up. There was only the one silent dragon overhead. These were multiple voices, and they seemed to be coming from the forest.

Can you hear me? she asked mentally, and a chorus of soft voices wafted into her mind.

Who was that?

She is not one of us. Ignore her.

She must not be one of the barbarians. They cannot hear us.

She must be Elf.

Then she is far from home.

Gwennore had counted at least five voices. They weren't speaking Norveshki, but something akin to the language of Woodwyn. *Who are you?* she asked mentally in Elfish.

She is Elf.

Why is she in the land of barbarians?

My name is Gwennore. May I ask—

"Are you communicating with someone?" General Dravenko asked, as he approached the railing where she was standing.

She gave him a curious look. "You're not hearing them, Lord General?"

"Call me Silas," he whispered. "What do you mean—them? How many are there?"

"I've counted more than five. Some are male, and others female."

"I'm hearing only half of the conversation—your half. You were using Elfish. Have some elves invaded my country?"

"I don't think so." Gwennore turned her attention back to the forest. *May I ask who you are?*

We are many.

We are the Kings.

Kings of the Forest.

You mean you're . . . trees? Gwennore asked.

"Trees?" The general gave her an incredulous look. "Are you seriously—"

She lifted a hand to stop him when the voices continued.

Do not confuse us with the twigs. They are not sentient.

We are the Kings.

We tower over the twigs.

Then I will find you in the forest? Gwennore asked mentally. *Where?*

You cannot miss us.

We stretch from the Southern Sea of Woodwyn to the far reaches of the frozen north.

We are taller than the castles built by barbarians.

We are older than the Ancient Ones.

Who are the Ancient Ones? Gwennore asked.

The first dragons who flourished a thousand years ago.

They were destroyed five hundred years ago.

Replaced by the new dragons.

"Is this a game you're playing on me?" the general interrupted with a worried look. "Are you getting revenge? Or did you have so much wine, you're imagining—"

"I'm not drunk," Gwennore muttered. "And I'm not making it up. They call themselves the Kings of the Forest. They say they are taller than castles and older than the Ancient Ones. Do you know of any extremely tall trees?"

His eyes narrowed. "The giant redwoods?"

"Are they tall?"

He nodded. "And rumored to be ancient. But they're trees, for Light's sake. I never thought they could speak. Are you sure you're communicating with them?"

She turned back to the forest. *How is it possible for me to hear you?*

Are you Elf?

You must be Elf.

Only a few Elves can hear us.

I am Elf, Gwennore admitted.

You are far from home.

Are you the giant redwoods? she asked.

That is what the barbarians call us.

They are young and ignorant. They know not what they do.

"They are the redwoods," Gwennore told the general.

He took a deep breath. "Then you're really talking to trees. I would have never believed it possible."

"They said only a few elves can communicate with them."

"But you can hear dragons, too," he muttered.

"I'll ask about that." *Kings of the Forest, do you know of any Elves who can talk to the dragons?*

No. Elves talk only to us.

Some of the barbarians can talk to the dragons.

Only the cursed barbarians.

The general leaned close. "What did they say?"

"According to the redwoods, the only ones who can communicate with the dragons are the cursed barbarians."

His brows lifted. "Barbarians?"

She smiled sweetly. "That's what they call you, my lord."

He snorted. "When are you going to call me Silas?"

"You're missing the point here, my lord. You can stop worrying that the elves are able to communicate with your precious dragons."

"That is a relief." He gave her a wry look. "Although I'm still dealing with one very stubborn elf, who refuses to say my name, but can communicate with both dragons and trees."

"I could hear you, too, if you dropped your shield."

He tilted his head, watching her carefully. "You said we wouldn't be even unless you could hear my thoughts.

Is that what it'll take to ease your anger? Shall I let you hear me?"

Her breath caught. Was he serious?

"I'm very serious. But I should warn you. I'm not a tree."

What does that mean? she wondered. *That he has the thoughts of a man?*

He nodded. "Are you willing to hear exactly how much I want you?"

With a gasp, she stepped back. "Don't say that."

"Then learn how to build a shield. Because the more I listen to your thoughts, the more I'm tempted to do every damned thing I've been imagining. And believe me, I'm barbarian enough to do it."

Her cheeks blazed with heat as she turned away. *Don't think about him.*

What is bothering you, Elf?

The redwoods were still hearing her, Gwennore thought. And the general and his friends. And the dragons. If she didn't construct a shield, she would never have privacy again. "All right, my lord. I'll do it."

"Silas," he growled.

She felt as if she were sinking. Drowning. "Silas."

Gwennore was exhausted, both physically and mentally, by the time they arrived at Draven Castle. Her rear end ached from another long ride on a horse, and her mind was tired from constantly building a wall. The act, itself, was easy enough to do. She only had to imagine herself constructing a wall, brick by brick, around her thoughts. The problem was she was never quite sure if she was doing a proper job, so she kept building it over and over.

Silas had assured her he could no longer hear her thoughts, but the scoundrel hadn't exactly proven himself trustworthy. She'd found herself calling him a bastard every five minutes just to see if he reacted.

They'd spent the rest of the trip coming up with plans, and they hoped to get started soon. When they dismounted in the courtyard of Draven Castle, Dimitri met them there and told Silas that His Majesty wanted to speak to him.

"I'll take care of your guest," a woman's voice called out as she hurried across the courtyard.

Gwennore turned toward her. She looked perhaps fifty years of age, with gray streaks in her red hair and a few wrinkles on her brow and around her eyes. But she was still slender and moved quickly. She flashed a smile at Gwennore, then stopped next to the general.

"Margosha." Silas greeted her with kiss on the cheek. "We'll talk later."

"Yes, don't leave the king waiting." She waved him off, then turned to Gwennore. "I've been looking forward to meeting you."

"Pleased to meet you, my lady." Gwennore curtsied.

"No need for formalities. Please call me Margosha." She linked an arm through Gwennore's and led her toward the entrance to the southern wing. "So did you return the little princess?"

"Yes, Eviana is back with her parents."

"Excellent." Margosha lowered her voice. "Thank you for coming back. We need all the help we can get."

"I'm concerned about you tasting Her Majesty's food and drink. It could be dangerous."

Margosha's eyes softened. "You're a sweet girl. But I believe you're the brave one. Silas told me how you hitched a ride with a dragon."

Gwennore snorted. "Not that brave. I was clinging to Puff for dear life."

"Puff?"

"The dragon who saved me and brought me here."

"You named him Puff?" Margosha's mouth twitched. "I can't imagine him liking that."

"You know him?"

"Of course. Come. Let me show you to your room." Margosha led her toward the double doors.

Gwennore glanced back at the western wing. "I was over there before. In the nursery."

"Yes, but you're not playing the role of a nanny this time." Margosha opened the doors. "I had all your clothing moved over here."

"I see." Gwennore followed her up a flight of stairs. This wing was much more decorated than the western one. Portraits lined the walls, and every now and then a small table was topped with a vase full of flowers.

"The royal apartments and those of all the ladies-in-waiting are here in the southern wing," Margosha explained as she led her down a corridor. "It's warmer and Her Majesty enjoys having a view of the garden."

Gwennore nodded. She would need to investigate the garden. Whoever was poisoning the queen could be using some of the plants that were growing there.

"You must be tired from the journey. A nice hot bath is what you need." Margosha opened a carved wooden door on the left. "I'm afraid it's not one of the best rooms. You'll only have a view of the courtyard."

"That's quite all right." Gwennore stepped inside and her mouth dropped open. The bedchamber was huge and richly furnished. The bed, with four massive posts of carved oak, was set up on a dais and surrounded by curtains of shimmering red silk. A coverlet of red velvet spread across the wide expanse of the bed.

Across from the bed, a fire burned in a hearth of polished pink marble. Two chairs, upholstered in red velvet, sat in front of the hearth. Between the two chairs, a delicately carved wooden table rested, topped with a vase of pink glass that held a dozen red roses.

"Will it do?" Margosha asked.

"It's beautiful," Gwen murmured as her slippers sank into a thick red carpet.

Margosha smiled. "I'm so glad you like it." She motioned to the red velvet curtains across the room. "The windows overlooking the courtyard are there. Now, let me show you the dressing room." She strode toward a door to the left of the hearth.

Inside, Gwennore gawked at the size of the marble tub. Across from it, shelves lined a wall.

"I put all your gowns and clothing there." Margosha motioned to the shelves, then to a dressing table. "And I made sure you would have everything you need."

"Thank you." Gwennore ran her fingers over a silver hairbrush and toothbrush.

"I heated up some water for you." Margosha lifted a kettle off a small stove, then poured it into the tub. Steam rose into the air. "Your maid will keep this stove hot, so you can have hot water whenever you want."

"My maid?"

Margosha nodded. "Nissa asked to be your maid. Is that all right?"

"Yes." Gwennore turned on a faucet and marveled at the water that gushed into the tub. "This is so amazing."

"You don't have that in Eberon?"

Gwennore shook her head.

"It's nice, but unfortunately, the water is always cold." Margosha filled the kettle again and placed it on the stove. "Shall I call Nissa for you?"

"I can manage, if you'll help with the laces."

"Of course." Margosha motioned for her to turn

around. "Did you know I was there when Sorcha was born? She was such a beautiful baby."

Gwennore sighed. "She's still beautiful." *And I miss her already.*

"Did Silas get to see her?"

"Yes."

"That's good." Margosha *tsk*ed. "You poor thing. Your back is bruised."

"It happened when Puff caught me."

"You need a nice long soak. There, finished."

"Thank you." Gwennore slipped out of her gown and draped it on the back of the chair by her dressing table.

"I'll leave you alone then." Margosha headed for the bedchamber door. "And I'll send Nissa to you in about an hour."

"Thank you." Gwennore noticed another door on the far side of the shelves. "Where does that door lead to?"

Margosha paused halfway into Gwennore's bedchamber. "Another dressing room. It belongs to Silas, of course."

"What?" Gwennore stiffened.

"His bedchamber is next door to yours," Margosha explained with an amused look on her face. "It's the best way to convince everyone that you're lovers."

"But—but we're not." Gwennore ran over to the door. There was no lock! She turned back to Margosha, but the woman had left.

Good goddesses. Gwennore cracked open the door. It was dark inside. She closed it, then wedged a chair under the knob. Then she shoved the dressing table up against the door.

With a wary glance at the blocked door, she slipped out of her shift. Her skin pebbled with gooseflesh, and she glanced down at herself. Her breasts felt full and heavy, the nipples tightened into hard buds. Because she was cold, she thought. Not because she was wondering what Silas would think of her.

Are you willing to hear exactly how much I want you? His words echoed in her mind.

She unbraided her hair and let the long, white-blond tresses hang loose to her narrow waist. *Lovers.*

Don't think about him.

She climbed into the tub and sighed as the heated water caressed her skin.

I'm tempted to do every damned thing I've been imagining.

She shuddered. No doubt Silas had a very healthy imagination. She glanced at the blocked door.

What would happen if she left the door open? Did she dare?

Chapter Eleven

◈

Silas and Dimitri headed across the courtyard for the king's offices in the northern wing.

"I can't hear Lady Gwennore's thoughts anymore," Dimitri whispered. "You must have taught her how to build a shield."

Silas nodded.

"Then you must have told her we could hear her thoughts." Dimitri jumped in front of him and looked him over. "No black eyes? She didn't clobber you?"

Silas gave his friend an annoyed look. "Did you see anything today?"

"Changing the subject, huh? So how pissed was she?"

Enough to torment Silas with images of her sitting in his lap and caressing his face. She'd nearly killed him. "She took it well."

Dimitri snorted. "Right. So how much did you have to grovel?" He snickered when Silas punched him on the shoulder.

"Did you see anything?" Silas asked again.

Dimitri nodded. "Someone sneaked away from the Eberoni camp and crossed the border, making his way north. He looked like a priest."

Silas narrowed his eyes. "I don't think Leofric sent him. Not when he was able to pass a message to King Petras directly through me." And if Leofric didn't send him, then who did?

"I'll keep watch to see whom the priest contacts." Dimitri opened the door to the northern wing and glanced around to make sure they were alone. "Why did Aleksi go to the army camp? Are you expecting a problem with the elves?"

Silas stepped inside. "He's bringing Annika here."

Dimitri froze for a moment, then slammed the door shut with more force than necessary. "Why?"

"She's trustworthy and has a good supply of medicinal herbs." Silas gave his friend a sympathetic look. "It can't be helped. I made a deal with the king and I have to deliver."

Dimitri sighed. "Fine."

Silas strode toward his brother's offices with Dimitri trudging along beside him. "If Lord Romak is there, keep him busy. I don't want him eavesdropping."

Dimitri nodded.

When they stepped into the outer office, Lord Romak looked up from his desk and pasted a fake smile on his weasel-like face.

"His Majesty wants to see me," Silas said.

Lord Romak stood and bowed. "I am aware of that, Lord General." His beady eyes narrowed. "I heard you brought the elfin woman back with you."

"Of course." Silas smiled. "Lady Gwennore and I are inseparable."

Lord Romak slanted a sly look at Dimitri. "I wonder if your dear friend Colonel Tolenko approves. After all, his uncle was probably murdered by those vicious elves."

Dimitri stiffened. "If my uncle is indeed dead, then he

died in service to his country, and his memory should be honored."

"Of course." Lord Romak folded his hands over his stomach, his numerous rings sparkling in the dim candlelight as he bowed low.

Silas knocked on the door to his brother's office, then entered.

Petras looked up from his desk. "You're back." He set down his quill and rose to his feet while Silas made a quick bow. "So you returned the princess?"

"Yes." Silas removed two letters he'd secreted inside his leather vest. "These are from the kings, Leofric and Ulfrid. They were both very grateful for the child's safe return."

Petras circled his desk and reached for the letters. "Then they don't know that I'm the one responsible for the kidnapping."

"No. I told them it was a rogue dragon."

Petras unfolded the first letter and read it, then the second one. "They want peace and prosperity for all the people of our countries."

Silas nodded. "Today's act went a long way toward ensuring them that we want the same thing."

With a sigh, Petras dropped the letters on his desk. "But it's not what Fafnir wants."

Not this again. Silas gritted his teeth. It had taken him an hour last night to convince his brother that following the dictates of a dragon were not in his best interests. "You're the king here. You know what's best for your people, and it certainly isn't war. We can't afford to lose any more of our population."

Petras rubbed his brow. "But the curse—"

"I told you." Silas stepped closer to him. "I will get rid of it. Give me one month. That's all I ask."

"You'll make Freya healthy again?"

"Yes." Silas nodded. "I'm bringing together a team of the best healers I can find. Trust me, brother."

Petras regarded him sadly. "I do trust you. But Fafnir doesn't. He thinks you want the throne for yourself."

"I was raised to be a soldier, not a king. I won't let you down, Petras."

The king sighed. "One month, then. That was our agreement. Get rid of the curse. Make Freya well again. But if you fail—"

"I know." Silas clenched his fists. "We'll do as Fafnir wants."

Petras nodded. "We'll invade Woodwyn. And attack Tourin."

Over my dead body, Silas thought. He had one month to set things right and figure out if this damned Fafnir was a hoax. "I'll get right to work."

Petras wandered back to his desk. "Fine. You may go."

On the way to his room, Silas whispered to Dimitri, "Did you keep Romak from listening at the door?"

"Didn't need to. Turns out he wanted to talk to me in private." Dimitri withdrew a small dagger from his sleeve. "He gave me this."

"What the hell?" Silas eyed the sharp dagger. "Does he expect you to assassinate me?"

"Not me." Dimitri slid the dagger back up his sleeve. "He's hoping Lady Gwennore will do it."

"What?"

Dimitri smirked. "Romak laid a huge wager on when the elfin woman would stab you to death in your sleep. He asked me to pass the dagger on to her and encourage her to wait till tomorrow night to do the deed. If she does as I ask, he'll give me ten percent of his winnings."

Silas scoffed. "Ridiculous."

"I know." Dimitri grinned. "I held out for twenty-five percent."

Silas cuffed him on the shoulder.

Dimitri laughed. "Don't worry. I won't give her the dagger."

"Go ahead and do it."

"Are you kidding? When she's pissed at you?"

Silas shot him an annoyed look. "She might need it for self-defense."

"From you?"

Silas punched him harder. "I would never hurt her."

"No, you just lie and deceive and—"

"Sod off."

Dimitri grinned. "I'll go then. See you at dinner."

Gwennore was dressed in a shift and lounging in front of the hearth, drying her hair, when Nissa arrived to help her dress for dinner.

"It's good to see you again." Gwennore smiled at her. "Thank you for agreeing to be my maid."

Nissa blushed. "The other maids are afraid of you, my lady, but I told them you're actually nice. Unfortunately, they're still convinced that you'll murder your lover—"

"Excuse me?"

Nissa bit her lip. "Maybe I shouldn't have mentioned that. How about a blue gown, since it's Sapphirday? It would look lovely with your eyes."

Gwennore followed her into the dressing room. "People are saying I'm going to murder General Dravenko?"

Nissa glanced at the chair and dressing table pushed up against the door to Silas's dressing room. "Oh, my, is the affair over?"

"No, it—"

"Oh, thank the Light. I can't imagine anyone turning

down an affair with the general. He's so handsome." Nissa selected a blue velvet gown.

"But I heard no one wants to marry him or Dimitri," Gwennore said as the gown slid over her shoulders.

"Or Aleksi," Nissa added. "Because of you-know-what."

"The Curse of the Three Clans?"

Nissa grimaced and looked around.

"We're alone here, Nissa. I hope to get rid of the curse, but it will be hard to do if I don't learn more about it."

Nissa grabbed on to the gold-painted wooden orb that hung from the leather thong around her neck. "May the Light protect us."

"There could be no harm in simply repeating the story," Gwen insisted. "Can you tell me how the curse started?"

"It was five hundred years ago," Nissa whispered. "When the Ancient Ones ruled the skies and the country."

Gwennore recalled that the giant redwoods had referred to the Ancient Ones. "Who are the Ancient Ones?"

"The first dragons." Nissa leaned close. "They were vicious and hoarded all the gold and jewels for themselves. If the Norveshki people didn't mine the mountains and give the dragons enough gold and precious jewels, the dragons would set their villages ablaze."

"That sounds terrible."

"Oh, it was." Nissa nodded, her eyes wide. "We were like their slaves. But about five hundred years ago, the dragons became lazy. All they wanted to do was lie about their caves, wallowing in piles of gold and jewels. And that's when a wealthy man named Magnus made a deal with them. Magnus owned several mountains that were said to be full of rubies and emeralds. If his seven sons mined the mountains for the dragons, then the dragons would let him rule over the Norveshki people in their stead, as long as he did whatever the dragons told him to do."

Gwennore nodded. "So this Magnus made himself king?"

"Yes, although he was more like a puppet for the dragons." Nissa tightened the laces on Gwennore's gown as she continued. "But then something terrible happened. One of the mountains caved in while the seven sons were inside, and the oldest two were killed."

"So five of them survived?" Gwennore asked.

"They were injured terribly," Nissa whispered. "Magnus was afraid they would die and he would have no heir to the throne, so he begged the dragons to help him. And one of them, by the name of Fafnir, said he would help."

"How?"

Nissa hesitated. "I—I dare not say. But two more of the brothers died because of it. Only three of them survived what Fafnir did. Their names were Draven, Tolen, and Maren. Even though they lived, they blamed the dragons for the deaths of their brothers. So eventually, they rebelled against the Ancient Ones and overthrew them. It made the old dragons furious, so they cursed the three brothers and their progeny for all eternity."

"So the Three Cursed Clans are the descendants of those three brothers?"

Nissa nodded. "The Dravenko clan is descended from Draven. And then, there's the Tolenko clan and Marenko clan."

So Dimitri was from the Tolenko clan and Aleksi from the Marenko, Gwennore thought. It made sense since she knew the word *ko* in Norveshki meant "son of." "And women are afraid to marry into those clans?"

With a wince, Nissa touched the golden bead on her necklace. "According to the curse, the descendants' seed will shrivel and die. And all those who thirst for power will go mad. So it is believed that any woman who marries into the three clans is doomed. She'll lose her children, go insane, or die a terrible death."

Gwennore scoffed. "Obviously, some of the children have survived, or the clans wouldn't still be here after five hundred years."

"Oh." Nissa tilted her head, considering. "Well, there aren't that many descendants. You can usually tell who the men are, since they all tend to have black hair."

Gwennore recalled that most of the people she'd seen in Norveshka had either red or blond hair. And from what she'd seen of the villages, it appeared that infant mortality might be a serious problem for the entire country. "I noticed when we were traveling today that there aren't many children in any of the villages."

Nissa heaved a mournful sigh. "That's because the curse has spread beyond the three clans, and now the whole country is suffering."

"But I doubt a curse could do that. It would make more sense if it was caused by something like the plague that swept through the country about twenty years ago."

Nissa hung her head. "Even if that's true, everyone believes the plague is simply part of the curse. Women all over the country are having trouble conceiving children."

Gwennore swallowed hard. No wonder Silas was desperate. If the Norveshki were suffering from widespread infertility, the country would not survive. "Thank you for telling me, Nissa. I will do my best to help."

"Thank you." Nissa selected a pair of blue slippers. "I knew you couldn't be vicious like the others say."

Gwennore rolled her eyes, then slipped her feet into the blue velvet shoes. All this time spent dressing up seemed like a waste. She and Silas had made plans on the journey, and she was eager to set them into motion.

"Come and sit." Nissa motioned to the chair. "We need to do your hair."

Gwennore winced when she realized Nissa had moved the table and chair away from the general's dressing room door. Now the rascal could come inside whenever he pleased.

Once Nissa had arranged her hair on top of her head, she stepped back. "All done. What do you think?"

Gwennore took a deep breath. She'd never looked this good before. "You worked a miracle. Thank you."

Nissa snorted. "Not really. Once I got used to your pointed ears, I realized how beautiful you are. It's no wonder the general fell for you."

I wish. The thought made Gwennore grow still and stare at herself in the mirror. Did she really want Silas to fall for her?

What did he really think of her? With her hair up, her neck seemed long and slender. And the cut of the gown made her waist seem tiny and her breasts practically pop out. He had said he was attracted to her, and even though a part of her had thrilled at his words, another part had suspected he was merely using flattery in order to gain her cooperation.

She sighed. The last two and a half years that she'd spent in Eberon and Tourin had made her distrustful of anyone other than her sisters.

"Hello?" a female voice called out from the bedchamber.

"Yes?" Gwennore strode into her bedchamber and discovered Lady Olenka, dressed in a dark-blue silk gown. She wore a matching blue ribbon around her neck with a small sapphire. She was also wearing two small sapphire rings. Of course, Gwennore thought. It was Sapphirday.

"Why, look at you!" Lady Olenka clasped her hands together. "You look fabulous!"

Gwennore blushed. "Thank you."

Olenka waved a hand at Nissa. "You may go." As Nissa

hurried from the room, Olenka's gaze drifted over Gwennore. "Oh, dear. Oh, no." She pressed a hand to her chest as a look of horror crossed her face. "I am shocked! Shocked and appalled!"

"Why? What's wrong?"

"You have absolutely no jewels!" Olenka cried. "Not even a single ring!"

"I'm not accustomed to wearing—"

"This is unbelievable!" Olenka fanned herself as if she were ready to faint from the shock. "How can the general call himself your lover and not give you any jewelry?"

"Well, I—"

"It's insulting! How dare he treat you like that." Olenka stepped closer and lowered her voice. "No wonder people are saying you're going to murder him in his sleep."

"I would never—"

"Oh, I know." Olenka touched her shoulder and gave her a sympathetic look. "All those terrible people wagering that you'll stab the general to death in his sleep. I mean, really, who could kill the man? He's so gorgeous!"

"Actually, I wouldn't stab anyone, regardless of their looks."

"Of course not!" Olenka sighed dramatically. "As your close friend, I know you're not the sort to go about killing someone."

"Well, thank you. I appreciate that."

"What are friends for?" Olenka waved a dismissive hand. "I'll have you know that I refused to participate in any wagers that you would kill the general. Everyone thought I was being foolish, but I bet that you would only wound the general."

Gwennore blinked. "What?"

"A small wound, that's all I ask. Just between us friends. All right?" Olenka winked.

"You expect me to stab him?"

"Just a flesh wound. Two nights from tonight." Olenka drew a small, jeweled dagger from her sleeve. "Isn't it lovely? It's my gift to you."

"I don't really need—"

"Oh, I'm sure you have your own knives, but I wanted to be helpful." Olenka dashed over to the bed and slipped the dagger underneath a pillow. "There! Now you're all set! You won't let me down, right?"

A knock sounded at the door, then Lady Margosha entered, carrying a blue velvet bag. "Oh, you wore blue. Perfect!" She nodded at Olenka. "Don't you both look lovely tonight."

"Thank you." Olenka eyed the velvet bag. "What do you have there?"

"A small gift from General Dravenko." With a smile, Margosha opened the bag. "This necklace belonged to his mother."

Olenka gasped when Margosha pulled out a sparkling necklace of sapphires and diamonds.

With a gulp, Gwennore stepped back. "I shouldn't have something that belonged to his mother. It should go to Sorcha."

"Now, now. You know how fond the general is of you." Margosha fitted the necklace around Gwennore's neck. "And here is the matching ring."

With her heart pounding, Gwennore slipped on the sapphire ring. This couldn't mean anything. Silas was just playing his role as her lover. When she left in a month, she would give these back to him.

And say good-bye. The thought made her heart tighten. *There's no one else like him. No one makes my heart race like him.* The scoundrel. No one exasperated her like him.

"They're magnificent!" Olenka cried, eyeing the jewels with an astounded look.

"Yes." Margosha smiled. "The general is quite generous."

With a wince, Olenka leaned close and whispered, "Don't hurt him too much. Just a tiny scratch, all right?"

"Excuse me?" Margosha asked.

"It's nothing!" Olenka dashed from the room.

Margosha shook her head. "Silas wanted me to escort you to the Great Hall for dinner. Are you ready?"

"Yes." Gwennore took a deep breath to steady her nerves and followed Margosha into the hallway. "Will there be many people there?"

"Just the usual courtiers." Margosha led the way down the hall toward the western wing. "But there is a group of traveling minstrels here tonight, so after dinner, there will be some dancing."

"I see."

Margosha leaned close. "Silas explained the plan you came up with. He thinks tonight will be the perfect time for us to do it. The queen will be busy at the dance tonight, so her dressing room will be vacant. I have readied everything we'll need to test her clothing and jewels."

"Excellent. Thank you." Gwennore smiled at Margosha. "I'm quite eager to get on with our investigation."

"Silas is eager, too." Margosha led her down some stairs. "After we reach the Great Hall, I'll have to leave you for a while. I need to taste everything before it's taken to the royal table."

"It worries me that you do that."

Margosha squeezed her hand. "Don't let it concern you. I'm glad to be of service."

"Silas is lucky to have you."

"He's a good man."

Hero or scoundrel? Gwennore thought. Perhaps a bit of both.

When they reached the western wing, Gwennore

paused a moment at the entrance. The Great Hall took up the entire length of the wing. A vaulted ceiling soared two floors overhead. As she glanced at the ceiling, she realized that the nursery was overhead. A balcony at the back of the Great Hall was filled with the minstrels who were tuning their instruments. At the front of the hall, a dais held a long table with three gilded chairs. Over each chair, a coronet of jewels hung from the ceiling.

Down each side of the Great Hall, there was a line of smaller tables and chairs. The center of the room was left vacant. For dancing, Gwennore assumed. On the side facing the outside of the castle, long windows overlooked the village of Dreshka.

Three enormous chandeliers hung from the high ceiling, providing several tiers of candles to illuminate the large room. More flames flickered in the candles of numerous wall sconces.

Margosha pointed at Dimitri, who was standing by a small table close to the dais. "You can eat there with the colonel. That table is reserved for nobles."

"I'm not noble," Gwennore whispered.

"You are here." Margosha leaned close. "And as the general's mistress, you automatically have a higher rank than the other women here. Except the queen, of course."

Gwennore swallowed hard. Already, she could see other courtiers eyeing her suspiciously. She looked around, but Silas was nowhere to be found.

"I'll see you soon." Margosha rushed away.

Gwennore squared her shoulders. After one more check that her mental shield was solidly in place, she strode toward Dimitri.

"My lady." A thin man with beady dark eyes stepped in front of her and bowed low. "May I introduce myself? I am Lord Romak, personal secretary to His Majesty, the king."

Gwennore curtsied. "A pleasure to meet you, my lord."

He gave her a brittle smile. "I must admit to a certain curiosity about you, my dear. General Dravenko has never brought a mistress to court before. He usually keeps his women at the army camp, where they belong."

"Is that so?" Gwennore affected a bored look, even though the man's rudeness was making her tense.

"How long have you been with the general?" Romak asked.

Gwennore waved a dismissive hand. "I doubt our affair is of any interest to you."

"Oh, but it is." Romak's eyes narrowed. "As the king's secretary, I must keep myself fully informed of everything happening in our country. I must say, I find it hard to believe that any woman would want to involve herself with the general. He's from one of the cursed clans, you know."

Gwennore snorted. The nerve of this man. He had black hair mixed in with the gray, so he was also a descendant of one the Three Cursed Clans. "I don't frighten easily."

"I suppose not. I've heard the elves are quite vicious when it comes to war. But I have to question how trustworthy the general is. After all, we are at war with Woodwyn, yet he has brought an elfin mistress to the capital."

"I am not here to cause any trouble, my lord."

Romak smirked. "How about we stop with the games and tell the truth?"

She arched a brow. "You first."

His mouth twisted into a sneer. "I know you're up to something. I have my own sources, you see, so I know the general's tale about you is false. You're not from Woodwyn. You're the adopted sister of the queens of Eberon and Tourin. Are you here to spy for them?"

"No, of course not."

He scowled at her. "Are you planning to tell your sisters about the curse?"

"No. Why would I, when I don't believe it is real?"

He stepped closer. "Then you think there's another explanation for the queen's illness or the deaths of her children?"

Gwennore grew increasingly tense. "Perhaps."

He gave her a speculative look. "Perhaps you should ask yourself who would benefit the most from the deaths of the royal children."

Her breath caught. "Are you saying they were murdered?"

"Anything's possible." Romak shrugged. "Who would gain the most, do you think?"

"I suppose it would be the next in line."

"The heir?" Romak's eyes gleamed with malice. "Then that would be His Majesty's younger brother. I believe you know him well."

"I do?"

Romak chuckled. "You're sleeping with him."

Gwennore stiffened. Silas was the heir?

Romak's eyes widened. "The general didn't tell you?" He snorted. "I always knew he wasn't to be trusted."

Chapter Twelve

Gwennore attempted to appear unaffected, even though her mind was reeling. How could Silas fail to tell her something so important? He had to know that she would find out. *What else is he hiding from me? How can I trust him when he doesn't trust me?*

"Oh, dear." Romak lifted a hand to his face, doing a poor job of covering a nasty sneer. "I seem to have given you a shock."

Gwennore's sense of pride shot to the surface, giving her a boost of strength. "Shock, yes. I am definitely shocked you could suggest that someone as honorable as General Dravenko could have possibly caused harm to his brother's children. I would hate for His Majesty to hear you are spreading such a horrific rumor."

Romak's smile quickly vanished as his eyes hardened. "I see you are loyal to the general. I just hope you haven't fallen in love with him. For you must know that whoever marries him will be doomed to lose her children and go insane."

Gwennore swallowed hard. "Your concern has been noted. Good day, my lord."

She strode away, her heart pounding. Would the people here think she was trying to marry into the royal family?

"Good evening, my lady," Dimitri greeted her as she came to a stop beside him. He tilted his head, studying her. "Is something wrong?"

She gave him an annoyed look. "You can't tell? Why don't you invade my thoughts and find out?"

He winced. "That was never intentional. And believe me, it was damned uncomfortable."

"So sorry to cause you discomfort."

"Exactly. If I had to hear you calling Silas General Gorgeous one more time, I thought I was going to puke." He smiled when she shot him a dirty look. "Seriously, though, I am glad you've learned to build a shield."

She crossed her arms, still glaring at him.

He leaned close and whispered, "I don't have to read your mind to know that Romak upset you. What did the weasel say?"

"He inferred that Silas may have killed the king's children in order to inherit—"

"Bastard." Dimitri clenched his fists. "I should rearrange his face so he'll find it hard to say any more crap."

"I warned him not to repeat it."

"Good."

Gwennore shook her head. "It's not good. I was caught completely by surprise. Why didn't the general tell me he was heir to the throne?"

Dimitri winced. "He didn't tell you?"

"No. Who's going to believe we're close when I don't know the most basic things about him? What else is he hiding?"

Dimitri looked away, frowning.

There is something. "What is it?" An alarming thought struck her. "Does he have a mistress somewhere else?"

"Not at the moment. Women are generally reluctant to get involved with any man from the cursed clans."

"People really believe that?"

A pained look crossed Dimitri's face. "It is true."

Gwennore sighed. As far as she was concerned, the curse was only true if you believed in it. But what else could Silas be hiding?

A loud, clanging sound interrupted her thoughts, and she turned toward the entrance. Using a carved wooden baton, a servant struck a gold gong, and another clang reverberated across the Great Hall.

The gong was suspended next to the double doors of the entrance. Precious jewels lined the perimeter of the gong and shimmered in the multitude of lit candlesticks.

"His Majesty, King Petras; Her Majesty, Queen Freya; and His Highness, Prince Silas," the servant announced in a booming voice.

The courtiers quickly parted to leave a wide path down the middle of the room, then all bowed and curtsied. Gwennore sank into a deep curtsy, her heart thudding in her chest. *Prince Silas? And everyone believes he is my lover?*

With her gaze downcast, she grew tense when the king and queen passed by her on their way to the dais. A pair of booted feet stopped in front of her.

Silas. She rose from her curtsy but avoided looking at him.

"We need to talk," he whispered.

She snorted. For someone who kept wanting to talk to her, he managed not to tell her much.

When he moved away, she stole a glance at him and watched him step onto the dais. He frowned, casting a wary look at the jeweled coronet hanging over his chair. Was she just imagining it, or did he seem uncomfortable?

When the royal family took their seats, the rest of the

courtiers rushed to the smaller tables to sit down. Servants came in, carrying huge trays of food.

Gwennore sat next to Dimitri, her heart still thudding as she occasionally glanced up at the dais. If she had met the king earlier, she could have guessed he was related to Silas. They were both tall, with black hair, green eyes, and similar jaws, although she had to admit that Silas was much more handsome.

Petras was probably in his mid-thirties, although he looked older. The weight of his office must be wearing on him, she thought, or perhaps he was becoming ill like the queen. There were dark circles under his eyes, wrinkles were etched deeply into his brow, and his shoulders slumped in a way she interpreted as sadness or weariness.

She glanced over at Silas. He looked wonderfully fit compared with his older brother. His gaze lifted from his plate of food to look at her, and she glanced away.

"He should have told me," she muttered. "Why didn't he tell me?"

Dimitri paused in the middle of slicing into a piece of roast mutton. "I don't think it's something he's comfortable with. He's actually spent very little time here with his brother."

"He grew up with you and Aleksi?"

Dimitri nodded. "We were all trained to be soldiers. It was always assumed that Petras would have several sons, so Silas never believed he would inherit the throne."

"He still should have told me."

"Probably so." Dimitri ate while he considered. "I can tell you this. He always introduces himself as General Dravenko. That is how he sees himself. He's spent most of his life with the army. That is his home. Not here."

"I see."

Dimitri offered her something underneath the table. "He wanted you to have this."

A dagger? "What is this for?"

"Slide it up your sleeve," Dimitri advised. "It's a gift from Lord Romak. He's hoping you'll kill Silas in his sleep."

She scoffed. "You might find this hard to believe, but I can be peeved without being homicidal."

He smiled. "I wasn't going to give it to you, but Silas told me to go ahead."

"He has a death wish?"

Dimitri chuckled. "No. He thought you might need it for self-defense."

A chill crept up her spine. "Are you saying our investigation will be dangerous?"

His smile vanished. "You'll have to careful. If there's anything I can do to help, please let me know."

She nodded. "Thank you." As she slid the small dagger up her sleeve, she reminded herself why she was here. To keep other children from being kidnapped. To help Silas save his people. To find a cure for the queen.

With a small shock, she realized that Silas's mother had been the former queen. His mother had fallen into madness and thrown herself into the Norva River. And now the current queen was in danger of succumbing to a similar fate. No wonder no one wanted to marry into the family.

Another startling realization skittered through Gwennore, making her stiffen in her chair.

Sorcha was a princess.

"That should do it." Gwennore looked over the collection of thirty bowls scattered about the queen's dressing room.

After dessert had been served, Lady Margosha had escorted her to the queen's dressing room. While Her Majesty and the rest of her ladies-in-waiting were occupied with the dance in the Great Hall, Gwennore and

Margosha were secretly testing the queen's belongings for poison.

After filling each bowl half full with water, they had selected different items for testing. The sleeve of a nightgown had gone into one bowl, the sleeve of a day gown into another. A glove, a scarf, a sock, a cap, several rings, bracelets, necklaces, and hairpins—anything that the queen might come into contact with on a regular basis.

"I didn't realize we could be poisoned through our skin," Margosha said as she peered into one of the bowls. "So you're hoping some of the poison will seep into the water?"

"If the poison is there, yes. Then we can test the water and return the items where they belong."

Margosha nodded. "If she notices any of the wet items, I'll just tell her I had them washed. She'll never know what we've done."

"Was Her Majesty angry when she found out that we'd returned Eviana?"

"Actually, she took it very well. But then she's surprisingly lucid today. Every now and then, she seems almost normal, and we get our hopes up." Margosha heaved a sigh. "But it doesn't last."

"I'm sorry." Gwennore wandered about the room, checking on each of the bowls. "I can't imagine the pain of losing five children."

Margosha sat at the dressing table, her shoulders slumped. "It's taken a great toll on the queen. The king, too."

"I heard that women all over the country are having trouble conceiving."

Margosha winced. "That is true, but it's considered a state secret. Silas and the king believe it would be disastrous for other countries to know that our population is dwindling. It has gotten so bad that Silas has allowed women to become soldiers in order to make it look like we have a full army. He worries that other countries will attack if they realize we're vulnerable."

"I don't think he needs to worry about Eberon or Tourin. They both want peace."

"Yes, but that's a new development because they have new kings." Margosha wrinkled her nose. "The former kings were so nasty, they would have attacked. And there's still the problem with Woodwyn. Silas has been trying to convince his brother that we should make peace with the elves. We can't afford to lose any more of our people in battle."

"Why is Norveshka at war with Woodwyn?"

Margosha shrugged. "Who knows? Every now and then, the elves attack one of our villages. We don't know why, but we have to defend ourselves."

"Mayhap—I mean, perhaps—you should send an envoy to Woodwyn to discover the motivation behind their attacks."

Margosha nodded. "Silas's father tried that about twenty years ago. He sent an envoy, Dimitri's uncle, but Lord Tolenko never returned. We can only assume the elves murdered him."

Gwennore winced.

"Has enough time passed?" Margosha motioned to the nearest bowl. "We can't be caught doing this."

"I'll start testing." Gwennore dipped a silver spoon into the first bowl. No reaction.

"What are you looking for?"

"The most commonly used poison reacts to silver by turning it black," Gwennore explained as she wiped the spoon dry. She went about the room, dipping the spoon into each bowl. No reaction.

"So the queen's not being poisoned through her belongings?" Margosha asked.

"We can't be sure yet." Gwennore removed the night-gown sleeve from the water and wrung it dry. "This only means that the guilty party is not using poison derived from the seeds of the darca flower. It's the most common poison, since darcas can be found in almost every garden on Aerthlan."

Margosha nodded. "There are some here in the castle garden."

"I'll go through the garden tomorrow to check for other plants that can be used to make poison." Gwennore poured the water from the bowl into a small glass vial, then rammed a cork in it.

"I was wondering why you wanted all those vials." Margosha motioned to the sack she'd brought into the room, along with all the bowls and a pitcher of water.

"Thank you for bringing all the items I requested." Gwennore wrote WHITE LINEN NIGHTGOWN on a label and tied it to the vial.

"I'm happy to help." Margosha watched as she moved on to the next bowl. "So you plan to keep a sample of water from each bowl?"

"Yes. So I can test for other kinds of poison." Gwennore removed a ring from a bowl and dried it. "Could you put this back?"

"Of course." Margosha helped her, and soon all the clothing and jewelry items were back where they belonged and they had thirty labeled vials of water.

They were drying the bowls and stacking them in a sack when a knock sounded on the door, startling them.

They whirled toward the door just as Silas peered inside.

"Oh, Holy Light." Margosha pressed a hand to her chest. "You scared the life out of me."

"Her Majesty is on her way here," Silas whispered. "You need to leave now."

"We're almost done." Gwennore quickly dropped another bowl into the sack.

"I said *now*," Silas ground out.

"You go." Margosha motioned for her to leave. "I'll finish up here and sneak everything out."

"Are you sure?" Gwennore gasped when Silas grabbed her arm and hauled her toward the door.

"It's part of my job to keep the queen's dressing room in order," Margosha quickly explained. "Hurry now!"

"We'll create a distraction," Silas said as he pulled Gwennore through the doorway, then shut the door.

"I don't like the way she keeps endangering herself," Gwennore whispered.

"Then help me distract the queen." He led her a short distance down the hallway, then stopped close to a doorway. "This is the queen's bedchamber. She'll be sure to see us here."

Gwennore tugged her arm free from his grip. "What are you planning?"

He turned his head toward the end of the hallway. "She'll be coming up the stairs soon with her ladies."

Gwennore shut her eyes, focusing on her extra-powerful sense of hearing. "They're on the stairs now."

"Your hearing is that good?"

She opened her eyes to find him peering curiously at one of her ears. "Stop that." She stepped back against the wall and covered her ears before he could see them turning red from embarrassment.

"Why are you hiding them? I think they're cute."

She gave him a wary look. "What does that mean?"

"Ah. Another word that's too modern for you. Cute is—" He glanced down the hallway as Queen Freya reached the top of the stairs. "Can you act as well as you can hear?"

"Excuse me?"

"Play along." He slammed a hand against the wall close to her head, making her jump.

He was trying to draw the queen's attention, she realized. She glanced toward the queen to see if it had worked, but he suddenly blocked her view, leaning in close.

She stiffened. "What are you—"

"Shh." He nuzzled her neck.

She shivered at the feel of his breath feathering the curve of her neck. Goodness, she could hardly breathe. Was that the tip of his nose trailing up to her ear? It made her skin prickle with goose bumps. "Is—is this the distraction?"

"Mmm." He nibbled softly on her neck.

She pressed her palms against the wall, seeking its support, for she feared her knees would give out. "You couldn't think of anything else?"

"No. We're having a moment of passion."

"We are?"

He nipped at her earlobe. "Do you always talk like this when you're having a moment of passion?"

"I—what makes you think I'm having such a moment?"

He paused, then drew back to look at her.

Was that a glint of gold in his eyes? It made him look wild. And hungry. She glanced away, biting her lip. Why did he have to be so appealing?

"You're not feeling anything?"

She shook her head. Thank the goddesses, he could no longer hear her thoughts.

"Then I'll have to try harder, won't I?" He pulled her close, locking one arm around her waist. His other hand cupped the back of her head.

She gasped. They were pressed against each other so tightly, she couldn't breathe without her breasts pushing against his hard chest. The hallway swirled before her, so she shut her eyes and grabbed on to him for support. If he tried any harder than this, she might melt into a puddle at his feet.

His breath warmed her neck, then she felt the soft brush of his lips, grazing her throat and moving to her cheek. Closer and closer, he came to her mouth. Good goddesses, was he going to kiss her?

"Gwen?" he whispered, his lips moving against her skin.

Was he asking permission? She drew in a shaky breath. She was tempted, so very tempted to turn her head and meet his mouth with her own.

"You stopped talking." His mouth reached the corner of hers. "Does that mean you're feeling the passion now?"

She blinked. Was he playing with her? Had this all been a game to him?

"Silas!" the queen screeched. "Whatever are you doing?"

He drew a deep breath, his chest moving against her. Then he released her as his mouth curled up. "Oh, dear. We've been caught."

Chapter Thirteen

❧

Damn, he wanted to kiss her. Silas slapped himself mentally to stop lusting for Gwennore and instead focus on the irate queen, who was hurtling toward them like a fired cannonball. He could practically see the steam coming out of her ears.

The three ladies-in-waiting accompanying the queen didn't appear at all angry. They remained behind Her Majesty, exchanging grins. No doubt, they were excited to witness such a scandalous moment. It wouldn't take long for them to spread the news around the castle that he'd been caught kissing his mistress in the hallway.

If only he had kissed her. That had been the original plan. But once he'd pulled her into his arms, he'd found himself unable to force a kiss without her permission. So he'd tried to make it look like he was kissing her. Unfortunately, the more he had resisted doing it, the more he'd wanted it.

If they had been alone, would she have let him? *Fool.* If they had been alone, he wouldn't have needed the distraction. Clearly, he was too overwhelmed with lust at the moment to even think straight.

Holy Light, he wanted to kiss her. He wanted to do more than kiss her.

"How dare you!" Freya stomped a foot on the wooden floor. "It's one thing to bring a mistress to our castle, but to fornicate in the hallways is really—"

"We hadn't progressed that far," Silas muttered. He glanced over at Gwennore and noted a blush creeping up her cheeks. Even her cute ears were turning pink. She must be embarrassed. Damn, now he felt guilty in addition to feeling frustrated. But it couldn't be helped. Until Margosha managed to make her escape, he had to keep this scenario going.

Freya scoffed. "If we hadn't interrupted you, you would have been fornicating."

He groaned inwardly. *I can only hope.*

"Do you realize you're misbehaving right in front of my bedchamber?" Freya continued.

"Ah." Silas glanced at the nearby door. "My apologies, Your Majesty. We were caught up in a blazing inferno of passion. Right, Gwennie?"

Her ears turned a brighter shade of red.

"See how hot she is?" He wrapped an arm around her waist and pulled her close. "My darling Gwennie is practically feverish with desire." When a sound escaped from her, somewhere between a groan and a whimper, he winked at her. "I know it's hard, snookums. I can barely wait, myself."

The glare she shot at him was so heated, he half expected sparks to shoot from her eyes and sizzle across his skin. Holy Light, if they did have a moment of passion, they might set the bed on fire.

"Patience, bunnykins. We'll find a bedchamber soon." He spotted Margosha slipping out the dressing room door, behind the queen and her three ladies. With her arms filled with supplies, Margosha scurried away from them, down the hallway.

Freya crossed her arms, scowling at him. "I have never seen you behave like this before. The elfin whore is clearly a bad influence on you."

Silas's hand tightened on Gwen's waist. "Disparage me if you wish, Your Majesty, but do not speak ill of Lady Gwennore."

Freya huffed. "You defend her? An elf?"

"She's beautiful," Silas declared, and he felt Gwennore stiffen beside him. Did she think he was lying?

"She can never be anything more than a mistress," Freya hissed. "Surely you know that Norveshka would never accept an elfin queen!"

With a gasp, Gwennore tried to pull away from him.

He held on to her, keeping her pressed against his side. "Whenever I marry, whomever I marry—that decision will be mine." He swooped Gwennore up in his arms, ignoring her small cry of surprise. "Good evening, Your Majesty." He strode toward his bedchamber, carrying her.

"What are you doing?" Gwennore whispered, her hands clutching at his shoulders.

"Making a dramatic exit. I want them to focus on us and not Margosha. Can you see her?"

Gwen peered over his shoulder. "She just went into a room on the other side of the stairwell."

"That's her bedchamber." He nodded. "We did good. And the queen?"

"She and her ladies have gone into her bedchamber." With a groan, Gwen ducked her head. "That was so embarrassing."

"Why? Are you embarrassed to have me as your lover?"

She gave him an incredulous look. "Has it never occurred

to you that I don't like being the subject of gossip? Or that I hate having my reputation ripped to shreds?"

He winced. "I am sorry about that. At the time, it seemed like the best way to keep you and Margosha safe."

"You don't find this embarrassing?"

"No. I'm actually flattered to have such a beautiful lover."

She scoffed. "This is not real."

Ouch. Why did that hurt? *Because you still want to kiss her, you fool.* "It . . ." *Don't say it. Once you say it, you can't take it back.* "It could be." *Dammit, why did you say it?* "It could be real, if you wanted—"

"Put me down." She squirmed, but he pressed her harder against his chest.

"You seem to have forgotten the first rule for dating." He angled his face close to hers. "When you go for a ride, you hang on tight and never let go."

"That's not for you. It's for dating a dragon."

"Ah. So you still want to date Puff."

"I never said that."

Silas let out a sad sigh. "Poor Puff. He'll be so disappointed. He's very sensitive, you know."

She blinked. "Then he does like me?"

"Ha! You do want to date him."

"Do not."

"You shouldn't toy with his feelings, Gwen. Rule number two for dating a dragon is to remember they have extra-large hearts. That means they can love fiercely, but they can also be terribly hurt."

Her eyes narrowed. "Extra-large hearts?"

He nodded. "So be careful if you decide to date him."

"I can't possibly date a dragon."

"Then date me."

Her mouth fell open.

She looked a bit dazed, but damn, he still wanted to

kiss her. He motioned with his head toward the nearest door. "Can you open that for me?" When she turned the knob, he kicked the door open and strode inside.

She peered around the room with a confused look. "This isn't my bedchamber."

"No, it's mine."

She gasped. "Put me down."

"As you wish." He headed for the bed.

"Stop!" She struggled against his hold. When he set her on her feet, she made a wild dash for the open door.

"You didn't answer me."

She paused in the doorway. "Answer what?"

"Will you date me?"

She gave him an incredulous look. "Are you being serious? Because I never know. As far as I can tell, everything is a joke to you. I'm just snookums and bunnykins, and you're playing with me."

He walked toward her. "I'm not playing now."

"How can I believe anything you say? Or don't say. You keep hiding things like the fact that you're the heir to the throne."

"I didn't think it was important."

With a scoff, she impatiently brushed her hair back from her brow. "It's extremely important, for it gives you motive. If the king's children were truly murdered, then the next in line—"

"*What?*" He halted with a jerk. Holy Light, what did she think of him? "You—you think I could harm children?"

"No." A pained look crossed her face. "Others might believe it, but I don't. I saw how you were with Eviana."

"You thought I would make a good father."

She hissed in a breath. "You heard my thoughts. Do you have any idea how mortifying that is for me?"

"Yes, I do. I heard your reaction."

With a groan, she covered her face.

"Don't be embarrassed. I like the way you think." *I like you.* He took a deep breath. "Hearing your thoughts helped me to get to know you well."

When she lowered her hands, her eyes were glimmering with tears. "It didn't work both ways, for I hardly know you at all. And it doesn't help when you deceive or trick me. Or when you neglect to tell me something important. I . . . I need you to stop hiding things from me."

He swallowed hard. There was one thing he could never reveal. "We all hide things, Gwen. Our worst fears. Our secret desires. What we truly think about each other."

She blinked away tears. "I don't know what to think about you."

"What would you like to know? How much are you ready to know?"

She bit her lip, then ventured a quick glance at him. "Do—do you truly think I'm beautiful?"

"Yes. You're more than beautiful. You're clever. Brave and loyal. Those are the qualities that are the most important to me."

She took a deep breath, and her breasts nearly popped out from her tight bodice.

Holy Light, he wanted to kiss her. "I have a question for you. Did you . . . when we were embracing, did you want to kiss me? Were you tempted?"

She looked away, her cheeks turning pink.

"No answer?" He stepped closer. If he took her into his arms, would she stop him?

She retreated a step. "This is happening too fast. I met you only yesterday."

"We can slow down. We have plenty of time."

"No, we don't." She met his gaze. "I'm leaving in a month."

He swallowed hard. He'd forgotten about that. "I could still see you. I could visit you—"

"To what end? It is true what Her Majesty said. I would never be accepted here."

"I don't give a damn what people think."

"If you become king, they will be your people. So you should care."

"Gwen—"

"No." She lifted her chin. "I won't date you. And I will not be . . . tempted."

It felt like a jab through the heart. He did his best not to recoil.

She strode through the doorway and shut the door.

In his face.

Dammit. He clenched a fist, ready to punch a hole in the damned door. He still wanted to kiss her. He wanted to tempt her. Hell, he simply wanted her.

To what end? Her words echoed in his mind, and he let his arm drop to his side.

If he started something with her, how would it end? Would he end up trying to separate her from her adopted sisters and making her miserable instead of happy? He'd never known anyone from the Three Cursed Clans who had managed to have a happy relationship.

He sighed. He needed to keep his priorities straight. They had work to accomplish, so he should be concentrating on that.

But he still wanted to kiss her. With a groan he realized what the real question was. Not if he wanted her. That was a clear yes. But she was leaving in a month. The real question was—if he fell for her, would he be able to let her go?

While Nissa untied the laces on Gwennore's gown, her thoughts kept returning to the scene in the hallway. She'd come so close to kissing him! Good goddesses, she'd been so tempted. And then he'd asked her to date him?

She shook her head. Of all the things to focus on, that's where her thoughts kept going? She should be making more plans on detecting the poison and debunking the so-called curse. But as she slipped on her nightgown, she kept wondering what Silas would think of her now. Would he still find her beautiful?

She glanced at the door that led into his dressing room. Was that the sound of running water? Was he bathing?

Don't think about him. But how odd that he'd mentioned that Puff had an extra-large heart. When she'd done a reading on him, she'd noticed the same thing about him. It seemed like a strange coincidence—

"All done, my lady." Nissa's words interrupted her thoughts.

"Thank you, Nissa. You may go now."

"Good evening, then." Nissa bobbed a curtsy and made a quick exit through the bedchamber.

Gwen glanced once again at the door to Silas's dressing room. He wouldn't dare . . . she winced, recalling how close he'd come to kissing her. And all those outrageous comments he'd made. She'd been feverish with desire? And they'd been caught up in a blazing inferno of passion?

Oh, he would dare, the scoundrel. She dragged a chair over and rammed it against the door. He could probably hear the noise she was making, but that should make it clear that he was not welcome.

She strode into her bedchamber, closing the door to her dressing room behind her. As tense as she was, she feared she would have trouble sleeping. But it had been such an awfully long day that within minutes of crawling into the large bed, she fell fast asleep.

Some time later, she stirred when a sound emanated

from her dressing room. *It's nothing.* She rolled over and snuggled deeper into the wide, comfy bed.

The door to her dressing room made a slight creaking noise. Her eyes fluttered open, but she couldn't see anything. The fire in her hearth had gone out during the night. A few glowing coals provided enough light that she could barely discern the blurred outlines of a few pieces of furniture. *It's nothing.*

A shadow moved into view.

With a gasp, she sat up. *It's definitely something.*

"Don't be alarmed."

It's Silas! "What—what are you doing here?"

"No one will believe we're lovers if the servants discover us sleeping in separate beds."

He meant to sleep with her? "No!" She dragged the red velvet coverlet up to her chin. "You're taking this lover pretense much too seriously!"

"Shall I take it lightly then?" He bounced onto the bed.

"What are you doing? You can't get into my bed."

"Oh, that reminds me." He pulled back the edge of the coverlet. "I need to be under the covers, so it looks like I slept here."

"You're not sleeping here."

His grin flashed in the dark. "You want to do something else?"

"No!"

"Ah, rejected again. How many wounds must I endure?" He pulled off his shirt.

"What are you doing?" She scooted to her edge of the bed.

He tossed the shirt onto the floor. "We have to make it believable. I never sleep with a shirt on." He fumbled underneath the sheet.

She eyed him warily. "What are you doing now?"

"Just a minute." He lay back and raised his hips.

"There." He sat up and pulled his breeches out from underneath the sheet. "I never make love with my clothes on."

She gasped as he tossed the breeches across the room. "This is outrageous! Are you totally . . ."

"Naked? No, I still have on some drawers. But it might be more believable if I take them—"

"No!"

"Very well." He flashed another grin. "Anything to make you more comfortable."

"I'm not comfortable!" She grabbed a spare pillow and jammed it between the two of them. "Don't you dare cross this line."

"So you're all right with me staying?"

"I didn't say that."

"Gwennie." He stretched out on his side, his head propped up on his hand. "I have the upmost respect for you. I won't do anything to upset you."

"I'm already upset."

"I'll stay on my side of the bed and leave you alone. In fact, you'll be even safer with me here, because I can protect you. So go back to sleep."

"How could I possibly sleep with you in my bed?"

He shrugged the shoulder he wasn't lying on. "You ignore me."

Ignore him? When he was practically naked and the sheet only reached his waist? And his chest looked so . . . interesting. She turned her head, focusing on nothing in front of her. "I won't be able to sleep."

"Are you not used to sharing a bed?"

"I am, actually."

"I'll kill him."

She snorted. "You're always joking."

"Not always. Who is the bastard who shared your bed?"

She gave him a wry look. "Your sister. And if you don't behave yourself, I'll tell her what you called her."

He grinned. "You slept with Sorcha?"

"At the convent, yes."

He lay down, crooking his arm beneath his head for a pillow. "What is she like? Are you close to her?"

"Very close. I'm only six months older than her. I . . . I can't remember a time when she wasn't a part of my life."

"You miss her."

Gwen pulled her knees up against her chest. "Yes. I miss all my sisters."

"You'll see them again."

Gwennore nodded. In a month. Brody had promised to check on her in a week. "Brody said he would bring me letters from them."

"That's good."

"The—the jewelry you loaned me tonight—"

"Not a loan. I gave it to you."

"You shouldn't have. Those pieces belonged to your mother, so they should go to Sorcha."

He shrugged his shoulder again, causing her gaze to return to his broad chest. "Would you mind telling me about her?"

She tilted her head. "Who?"

"Sorcha. Unless you'd rather sleep."

With an inward wince, she realized she'd been staring at the curious-looking ripples along his abdomen. She turned her head away and scooted back so she was sitting against the headboard with the coverlet up to her chin.

"Are you cold? I could build up the fire."

"No!" The thought of him wandering about in his underpants was too much. "I—I'm feeling warmer." Her face flushed with heat. "Do you still want to hear about Sorcha?"

"Yes. She seemed very . . . straightforward. And strong."

"She is strong. I've always envied that about her."

"Why would you? You're strong, too."

Gwen shook her head. "I let people look down on me. If someone sneered at Sorcha, she'd probably punch him in the face."

He chuckled. "Probably so. But I still think you're strong. You have an inner strength that doesn't give up. And once it's added to your cleverness and sense of loyalty, it makes you formidable. Just look at what you've been through the last two days."

Her heart softened. Even though he was a scoundrel, somehow he knew exactly what she needed to hear the most. "I'm not used to . . ."

"To what?"

Her blush grew hotter, and she hoped he couldn't see it in the dim light. "You seem to think highly of me."

"I do."

She ventured a quick glance at him. Good goddesses, his face looked so sweet against that pillow. *Don't think about that!* She hastily made sure her mental shield was intact. "I'm afraid I'll disappoint you. I can't be sure I'll succeed—"

"I know. I've fought enough battles, seen enough of my people die, to know that success is never guaranteed. We can only do our best."

With a sigh, she closed her eyes and leaned her head back. He did have a serious side. How could he not when he'd witnessed so much war and death? His habit of joking had to be the way he dealt with stress and hardship. It was . . . endearing.

"Margosha told me you didn't find any poison earlier."

She opened her eyes. "That's true, but we did make some progress. We ruled out the possibility that the poison being used comes from the darca flower. Tomorrow, I'll check the garden for any other plants that could be used to make poison."

"Sounds good." He yawned. "I have some meetings I have to go to, but I'll catch up with you at the midday meal."

"All right." The sight of his yawn made her yawn, too.

"We're tired. Try to get some sleep." He rolled over toward the edge of the bed. "Good night, Gwen."

"Good night." She stared at his back for a while. So strong. And muscular. The tanned skin looked like it would be warm to touch. *Don't think about that.*

She scrunched down, curling into a ball on her edge of the bed. Behind her, she could hear the sound of his soft breathing.

Sorcha's brother. She smiled to herself. If Sorcha knew what her brother was doing, she'd clobber him for sure.

But he wasn't causing her any harm. He hadn't tried to touch her. In fact, he'd told her the things she'd most wanted to hear. With a sigh, she stretched out and closed her eyes.

Perhaps he could be trusted, after all.

Chapter Fourteen

❧

She should have known not to trust him. Some hours later, she was jerked abruptly awake when he suddenly wrapped an arm around her and pulled her back against him.

She gasped. "What—?"

"Shh," he whispered in her ear. "Play along."

She elbowed him and when he scooted back, she rolled onto her back to glare at him. The scoundrel had moved the pillow and crossed the line. "You—" She halted when he rested his hand against her cheek.

He leaned close. "The sun is up. Your maid will be coming—"

The door creaked open, causing a narrow shaft of light to beam into the room and fall across the bed.

Gwennore blinked, suddenly able to see Silas's face so close to her. His hair was tousled, and her fingers itched to brush back the dark curls falling over his brow. There was a quiet determination in the gaze of his green eyes, and a shadow of dark whiskers along his sharp jawline.

A gasp emanated from the doorway along with a clunking noise.

Silas sat up. "Oh, dear. We've been caught."

"My apologies, Lord General." Nissa curtsied, focusing on the floor as her face grew pink. "Please forgive me. I was just coming to light the fire." She motioned to the basket of firewood that she'd dropped.

"That's quite all right." Silas smiled at her. "But I suggest you knock from now on. I have a hard time resisting my darling Gwennie in the morning."

With a groan, Gwennore pulled the sheet over her face.

"That's my snookums," he teased. "Always trying to sneak a peek at the crown jewels."

With a huff, she lowered the sheet and scowled at him.

Nissa gathered up the basket. "I'll come back in a few minutes."

Silas gave her a wry look. "Give me an hour at least."

"Of—of course, Lord General." Nissa's eyes widened as she observed his broad, muscular chest. "You can take all day, if you like."

Gwennore winced. Could this get any more embarrassing?

"You can leave the firewood," Silas told the maid. "I'll get the fire started."

"Yes, my lord." Nissa set the basket on the floor, then backed out and shut the door.

The room grew dim and Gwennore took a deep breath. They were alone again. In bed.

With a gasp, she suddenly remembered the dagger underneath her pillow. Why hadn't she thought of that last night? She could have used it to chase Silas away. Why hadn't she? Had she been too busy eyeing his chest?

"Is something wrong?" he whispered.

"I just recalled I have a knife under my pillow."

"Ah. I guess I'm lucky I survived the night."

She nodded. "I missed my chance."

"What a shame. But there's always tomorrow."

"What? You intend to come back?"

"Of course." He leaned over her and stroked her cheek. "How could I resist?"

She pushed his hand away. "Don't tempt me."

"To do what? Kiss?"

"No. To use the dagger."

With a chuckle, he sat up. "So is it the one from Lord Romak?"

"No." She motioned toward her bedside table. "That one is in the drawer."

"Holy Light, snookums. How many knives do you have?"

"Keep calling me that and you'll find out."

With a smile, he stretched out beside her. "I enjoy being with you, Gwen."

Her face grew warm. Goddesses help her, she enjoyed his company, too. But there was no future for her here. Only heartbreak if she fell for him. "We should be focusing on our mission. Instead you keep wasting time, trying to prove a fake relationship with embarrassing scenes."

There was an awkward silence, then he scooted across the bed. "Since you find our fake relationship embarrassing, I'll be on my way."

She winced. Had she hurt his feelings? "It's not you that embarrasses me. Well, the *snookums* stuff is a bit embarrassing, but the real problem is the fact that everyone thinks I'm . . . that I'm . . ."

"Having the best sex in your life five times a day?"

She huffed. "You must think highly of yourself."

"I have to. I keep getting rejected, and it's crushing me."

"I—we hardly know each other. How can I be hurting you that badly?"

He was silent for a moment, sitting at the edge of the bed. "That is a good question."

A few more awkward minutes passed, then Gwennore

said, "Please understand. I was raised in a convent. I have no experience with men. So it is only natural that I would be embarrassed for people to think I'm behaving in a wanton manner."

He nodded. "I can understand that."

"Thank you."

"But we have a saying in Norveshka that the chicken has already been plucked. Meaning the feathers can't be put back on. It's too late now to convince people that we're not . . ."

"Copulating?"

His mouth twitched. "That's a nicer word than I was going to use. But I like the way you talk."

She snorted. "Because my speech is archaic?"

"Because it's one more reason for me to think you're beautiful."

Her gaze met his, and for a few seconds, it felt like the air was sizzling between them. It made her feel hot, breathless, and . . . needy. As if she desperately needed something.

"I'll get the fire going." He tossed back the covers to get out of bed.

She turned away, fanning herself. Good goddesses, but the fire had already started. When he picked up the basket of firewood, she ventured a quick glance at him. Long muscular legs. White linen underpants that clung to the contour of his buttocks.

Don't look. She pulled the sheet up to her brow and listened to the sound of him working by the hearth.

After only a minute, the room flooded with light, and she lowered the sheet. There was a blazing fire in the hearth, and he had put on his breeches and pulled open the curtains.

"How?" She glanced at the fire. "How did you get it going so quickly?"

"I'm good with fire." He scooped his shirt off the carpet and strode toward her. "I'll see you at the midday meal in the Great Hall, all right?"

She nodded, her eyes widening now that she was seeing his bare chest in full daylight. There were indeed some interesting ridges across his abdomen. The battle scars she'd discerned during her reading were there. One on the shoulder and one below his ribs.

And the tattoo was there on his left shoulder. Goodness, it was big. "Is that a dragon?"

He glanced down at it. "Yes."

"You had it done because you can communicate with the dragons?"

He motioned to a bell pull by her bed. "That's attached to a bell in the small room next door. Your maid's room. She can help you get dressed." His mouth curled up. "Unless you'd prefer my help."

She scoffed. "You may go."

With a sigh, he trudged toward her dressing room and his rooms that lay on the other side. "Rejected again."

After shaving and getting dressed, Silas hurried to the Great Hall, where only a few courtiers were having breakfast. Most of them were sleeping late, since last night's dance had kept them up well past midnight.

He helped himself to some eggs, ham, and bread with jam at the buffet table, then sat across from Dimitri at a small table.

Dimitri shot him a wry look. "Congratulations."

"Why?" Silas took a big bite of eggs.

"You've become a legend due to your phenomenal performance in bed."

Silas choked, then managed to swallow, his eyes watering. "What?"

"You survived the night in Lady Gwennore's bed,"

Dimitri muttered. "So the servants have spread the word that you avoided being stabbed to death by wearing the poor woman out. Now they're laying bets on whether she'll be able to walk."

Silas coughed, then quickly downed a cup of cider. "I barely touched her."

"But you did climb into her bed," Dimitri grumbled. "You barely know the woman. What the hell are you doing?"

Silas scoffed. "Are you my mother?"

"If you care about her at all, stay away from her. You know what happens to women who marry into the Three Cursed Clans."

Silas sat back. "Who said anything about marriage?"

Dimitri grimaced. "Don't fall for her, all right?"

"It'll be fine. Don't worry." Silas spread some strawberry jam on his bread. He'd always been careful in the past to keep his heart at a distance.

He glanced at his old friend. Dimitri had married his first love six years ago, but then she had died nine months later in childbirth, along with his newborn son. Ever since then, he'd believed in the curse. And he had vowed never to marry again, so he could never cause another woman to suffer.

Silas took a bite of bread. "Aleksi should be arriving soon with Annika."

Dimitri shrugged with a disinterested look.

"She's going to help Gwennore—"

"Just keep her away from me."

Silas sighed. When Annika had joined the army a year ago, she'd immediately fallen for Dimitri. He'd brushed her off, trying to scare her away with dire warnings about the curse, but as far as Silas could tell, her feelings had not withered away. She simply admired Dimitri from afar.

Silas had thought that was the end of it, but then he'd

secretly caught Dimitri gazing at her with a look of longing. "I don't believe in the curse."

Dimitri was quiet for a moment, then muttered, "I do."

"I know. But believe in this, too. I'm going to get rid of it."

Dimitri sighed. "I'll believe it when I see it."

Silas nodded, then lowered his voice to a whisper. "Did you see where that priest went?"

Dimitri glanced around the room, then leaned forward. "He met Romak in the woods. They exchanged letters, then the priest handed Romak a small bag. Romak looked inside, removed a gold coin, then dropped it back in."

"He's getting rich spying for someone," Silas concluded.

Dimitri nodded. "Someone from Eberon, I assume, since that's where the priest came from."

Silas drummed his fingers on the table. "Given the fact that the courier is a priest, I would guess Lord Morris from Eberon is the one paying for information."

"Lord Morris?"

Silas nodded. "He was head priest and chief counsel for King Frederic. Morris would like to get rid of the new king, Leofric, and go back to the good old days when the priests held the power of life and death over their followers."

Dimitri winced. "Thank the Light our priests here in Norveshka never wielded that kind of power."

"But what could Morris want with our country?" Silas gazed out a window while he considered. "If he wants to overthrow King Leofric, then he would need an army."

"Our army?"

Silas nodded. "He could be using Romak to persuade our king into waging war on Eberon."

"That would be disastrous for us."

"Both countries could end up destroyed, but maybe

that's what Lord Morris wants. When a country is in ruins, it's easier to take over." Silas recalled the dragon his brother had talked about. The Ancient One, Fafnir. The dragon also wanted war. Was there some connection here?

"We could arrest Romak and the priest," Dimitri suggested. "If we interrogate them, they'll tell us what they're up to."

Silas thought it over as he ate. "Let's leave them be for now so we can see what they do next. When Aleksi returns, have him follow the priest. You keep an eye on Romak. I need to visit the Sacred Well."

Dimitri blinked in surprise. "Why? There's nothing there but a spring of boiling water."

"That's what I need to check." Silas gulped down the last of his cider. Either his brother was right and there was an old dragon lurking in the cave, or Dimitri was right, and there was only a spring.

Silas banged his empty cup on the table. If there was no dragon there, he would have to admit that his brother was completely delusional.

She'd slept with a man. Gwennore lay in bed for a few minutes digesting that thought. General Gorgeous had slept with her, wearing nothing but his underpants, and she'd seen his bare chest, his broad shoulders, his battle scars, and the dragon tattoo on his shoulder.

When he'd leaned over her and touched her cheek, a part of her had wished they wouldn't be interrupted. With a sigh, she rolled over. What foolish thinking! He'd only behaved like that because he'd known the maid was coming in. It was nothing but pretense to him.

Or was it more? There had been that moment when they had looked at each other and time had frozen while the air between them had heated with desire.

Dear goddesses, the man tempted her. She sat up and

glanced at the pillow he had used. There was still a slight indentation where his head had rested through the night. She reached out to touch it, then jerked her hand back.

Stop thinking about him! There was work to do. She needed to gather up samples of any poisonous and medicinal plants she could find in the castle garden.

She headed to her dressing room and shoved a chair against Silas's door. After relieving herself, she filled a bowl with water and rolled up her sleeves to wash her face.

To her surprise, there was a pink, inflamed area on the underside of her left forearm. Had the fancy gown she'd worn last night irritated her skin?

She washed her face, then the pink area on her arm. With her hands still wet, she reached for her toothbrush, and it slipped from her grip and tumbled into the water.

"Of all the silly—" She grabbed the toothbrush, then dropped it again with a gasp. The silver handle had turned black.

Her skin chilled as she gazed once again at the pink spot on her arm. A side effect of the seeds of the darca flower. Someone was trying to poison her.

Chapter Fifteen

❧

Don't panic. Gwennore gripped the edge of her dressing table and took a deep breath. She needed to remain calm and act like the healer that she was.

First, she should take a reading on herself. She gripped her left wrist, and instantly her gift was activated. Pulse was fast, but that was probably due to shock. *Don't panic.*

She mentally searched her body for signs of poison. It was mostly concentrated around the inflamed area on her arm. Thankfully, she'd received a small dose. She could expect some dizziness and perhaps some nausea, but as long as she wasn't exposed again, she should be all right.

Just to be sure, she quickly stripped and examined herself for any other signs of inflammation. None. Thank the goddesses.

The next step was discovering what had transferred the poison to her arm, so she could avoid coming into contact with it again. The pink area hadn't been there before dinner last night, so the most likely culprits were the gown she'd worn or the nightgown she'd worn to bed. But why would someone treat only the left sleeve with poison?

Had something else touched her forearm? The knife! She'd slipped the dagger from Lord Romak up her sleeve.

She ran into her bedchamber and opened the drawer of her bedside table. Using a handkerchief, she picked up the dagger and returned to the dressing room. After emptying the bowl and rinsing it out, she filled it partway with fresh water, then slipped the dagger into the water. While she waited, she put on a clean shift.

After a few tense minutes, she dunked the silver handle of her hairbrush into the water.

It turned black.

She dropped the hairbrush on the table as a startling thought occurred to her. The toxic effect of darca poison was slow when absorbed through the skin, but if the knife had pierced her flesh, the poison would have instantly entered her bloodstream. It could have killed her.

Don't panic.

She inhaled slowly. So Lord Romak wanted her dead? *No, wait.* He had wanted her to use the dagger on Silas. He wanted Silas dead. And he wanted her to take the blame for it. Even the smallest of nicks could have killed Silas.

Her heart clenched at the thought of accidentally killing him, and she leaned over, pressing a hand to her chest. *Calm yourself.* Romak's plan would have never worked, for she could never attack Silas.

Not when she was falling for him.

With a groan, she covered her mouth. It was true. Her initial attraction to him had grown to the point that she was falling for him. And it was impossible. No one would accept her here. She was considered an enemy from Woodwyn, a malicious elf who could stab her lover to death. And if anything happened to Silas, they would hold her responsible. She would end up in a dungeon. Or executed.

Romak could be rid of both her and Silas in one fell

swoop. And with Silas gone, there was no heir to the throne. Was Romak planning to steal the crown?

She had to tell Silas about this immediately.

Even though the Cave of the Sacred Well was considered a holy place, Silas had never considered it a pleasant place to visit. As he approached, the smell of rotten eggs forced him to breathe through his mouth. He also had to watch his step or he could get seriously burned.

The stream that emerged from the cave was so hot that nothing could live in it or around it. The banks were white ash, and hot enough to sting through the soles of his boots. Any rocks that had fallen from the mountainside into the stream were blanched white like hard-boiled eggs.

Farther down the valley, where the stream was cooled off by snowmelt, the water gathered in a series of pools. It was believed that bathing in those pools could heal certain diseases, but as far as Silas knew, they hadn't helped the queen. They certainly hadn't helped his mother.

The entrance to the cave was narrow and dark. His vision adjusted quickly as he maneuvered down the tunnel, avoiding the white ash close to the stream. If he slipped here and fell into the water, he would be cooked.

After a few yards, the entrance opened into a huge cavern, big enough for more than a dozen dragons. The source of the stream, the Sacred Well, was situated in the center of the room. Wisps of steam rose from its clear blue depths, the water in it fed by an underground spring. Too hot for humans, but not for dragons.

Giant pillar candles were set onto boulders, held in place by pools of melted wax. Rivulets of wax had run off the edges of the boulders, only to cool and harden into stalactites that reached for the stone floor of the underground room.

Once a week, a caretaker ventured inside the cave to light the candles, but only a few remained lit now. The other flames had probably been extinguished by the breeze that wafted in from the large gap in the ceiling overhead. It was through that opening that the Ancient Ones had flown down into the cavern.

The old dragons had felt safe congregating here. Any human that tried to enter through the gap in the ceiling would fall into the Sacred Well and be boiled to death. The other entrance, the one Silas had just used, was easily guarded, since it was narrow enough that humans were forced to enter in single file. That made it easy for the dragons to roast an unwanted intruder with a breath of fire.

But the Ancient Ones had been killed off five hundred years ago in the Great War of the Dragons. The new dragons had quickly declared themselves the new guardians of the Sacred Well, and the place had been opened to all the Norveshki. Now the site was considered a holy place to pray, for any human who was brave enough to risk the danger of coming here would supposedly be rewarded by having his request granted.

Had Petras come here often to pray? And in his desperation, he must have considered Fafnir the answer to his prayers. Silas lit a torch and wandered about the cavern, examining all the nooks and crannies. No sign of a dragon.

But there were seven tunnels that branched off from the main cavern. The dragon could be hiding down one of those tunnels and only showing himself to Petras.

Silas ventured down the first tunnel. Dead end. Same with the second and third.

The fourth tunnel led to a small room. Just as Silas stepped inside, a large rat scampered past him, dashing for the main cavern. Toward the far side of the room, Silas found the doused remains of a campfire, and nearby some discarded bones. Odd. A dragon didn't need to cook his meals over a fire. He could simply breathe fire on an animal, then gobble it down.

Silas examined the room more carefully and discovered a narrow opening into a sheltered alcove. Inside, there were blankets. A man's clothing. But no man in sight.

He checked the other tunnels but found nothing. It didn't look like an Ancient One was living here. But possibly, a homeless man was.

Who was Petras meeting? If Fafnir was real, he must have flown away when Silas had approached the cave. But he hadn't seen a dragon in the sky.

He groaned. Whatever was going on here stank as badly as the Sacred Well.

Gwennore whispered a prayer of thanks to the goddesses when she discovered a verna plant in the castle garden. She pulled off several leaves, still damp from morning dew, and pressed them against the inflamed area on her arm. Within seconds, the itching and burning subsided.

She hadn't mentioned the poisoning to Nissa when she'd asked the maid to help her dress, for she hadn't wanted the news to spread around the castle. But as soon as she was dressed, she'd dashed to Lady Margosha's bedchamber to tell her. Margosha had quickly agreed that the situation had to remain a secret. Lord Romak couldn't know that they knew what he had done, or he might try to flee.

So they had agreed to go about their day as normally as possible. Margosha had provided Gwennore a canvas bag and a pair of shears for working in the garden. While Gwennore had hurried down the stairs, Margosha had gone to find Silas.

Now, in the garden, Gwennore stuffed more verna leaves into her bag in case she needed them later. Then she clipped off samples from other plants. Some could be used to make poison, others medicine, and some could actually do both, depending on how potent a concoction was made.

As she worked, she kept glancing toward the southern gate, hoping to see Silas. Had Margosha told him the news yet? If he cared about her, wouldn't he come running to make sure she was all right?

Her gaze drifted to the green lawn where she and Eviana had been dropped that first day. Only two days ago. So much had happened since then. It felt like she'd known Silas for two months instead of two days.

And what had happened to Puff? She glanced up at the sky. No dragon in sight. When would she see him again? When would she hear his beautiful voice in her mind? It had a soothing quality that she would welcome right now when her head was beginning to hurt.

An effect from the poison, she thought as she glanced once again at the southern gate. Where was Silas? His voice was soothing, too, when he lowered it and spoke softly. Goodness, she'd forgotten how similar their voices were. But now that she thought about it, it seemed odd. Even their word choices were similar.

A wave of dizziness caught her off guard and caused her to stumble. There was a bench nearby, so she took a seat and breathed deeply until she felt steady once again.

Movement at the southern gate caught her attention. Silas? No, it was Margosha. A pang of disappointment reverberated deep in her chest. How annoying, she chided herself as the pain in her head increased. She shouldn't have fallen for that scoundrel so quickly. Especially when he kept hiding things from her.

But he made her pulse race when he looked at her. He made her breathless when he touched her or spoke softly to her. He made her heart melt when he did sweet things like giving Eviana a birthday cake. He made her laugh when he was outrageous. He made her heart sing when he defended her in front of others.

He made her want more.

How could she not fall for such a man?

"Are you all right?" Margosha asked as she sat next to Gwennore.

"I was dizzy for a moment and my head hurts. Did you talk to Silas?"

"No, but I told Dimitri everything. He said Silas has gone somewhere, but he wouldn't say where."

Gwennore heaved a sigh. "I hate it when they keep secrets."

"Me, too." With a frown, Margosha crossed her arms. "They should trust me."

Gwennore winced. "I'm sure they do. The problem is they know you're going to tell me, and they don't trust me."

Margosha gave her a sad smile. "They will, in time."

"Dimitri had the knife hidden up his sleeve. Does he have an inflamed area, too? Is he suffering at all?"

"He said he was fine." Margosha snorted. "But then he's a soldier. His guts could be falling out, and he'd say it was just a flesh wound."

"Men," Gwennore muttered.

"Exactly." Margosha nodded. "I told him to come with me so you could treat him, but he refused. He's busy keeping an eye on Romak to make sure the weasel doesn't escape."

"Why doesn't he arrest him?"

"He wants to, but he's waiting for Silas to give the order."

Where had Silas gone? Gwennore wondered as she pulled a few verna leaves from her canvas sack. "Can you give these to Dimitri? Just tell him to press the leaves against the inflamed area."

"All right." Margosha stood. "You're not done here?"

"I still have that area over there to check." Gwennore motioned to a shaded area close to the forest. "I'll be along soon."

"Very well. I'll see you at the midday meal." Margosha headed for the southern gate.

Gwennore rested awhile longer on the bench. Even with her head hurting, she was enjoying the view. And the sounds of the garden. A red cardinal was flitting about, and the trill of birdsong drifted toward her. In the distance, she detected the buzzing of bees around the flowering fruit trees. Pink and white flowers. A breeze blew a few petals across the garden and deposited them on the green lawn. Such a beautiful country. And yet the people were suffering from a so-called curse.

A stronger breeze unleashed more cherry blossoms, and she smiled at the pink petals swirling in the sky. A murmur of voices caught her attention, and she closed her eyes to concentrate.

Soft voices speaking in a language much like Elfish. The Kings of the Forest? Were they in this area, too?

Since she was alone at the moment, she figured it was safe enough to drop the shield around her mind. That way, the giant redwoods would be able to hear her call out to them mentally. *Kings of the Forest, can you hear me?*

It is the Elfin woman.

We have heard of you.

The Kings in the south told you about me? Gwennore asked as she rose to her feet.

Yes. The news has spread north with the wind.

Where are you? Gwennore asked. *I'd like to meet you.*

Go north along the Norva River.

Past the waterfall. We are by the lake.

Gwennore hesitated, reluctant to venture off on her own. But she knew the lake wasn't far and as long as she could see the towers of the castle, she couldn't actually get lost. She remembered from her travels the day before that the path down to the village of Dreshka went in a southerly direction. So she should take the other path, the one that circled around the eastern side of the castle, headed north.

When Puff had left her in the garden, he'd flown off that direction. If she followed the path, would she find him? And the Kings of the Forest?

She was too curious not to try it. So she hitched the canvas bag over her shoulder and headed for the path. After circling the castle, she noticed that the path split—one branch leading to a dead end at the northwestern tower, and the other widening into a road that led into the forest.

As she wandered down the road, the sound of rushing water grew stronger. She had to be close to the river. She gazed into the forest, searching for giant trees. The pines and firs were tall, but slender.

Are you close to the castle? she asked the Kings of the Forest.

Not far.

Why are you in the land of the barbarians?

I'm a healer, Gwennore explained. *I'm trying to discover what is causing the health problems here.*

You mean the curse?

You know about that? Gwennore asked.

There is little we do not know.

Would you be willing to tell me about it? Gwennore asked. *I would really appreciate your help.*

There was a pause, then she heard multiple voices whispering to one another. They seemed to be arguing. Some were objecting to helping the barbarians who had no respect for them.

Gwennore was wondering if she should join the argument when suddenly, she discovered a large clearing to the left. A field had been cleared of trees, and situated close by was a log cabin with a grass roof. No smoke drifted from its stone chimney.

"Good morning!" Gwennore called out, but no one emerged from the small house.

"Hello?" She stepped up onto the front porch and peeked inside a window. No one inside, but there was a table and chairs. Boots on the floor. Piles of clothing on the table.

A gust of wind caused the door to creak open. She peeked inside. No bed. No cooking utensils. Apparently, no one lived here. The clothing on the table seemed familiar, so she ventured inside for a closer look.

Brown breeches, some made of leather, some of linen. Green linen shirts. White linen underpants and woolen socks. Leather breastplates. Green, hooded capes. These were uniforms worn by soldiers. What on Aerthlan were they doing here?

She picked up one breastplate and noticed the two brass stars. Could it belong to Aleksi? But then there was probably more than one captain in the army. Another breastplate had three brass stars. A colonel like Dimitri would wear this.

Her breath caught when she spotted a breastplate with four stars. This had to belong to Silas. She ran her fingers over the stars. They needed polishing, for the star on the left had turned green. Why was he keeping a stash of clothing out here in a cabin?

A sudden creak made her jump, but it was just the wind pushing the door further open. She adjusted her canvas sack on her shoulder, then left, closing the door behind her.

She glanced back at Draven Castle. It was a quick walk from here. Since Silas, Dimitri, and Aleksi all had rooms at the castle, why did they have clothes out here?

It was strange, she thought, but her head hurt too much to dwell on it. As she wandered down the road, she was soon surrounded again by forest. The sound of rushing water grew increasingly loud.

The road narrowed into a path that led her straight to the Norva River. Holding on to a tree, she gazed down into the ravine and spotted the river below, crashing and foaming around numerous boulders. So beautiful! She would really miss this place when she returned to the palace at Ebton. Eberon was a pretty country with its green rolling hills, but not nearly as stunning as Norveshka.

The sound of roaring water became louder as she walked around a bend. She stopped with a gasp. The waterfall! The water spilled over a cliff to crash into the ravine far below. She stood still for a moment, letting the beauty of the scene soothe her soul. Mist dampened her skin, and a cool breeze kissed her face. Her headache faded away.

She loved it here.

The thought struck her unexpectedly, but she realized it was true. Somehow she felt at home here in the mountains and forest. As if she belonged here. Perhaps it was in her elfin blood, for she'd always heard that Woodwyn had vast forests and mountains, too.

On the other side of the waterfall, a lake stretched out before her, its color a lovely shade of turquoise. A green field of wildflowers surrounded it, and in the distance— she gasped.

The trees were enormous! The Kings of the Forest had not been boasting. They really were taller than a castle.

She strode toward the grove of giant redwoods. *I'm here.*

We know.

Welcome.

She rested a hand against the trunk of one. *You're*

amazing. I never knew something as wondrous as you existed.

We know.

We have decided to help you with your quest. But you must do something for us.

What? Gwennore asked.

You must tell the barbarians who we are.

We have been here longer than they have.

Storms cannot hurt us. Earthquakes cannot uproot us. Fire can only scorch us.

Then you are indestructible? Gwennore asked.

The barbarians can kill us with their axes and saws.

They know not what they do.

They must stop.

I will tell them, Gwennore promised. *I'll tell General Dravenko. He already knows about you. What can you—* She paused when she heard a cry in the distance. *What is that?*

One of the wild barbarians has fallen into the stream.

Just north of the lake.

Gwennore strode toward the northern end of the lake, where a stream fed into it. Another howl of pain sounded in the distance.

"I'm on my way!" she called out in Norveshki as she hurried along the eastern bank of the stream. On this side, the ground was level with the water, but on the opposite side, a high ridge bordered the stream. Perhaps the man had fallen off the ridge and onto the rocks in the stream.

She spotted him, hunched up on a flat boulder in the middle of the stream, holding his leg. Blood seeped from a gash to color the boulder red.

"I'm coming!" she yelled, but he ducked his head down and looked away. He seemed short. Only a boy.

"It will be all right." She waded into the shallow stream,

wincing at how frigid the water was. "I'm a healer. My name is Gwennore. And your name?"

He shook his head, his thick mane of hair concealing his face.

Poor child, Gwennore thought, as she noted the dirty clothes he was wearing. His hair was unkempt and matted.

She climbed up onto the boulder. "Let me see your leg."

He flinched when she pulled his ragged breeches up to his knee. The gash on his shin was bleeding so much, it was hard to see how big it was.

"I need to wash this off a bit." She set her canvas bag on a dry section of the boulder, then scooped up some water in her hands to rinse off his leg.

With a groan, he shuddered.

"It's not that bad," she assured him. How lucky that she had some of the verna plant with her. The leaves would keep the wound from getting infected.

She pulled out some of the leaves then, using a small rock, ground them on the boulder and added some water till she had a green paste. She smeared it onto the wound, then used her shears to cut a strip of white linen from the hem of her shift. She wrapped it around the treated wound and tied off the ends.

"There." She patted the boy on the shoulder. "You'll be fine. Do you live close to here? Do you need help getting home?"

A series of shouts drew her attention, and she glanced up at the ridge. There were a dozen men there, yelling at her and shaking their spears.

More shouts came from the other bank, and she gasped when she saw a dozen more men.

No, not men. They were close enough that she could get a good look at them. They were short, dressed in dirty clothes, with long hair and beards. The language they were yelling was not Norveshki. And they all had spears pointed at her.

The boy she had just treated yelled back at them, his voice deep and guttural.

With a gasp, Gwennore jumped back, falling off the boulder and landing knee-deep in the frigid water.

He wasn't a boy. With his face now visible, she saw he had the beginnings of a beard. His nose was large and bulbous.

Her blood ran cold.

Mountain trolls were real. And these were ready to attack.

Chapter Sixteen

❧

Gwennore stumbled back, her gaze darting from one side of the stream to the other. Goddesses help her! The trolls looked every bit as frightening as the illustrations in *Torushki's Bedtime Tales of a Mountain Troll*. But this wasn't a nightmare. She was awake, and they were real. Their spears were definitely real.

The injured troll on the boulder was telling the others something and motioning to his leg.

"Yes! I'm a healer," Gwennore called out in Norveshki, hoping they could understand. "I mean you no harm."

The trolls started jabbering to one another, but she couldn't tell if they were excited or angry. She backed away slowly, ignoring how much her feet were burning from the icy water.

One of them on the ridge noticed her sneaking away, and with a shout, he pointed his spear at her. Another one on the opposite bank lunged toward her.

Goddesses protect me! Gwennore lifted her skirts and ran, splashing through the stream toward the lake.

There is no need to fear, one of the Kings of the Forest said softly.

She scoffed. Easy for the Kings to say. They were

practically indestructible. The water grew deeper, up to her thighs, then her hips. In desperation, she ripped away any remaining shield around her mind and envisioned herself mentally screaming. *Puff! Can you hear me? I'm in trouble!*

A spear shot past her, bouncing off a boulder. *Puff! They're attacking me! Help me!*

Where are you? His voice sifted into her mind, and she almost wept from relief.

He'd heard her! Puff was there for her. *I'm north of the castle, close to the lake.*

The stream's current knocked her off her feet, and with a squeal, she plunged into icy water that was up to her shoulders. As the current swept her along, it took all her concentration to keep her head above water and avoid being slammed into any boulders. Before she knew it, she was dumped into the lake.

She treaded water as the current carried her toward the center of the lake. Thank the goddesses she'd learned how to swim on the Isle of Moon. And she no longer had to worry about crashing into any rocks. Glancing around, she spotted the trolls. They had followed her to the lake and were shouting at her, gesturing for her to swim ashore.

Were they hoping to take her captive? She couldn't let that happen. But the freezing cold was seeping into her bones. If any of her muscles cramped, she could drown. *Puff?*

I'm coming.

Her heart squeezed at the sound of his sweet voice. He would save her again. Goddesses help her, if he wasn't a different species, she would date him.

Have you reached the lake? he asked.

I'm in the lake.

What? Dammit, Gwen, get out. It's dangerous.

I can't, she replied. *The trolls will attack me.*

I'm almost there. Don't get caught in the current.

A little late for that, she thought as the current swept her slowly south. If she just stayed afloat, she would eventually make it all the way to the village of Dreshka. With a gasp, she recalled the waterfall.

She was slowly moving toward it. And the current was getting stronger. Holy goddesses, she could either plummet to her death or be captured by the trolls.

Panic threatened to overwhelm her, but she channeled the frantic feelings into a burst of energy, swimming hard for the shore. The trolls pranced about, shaking their spears. *Puff, where are you?*

A burst of fire shot from the sky, hitting the shoreline and forcing the trolls to retreat.

Puff! She spotted him, coming from the north and flying straight for her. Good goddesses, he was magnificent. Smoke curled up from his mouth, and his scales shimmered green and purple in the sunlight. He had to be the most incredible creature on all of Aerthlan.

And he was coming for her.

His wings folded in as he dove downward. His forelegs hit the water, skimming along the surface, then he scooped her up as easily as if she were a kitten.

She flung her arms around one of his legs, squeezing him tight.

I have you.

His great wings batted the air, lifting him slowly as he continued to fly south. Just as he rose above the lake, she glanced down and saw the water cascading over the falls. Oh dear goddesses, she'd come too close to dying.

But she was safe now, thanks to Puff. Tears burned her eyes, and a shudder racked her body.

He curled up his forelegs, cradling her against his chest. *Are you all right?*

"Yes." She shivered. "No. I'm freezing. And I was

so . . . afraid." A sob escaped and she burrowed her face against his soft leathery skin. "You saved me. Again. You're the best dragon in the whole world."

He held her tighter against him. *I was afraid, too.*

"Oh, Puff." She pressed a hand against his chest. "I missed you. It seems like ages since I last saw you."

It hasn't been that long. And you had others to keep you company. Like the general.

"He doesn't come dashing to the rescue like you. You've saved me twice now."

One of Puff's claws flinched. *Then you prefer me?* He angled his head downward, his golden eyes gleaming as he looked at her. *I heard you wanted to date me.*

"Wh-what?" she stuttered. "Who told you that? The general? The man is always joking. You can't take anything he says seriously."

A huffing sound emerged from Puff's nostrils as he shifted his gaze forward. *So you ignore what the general tells you? Didn't he warn you about the dangers of the forest?*

Gwennore winced. While it was true that she'd made a mistake, wandering off on her own, she still felt that Silas shared part of the blame. "I wouldn't have gone if I'd known the trolls were real. Silas should have told me."

But he warned you about the bears, wolves, and wildcats, didn't he?

"I don't want to talk about him," she grumbled. "He's always neglecting to tell me important things."

Another huff from Puff. *Maybe he's trying to protect you.*

"Why are you defending him?" She smoothed a hand across the soft leather of Puff's chest. "No one protects me as well as you."

His claws tightened, then relaxed. *Then it's true. You want to date me?*

"Well . . ." She winced. How could she let this beautiful dragon down gently? "I am very fond of you, but . . ."

Have you heard of the rules for dating a dragon? When I take you for a ride—

"Hold on tight and don't let go," she finished for him. "And the second rule is about your extra-large heart." She sighed. "I would never want to hurt you, Puff. Not when you're sweet enough to come to my rescue."

Then you should know the third rule, he said softly in her mind. *Whenever you need me, you only have to call and I will come.*

Dear goddesses, he made her heart ache. What a shame that he was a different species. For he was so much sweeter than that rascal Silas.

Puff's claws flinched once again.

"Ouch."

Sorry. He paused for a moment, then continued, *I have to admit to some anger that you ventured away from the castle by yourself. Why did you?*

"I wanted to meet the Kings of the Forest. And I did. They're truly magnificent." She patted his chest. "Almost as magnificent as you."

Another huff. *The general will be upset, too.*

No doubt Silas would want to fuss at her. But she was annoyed with him, too. "You can communicate with him, right?"

Yes.

"Good. Then tell him I don't want to talk to him. After all, whenever I'm in trouble, you're the one who saves me. Not him."

Puff's grip tightened as another huff escaped his nostrils. *We're at the castle now. I'll tell the colonel that you have arrived.*

He zoomed down and dropped her with a thud on the lawn close to the southern gate.

Oof. Had he done that because he was angry? Gwennore sat up and saw him flying around the castle, headed back north. *Puff, when will I see you again?*

Why do you ask? Are we dating?

She scrambled to her feet. *I haven't thanked you properly.*

Thank the general. He's the one who sent me.

Silas had sent Puff? Gwennore pondered that as she watched the dragon disappear from view. If Silas had been communicating with Puff, why had she heard only Puff's voice in her mind? That reminded her that her mind was still open, so she quickly erected a mental shield.

A cool breeze wafted against her wet clothes, causing her to shiver. She needed to warm up quickly, or she'd catch a cold. As she hurried through the gate, she realized she'd left her canvas bag behind at the river. Blast. She'd have to do all that work in the garden again.

This day was not going well. And it wasn't going to get any better if Silas was intending to give her an earful.

"Dammit, I'll wring her neck!" Silas strode down the hallway on the ground floor of the northern wing. He'd just returned to the castle through the northwestern tower, where Dimitri had met him.

"Not so loud," Dimitri grumbled. "Everyone in the castle is eager for more gossip about your turbulent love affair with Lady Gwennore."

Silas took a deep breath to calm his anger. "Did you send Margosha to her?"

"Yes." Dimitri opened the door to Karlan's office. "We can talk in here."

Silas glanced around as he entered. "Where is Karlan?"

"I asked him and a few of his most trusted guards to help me keep an eye on Romak and the priest. We're taking turns, so they won't realize they're being watched."

"Where is Romak?"

"In the king's outer office, going about business as usual." Dimitri rolled up a sleeve to show a few wet leaves plastered against his forearm. "Lady Gwennore sent these earlier." He peeled off the leaves to show a red, inflamed patch of skin.

"What is that?" Silas asked.

"It was caused by poison. Lady Gwennore has a similar spot on her arm."

"What?" Silas's heart lurched. "She's been poisoned?"

Dimitri snorted. "I was, too, but I can see where all your concern lies."

Silas gave him a wry look. "You're obviously still alive. Where did the poison come from?"

"The dagger that Romak had me pass on to Gwennore."

Silas's heart grew still for a moment. "The weasel wants me dead."

Dimitri nodded. "I figure he wants rid of both you and Lady Gwennore. If she stabbed you with the poisoned dagger, it would kill you. And then she would be executed."

"Bastard." Silas clenched his fists. "How dare he abuse her like that? If she had accidentally cut herself, she could have died!"

Dimitri cleared his throat. "Me, too."

"Yes." Silas paced about the room. "So Romak didn't receive that gold just for spying. He was being paid to assassinate me."

"Say the word, and I'll arrest him."

Silas paced some more as he considered. "Where is the priest?"

"In the village at a tavern."

"Probably waiting for news of my death." Silas stopped. "As soon as Aleksi returns, spread the word in the village that I'm deathly ill and not expected to live. When the priest leaves, have Aleksi follow him. I want to know where he goes and who is behind all this."

"I thought you suspected Lord Morris."

"I do, but I need to be sure. Once the priest is gone, we arrest Romak."

Dimitri nodded. "Got it."

Silas glanced at his friend's inflamed arm. "Did the poison make you sick?"

"Now you ask?" Dimitri smirked. "My head hurt like hell."

So did that mean Gwennore had a headache, too? Silas grimaced. "She should never have wandered off like that."

"But I'm feeling much better now, thank you." Dimitri smiled when Silas gave him an affectionate swat on the shoulder. "I suggest you refrain from wringing her neck. After all, she's the one who figured out that the dagger was poisoned. We need her."

"I know. She's wonderfully clever." Silas thumped a fist on Karlan's desk. "That just makes me more upset with her. How could she do something so foolish?"

"Calm down. She's fine. No harm done."

"She almost went over the waterfall! And if I have to hear one more time about how sweet that damned Puff is—"

"What? Puff?"

"The dragon," Silas growled. "She keeps going on and on about how he always comes to the rescue, while I do nothing! It's Puff who protects her, not me! It's Puff that's a sweetheart—"

"By the Light!" Dimitri laughed. "Do you hear what you're saying?"

"It's what she's saying that's pissing me off!"

Dimitri punched him on the shoulder. "Idiot. You're jealous of yourself."

Silas hissed in a breath, then shot his friend a warning glare. "Don't say it. We can never let her find out."

"If she's as clever as you think, she'll figure—"

"No!" Silas shook his head. "She wants to go back to her family in a month. If she finds out, we won't be able to let her leave."

Dimitri gave him a sympathetic look. "Then you have no choice. You have to let her think Puff is the hero."

Silas sighed. The true nature of the dragons was Norveshka's most guarded secret. No foreigner was ever allowed to know the truth.

"And you should keep your distance from her," Dimitri added. "Any woman who gets involved with us could be affected by the curse."

"I don't believe in the curse."

"Fine. But even without the curse, you could hurt her. So be careful."

Silas winced. He knew deep down he shouldn't get involved with Gwennore. Not when her greatest desire was to return to her adopted family in Eberon. But how could he stay away from her when he was working with her? He had to be by her side.

Or was he just using that as an excuse? With a silent groan, he realized the truth. He didn't want to stay away. He enjoyed being with her.

She made him laugh. She made him lust. She made him want more and more of her.

But to what end? She'd already asked him that. If he had any honor, he would stop lusting for her. Stop trying to pull her into a relationship that had no future. "I need to warn her not to wander off by herself. After that, I'll stay away."

Dimitri gave him a wry look as if he doubted Silas would heed his own words.

As Silas left the northern wing and crossed the courtyard, he wondered if he was capable of staying away from Gwennore. He'd been so terrified earlier that she would come to harm. Or die.

By the Light, he had to be suffering from more than a bad case of lust. He wanted to grab on to her and not let go. And it was so damned tempting to do that when he knew from overhearing her thoughts that she was also attracted to him. Whenever their eyes met, he could feel the pull between them. The yearning. It was so strong, it felt like a cord had connected them, and it was slowly being reeled in.

But she was going home in a month. If he truly cared about her, he needed to cut the cord. He shouldn't send her home with a broken heart.

His hands curled into fists. What about his heart? She'd nearly killed him when she'd put herself in danger. And then she'd trampled all over his traumatized heart by declaring Puff the real hero. She'd called the general a jokester, a man who wasn't to be taken seriously.

Dammit to hell! How could she dismiss him like that? Was that any way to treat a man she was attracted to? He strode into the southern wing, then darted up the stairs, two at a time, headed for her bedchamber.

She was going to take him seriously. Now.

Gwennore settled on a pillow in front of the hearth to let the heat from the fire dry her long, wet hair. After a hot bath, she was feeling much better. Margosha had taken away her sodden clothes with a promise to return later with some hot tea and soup.

Now she was dressed in a clean shift and trying to relax, but it was difficult to do when she knew Silas was going to fuss at her. *Stop worrying about him*, she told herself. It didn't matter what he thought, not when she was leaving in a month. And there was no point in wanting a relationship with him. No one else would ever accept her here. So it was better to keep her thoughts private and never let him know how much she had fallen for him.

She carefully reconstructed her mental shield once again, placing each imaginary brick into place until she had a sturdy wall that Silas could never penetrate.

A knock sounded at the door. Probably Margosha. Gwennore rose to her feet, suddenly realizing how hungry she was. "Come in!"

The door swung open, and Silas strode inside.

She gasped. "What . . . ?"

He halted with a jerk, his eyes widening.

She grabbed the pillow off the floor to hold in front of her. Good goddesses, she was wearing nothing but a thin shift. "You can't come in now!"

His jaw shifted. "I have a few things to say to you." He reached back and slammed the door shut.

He wasn't leaving? "I'm not properly dressed!"

"I noticed." He strode toward her.

She stepped back. "You need to go. Now!"

He stopped a few feet away from her. "I see you're taking me seriously now."

"What?"

"For your information, I was the one who sent the dragon to you. He didn't want to go, but I insisted. I knew he could get to you faster than I could."

"Oh. All right." Why was Silas making a big deal over who did the rescuing? Gwennore looked him over. He was as handsome as ever, dressed in full uniform with brown linen breeches, green shirt, and his leather breastplate. His hair was disheveled, though, as if he'd dressed in a hurry, and his green eyes were glittering with emotion.

She hugged the pillow, making sure it covered her breasts and private parts. "Then before you go, I would like to thank you."

"You're welcome."

When he didn't budge, she motioned toward the door with a pointed look.

He frowned at her. "I heard the dragon told you that he would always come if you called him."

"Yes. It's rule number three for dating a dra—"

"What you need to know is that the same rule applies to me. You can always count on *me*." Silas thumped his chest, drawing her attention to his leather breastplate.

Her eyes narrowed on the four stars. The one on the left was tarnished. Green, just like the one she'd seen in the small cabin in the clearing. Were these the same clothes? Why had Silas dressed there? And how did he know what she and Puff had talked about? "Did you listen in on my conversation with Puff?"

"Of course I could hear you. Your shield was down."

"I didn't hear you," she muttered. Or had she? Silas's voice was similar to Puff's, although it was hard to distinguish the two since she heard Silas's voice with her ears and Puff's voice in her mind. And Puff was usually speaking kindly to her with a soft voice, while Silas was either fussing at her or joking.

Scowling at her, he shifted his weight, "I told you how dangerous the forest could be, but you failed to heed my warning."

She lifted her chin. "You failed to tell me about the trolls."

He scoffed. "Telling you about bears, wolves, and wildcats wasn't enough? Warning you that children get lost in the—"

"I was never lost! I knew exactly how to get back. And I'm not a child."

His gaze drifted down to the pillow, then back to her face, his eyes blazing with a fierce intensity. "You shouldn't have gone off by yourself."

She winced inwardly. That much was true, although she hadn't thought there would be any wild animals close to the castle. She'd assumed there were game wardens who kept the area surrounding the castle free from any danger. It was that way at the palaces where Luciana and Brigitta lived. "I would have asked you to accompany me, but you weren't here. Where did you go?"

He shrugged. "Official business."

"Meaning you won't tell me. Just like you didn't tell me about the trolls."

"They're harmless."

"They were chasing me! One of them threw a spear at me."

"They're excellent hunters. If he'd wanted to hit you, he would have."

She huffed. "And that makes it all right? I was terrified!"

"It wouldn't have happened if you'd stayed here!"

"I wouldn't have left if I knew the trolls were out there! You should have told me."

"You were already terrified of them. I didn't want to scare you even more by saying they were real."

She pointed a finger at him. "That's not your decision to make. From now on, I want honesty from you, whether it frightens me or not. Don't you dare keep things from me again!"

"You want honesty?" He stepped closer. "You think you can handle it?"

"Yes!"

"Then here's some for you. I wish I had kissed you yesterday. I wish I hadn't been so damned honorable about it, because ever since then, it's been driving me berserk."

Her mouth dropped open, then snapped shut when his gaze lowered to her lips.

"You want more honesty?" He took another step closer. "You scared the crap out of me today."

"I was afraid, too." She glanced at his eyes and for a second, before he blinked, they looked gold. Like Puff's. How? Why did she keep getting this odd feeling? Her mind raced. Golden eyes, similar voices, an extra-large heart. The tattoo of a dragon on Silas's shoulder. There had even been times when Puff and Silas had used the exact same words.

She stepped back, bumping into a chair. No, it was too bizarre. It couldn't be possible.

"Do you want more?" he asked.

She clutched the pillow tightly with her fists, suddenly afraid she couldn't handle more truth. "We . . . we should stop now."

"Stop what? Pretending I don't want you? That you don't want me?"

"I never said that!"

"You were thinking it. Ever since you met me."

"No!"

He scoffed. "How about some honesty from you?" He ripped the pillow out of her hands and pulled her into his arms. As she slammed against his chest, he gripped the back of her head and planted his lips on hers.

Chapter Seventeen

When she stiffened with a jolt and pushed at his chest, Silas broke the kiss and looked at her. Gwen's lavender-blue eyes were so wide, and her lips so pink and beautiful, it took all his control not to pounce on her again. But then he noticed she was searching his face as if she was trying to detect something.

Was something wrong? "Gwen?" He almost wished he hadn't taught her how to erect a shield, for he had no idea what she was thinking.

Her gaze fell to his chest, where her hands still rested against his breastplate. She touched the brass stars, her fingertips lingering on the tarnished one. The sleeves of her shift had fallen back to reveal the pale skin of her forearms.

"I heard you were poisoned." He grasped her wrists and held up her arms till he could see the pale-pink area on the underside of her left arm.

"Damn," he whispered as he examined the inflamed area. "Is it hurting you? Are you in pain?"

"I'm all right now, but earlier I had a headache and some problems with dizziness."

So she hadn't been thinking clearly when she'd gone off by herself. And he'd yelled at her. "I'm sorry."

"It's not your fault Romak tried to poison us. Are you going to arrest him?"

"Yes." Silas stroked his fingers over the delicate pink skin. "I can't bear the thought of you being hurt." He leaned over to kiss the inflamed area.

"No!" She stepped back, yanking her arm from his grip. "You mustn't risk getting any poison on your mouth."

"Then where is it safe to kiss you?" He took hold of her shoulders and moved close enough to brush his lips across her brow. "Is that all right? Or maybe here?" He kissed her temple.

When she placed her hands back on his chest, he took that as a *yes*.

"How about this?" He skimmed his mouth across her damp hair, then kissed the tip of her ear.

With a small gasp, she shivered.

So her pretty ears were sensitive. He ran his tongue along the contour and was rewarded with a soft moan that was so sweet, his groin tightened. "Gwen." He pulled her back into his arms and nuzzled her neck.

She wrapped her arms around him, her hands delving into his hair. "Silas . . ."

"Yes." He kissed a path toward her mouth.

"I'm not sure if this is safe," she whispered.

He hesitated, his mouth close to hers. What did she mean? Was she afraid of losing her heart? Or was the unthinkable happening, and she was figuring out the truth? He blinked, making sure his sight was normal. Sometimes, when his emotions grew too intense, the power of the dragon flared hot and turned his eyes gold.

He leaned back to look at her. "If you're worried about getting hurt, all I can say is we're in this together. My heart is just as much at risk as yours."

She placed a hand on his cheek, then ran her fingers over the whiskers along his jaw. "I must be letting my imagination get the better of me. I didn't think trolls were real, but they are. So now, I'm—" She shook her head. "I must be mistaken."

His nerves tensed. "About what?"

"It's nothing. I'm just being paranoid. For over two years now, I've hidden in the shadows, afraid to be myself and suspicious of everyone around me. But I don't want to be that person anymore. I want to be brave. And bold."

"You're the bravest woman I've ever met." He smiled as he smoothed a hand down her silky hair. "But I'd like to see how bold you can be."

A pretty blush crept into her cheeks and colored the tips of her ears. "All right." She slipped her hand around his neck and gave him a shy smile. "I'm ready for you to kiss me, if you like."

"You brazen hussy."

When she laughed, he pulled her into his arms. By the Light, the peal of her laughter was so sweet to his ears.

She took a deep breath, and the pressure of her breasts against his chest sent his blood rushing to his groin.

"Gwen, I might go insane if I don't kiss you."

She touched his cheek. "Then I recommend you go ahead." Her eyes fluttered shut when he bent down to press his lips against hers.

Sweet. He kissed her again, and when she leaned into him, he deepened the kiss, molding his mouth against hers.

A thrill of victory shot through him. *Yes.* He'd known it would be this good with Gwennore. It was more than good. It was glorious. His heart thundered in his ears, and the fire of the dragon flared in his chest. Somewhere in the dark reaches of his lust-filled brain, he realized he'd never reacted this strongly before to a mere kiss.

When she moaned, he slipped his tongue into her mouth. By the Light, she was warm and sweet. And bold, for she hesitated only a second before welcoming him with a stroke of her own tongue.

He wanted her. He wanted her more than any woman he'd ever met. And he wanted her now.

He pulled back for a second to let her catch her breath, then dove in for a hot and ravaging kiss. She melted against him, kissing him back, her fingers entwined in his hair. His sweet and bold Gwennie.

She gasped against his mouth when he cupped her breast. Through the thin material of her shift, he felt her nipple harden against the pad of his thumb. And that just made him grow harder. He needed her now.

As he smoothed his hands down her back, he reveled in how beautifully she arched against him. The small of her back, the curve of her waist, the flare of her hips: It was all perfect and perfectly in tune with him.

More, he wanted more. He splayed his hands over the sweet curves of her rump and pressed her hard against the swollen bulge in his breeches. *Yes.* She belonged there.

"What?" She jerked back, and her gaze dropped to his breeches. "Holy goddesses."

"Gwen." They weren't finished. He attempted to pull her back, but she jumped away.

"I wasn't expecting anything more than a kiss." She shot an incredulous look at his breeches. "Surely you weren't planning to . . . to copulate with me? We just met three days ago!"

"I didn't plan anything. It just happened while we were kissing." And they weren't finished. He reached for her.

She stepped back, frowning. "If that's the case, we had better not kiss again."

"What?" His lust-hazed brain was having trouble following this. "Why?"

"Because I have no intention of copulating with you."
She shifted her weight nervously. "I—I only wanted a kiss.
I've never experienced it before, so I was curious—"

"You did this out of curiosity?" The fog of lust in his
brain faded away, leaving behind a knot of frustration.

"Well, yes. Partly." She winced. "I also wanted to be
bold for a change. And I wanted to make sure that you
were . . ." She bit her lip as she glanced away.

"That I was what? Going insane?"

"That you're a genuine human male," she mumbled.

"What else would I be?" He raked a hand through his
hair. Dammit, was she suspecting the truth?

She stole another glance at the bulge in his breeches.
"I would say you're definitely male. But it hardly matters,
since I never intend to copula—"

"I got it!" He held up a hand to stop her. If she mentioned her objection to *copulating* one more time, he
might end up punching a stone wall. "But you should
know, for future reference, that I definitely want to kiss
you again, and in a moment of passion one thing can lead
to another."

She crossed her arms over her chest. "That's precisely
why we should never kiss again."

"You were enjoying it."

She waved a dismissive hand. "That may be true,
but—"

"*May be*? Hell, woman, you were on fire."

Her cheeks turned pink. "It was my first time to experience a moment of passion, so I may have gotten a bit
carried away. But I'm sure that in time, I would learn to
control myself—"

"Don't you dare. I want you out of control."

Her blush spread to her ears. "Thankfully, I was still
rational enough to come to my senses and stop this before something terrible happened."

"Terrible?" he repeated. Why didn't she just slap him? It would hurt less.

She nodded. "It would be terribly improper for us to copulate when we hardly know each other."

"Don't—" He gritted his teeth. "I do know you."

She scoffed. "You're obviously not thinking very clearly." She motioned toward his breeches. "No doubt you're suffering a diminished mental capacity due to your extreme reaction."

"What?" Did she just call him stupid? "Gwen. How would you know what's extreme? How many men have you kissed?"

She winced. "None, other than you. But I have treated male patients in the past, so I feel reasonably certain that this is not normal." She tilted her head, studying his breeches, and her eyes widened. "Good heavens, I think it's getting even bigger!"

"Because you're looking at it!"

Her gaze lifted to his face. "That's all it takes?"

"Apparently so." He clenched his fists. "You should be flattered you have that much power over me."

She blinked. "I . . . do?"

"Yes. Now, before I go totally insane, I'll go to my dressing room to take care of this problem."

"Really? How?"

"Why do you ask?" He arched a brow. "Would you like to lend a hand?"

She looked confused. "I don't think so."

"That figures." He trudged toward her dressing room. "Rejected again."

"Don't come to my bed tonight."

He paused by the door. "Why not?"

"I think the reason is obvious."

"You don't trust me." He glanced back at her. "Or could it be you don't trust yourself?"

Her face grew pale. "I'm going to spread the news that our affair is over."

"Then what will be your excuse for remaining here for a month?"

"I'll try to finish in a week. Then I'll be able to go home."

He gripped the door hard, suddenly tempted to punch a fist through it. "I see." She'd kissed him and wanted no more of him.

Crap! He strode into his dressing room and slammed the door behind him. A glance down at his breeches confirmed he no longer needed a cold bath. He'd been thoroughly rejected, so his problem was quickly shriveling away.

And his heart was hurting.

"Dammit." He stalked into his bedchamber. A pain shot through his heart, and he pressed a hand against his chest.

By the Light, he didn't want her to leave in a week. He didn't want her to ever leave.

He collapsed in a chair. Usually, his half-dragon heart made him stronger, healthier, and more formidable in battle. But with Gwennore, it was having the opposite effect.

For rule number two stated that a dragon could love fiercely, but if his heart was broken, he would feel the pain with an equally fierce intensity.

He rubbed his chest. The pain was bearable at this point, but the fact that it was there could only mean one thing.

He was falling in love.

Gwennore paused in the doorway of her dressing room, studying the closed door that led to Silas's suite. There was a small part of her that wanted to be brave and fling that door wide open. But another part, a larger part, wanted to run back home to her sisters.

She was a coward after all.

With a sigh, she trudged toward her bed. What was she doing here? She was so far from home, all alone in a foreign country where most people saw her as an enemy and a wanton woman who could kill her lover in his sleep. She'd been poisoned, attacked by trolls, and propositioned by a man she wasn't sure was even human.

But holy goddesses, he could definitely kiss.

She wrapped her arms around a bedpost and closed her eyes, letting herself remember for a few minutes just how glorious the kiss had been. It had encompassed her, enveloped her, entranced her.

All her worries and suspicions had melted away with the heat of his embrace and the soothing timbre of his deep voice, and for a few precious minutes, she had felt absolutely certain that he was human. His voice, his lips, his shoulders, his hair, the whiskers along his jaw—it had all felt completely human. And totally male. Didn't the bulge in his breeches prove he was undeniably a man?

But his sudden desire to bed her had given her such a shock that all her doubts had come crashing back. How could she become the lover of a man who might not be a man?

The room spun around her for a few seconds, and she hugged the bedpost to keep her balance. Then a pain shot across her brow, reminding her that the poison was still in her body. She glanced at the pink area on her forearm. The verna leaves she had placed there had washed away in the rushing stream. She ought to get dressed and fetch more leaves from the garden, but she felt too drained right now to do any more work.

With a groan, she crawled into bed. As she lay her head

on a pillow, she realized this was where Silas had rested last night. She nuzzled her nose against the linen, hoping to catch a whiff of the cedar-scented soap he used.

You're hopeless. She rolled onto her back and stared at the red velvet canopy overhead. How could she long for him when she wasn't sure who or what he was? How could she yearn for him when she was never sure if he was being completely honest with her?

If only her sisters were here. They would listen to her, comfort her. The Song of Mourning came to her mind, the rhythm pounding in time with the throbbing pain in her head.

My true love lies in the ocean blue. My true love sleeps in the sea. Whenever the moons shine over you, please remember me.

My lonesome heart is torn in two. My grief runs deep as the sea. Whenever the waves roll over you, please remember me. Please remember me.

Tears burned her eyes. Oh, how she missed her sisters! What would they say if she told them she suspected Silas and Puff were one and the same?

As the oldest and most responsible, Luciana would warn her to proceed with caution. Trust no one but herself.

Brigitta would tell her to throw caution out the window and follow her heart. Gwennore smiled to herself, imagining Brigitta turning Silas into a dashing hero in one of her dramatic stories.

Maeve would find her suspicions wildly exciting. After all, she shifted into a seal every month. And she was very fond of Brody when he was in the guise of a dog. She'd have no trouble believing Silas could be a shifter.

But a *dragon* shifter? How could that be possible? Dragons were so much bigger than humans. And they could breathe fire. When Silas had first kissed her, Gwennore had panicked for a moment, remembering the burst of fire that Puff had used at the lake to force the trolls to retreat.

That would be Sorcha's reaction, too. Gwennore could imagine her sister fussing at her. "You think he's a fire-breathing dragon and you kissed him? Are you crazy? He could have set your innards ablaze!"

She had felt inflamed, but in an entirely different way. Gwennore covered her face as heat rushed to her cheeks. Why had she kissed him when she'd been afraid it wasn't safe?

Afterward, she'd blamed it on curiosity, or on a need to prove he was human. But the truth had been very simple.

She'd wanted her first kiss to be from Silas.

A tear rolled down her cheek, and she angrily brushed it away. The relationship couldn't happen. He was heir to the throne, and no one in Norveshka would ever accept an elf for their queen. She wasn't being a coward. She was simply being realistic. It was best for her to leave as soon as possible.

That was the only way to protect her heart. For she had no doubt that if she stayed here an entire month, she would fall completely and irrevocably in love with him. Indeed, she feared the fall had already begun, for she still longed for him, even when she didn't know the truth about him.

If Silas was actually a dragon, did that mean his brother, the king, was one, too? Were Dimitri and Aleksi dragons? Was that what happened to the descendants from the Three Cursed Clans?

Gwennore shook her head. She was letting her imagination run amok. Sorcha was Silas's sister, which meant she was also a member of the Dravenko clan, and she certainly wasn't able to shift into a dragon.

Silas had to be human. Gwennore took a deep breath. He was human. *Completely human.*

She groaned. No matter how many times she repeated it to herself, the doubt refused to fade away.

Chapter Eighteen

About an hour later, Gwennore was woken from a light sleep by a knock at the door.

Margosha peeked inside. "Are you hungry? I brought some food."

"Oh, thank you." When Gwennore sat up, the room swirled for a second, and she rubbed her brow. At least the pain in her head had subsided a little.

Margosha entered the bedchamber, carrying a basket. "I was afraid you wouldn't be feeling well, so I asked Annika to join us. She arrived just a few minutes ago."

A young woman followed Margosha through the door, her hands filled with another basket and a leather satchel.

Gwennore watched her curiously. So this was the trustworthy army physician Silas had said would help. She was pretty with her tall and slender form and her red hair and green eyes. In fact, she looked so much like Sorcha that Gwen felt a pang of homesickness.

But this was not Sorcha. Annika was dressed in an army uniform, much like the ones Silas and his officers wore. And she'd been ordered to come here. Gwennore winced inwardly. No doubt, this Annika would be reluctant to help an elf when most of her patients in the army had received their wounds from elves.

Gwennore gave her a hesitant smile as she introduced herself. "Thank you for coming." She slipped out of bed and tucked her loose hair behind her ears. "I'm afraid I'm not properly dressed."

Annika shrugged. "Neither am I, by court standards. The ladies have been scandalized by my breeches."

"They look comfortable to me," Gwennore said.

Annika smiled. "They are. I hope you don't mind us invading your room to have a meal." She motioned with her head to the large picnic basket she held in one hand.

"Not at all." Gwennore watched as the young woman and Margosha set down their things in front of the hearth. Then they pushed back the table and chairs to make room for the three of them on the carpet in front of the fire.

Annika sat cross-legged on the floor and proceeded to empty the baskets. "They're finishing up the midday meal in the Great Hall, but I didn't want to eat there."

"Why not?" Gwennore sat beside her.

"She's avoiding someone," Margosha whispered, then grinned when Annika shot her an annoyed look.

Most probably a man, Gwennore thought, then her breath caught. *No, don't let it be Silas.* She cleared her throat. "Are you referring to the general?"

Annika snorted. "Of course not."

Thank the goddesses. But Gwennore's sense of relief was rapidly followed by annoyance. How foolish of her to feel possessive when Silas could never be hers.

Annika's mouth twitched. "Were you worried?"

"No, not at all," Gwennore said. *Blast.* The warmth in her cheeks was giving her away, and that made her blush even more.

Margosha chuckled. "Annika, why don't you look at her injury? She looks a bit feverish to me."

"It's not that bad—" Gwennore paused when Annika grabbed her arm and inspected the inflamed area. "I can treat it myself. I just need some more verna leaves—"

"I have some." Annika opened her leather satchel and removed a clay jar and linen bandage. She smeared some green paste from the jar onto the pink skin, then wrapped the bandage around it. "I make it myself. Ground verna leaves with honey."

"Oh." Gwennore was impressed. "That's very clever."

Annika smiled as she tied off the bandage. "I don't usually treat a poisoning. Most of my patients are wounded in battle, but the paste helps them to heal."

Gwennore nodded. "The wounds you treat are caused by elves."

Annika's smile faded as she lifted her gaze to Gwennore's face. "You think I'll hold that against you?"

"I'll understand if you're reluctant to work with me."

Annika placed her hand on Gwennore's. "You volunteered to help us be rid of the curse. I want the same thing, so I'm grateful that you're here."

Gwennore's heart softened. "Thank you."

"No, thank you." Annika squeezed Gwennore's hand, then let go. "Besides, Aleksi told me all about you. How you grew up on the Isle of Moon with the queens of Eberon and Tourin as your adopted sisters. How you hitched a ride with a dragon to save the Eberoni princess. How the general pulled a sneaky maneuver to make you stay, but then you bravely offered to do it. Aleksi thinks very highly of you."

Embarrassed, Gwennore turned her attention to filling her plate with food. "Aleksi talks too much."

"That's true." Annika snickered as she put away the clay jar. "He even said you were calling a certain someone General Gorgeous."

Gwennore winced. "I should clobber Aleksi."

"Don't worry." Annika opened a bottle of wine. "I punched him for you."

Gwennore's mouth twitched. She couldn't help but like Annika. "Thank you."

"Aleksi mentioned something else." Annika filled three cups. "He thought you and Silas might be having an affair."

Gwennore waved a hand. "Tha-that's not true."

"Silas is only pretending to have an affair, so he can explain her presence here," Margosha said as she loaded her plate with food.

Gwennore gulped down some wine. "I'm going to tell everyone that it's over."

"What?" Annika's eyes widened. "Why? You don't believe in the curse, do you?"

Gwennore shook her head. "No."

Annika bit into a crusty roll and chewed while she considered. "Then it must be that you don't care for him."

Gwennore paused with a bite of cheese halfway to her mouth. Memories of their embrace came rushing back, the feel of his hands on her breast, her hips, her buttocks. The heat of his mouth on hers.

Annika leaned closer to peer at her. "You're blushing again. I think you do like him."

Gwennore set the cheese down. "Surely you must know that a relationship between the general and myself is impossible. No one will accept me here."

Annika scoffed. "I do."

"Me, too," Margosha added.

Gwennore's heart squeezed. "That's very kind of you, but you're only two out of an entire country."

"If you can get rid of the curse, the entire country will love you," Annika declared.

Gwennore's mouth fell open. Could that be true?

Annika bit into a slice of ham. "I know I would be

eternally grateful. The minute the curse is gone, I'm jumping that man's bones."

"What?" Margosha laughed.

"I'm serious," Annika said with her mouth full.

Margosha shook her head. "I must be getting old. What happened to the style of courtship where the man did the pursuing?"

Annika waved a dismissive hand. "That might happen here at court, but at camp, it's entirely different. Women make up one-fourth of the army now, and since many of them are infertile, they aren't worried about getting pregnant."

"So they're . . . jumping men's bones, as you put it?" Gwennore asked.

Annika nodded, her eyes twinkling. "If we want a man, we go after him." She made a fist. "And we capture him."

Margosha pressed a hand to her chest. "Such behavior."

Annika shrugged. "Why shouldn't we take charge of our own destinies? Besides, men can be too slow sometimes."

"Or too fast," Gwennore muttered.

Annika gave her a curious look. "Don't tell me Silas tried to jump your bones."

Gwennore drank from her cup to avoid answering.

With a snort, Annika popped a slice of apple in her mouth.

Margosha shook her head. "I don't think this new method of yours is working. Not when you have to eat here in order to avoid you-know-who."

Annika frowned. "What can I do? The silly man believes in the curse, so he keeps telling me to get lost."

"The man you want to capture is eating in the Great Hall?" Gwennore asked.

Annika nodded. "He lost his first wife and infant son six years ago, and he thinks the curse is responsible."

Then he had to be from one of the Three Cursed Clans, Gwennore thought. It couldn't be Aleksi, since he wasn't avoiding Annika. "Are you talking about Dimitri?"

"That obvious, huh?" Annika gave her a wry look, then heaved a sigh. "When I joined the army a year ago, I saw him for the first time and right away, I knew he was the man for me. But he keeps rejecting me."

Margosha refilled their cups. "Maybe he hasn't recovered yet from the loss of his wife and child."

"I thought that, too, but I wanted him to know that he was still loved. So I confessed." Annika made a face. "And then he tried to chase me away with all that rubbish about the curse."

Margosha shook her head. "If he's not interested, you can't—"

"Then why did he kiss me?" Annika cried.

With a gasp, Gwennore turned toward the young woman. "He kissed you?"

Annika nodded. "About six months ago. He came into my tent drunk, hauled me to my feet, and kissed me senseless. Then he passed out, so I let him sleep on my pallet." She clenched a fist. "I should have lied the next morning and told him we'd made love, but I couldn't bring myself to do it. And now he's avoiding me like the plague."

"So he really does want you," Gwennore said softly.

Tears glimmered in Annika's eyes. "That's what I think, too. But he's going to ignore me until we can get rid of the curse."

Gwennore squeezed her hand. "We'll do it."

Annika smiled. "I knew I would like you."

Gwennore returned the smile. It looked like she wasn't alone here, after all. Margosha was looking out for her, much like Mother Ginessa would. And Annika—"You remind me of one of my adopted sisters. Sorcha."

Annika laughed. "I should. She's my cousin."

"What?" Gwennore's mouth dropped open. "Then you're—"

"Cousin to Silas and His Majesty, King Petras." Annika ate another apple slice. "My mother and the late queen were sisters, but they didn't come from one of the Three Cursed Clans. My father didn't, either, so the curse doesn't apply to me. But it would to Sorcha."

Gwennore took a closer look at Annika. "You do look quite a bit like her."

Annika tilted her head, studying Gwennore. "There's something different about you. I can't figure out what, but you don't look quite like the other elves I've seen."

Gwennore shrugged. "I wouldn't know. I've never met another elf."

"Well, the ones I've seen are all male, so maybe the females just look a bit different." Annika's eyes narrowed. "I think your ears are smaller."

"Women usually do have smaller ears," Margosha pointed out.

Annika nodded. "That must be it. Did you know they don't all have white-blond hair like you?"

"No, I didn't," Gwennore admitted.

"The wood elves tend to have brown or red hair, while the river elves from the mountains have white hair," Annika continued. "The royal family has hair like yours. Do you know who your parents are?"

Gwennore shook her head. "I have no idea. You actually know more about the elves than I do."

"Enough with the gossip," Margosha announced. "We need to get to work, since Gwennore is leaving in a month."

Gwennore winced. "I just told Silas I wanted to leave in a week."

"What?" Annika gave her an incredulous look. "The curse has been going on for five hundred years, and you think you can figure it out in a week?"

"Well, I—" Gwennore hesitated.

Annika's eyes narrowed. "Is this because he jumped your bones?"

"I'm not comfortable with him right now," Gwennore admitted.

"Then work with us," Margosha insisted. "The three of us can do it. I want to see the queen get better. I want there to be children in our country again."

Annika nodded. "We want our country to have a future." She ducked her head. "And I want a future with Dimitri."

Gwennore rested a hand on Annika's shoulder. "I'm going to try my best."

"But for only a week?" Annika gave her an injured look.

"It might not take as long as you think," Gwennore said. "The only reason the curse has lasted this long is because no one has ever tried to be rid of it before."

"Here's to us, then." Margosha lifted her cup.

"The three of us." Annika lifted hers. "We can do it."

Gwennore clinked her cup against theirs. "Death to the curse."

"I've been hearing a rumor that people are disappearing," Silas told Karlan in the captain's office. "What can you tell me about it?"

With a sigh, the captain of the king's personal guard took a seat behind his desk. "There are too many courtiers with nothing to do but gossip."

Silas moved his chair closer to the desk. "From what I heard, the people go missing after they talk about the queen's illness."

Karlan winced. "You know how devoted His Majesty is to his wife. He's desperate to keep her from harming herself."

"I understand that." A flash of memory pricked at Silas. The devastation of a six-year-old boy learning that his mother had thrown herself off the bridge in Dreshka. He would have done anything to stop her, anything to convince her to live.

Or maybe not. He doubted he could ever kidnap children like his brother was doing. Knowing that the children were now in loving homes didn't do much to lessen the guilt Silas felt. There had been too many kidnappings that he had failed to stop. And now he was worried that his brother might be doing something even worse. "Karlan, I trust you more than anyone else at court. Please tell me what's happening."

Karlan was quiet for a moment, then nodded. "All right. Two noblemen requested an audience with the king, so they could tell him that the queen was too mentally unstable to keep her office. They petitioned His Majesty to divorce her and remarry."

Silas winced. "I doubt that went well."

Karlan gave him a wry look. "That's putting it mildly. After throwing a few things across the room, the king calmed down a bit. He gave the two men assignments far away from court, and I was ordered to have some soldiers escort them away that night. So it looked like they had disappeared. His Majesty has allowed everyone to believe it, so they'll keep their mouths shut about the queen."

Silas clenched the arms of his chair. "Are the men still alive?"

Karlan snorted. "I wasn't ordered to kill them, if that's what you're thinking. They're . . . resentful, but still alive."

Silas heaved a sigh of relief that his brother hadn't

become a murderer. But still, the situation was not good. "So now there are noblemen in the countryside with a grudge against the crown."

Karlan nodded. "True."

"Are you watching them? They might try to join forces with Lord Morris."

Before the captain could answer, the door burst open and Dimitri rushed inside. "I just received word from Aleksi. The priest has left Dreshka and is moving south. Aleksi is following him."

"Good." Silas stood. "We can arrest Romak now." He helped himself to one of the swords Karlan kept in his office and passed another one to Dimitri.

Karlan grabbed his sword as he circled his desk. "I've been wanting to arrest that weasel for months."

As they strode down the hallway, Karlan called several of his guards to accompany them.

Silas flung open the door and marched inside. Romak and several courtiers jumped to their feet.

"What is the meaning of this?" Romak demanded. His eyes widened at the sight of more armed soldiers entering his office.

Silas motioned to the two courtiers who were waiting for an audience with the king. "Out."

As they scurried away, Romak eased toward the door.

"Halt." Silas pointed his sword at the weasel.

"There must be some sort of misunderstanding," Romak said, his voice becoming a shout. "I have been His Majesty's faithful servant!"

The door to the king's office opened, and Petras peered out, his eyes widening with surprise.

"Your Majesty!" Romak dropped to his knees. "I've done nothing wrong, I swear it!"

"You're under arrest for espionage against the crown, accepting bribes, and attempted murder," Silas began.

"No!" Romak shot the king a pleading look. "Please, Your Majesty, don't believe—"

"You have proof?" Petras asked.

Silas nodded. "He met a spy, a priest from Eberon, whom I believe is connected to Lord Morris."

"Speculation!" Romak shouted.

"You were seen delivering a message to this priest and accepting a purse of gold coins," Silas said. "And before that you handed Colonel Tolenko a dagger to be used to murder me."

"*What?*" Petras strode into the room.

"The dagger was coated with poison." Silas motioned to Dimitri, who lifted his sleeve to show the inflamed area. "If anyone had been pricked by that dagger, they would now be dead."

Romak turned pale. "I—I didn't know about the poison! I didn't know! I—I'm being framed!"

"Where did you get the dagger?" Petras demanded.

"S-someone gave it to me," Romak insisted. "I didn't know it was poisoned!"

"But you still intended it to be used on my brother!" Petras shouted.

Romak crawled toward the king. "I was doing it for you, Your Majesty. I'm trying to protect you. You can't trust the general. He wants your crown."

"Bullshit," Silas growled. "You're a spy. Once we find out who the priest reports to—"

"I was only doing my job!" Romak cried as he grabbed on to the king's boot. "I was gathering information for you, my liege. I've been risking my life spying for you!"

"Then why were you accepting gold instead of giving it?" Silas asked.

"Your Majesty!" a female voice screamed in the hallway.

The soldiers moved aside to let Lady Olenka enter. She glanced around, her eyes widening at the sight of drawn swords and Romak on the floor, clinging to the king's leg.

"Your Majesty!" She curtsied low. "I have dire news. Her Majesty has collapsed! She's unconscious, and we fear—"

"Where is she?" Petras pulled his leg away from Romak's grasp.

"Her bedchamber," Olenka replied. "We put her in bed."

As Petras hurried out the door, he glanced back at Silas. "Take Romak to the dungeons. We'll have his trial at the next Summoning."

"Your Majesty!" Romak screamed as the king dashed down the hallway.

When Olenka started to follow him, Silas called out to her. "Lady Olenka, send Gwennore to the queen. She might be able to help."

"Yes, my lord." Olenka dipped into a quick curtsy, then ran after the king.

"You heard His Majesty." Karlan motioned to two of his guards. "Take Romak to the dungeons."

"This isn't over!" Romak shouted as he was hauled to his feet. He glared at Silas. "You bastard. You'll never be king."

Silas scoffed. "You'll never be alive to see it."

While the guards dragged him into the hallway, Silas turned to Karlan. "Remove all his jewelry and check his clothing for any hidden jewels or money. I don't want him trying to bribe any of the guards."

Karlan nodded. "Understood."

Romak dug in his heels and twisted to look back at Silas. "I can make a deal with you! If you release me, I'll give you information."

Silas gave him a bland look. "Not interested."

Romak scoffed. "You don't want to know who Lady Gwennore's parents are?"

Silas's heart stuttered in his chest, but he merely shrugged, feigning disinterest.

"Go on," Karlan ordered, and his guards proceeded to drag Romak down the hallway.

"I know who Fafnir really is!" Romak screamed as he was hauled out the doorway into the courtyard.

Silas hissed in a breath.

"Fafnir?" Dimitri asked. "One of the Ancient Ones?"

Karlan shook his head. "They all died five hundred years ago."

I know who Fafnir really is. Silas narrowed his eyes. That had to mean his suspicions were correct, and Fafnir wasn't who he claimed to be. Was he a rogue dragon shifter who was tricking Petras? To what end? To steal the crown or destroy the country?

"Karlan," Silas said quietly. "I want that information." And not just about Fafnir. He wanted to be the one to tell Gwen who her parents were.

"We could rough him up a bit," Karlan offered.

Silas shook his head. "Only give him water. Tell Romak if he wants to eat, he'll have to tell me what he knows."

Chapter Nineteen

As the sun began to set, Gwennore paced about the new workroom. It had been almost an hour since Margosha and Annika had been admitted into the queen's bedchamber, and there was still no news.

After her midday meal with Margosha and Annika, Gwennore had spent the afternoon with them making a workroom on the third floor of the western wing, next door to the nursery. With the help of some servants, they had cleaned the empty room and fireplace, polished the long line of westward-facing windows, set up a row of tables, and brought in some chairs.

Several of the tables were now covered with bowls filled with the water left over from soaking the queen's belongings. Each bowl was labeled with a description of the item being tested.

Gwennore had decided to use plants to check the water for poison. She and Annika had rushed down to the garden to gather up lily pads from the ornamental pond. Now each bowl had a lily pad floating on the water, and they were waiting to see if any of the plants shriveled and turned brown.

They had gone to the garden a second time to collect

more verna leaves. Since the leaves were so good at drawing out poison, Gwennore had theorized that a drink made of them might help cleanse poison from within the body. Annika had agreed, and the two of them had concocted a hot tea spiked with verna and honey. Since Gwennore had been exposed to poison, she'd tested the drink on herself.

So far, no ill side effects. Her headache was completely gone, and the pink spot on her arm was fading away. Even so, she wasn't sure if her recovery was due to the verna tea or her own body's recuperative ability. But since the tea was safe and possibly helpful, she thought it would be a good idea for the queen to drink some every day.

She glanced over at the hearth where the kettle filled with verna tea was resting close to the fire. Margosha or Annika would have to give it to Her Majesty, for it was now clear that the queen would not accept any help from Gwennore.

An hour ago, Lady Olenka had burst into the workroom to announce that Her Majesty was deathly ill. Annika had snatched up her leather medicine bag, and then they had dashed to the queen's bedchamber. The king was already inside, and two soldiers were guarding the door, surrounded by a crowd of gossiping courtiers.

Since they were official ladies-in-waiting, Margosha and Olenka had automatically been allowed inside. Olenka had quickly informed the queen that General Dravenko had sent the healers Gwennore and Annika to take care of her.

Waiting outside, Gwennore had heard the queen's screeching reply. "You can let Annika in, but send that horrible elf away! She'll try to kill me!"

Gwennore had flinched inwardly. Thoroughly humiliated, she'd tried not to let it show, but it had been hard to do with all the courtiers glaring at her. While she'd waited for confirmation that the king had barred her from entering, the crowd of courtiers had speculated on her breakup with General Dravenko.

"Thank the Light he came to his senses and dumped her," one hissed in an angry voice. "No doubt he was afraid she would murder him in his sleep."

Determined not to cry, she'd hurried back to the workroom where she could be alone. After furiously grinding up the rest of the verna leaves, she'd still felt tense, so now she was pacing up and down the length of the room.

The humiliating experience had only confirmed what she already knew. The people of Norveshka would not accept her.

Why should I care? a hurt inner voice protested. She was leaving soon. Let them all suffer from the curse.

She slowed to a stop. Now she was being as petty as they were. She shouldn't judge an entire population by a few rude nobles. If she could help this country, she should. And if she got rid of the curse, wouldn't they accept her then? Annika had said they would love her.

Was it possible to have a future with Silas? Her heart tightened in her chest. How could she not want a future with him? He had a way of looking at her like she was the most beautiful and clever creature on all of Aerthlan.

When she was with him, she felt so alive. Smart, capable, brave, and happy. No more hiding in shadows; she was free to be herself. She was her best with him. And goddesses help her, she thought he was his best when he was with her.

How could any other man make her feel this way? She wrapped her arms around herself, wishing he could kiss her one more time, that she could feel herself melting in that fiery moment of passion one more time.

If she went back to her sisters, she might be safe, but she might never experience passion again.

So, should she throw herself into the fire? Even if he might be a fire-breathing dragon?

The door opened and the ladies trudged inside. Annika looked crestfallen, while Margosha's eyes were glistening with tears.

Gwennore swallowed hard. "How bad was it?"

Margosha turned away, wiping a tear from her cheek.

With a sigh, Annika set her satchel on a table. "I don't think Her Majesty will be with us for very long."

Gwennore winced. "I thought the same thing when I did a reading on her a few days ago." She'd explained her gift to the ladies that afternoon. "Did you break the news to the king?"

"I tried," Margosha said, "but he doesn't want to believe it. He kept saying she would recover once the curse was gone." She motioned toward the kettle. "Why don't we give her some tea every day?"

"I'd like that," Gwennore admitted. "But even if the tea cleans some of the poison out of her system, I don't think it can repair the damage that has already happened to her internal organs."

Annika nodded. "I agree."

Margosha pressed the back of her hand against her mouth. "So there's nothing we can do?"

Annika collapsed in a chair. "From what I could tell, it's a wonder she's still alive."

When Margosha stifled a sob, Gwennore wrapped an arm around. "I'm so sorry."

The door burst open suddenly and Lady Olenka rushed inside.

Margosha gasped. "Is it the queen? Has she—"

"No, she's the same." Olenka closed the door. "But have you heard the latest news? Lord Romak has been arrested and taken to the dungeon!"

"About time," Annika muttered. "He poisoned Gwennore and Dimitri with that dagger of his."

With a worried look aimed at the other women in the room, Olenka edged toward Gwennore. She lowered her voice to a whisper. "Do—do you still have that little gift I gave you?"

"You mean the dagger you put under my pillow?"

With a hiss, Olenka put a finger against her mouth. "You won't tell anyone I gave it to you, right? You know I would never want anyone to be hurt!"

Gwennore gave her a wry look. "You asked me to stab the general."

"Just the tiniest of pricks!" Olenka protested, waving her hands. "But I've changed my mind. Please don't do anything!"

"I wasn't intending to."

"Oh, thank the Light." Olenka struck a dramatic pose, her hand pressed against her brow. "I was so afraid I might be arrested."

Gwennore rolled her eyes. "There was never any danger of that."

Annika smirked. "Unless you put poison on the dagger."

Olenka gasped. "I would never! I wouldn't even know how!"

Margosha clucked her tongue. "Why on Aerthlan did you do such a foolish thing?"

Olenka lowered her head, looking properly chastised. "I wanted to win the wager everyone's betting on."

Margosha snorted. "You're already receiving free room and board. And beautiful gowns and jewels to wear. Isn't that enough?"

Olenka winced. "Two months ago Lord Darnhill asked me to marry him. I was considering it, but then his parents said we couldn't marry because I didn't have a large enough dowry. So I thought if I had more money—"

"Why would you want to marry Darnhill?" Margosha grimaced. "The man is an ass. Everyone calls him Lord Dunghill."

While Annika choked back a laugh, Olenka's bottom lip quivered.

"Don't waste any tears over a man who gives up on you that easily." Gwennore wrapped an arm around Olenka's shoulders and gave her a hug. "I would say you're better off without Lord Dung—Darnhill."

Annika laughed out loud.

Olenka shot her an injured look. "It's not funny. There are only a few eligible bachelors here at court. I don't have much to choose from."

Annika waved a dismissive hand. "Then join the army like I did. You'll have hundreds of men to choose from. And they won't be like these limp, pasty-faced men at court. I'm talking strong, handsome, virile young men."

Olenka's eyes widened. "Do they look like Aleksi and Dimitri?"

Annika stiffened. "Dimitri is mine, but you can have your choice of the others."

Olenka's eyes gleamed for a moment, then she slumped. "My parents would never allow it."

"How would they stop you?" Annika scoffed. "Can they defeat an army?"

Olenka gave her a wary look. "Would I have to fight like a soldier?"

"Not if you have a skill like I do," Annika replied. "I could use an assistant, actually, if you're willing to learn."

"What about my pretty gowns and jewelry?" Olenka smoothed her hands over her silk skirt.

"What about them?" Annika gave her a pointed look.

"Hundreds of strong, handsome, virile young men. And if you want one of them, you can jump his bones."

Olenka's eyes lit up. "I'll do it!" She turned toward Gwennore. "And I'll help you. I'm on your side, really. When I heard how the other courtiers were treating you, I wanted to punch them!"

"You'll have to get in line," Annika growled.

Gwennore smiled. Her circle of friends was growing. As she watched Margosha giving Olenka a hug and then Annika showing her how to salute, her heart squeezed.

She had wanted to leave in a week to keep from getting hurt. But it was already too late. It would hurt to leave her new friends behind.

And it would hurt like hell to leave Silas.

The next morning, Gwennore woke to find the sun was already up. She'd overslept, even though she'd gone to bed early. But yesterday had been far too exhausting. She closed her eyes, remembering the troll attack, her near plummet over the waterfall, Puff's dramatic rescue, and then Silas's kiss.

Were they the same? Was Silas actually a dragon?

She rolled onto her side and rested her hand on the pillow where he had slept. *Why don't you just ask him?*

No. She sat up. She'd asked him before to be honest with her. If he couldn't do it, then there was no point in seeing him.

But it was so tiresome having to avoid him. She'd eaten dinner in the workroom last night with her friends. And today she'd probably have all of her meals there.

She climbed out of bed and rang the bell for Nissa. Then she relieved herself in the privy next to the dressing room. As she filled the tub with water, she heard similar noises from the dressing room next door.

Silas was there. Had he overslept, too? Was he miss-ing her? She tiptoed over to the door to listen. Yes, he had to be bathing. Or shaving, perhaps.

"My lady?" Nissa rushed into the dressing room.

Gwennore jumped back from the door. "Oh, good morning. I—I've started the bath."

"I'll heat some water for you." Nissa held the kettle under the spout of running water and gave Gwennore a curious look. "Are you considering taking him back, my lady?"

"No, of course not." Gwennore glanced at the door once again as she stepped away.

Nissa set the kettle on the stove, then added some wood to the fire. "It must be hard to turn down a man like the general."

Gwennore sighed. Definitely hard.

She must be bathing, Silas thought, as he pressed his ear against the door. How many times had he stopped him-self from knocking on her door last night? He'd been up half the night, fighting temptation.

With a sigh, he stepped back. He wanted to respect her wishes, but weren't they supposed to be working together? Didn't that give him a legitimate reason to talk to her? He'd heard about her new workroom in the western wing. Maybe this afternoon, he could drop by for an official report.

He clenched his fists. How could he wait till this after-noon? Maybe, if he timed it right, he could run into her in the hallway?

What a lovesick fool he was. He quickly washed, shaved, and threw on his clothes, all the while listening to the noises next door. When the noises stopped, he rushed to his bedchamber door and peeked out.

When she stepped into the hallway, he quickly exited, then stopped as if surprised to see her.

Damn. He was surprised. She was wearing breeches!

"What?" He strode toward her. "What are you doing?"

Her cheeks turned a lovely shade of pink, but she avoided looking at him. "Good morning."

"You're wearing breeches."

"I am aware of that." Her pretty ears turned pink. "Annika loaned me a pair. We're going to collect wild herbs and such from the forest today, so I thought—"

"You're going into the forest?" Silas scowled at her. "You should take an armed soldier with you—"

"I am." Gwen gave him a wry look. "Annika."

His mouth twitched. No one could set him straight as well as Gwen. Even so, he would ask Karlan to send some guards to make sure the ladies were safe. No matter how capable Annika was, she'd have trouble fighting off a bear all by herself.

He crossed his arms over his chest as he studied Gwen. "So did you want to join the army?" He leaned close. "I have a really nice tent you could share with me."

She snorted. "If you'll excuse me, I have work to do." She walked past him, and as he turned to follow her progress, his gaze dropped to the lovely sway of her hips, so well defined in those tight breeches.

Damn. He stalked after her. "It's against regulation not to wear the complete uniform. You're missing the breast-plate."

Gwen stopped. "Annika had only one of those."

The breastplate was long enough to cover most of a woman's hips. Didn't Gwen realize how much of her sweetly rounded rump was on display? He grabbed her shirt and started pulling it from the waistline of her breeches.

Gwennore stiffened. "What are you doing?"

"Hiding your sweet ass," he grumbled as he let the shirt fall around her hips.

She huffed. "I'm hiding enough, already. I'll be in the workroom most of the day."

"Hiding from me?"

She pushed his arms away. "Avoiding you."

"I miss you."

A pained look crossed her face before she affected a bland expression. "It hasn't been that long. You saw me yesterday."

"I kissed you yesterday." He reached for her, but she stepped back.

"I told you, the make-believe affair is over. I have no intention of copula—"

"It wouldn't be copulating, dammit! It would be making love!" He froze, stunned by the words that had come out of his mouth. Damn, had he just confessed?

Her eyes widened with shock.

"Gwen." There was no point in denying it now. "It's true. I have fallen for—"

"I have to get to work!" She darted down the hallway.

Crap! He slammed a fist against the wall. She was running away again.

How could he convince her to stay? What could he do to impress her?

The truth about her parents. Gwen was a person who appreciated the truth. And he could do that for her.

He dashed down the stairs and strode across the courtyard. Hopefully, after missing dinner and breakfast, Romak would be hungry enough to spill a few secrets.

As Silas neared the dungeon, he spotted Karlan at the entrance, yelling at two of his soldiers.

"How could you leave your post?" Karlan growled.

"What's wrong?" Silas asked.

"These two were supposed to watch Romak last night."

Karlan cuffed the nearest one on the head. "Come on, I'll show you."

Silas followed Karlan and the guards down the stairs into the dungeon, lit by torches along the stone wall. They passed two empty cells, then stopped at the last one, where the gate was open.

Silas's breath caught. Romak was inside, lying in a pool of blood, a knife protruding from his chest.

Dammit. Silas rushed inside. One look at Romak's glazed eyes and he knew the man was dead. He'd been dead for several hours. "How?"

The captain scowled at his soldiers. "These two were supposed to watch him last night, but when I arrived this morning, they were lounging around outside the door."

Silas gritted his teeth as he strode toward the guards. "You left your post?"

The two men exchanged nervous looks.

"We—we were ordered to, my lord," one answered.

"That's right," the other one agreed. "We were told to wait outside until morning."

"Who would tell you that?" Karlan demanded.

The two men turned pale as they exchanged a frantic look.

Karlan grabbed one by the collar. "Who?"

The man gulped. "It was . . . you, Captain."

Karlan released the man, his eyes wide with shock.

The second soldier gave Silas a pleading look. "It's true, my lord. The captain told us to leave. Then he went inside."

"He was carrying that knife." The first soldier pointed at the knife embedded in Romak's body.

"What?" Karlan stepped back with an incredulous look. "I didn't kill him!"

What the hell? Silas clenched his fists as his heart squeezed in his chest. Had Karlan betrayed him? Was he in league with someone like Lord Morris who had ordered him to kill Romak before the man could talk?

But dammit, Karlan looked as shocked as Silas felt. It didn't make sense for Karlan to be the murderer. He'd always been loyal. And he was too smart to leave such obvious evidence. He would have covered his tracks better than this.

"You had better be sure about this," Silas growled at the guards. "I can easily check Karlan's whereabouts last night. And if I discover you two have been lying—"

"It was him! I swear it!" the first soldier cried, and both men dropped to their knees. "Please forgive us, my lord. We thought we were following orders."

"It wasn't me," Karlan whispered, his face pale. "I swear it wasn't me."

Silas glanced at the dead body in the cell. What the hell was going on here?

Chapter Twenty

❧

Gwennore's heart pounded as she rushed to the workroom in the western wing. *It would be making love.* Goddesses help her, how could she resist falling in love if Silas was feeling the same way?

She shut the door behind her, then leaned against it to catch her breath.

"How does it feel?" Annika asked.

Frightening. Gwennore pressed a hand against her still-thudding heart. No, it was exciting. And so tempting.

Annika motioned to her breeches. "Doesn't it feel strange at first?"

"Oh." She meant the breeches. Gwennore pushed away from the door. "It made it much easier to run up the stairs."

Annika gave her a curious look. "Why were you running?"

Gwennore hesitated, then changed the subject. "Did you check on Her Majesty this morning?"

"Yes, she's about the same. Margosha and Olenka are with her, giving her some verna tea. They should be here soon." Annika motioned to a table where the plates contained small portions of bread, cheese, and fruit. "You missed breakfast, but we left some food for you."

"Thank you." Gwennore grabbed a slice of cheese and ate it as she approached the bowls of water and lily pads. "Has there been any change?"

"One is starting to look bad." Annika pointed at a lily pad that was turning brown along the edges. "But it could be a natural reaction from being transplanted."

"Or it could be caused by poison." Gwennore picked up the slip of paper next to the bowl.

EMERALD RING, RECTANGULAR, SURROUNDED BY EIGHT SMALL DIAMONDS

"We need to examine this ring." Gwennore studied the bowls on the table. Only half of them had tested jewelry, and that was only a small sampling of the large amount the queen owned. "Actually, I think we should test all of Her Majesty's jewelry."

Annika's eyes widened. "That will take a while."

"Yes, but I suspect there could be other tainted pieces." Gwennore tapped her finger on the label. "This is an emerald ring, so the queen would wear it only once a week on Emeralday. I'm not sure that would produce the amount of poison she has in her system."

The door opened and Margosha and Olenka came inside.

"Any progress?" Margosha asked.

"Perhaps." Gwennore handed her the slip of paper. "What do you know of this ring?"

"It's one of the Her Majesty's favorites." Margosha frowned. "Are you saying it's poisoned?"

Olenka snatched the paper away and read it. "Oh, I know about this. It was a gift to Her Majesty last summer after she suffered her last miscarriage."

"A gift?" Gwennore asked. "Who gave it to her?"

Margosha winced. "Her husband."

The king. Gwennore swallowed hard.

"King Petras gave her a poisoned ring?" Annika asked. "Is he hoping to replace her with a healthy—"

"He's devoted to her," Margosha interrupted. "He would never . . ."

"Oh, my." The piece of paper slipped from Olenka's hands. "Then it's not a curse, after all? Someone is trying to poison the queen?"

"They already have," Annika muttered.

"It can't be His Majesty," Margosha insisted. "He's with her now. He's beside himself with worry."

Gwennore nodded. "Then we need more information. Where did the king buy the ring? Or did someone give it to him?"

"I'll ask around and check the jewelry shop in the village," Margosha offered.

"Good. But before you go, could you bring us all of the queen's jewelry?" Gwennore asked.

"All of it?" Olenka scoffed. "She has three caskets. We can't just walk out of the queen's bedchamber with them. She'll throw a fit!"

"We need to test everything," Gwennore insisted. "I seriously doubt that this one ring is responsible for the amount of poison in Her Majesty's system. Especially if she received it only last summer. She's been ill for longer than that, right?"

"Right." Margosha nodded. "We'll tell her that we're cleaning her jewelry. She's been complaining lately that it doesn't sparkle enough." She motioned to Annika and Olenka. "The three of us can bring the caskets here."

Gwennore sighed as the women left. Obviously, she was still not welcomed in the queen's quarters.

Two hours later, they had the contents of the first casket all soaking in fresh bowls of water, each one topped with a lily pad. After raiding the castle garden of all of its lily pads, they'd resorted to taking them from the pond in the village.

"Whew." Olenka collapsed in a chair. "So what do we do now?"

Annika ate the last piece of cheese left over from breakfast. "After lunch, we're going into the forest to collect medicinal plants. If you're serious about becoming my assistant, you should come along."

Olenka saluted her. "Yes, Captain."

Margosha shook her head, but smiled.

"Silas wants us to take some armed soldiers with us." Gwennore nabbed the last crust of bread from the breakfast table.

Annika snorted. "We can take care of ourselves. When did he tell you this?"

"This morning."

"Ah." Annika's eyes twinkled with mischief. "Before you had to run up the stairs?"

Gwennore tossed the piece of bread onto the tray. "This is stale. Why don't we have lunch?"

Annika's mouth twitched. "Why don't we change the subject?"

Gwennore gave her a wry look. "Nothing happened."

"Well, isn't that a shame?" Annika nudged her with an elbow. "You should have jumped his bones."

Olenka giggled.

"Go get some food," Gwennore fussed at her friends. "I'm hungry."

Annika grinned. "All right, let's go." She waved at the others as she headed for the door. "Of course, Gwen wouldn't be so hungry if she was satisfying her other appetites."

"Go!" Gwennore threw the crust of bread, missing Annika, who laughed as she left with the other women.

Gwennore smiled. It was almost like being back with her sisters.

Her smile faded. She would miss her new friends here. And goddesses help her, she would miss Silas something terrible. It was like her heart was being torn in two different directions.

She wandered over to the long line of windows to gaze at the beautiful view. The charming village of Dreshka was nestled along the banks of the Norva River. And across the valley, green pastures dotted with fluffy white sheep swept up the hillsides. Then the forest began, stretching up the mountainsides till they gave way to patches of snow.

Gwennore sighed. *I would never grow tired of this.* Once again, she had the odd feeling of coming home, as if this place had been secretly harbored in her heart all her life.

What had Annika said about the elves? It was the river elves who lived in the mountains and had white-blond hair like hers. That had to be why she loved mountains so much. They soothed her soul, because they were in her blood.

A movement in the sky drew her attention. An eagle? It flew straight for the castle, then swooped along the windows on the western wing.

Brody? Gwennore quickly opened a window and waved. "Brody!"

The eagle circled around then came straight for her. She jumped to the side as it shot through the open window. It landed on the floor, then turned into a black-and-white shaggy dog.

"Brody!" Gwennore gave him a hug. "I didn't expect you for a few more days."

He grinned at her, then barked.

"Oh, you must have news." No doubt, he wanted to shift into human form. She glanced around the room, but there were only a few small towels, not big enough to wrap around him. "Wait here a minute. I'll bring you some clothes."

She dashed off to Silas's dressing room, wondering what had happened to cause Brody to come early.

Silas pulled off his shirt as he entered his bedchamber. He'd managed to stain the sleeves with blood while examining Romak's body, so he wanted to put on a clean shirt before making his report to the king.

Although there wasn't much he could tell Petras, since nothing was making any sense.

As he opened the door to his dressing room, he tossed the dirty shirt into a basket and heard a gasp from across the small room.

He spun around. *Gwen?* She was next to the shelves of clothes, holding up a pair of his underpants. At first she looked stunned; then her gaze drifted over his bare chest, and her lovely eyes grew even bigger.

His mouth twitched. "Have you acquired a sudden interest in my underwear?"

"What? No!" She hastily dropped his underpants on his dressing table. "I can explain."

"No need to. I'm thrilled you want to see my underpants. Here, I'll show you the more exciting version." He unfastened the top button of his breeches.

"Stop that!"

He choked back a laugh. "Gwen, sweetheart." He stepped toward her. "Why are you here? Did you miss me?"

She huffed. "I just saw you this morning."

"You ran away from me this morning."

A blush invaded her cheeks as she quickly folded up

his underpants. "If you must know, I was simply checking the size of these to make sure they would fit—"

"Why? Were you planning to wear them?"

"They're not for me!" She placed the folded underpants on top of some folded breeches. "I could explain if you weren't so determined to distract me."

"You find me distracting?"

Her gaze drifted to his bare chest again, then lingered on the dragon tattoo.

How much did she suspect? He motioned toward the shelves. "Could you hand me a shirt?"

"Of course." She passed him one, then placed a second one on her stack of clothes. "I'm in a bit of a hurry. Brody is in the workroom, stuck as a dog until I—"

"Brody's here?"

"Yes." She gathered up the stack of clothes. "This was the only place I could think of that would have some male clothing. So if you don't mind . . ."

"Of course not." He slipped on his shirt. "Let's go."

She followed him into his bedchamber. "You didn't button your shirt."

"It can wait." He glanced at his bed, then at her. "Unless you have something else in mind."

She scoffed. "You seem to have only one thing on your mind these days." She darted past him to open the door.

"It's what happens when a man falls in love."

She froze in his doorway, then whispered, "Don't."

"Don't what? Fall in love?"

"Don't tempt me." She stepped into the hallway.

Did that mean she was tempted? He ran after her, slamming his door behind him. "Gwen."

In the hallway, a few doors down, a servant gasped at the sight of them and dropped her armful of bed linens on the floor.

"Are you all right?" Silas picked up the bedsheets

and handed them to the servant. "We didn't mean to frighten you."

"I—I'm fine, Your Highness." The young woman curtsied, then dashed away.

Gwen shot him a wry look as she headed for the western wing. "I told you to button your shirt."

He snorted. "Are you saying my chest is scary?"

"Not exactly," she muttered.

He followed her as he fastened the buttons. "I've been wondering how you were doing. Have you made any progress?"

She explained how they were examining the queen's jewelry and that so far, there was one ring they suspected was poisoned. "It was a gift from the king last summer."

"Petras gave it to her?"

Gwen nodded. "Margosha said she would ask around to see where it came from."

"I'll ask him."

Gwen gave him a worried look. "That could end badly if the king thinks we suspect him."

"He'll cooperate. He wants rid of the curse more than anything. He believes his wife will improve if we—" Silas stopped when a pained look crossed Gwennore's face.

"I don't think it's possible for her to improve. She's been poisoned for too long, and it's affected all her internal organs."

Silas swallowed hard. He'd told Petras that he would help the queen. And if he failed, he would go along with Petras's wish to do what Fafnir ordered. Invade Woodwyn and declare war on Tourin.

"I'm sorry," Gwennore whispered.

"So am I." Silas remained silent for a while as they walked, then something occurred to him. "The queen received the ring last summer, but she's been ill for longer than that. And my mother suffered from madness, too."

Gwennore nodded. "That's another reason why I suspect the jewelry. It's the only thing that gets passed on from one queen to the next. Everything else changes."

When they reached the workroom, they found Annika, Margosha, and Olenka inside. They'd brought up several baskets of food and were arranging it on a table. Brody, in dog form, was wolfing down a plate of ham that had been placed on the floor.

Annika saluted Silas then motioned to Brody. "We found this dog in the room. I don't know where he came from."

"But he's so cute." Olenka patted Brody's head, and he grinned at her.

Gwen set the stack of clothes on the floor next to Brody. "We should leave the room for a few minutes."

"What?" Annika eyed the clothes. "Why?"

"We were just about to eat," Margosha protested. "Would you like to join us, my lord?"

"In a moment," Silas said. "First, I'd like to talk to Brody. So if you don't mind . . ." He motioned to the door.

"Brody?" Margosha looked confused. "You mean the dog?"

Annika snorted. "You want to talk to a dog?"

Gwennore picked up a plate of ham and cheese and headed for the door. "I'll explain outside. Come on."

Margosha grabbed the bottle of wine, while Olenka and Annika gathered up some cups and a loaf of bread. Then they followed Gwen out the door.

As soon as the door shut, Brody's form wavered for a few seconds, then snapped into the shape of a man. He reached for the underpants. "I smelled death on you. What's going on here?"

Silas wandered about the room, studying Gwen's experiment. "Lord Romak was murdered last night. I've been investigating the matter."

"Who is he?" Brody fastened the waist of the underpants.

"The king's personal secretary." Silas explained how he'd discovered Romak's spying activity. "I sent Aleksi to follow the priest, so we can figure out who was paying Romak. I suspect Lord Morris or one of his minions."

Brody pulled on the pair of breeches. "Is this Aleksi one of your dragons?"

When Silas stiffened, Brody gave him a wry look. "I can smell a fellow shifter."

Silas clenched his fists. Dammit, he should have realized this, since he'd always been able to tell that Brody was a shifter. "Have you told anyone?"

"No." Brody smiled. "You can relax. I don't intend to tell anyone. Shifters' code of honor."

Silas flexed his hands. "I'll hold you to that."

"So someone killed the spy you arrested." Brody buttoned the breeches. "Sounds like you may have more than one spy around here."

Silas nodded. "Someone made sure Romak couldn't talk. Romak had planned to kill me and frame Gwennore for it."

"What?"

"She was given a poisoned dagger—"

"Is she all right?"

"Yes." Silas motioned toward the door. "You saw her. She's fine."

Brody frowned as he put on the shirt. "So any idea who killed this Romak?"

With a grimace, Silas ran a hand through his hair. "It's not making any sense. The two guards said their captain ordered them to stay by the dungeon entrance all night. And they saw him go inside with a knife, the same knife that is now protruding from Romak's chest."

"Then he's your man." Brody buttoned the shirt.

Silas shook his head. "Karlan swears it wasn't him. And I checked with the other soldiers. He was in the barracks with them all night."

"Then the two guards are lying."

Silas sighed. "They swear they're telling the truth. And even Karlan says they are trustworthy. He's completely baffled. Hell, we all are."

Brody paused in the middle of fastening a button. "The murderer looked like the captain, but he wasn't him?"

Silas nodded. "Right."

"You still have the body?"

"In the dungeon, yes."

"Take me there." Brody finished buttoning his shirt. "If it was the Chameleon, I might be able to pick up his scent."

"The Chameleon?"

Brody nodded. "I'll explain on the way."

"No need. I've heard of him." The Chameleon had tried to steal the throne in Eberon and Tourin. Silas headed for the door. "You think the Chameleon is here? Making a play for Norveshka?"

"Could be." Brody followed him out the door.

Gwennore was sitting with the other women in the hallway, enjoying a meal. "Brody!" She jumped to her feet and hugged him.

Annika looked him over curiously. "He was the dog?"

"Gwennie." Brody took hold of her shoulders. "I heard you were poisoned. Are you all right?"

"Yes, I'm fine. How are my sisters? You came early. Is something wrong?"

Brody smiled as he gave her shoulders a squeeze. "Everything's fine. They were just worried about you."

Silas cleared his throat. "Are you going to hug each other all day? We need to be going."

Brody released her. "I'll be back soon." He followed Silas to the stairwell.

"What's going on?" Gwen ran after them.

"Stay in the workroom for now," Silas called back to her. "I'll send some guards to watch over you."

"Why do we need guards?" Annika yelled.

"Just to be safe." Silas bounded down the stairs.

Brody kept up with him. "Do they know about the murder?"

"Not yet."

"Has Gwennie made any progress with figuring out the curse?"

"Maybe."

Brody snorted. "You're not very forthcoming."

"Neither are you." Silas glanced at the shifter as they reached the ground floor. "Why did you come early?"

Brody shrugged. "Leo and Luciana wanted to make sure Gwennore was safe."

"Why?" Silas opened the door to the courtyard. "Has something happened?"

Brody squinted as they stepped out into the sunlight. "A special envoy from Woodwyn came to the Eberoni camp."

Silas halted. The elves never sent envoys. They were the most reclusive people on the planet. "What did he want?" When Brody hesitated, a lump of dread caught in Silas's throat. "They want Gwennore."

Brody nodded. "The royal family is requesting her return."

Silas fisted his hands as his heart started to pound. "Why? Is she a member of the royal family?"

"They wouldn't say. They just demanded her back."

Silas scoffed. "They rejected her as a baby, and now they think they can simply demand her back?"

"Leo and Luciana are as suspicious as you are. They were actually relieved that she's here, since it gave them a good excuse to turn the elves down."

Silas strode toward the dungeon. "We can't let her go, not when we don't know what they plan to do with her."

"I agree." Brody walked barefoot beside him. "That's why I came here to make sure she was all right. Leo thought the elves might have a spy here."

Romak? Silas wondered. Could Romak have been spying for Woodwyn?

"I did some spying, myself, around the envoy and his secretary," Brody continued. "People don't watch what they say in front of a dog."

"What did you learn?"

"They called Gwennore a princess."

Silas stopped again. Had he fallen in love with an elfin princess?

"They had another name for her." Brody winced. "But they said it with such disdain, it made me worry that if she did go to Woodwyn, she would be mistreated. She's already endured enough prejudice. So I told Leo and Luciana that I didn't think she should ever go."

Silas frowned. "What did they call her?"

"Half-breed."

Silas blinked. "Half . . . ?

Brody nodded. "Obviously, she's half elf. But the other . . . we have no idea."

Half-breed. Silas resumed his walk across the courtyard. Romak had known who her parents were, but he'd died before he could talk. Did that mean her parents were important? Powerful enough to silence a prisoner in another country?

When Silas reached the group of soldiers at the entrance to the dungeon, he asked two of them to guard the workroom. As they dashed off, he led Brody inside.

Half-breed. Silas had never heard of any elf coming

across the border to have a child. And Gwennore had been born in Woodwyn. That meant someone, who was not an elf, had traveled to Woodwyn. And since Gwennore was a princess, that someone had had an affair with a member of the royal family.

"You're back," Dimitri said as Silas approached with Brody. His eyes narrowed. "You brought the shifter."

Brody snorted. "Takes one to know one."

Dimitri stiffened.

"It's all right." Silas motioned to last cell. "The body's in there."

Brody slipped into the cell.

"What's he doing?" Dimitri whispered.

"Seeing if he can detect the smell of the Chameleon," Silas said. "It would explain why the murderer looked like Karlan but wasn't Karlan."

Dimitri nodded, then leaned close. "Can we trust the shifter?"

"I believe so." Silas's breath caught as a sudden thought occurred to him. "Dimitri, when did your uncle go to Woodwyn as an envoy? How long ago, exactly?"

Dimitri tilted his head, considering. "It must be twenty-two years. Why do you ask?"

Silas swallowed hard. The timing was right. Was Gwennore the daughter of Lord Tolenko? If so, she was Dimitri's cousin and a member of one of the Three Cursed Clans. The daughter of a dragon shifter. Shit. That would explain why she could hear the dragons. Somehow, she'd inherited the gift from her father.

"What is it?" Dimitri watched him with a worried look.

"I—I need to be sure before I . . ." Silas took a deep breath. If his theory was right, then Gwennore belonged in Norveshka just as much as she did in Woodwyn. By the Light, he wasn't giving her up.

"It's a good thing I'm here," Brody said as he exited the cell. "I can tell you for sure who the murderer is."

Silas grew tense. "The Chameleon? He's here in Norveshka?"

Brody nodded. "I'll help you find the bastard."

Chapter Twenty-One

❧

"The Chameleon is here?" Petras asked with an incredulous look. "In the castle?"

"It's possible," Silas admitted.

He'd asked for a private word with his brother, and Petras had taken him to his suite of rooms next door to the queen's bedchamber. The king couldn't bear to be separated from his ailing wife for very long.

"Dimitri is taking the shifter, Brody, through the castle right now," Silas reported. "If the Chameleon is still here, Brody will be able detect his scent."

"You can detect shifters, why don't you do it?" Petras asked.

"I've never met the Chameleon before, so I'm not familiar with his scent."

Petras frowned. "I don't want that Brody staying here for long. He's a spy for King Leofric."

Silas didn't want to admit that Brody already knew their biggest secret, that some of the men from the Three Cursed Clans were dragons. "No one knows what the Chameleon actually looks like. Brody is our best bet at finding him."

"All right." Petras paced nervously about his sitting room. "Do you think Romak was working for the Chameleon?"

"Possibly, since the Chameleon killed him to keep him from talking. But there may be more people involved in this. The priest who paid Romak is currently headed south. Aleksi is following him to see who he reports to."

Petras slowed to a stop. "I was afraid something like this would happen. There could be a group of people trying to take over our country."

"That's certainly possible, but don't worry. I'll get to the bottom of it."

"I have to worry! It's my crown!" Petras slapped his chest, then fisted his hand. "The nobles are restless. I can hear them whispering about me. And my wife. They think I'm too distracted to rule. They think Freya's going to die."

Silas groaned inwardly, recalling Gwen's warning that the queen would not last much longer. "I hate to tell you this, Petras, but the queen—"

"She'll get better!" Petras shouted. "We just have to get rid of the curse. And then she'll be healthy again, and we'll have children. All the families will be able to have children."

"We're working on it."

"You have to succeed!" Petras resumed his pacing. "The curse has made our entire country sick. It's causing the madness, causing the plague, and it won't stop until we're all mad or dead!"

Silas winced at the frantic gleam in his brother's eyes. "Petras—"

"Summer is coming soon." Petras paced even faster. "That means the plague will come back. More people will die. And they'll blame me for it. They'll want my head!"

"Petras!" Silas grabbed him by the shoulders. "It will be all right."

Petras's eyes glimmered with tears as he clutched Silas's shirt. "You're the only heir I have. Don't let them assassinate you."

Silas squeezed his brother's shoulders. "I won't."

"You should get married. Right away. Have some children. That will stop the nobles from conspiring behind our backs."

Marriage? An instant picture of Gwen popped into Silas's mind and he stepped back, releasing his brother. Marry Gwennore?

Why not? He didn't want to let her go. Wasn't marriage the best way to keep her by his side? *Forever.*

He stood still, waiting for some sort of uneasy feeling to swamp him. After all, this would be a commitment for life.

Gwen forever. *Yes.* A calmness spread through him, a peaceful feeling that he'd found his home, his strength, his refuge from any storm. Gwennore. Who could heal his heart and soothe his soul like her?

"You're smiling." Petras studied him closely. "You must have someone in mind."

"Yes. Lady Gwennore."

Petras stiffened with a jerk. "No! Anyone but her."

Silas gritted his teeth. "There is nothing wrong with her."

"The nobles will never accept an elf for their queen. You'll cause a rebellion!"

"On the contrary, I believe she could bring peace between our country and Woodwyn. The Norveshki people will appreciate not losing their loved ones to war."

"The elves will never want peace!" Petras hissed. "Look what they did to our last envoy. They killed him!"

Silas shook his head. "We don't know that for a fact. Lord Tolenko might be living quite happily in Woodwyn. I have reason to believe that he and an elfin princess are Gwennore's parents."

"What?"

"Lady Gwennore is only half elf. I believe the other half is Norveshki. She belongs here just as much as—"

"That's all speculation." Petras waved a dismissive hand. "What proof do you have?"

"She can hear the dragons. No elf can do that. She must have inherited the gift from Lord Tolenko. That makes her the daughter of a dragon shifter."

Petras frowned. "Then she's too closely related to us."

Silas snorted. "It would mean that Gwen and I have ancestors who were brothers five hundred years ago. None of your objections will deter me, Petras. She's the one I want. I love her."

"No one will accept her!"

"They will." Silas gave his brother a pleading look. "You married for love. Allow me to do the same."

Petras glanced at the door that led to his wife's room. "What will you do when you see the woman you love succumbing to madness just like our mother did?"

Silas swallowed hard. He and Gwennore had to succeed. The Light help him, if he had to watch Gwen grow sick and lose their children, he would go mad with despair.

Was that why Petras had become so paranoid?

Petras shook his head. "You can't marry her. It will cause trouble."

"Give me some time. When Gwennore and I get rid of the curse, you'll think differently."

Petras started pacing again. "That's the problem. This damned curse. All our troubles go back to the curse." He halted, giving Silas a pointed look. "If you fail, I'm going to do what Fafnir tells me to do."

"I know." Go to war on multiple fronts and destroy the country. Silas sighed. "I'd like to find a special ring for Lady Gwennore. She was admiring the emerald ring you gave Freya last summer. Can you tell me where you got it?"

Petras waved a hand. "You won't find another one like it. He had it made especially for the queen."

"Who?" Silas asked softly.

"Fafnir."

Silas's breath caught. The dragon had given the king a poisoned ring?

"In the last year, he's had a few pieces of jewelry made for Freya," Petras continued. "He wanted to prove that he's on our side."

"Since he's on our side, I'd like to meet him."

Petras shook his head. "He talks only to me." He headed for the door. "Keep me informed. The Summoning is in a week, next Diamonday. I need some answers by then."

"I went to the Sacred Well."

Petras spun around. "What?"

"Fafnir wasn't there."

Petras's gaze darted frantically around the room. "O-of course he wasn't there. He refuses to see anyone but me."

Silas's heart clenched once again with the fear that his brother was not only paranoid, but delusional. But if Petras was imagining the dragon, then where had the poisoned ring come from?

Petras stalked toward him. "You shouldn't have gone there. You might have frightened him off!"

"He's a fire-breathing dragon. Why would he frighten so easily?"

"He—he was injured by one of our ancestors. He's

afraid to trust us!" Petras scrubbed a hand over his face. "How could you do that? He might be the only way we can get rid of the curse!"

"My apologies, Your Majesty."

Petras frowned at him, then finally nodded. "All right. We're agreed, then. You'll leave Fafnir to me." He hurried through the door to his wife's bedchamber.

Silas took a deep breath. There was no way he was leaving his brother to deal with Fafnir. Whoever the hell this bastard was, he was poisoning the queen and trying to destroy their country with hopelessly suicidal wars.

The next morning, while Gwennore was putting on a clean shift in her dressing room, she realized she might have to wear one of the fancy gowns that Margosha had lent her. The breeches she'd worn yesterday had gotten dirty during their afternoon tromp through the forest to collect medicinal plants. "Did you wash the breeches?"

"Yes, my lady, but they're not quite dry." Nissa pointed to a green brocade gown. "Perhaps you should wear this one since it's Emeralday."

Gwennore sighed. It seemed silly to wear such an elaborate court dress when she was going to spend the entire day in the workroom. "What I need is some work clothes. Do you have anything I could borrow?

Nissa gasped. "My lady, you can't wear a servant's clothes. Not when you're . . ." She ducked her head, blushing.

"What?"

With a shy smile, Nissa pointed at the door to Silas's dressing room. "I'm so happy for you, my lady."

Gwennore glanced at his door. She could hear running water. Silas must be washing up. "Why are you happy?"

With a grin, Nissa clasped her hands together. "You're back together with His Highness."

"What? No!"

"You were seen, my lady." Nissa lowered her voice to a whisper. "The two of you left his bedchamber yesterday, and he was still getting dressed." She turned away, her face blushing.

"That doesn't mean we . . ." *Oh dear goddesses.* Gwennore grabbed the green brocade gown and slipped it over her head. At least she could stay in the workroom all day, far away from the ridiculous gossip. "Could you do the laces, please?"

"Of course." Nissa stepped behind her. "Everyone's talking about it. Some people are saying you've bewitched the general."

Gwennore snorted. "So now they think I'm a witch."

"I told them you're not." Nissa tugged at the laces. "Others are saying the general has succumbed to madness like the queen."

Gwennore closed her eyes briefly. That was even worse. How could Silas inherit the throne if everyone thought he was insane?

"At least no one is saying you want to kill him anymore."

Gwennore scoffed. "Well, that's nice of them."

Nissa tied off the laces. "They're saying you want him alive, so you can marry him and become the next queen."

Gwennore turned to face her maid. "That's not true. I'm leaving in a few days." Perhaps. She wasn't so sure anymore. Her heart was being torn in two.

"How can you leave?" Nissa's eyes widened. "Don't you care for the general?"

Goddesses, yes. She more than cared for him. "I care enough not to cause him any trouble." She recalled the scornful glares outside the queen's bedchamber. "There are too many people here who hate me."

"Oh, you must have heard." Nissa grimaced.

"Heard what?" When her maid ducked her head, Gwennore touched her shoulder. "Tell me."

Nissa grabbed hold of the gold-painted bead that hung from a leather cord around her neck. "Some people are saying it's not the curse that's killing the queen. They think it's you."

Gwennore gasped. *Dammit.* She was so damned tired of being misjudged and reviled. Why should she stay here and help these ungrateful people?

"I told them they were wrong!" Nissa insisted. "I know how hard you're working to get rid of the curse." A tear rolled down her cheek. "Please don't leave us. We need you. The general needs you."

Tears burned Gwennore's eyes when she imagined Nissa all alone, trying to defend her. "I'll stay awhile longer."

"Thank you." Nissa wiped her cheeks dry.

Gwennore pulled her into a hug. "No, thank you for reminding me that I have true friends here."

Nissa gave her a tremulous smile. "Let me know if you need anything." She ran from the room.

Gwennore let out a groan as she dropped her head back and stared at the ceiling. Wherever she went, it was always the same. People gossiped about her in Eberon and Tourin, too. If she truly wanted to escape prejudice, she would have to spend the rest of her life in the convent on the Isle of Moon.

No. She would not be chased off the mainland. She had to be stronger than that. After splashing some cold water on her face, she dried herself with a towel and glanced at the door to Silas's dressing room. Was he aware of the rumors circulating in the castle?

The quickest way to set everyone straight would be for

him to denounce their relationship. She pressed an ear to the door. The water had stopped some time ago. He should have had time to dress.

She tossed her towel onto the dressing table, then cracked the door open. "Hello?"

"Ah! Dammit!"

She gasped as the door swung open. Silas was standing in front of a mirror, wearing only a towel around his hips while he shaved. A trickle of blood ran down his jawline, mingling with the white lather.

She stepped toward him. "You cut yourself!"

"You surprised me." He turned to face her as he pressed a handkerchief against the cut.

"I-I'm sorry." She backed toward the door. "I thought you would be dressed."

"Don't leave now." He gave her a wry look. "Or I will have been wounded in vain."

She lowered her eyes to keep from gawking at his chest. Unfortunately, that just brought his towel into view. She dropped her gaze some more. What muscular calves he had.

The floor. That was the only safe place to look.

"That's a pretty gown. You look beautiful in green."

She glanced up. He had turned toward the mirror again and was finishing his shave. She winced as he scraped the sharp blade up his throat.

He rinsed the blade off in a bowl of water, then glanced at her. "I like your hair loose like that."

Oh. She tucked her hair behind her ears. In her hurry, she'd forgotten to braid it.

He made another swipe up his throat. "Was there something you wanted?"

Her gaze drifted to his broad shoulders and muscular back. His spine caused an interesting valley at the small of his back. And his rump seemed wonderfully firm.

"Gwen?"

She looked up and discovered him watching her in the mirror. Good goddesses, he'd seen her ogling him. "There's a . . . a rumor going around."

"About the Chameleon?" He finished shaving his neck, then returned to his jawline. "It's true. Brody confirmed that he's the one who murdered Romak. But he's no longer in the castle. Brody and Dimitri searched everywhere."

"I know about that. Brody told us last night. He's sleeping in the workroom."

"There's no bed there." Silas rinsed his face with water, then grabbed a towel to dry himself.

"I made a pallet for him. He had to switch back to a dog, because he can't keep his human form for more than a few hours each day."

"Really?"

Gwennore winced. Her nervousness was causing her to say things that she shouldn't. Brody was rather sensitive about the witch's curse that kept him from being human for most of his life.

"Can you hand me some underpants?" Silas's mouth twitched. "You know where they are."

She nabbed a pair off a shelf and tossed them to him. Unfortunately, they didn't quite reach him, and when he lunged forward to grab them, his towel slipped.

With a gasp, Gwennore spun around. "I need to be going." She sidestepped toward the open doorway.

"You never told me why you're here."

She tried not to think about him standing naked behind her. "The servant who saw us yesterday misinterpreted things, and now everyone believes that we're . . ."

"Copulating?"

Making love. She paused in the doorway. "I think it would be for the best if you made it clear to everyone that we're not . . . lovers."

He placed a palm against the wall next to her and leaned forward to look at her. "We could be."

She blinked a few times, struggling against a desire to drop her gaze. When she did, she saw he had put on the underpants.

"Disappointed?" he asked softly.

Her cheeks grew warm. "Of course not."

"I'm ready to take them off. And it wouldn't take me long to remove your gown."

She scoffed. "I'm not making love to a man I've known for less than a week."

"Ah." His eyes twinkled as he leaned toward her. "You said *love* instead of *copulate*. I wonder why."

She winced inwardly.

"So how much time do you need?" His mouth curled up. "A week and a half?"

His gorgeous smile and beguiling voice made her heart ache, yearning for the impossible. "Is this a joke to you?"

His smile faded. "No. I'm quite serious. And if you ever say yes, you had better be serious, too, for I won't be able to let you go. We'll be more than lovers. We'll be man and wife."

She gasped. Marriage? "You—you can't say that. You're the heir to the throne."

"I'm aware of that."

"Don't you know what people are saying? They think I'm killing the queen! If I ever marry you, they'll say I murdered my way to the throne!" She stepped through the open doorway.

"Gwen." He reached out to stop her.

"They're already questioning your sanity. I'll question it, too, if you refuse to accept that a relationship between us is impossible." She slammed the door shut.

Marriage? How could he even contemplate something that would cause him so much trouble?

She slipped on a pair of shoes and dashed to the work-room.

Chapter Twenty-Two

Gwennore nibbled on a piece of bread while her mind replayed her last conversation with Silas for the hundredth time. He couldn't have been serious. What man proposed marriage in less than a week?

She sighed. To be honest with herself, she had to admit that she'd fallen for him very quickly, too. And she still didn't know if he was actually a dragon.

"Gwen?" Annika waved a hand in her face to get her attention. "What do you think of my great idea?"

"Oh." She glanced at Annika and Margosha, who were sitting with her, eating breakfast in the workroom. Brody had scampered off in dog form the minute she'd opened the door. She assumed he was spying around the castle. "It sounds good to me."

Margosha snorted, while Annika rolled her eyes.

"I suggested making a tonic out of horse dung," Annika muttered. "What's going on with you?"

Gwennore set the slice of bread on her plate. "People are saying Silas and I are back together."

"Really?" Annika smirked. "Did you jump his bones?"

Gwennore shook her head. "It's not amusing. Because of me, people are questioning his sanity, and that puts his inheritance at risk. They're also saying it's not the curse that's killing the queen, but me."

Margosha winced. "Don't pay any attention to them. There will always be cruel and nasty people."

Annika pounded a fist on the table. "They had better not let me hear them spouting that crap! I'll punch their faces in."

Gwennore smiled. "Thank—"

The door burst open, and Olenka ran inside.

"My lady!" She dashed toward Gwennore and flung her arms around her. "Have you heard the news?"

"You mean the rumors?" Gwennore asked as she rose to her feet.

"It's not a rumor. It's true!" Olenka reached into her gown's pocket and pulled out a velvet bag. "I won!" She shook the bag to make a clinking noise. "Fifteen pieces of gold!"

"What?"

With a laugh, Olenka nudged Gwennore with her elbow. "You silly goose, acting like you don't know." She glanced at the other ladies. "She's the best friend in the world!"

"What are you talking about?" Margosha asked.

"I won the wager!" Olenka opened the bag and let the gold coins spill out onto the table. "Gwennore cut the general last night, just like I asked her to!"

Annika jumped to her feet, giving Gwennore an incredulous look. "You cut Silas?"

"No!" Gwennore shook her head.

Olenka pulled her into another hug. "How can I ever thank you?"

"You cut Silas?" This time Annika and Margosha said it in unison.

"No!" Gwennore pushed Olenka back. "It was—"

"Don't worry," Olenka interrupted. "It was only a tiny

nick. Although it is a bit sad that you aimed at his gorgeous face." She gave Gwennore a disapproving frown.

"I didn't do it," Gwennore protested. "Silas cut himself."

Olenka gasped, pressing a hand to her chest. "You asked him to do it for you, and he did?" Her eyes glimmered with tears. "That's so romantic!"

"No, it's not!" Gwennore grimaced. "Holy goddesses, I could never ask someone to hurt himself. It was an accident. Silas nicked himself while he was shaving this morning."

Olenka blinked. "Are you sure?"

"Yes." Gwennore planted her hands on her hips. "I saw it, myself."

"Wait a minute." Annika stepped closer. "You were with him while he was shaving?"

Gwennore bit her lip. "Well, I dropped by for a few minutes."

Annika snorted. "Right." She gave the other women a knowing look.

"I should have known." Olenka's shoulders slumped as she picked up the coins and dropped them back into the bag. "I'll have to return the money."

"Why should you?" Gwennore asked. "If they were foolish enough to—"

"Because if I accept it, it's the same as me saying that you did cut the general. I should have known you would never do such a thing." Olenka stuffed the bag back into her pocket. "I let a moment of excitement and greed cloud my judgment."

Gwennore touched her shoulder. "I won't be offended if you keep it."

"No." Olenka raised her chin. "If I had acted like a true friend, then I would have been offended on your behalf.

I'm taking it back, and I'm going to tell them the truth, that you would never hurt anyone."

Gwennore hugged her. "Thank you."

Olenka gave them all a grin, then scampered out the door.

Margosha chuckled. "There's hope for her after all."

With a smile, Gwennore wandered over to the bowls where the first casket of jewelry was being tested. Her smile faded when she noted that two of the lily pads were starting to shrivel around the edges.

"We may have found more poisoned jewelry." She fished out the ring resting at the bottom of the first bowl. A large sapphire. The metal seemed a bit dull to be silver. "What do you think this is? Pewter?"

Margosha examined the ring. "Perhaps. This was a birthday present for Her Majesty, so she's had it about four months."

"A present?" Annika frowned. "From her husband?"

Margosha nodded as she dropped the ring back into the bowl.

Gwennore fished out the second suspicious piece of jewelry. Another ring, this one an opal. Once again, the metal was a dull grayish color.

"The queen received that one last summer as an anniversary present," Margosha said.

"From her husband," Annika muttered.

Gwennore glanced at her. The king was Annika's cousin, so she obviously didn't want to see him as a villain. "I don't think he's the one trying to hurt her. The culprit would be whoever is supplying him with this jewelry."

Margosha nodded. "I agree. And these rings couldn't be the only things hurting Her Majesty. She's been ill for several years, but these rings were given to her this last year."

Gwennore located the emerald ring that they also suspected was tainted. It was also set in a dull silver-colored metal. "But it's true that in the past year, her illness has worsened quite a bit?"

Margosha winced. "Yes."

So the rings had accelerated a problem that already existed. Gwennore set the ring down and looked at her hands. Was she exposing herself and her friends to poison? "Let's heat up some water and wash our hands."

"Good point." Annika filled up a kettle and put it over the fire.

"We should wear gloves from now on." Margosha rushed out the door.

After she returned and they had washed up, Gwennore wandered to the window to look at the village below. She'd always thought it was charming, but Silas had to see it differently, knowing that his mother had thrown herself off the bridge that spanned the Norva River. "The late queen suffered from madness, too. How many queens have been affected over the centuries?"

"A few." Margosha joined her at the window. "Some of the queens died in childbirth. Others died from the plague. But all the ones who survived to their old age went mad."

Gwennore recalled how her sisters Luciana and Brigitta always said it was good to be queen. Apparently, that wasn't true in Norveshka. "So there's never been a happy queen here."

Margosha shook her head. "Not for five hundred years. That's why people believe in the curse."

"And why men from the Three Cursed Clans are reluctant to marry," Annika grumbled.

She had to be referring to Dimitri, Gwennore thought. Silas didn't seem at all afraid of marriage. "There must be something that all the queens have had in common. Something that links them together."

Annika joined them at the window. "You mean something other than marrying into a cursed clan?"

Gwennore nodded. "Something tangible. Something that could be poisonous." She glanced at the caskets. "Does any of the jewelry date back to the first queen?"

Margosha frowned while she considered. "There might be a few pieces, but they're so old-fashioned that Her Majesty never wore them."

"There has to be something—" Gwennore stopped with a gasp. "The crowns. How old are they?"

Margosha turned pale. "Oh, my." She pressed a hand to her chest. "They—they were a gift to the first king, Magnus, when the Ancient Ones agreed to let him and his wife rule in their stead."

"So the Ancient Ones made the crowns?" Annika asked, and Margosha nodded.

Had the Ancient Ones knowingly given poisoned crowns to the humans they'd selected to rule? Gwennore winced. If so, that had been a cruel and vicious trick. "How often are the crowns worn?"

"At all the royal functions," Margosha replied. "The annual ball, any weddings or funerals involving the royal family, and the Summoning."

"What is that?" Gwennore asked.

"It's when the king listens to complaints and disagreements from the people," Annika explained. "And then he makes a judgment."

Margosha nodded. "Centuries ago, the Summoning only happened twice a year. There weren't many roads, so it was difficult for people to travel to the royal court. But now, the journey is much easier, so the Summoning happens every month."

"That means the more recent kings and queens are wearing the crowns more often," Gwennore concluded. That would explain why the curse seemed worse now and why the queens were going mad at a younger age. "I have to see these crowns."

"They're in a locked room in the cellar," Margosha said. "Only a member of the royal family can take you inside."

The queen was too ill and the king didn't trust her. Gwennore sighed. "I'll have to ask Silas."

"Any idea where Silas is?" Gwennore asked Annika as they ventured into the courtyard.

"No, but you could ask Karlan. His office is over there." Annika pointed at the northern wing.

"Let's go then." Gwennore took a few steps before realizing that Annika hadn't budged. "What's wrong?"

"I think I'd better go back to the workroom."

"I need you." Gwennore linked her arm with Annika's. "Come on."

Annika frowned as she walked beside her. "Am I a chaperone? Are you afraid to be alone with Silas?"

"Something like that."

"Coward," Annika muttered.

"You're one to talk." Gwennore gave her a wry look. "You've managed to avoid Dimitri for two days."

Annika winced. "It hurts when he ignores me."

"Then don't let him ignore you. If I were you, I'd make sure he saw me several times a day."

Annika shook her head. "It would be too awkward. He's made it clear he wants me to stay away from him."

Gwennore opened the door to the northern wing. "Maybe he'll change his mind once we get rid of the curse."

"I hope so." Annika led her down the hallway. "Here it is." She opened the door and stepped inside. "Karlan, do you know—" She came to an abrupt halt, causing Gwennore to bump into her.

One quick glance around the room, and Gwennore

spotted the problem. Dimitri. He was standing across the room, next to Brody in dog form.

Dimitri's reaction had been equally quick. He'd stiffened, then turned to stare out the window.

"Can I help you?" Karlan rose from his seat behind his desk.

"We were looking for General Dravenko," Gwennore said, noting how pale Annika's face had become. "Do you know where we might find him?"

"He said he was going somewhere, but I don't know where." Karlan glanced at Dimitri. "Do you know?"

Dimitri's jaw shifted as he stared out the window.

Annika stood deathly still as she gazed at the floor.

Karlan looked perplexed as an awkward moment of silence hovered over the room, growing longer and longer.

Gwennore winced. This was not a peaceful silence. She could practically feel the tension radiating between Dimitri and Annika. Even Brody was moving his head back and forth, glancing at one, then the other.

Finally, Dimitri cleared his throat. "The general is on his way."

"Ah. Good." Karlan motioned to a pair of chairs. "If my ladies would like to be comfortable while you wait?"

Annika drew in a sharp breath. "I need to go. Brody, didn't I promise you a nice bone from the kitchen?"

Brody barked and gave her a grin.

"All right. Let's go!" She dashed out of the room with Brody trotting behind her.

Dimitri closed his eyes as a pained look stole over his face.

He loves her, Gwennore thought. But he was trying to protect her. "I think we're making progress in defeating the curse."

"Really?" Dimitri glanced at her, and there was a golden glint in his eyes before he blinked it away.

Dragon eyes. Gwennore nodded. "Yes."

After a few more minutes, her superior hearing caught the sound of rapid footsteps coming down the hallway. Someone was running toward them.

Silas skidded to a halt in the doorway. "Gwen." He breathed heavily. "You wanted to see me?"

Somehow he had known she was waiting, so he had rushed here. Gwennore glanced at Dimitri. During that long moment of silence, had he communicated mentally with Silas? If she had lowered her shield, would she have heard them?

She recalled Puff telling her the third rule for dating a dragon. *Whenever you need me, you only have to call and I will come.*

Silas had come.

He was in uniform, as usual, but once again, he was wearing the breastplate with the tarnished star. Had he dressed in the cabin and run all the way here?

"Gwen." His mouth curled up. "Did you need me?"

Did the rascal have any idea what his smile did to her? She had better keep strictly to business. "I would like to examine the crowns. Could you take me there?"

He blinked with surprise. "All right." He strode over to Karlan's desk and retrieved a key from a drawer. As he approached her, he smiled. "Let's go."

She winced inwardly. With no chaperone, she was going to be alone with Silas.

Silas shut the thick metal door so the guard outside wouldn't be able to hear them. "Alone, at last."

Gwen stepped away from him. "Could you light more candles, please?"

Did she think he was going to jump her just because it was dark? It was tempting, he thought as he went around the room lighting the candles with the candlestick he'd brought inside.

As the small underground room slowly brightened, he could see her better. Her skin looked luminous in the candlelight. Her hair, a shimmering white. Her appearance was so beautifully feminine, her movements so graceful, he still found it amazing that underneath that delicate exterior, there was an inner strength as mighty as a powerful sword. And her clever wit was as sharp as any blade. She'd certainly pierced his heart.

How could he ever let her go?

She moved toward the middle of the room, where a table rested, covered with a red velvet tablecloth. The crowns sat on top, draped with another cloth of red velvet, edged with gold braid. A gold-colored tassel hung from each corner.

After lighting all the candles, he set the candlestick on a small table by the door and noticed that one of his cuffs was unbuttoned. He'd dressed in a hurry at the cabin.

He'd spent the morning at the Sacred Well, searching once again for a clue that Fafnir was indeed alive and living there. But there had been nothing other than the dirty pallet and men's clothing, belonging perhaps to the caretaker who kept the candles lit inside the cave. Silas had looked for him, but he was nowhere to be found.

After flying back to the cabin, Silas had been dressing when Dimitri had alerted him that Gwennore wanted to see him.

He buttoned the cuff as he approached her at the table. "Why did you want to see the crowns?"

"We were trying to think of something tangible that all the queens would have had in common."

"So you suspect this?" He grabbed a tassel and pulled the cloth back.

She gasped.

"I know." He gave the crowns a dubious look. "They're a bit much, aren't they?"

"I . . . suppose they're meant to impress."

He snorted. "Are you being tactful? They're gaudy as hell."

Her mouth twitched. "Since you'll probably have to wear one of them someday, I'll refrain from comment."

With a chuckle, he pointed at the larger one. "You mean this one? It belongs to the king."

"It must have ten times the jewels as the one Leo wears."

Silas nodded. "You can safely say that the Norveshki have been obsessed with jewels for centuries." He motioned to the smaller crown. The gold rim and five golden arches were heavily encrusted with all kinds of jewels, and perched on top was a sparkling ruby dragon. "That one is for the queen."

Gwen winced. "It looks like they tried to cram as many jewels on it as possible."

He reached for it, but she grabbed his arm to stop him.

"We suspect it may be poisonous." She pulled some dainty white gloves from her pocket. "Margosha gave me these. We should wear them just to be safe." She set one pair on the table, then pulled on the second pair.

With a wry look, he picked up a glove. There was no way his hand would fit in this. Cupping it around his fingers, he lifted the queen's crown. "You want a closer look at it?"

She took it in her hands. "Goodness, it weighs a ton. Wearing it must be a huge pain in the neck."

"So you think this crown is the main cause of the queen's madness?"

"Perhaps." Gwen set it on the velvet tablecloth. "We

can't think of anything else that every queen has had in common."

"But if someone had coated the crowns with poison five centuries ago, wouldn't it have worn off years ago?"

"You would think so." Gwen retrieved a small bag from her gown pocket. "We suspect these rings are tainted." She upended the bag, and three rings tumbled onto the velvet tablecloth. "They were all given to Her Majesty in the past year."

Using a glove, Silas picked up the emerald ring that he'd asked his brother about the night before. "This was a gift from the king." And Fafnir had given it to him.

"They were all gifts from the king." Gwen motioned to the other rings. One held a sapphire and the other, an opal. "As you can see, the stones are all different. What the rings have in common is the metal that was used."

As Silas examined the rings, he grew increasingly alarmed. The Norveshki tended to focus only on jewels and ignore the setting. "Are you saying the metal itself could be poisonous? I've never heard of such a thing."

Gwennore shrugged. "If some plants and animals are poisonous, then why not metal, too?"

He winced as he set the rings down. "The kings have always wanted everyone to believe the crowns are made of pure gold. But the jewels are so heavy that the crowns were reinforced with another metal. Here, I'll show you." Using the velvet square-shaped cloth to protect his hands, he picked up the crown and turned it upside down.

Gwen gasped.

The inside of the crown was made with the same dull silver metal that had been used for the rings. A poisonous metal? Silas set it down with a thud. "For five hundred years, the Norveshki rulers have worn these crowns. And for five hundred years, they have suffered from illness and madness. Is it our own greed for jewels that has caused the curse?"

Gwen ran a gloved finger over the ruby-encrusted dragon. "Margosha told me the Ancient Ones made the crowns and gave them to the first king and queen."

"That's true." Silas narrowed his eyes. And another Ancient One, Fafnir, had probably given all three of the tainted rings to his brother.

Gwen gave him a worried look. "If the metal is indeed poisonous, and the Ancient Ones knew it, then—"

"They set us up to fail," Silas muttered. Dammit, they'd set the human kings up to die. "They never intended for us to last. They just planned to use us for a while."

Gwen winced. "It looks that way. But before we draw any conclusions, we need to test one of the crowns."

"You have a lily pad big enough?"

"I thought we could use a bigger plant. A much bigger one that can communicate with me."

"The giant redwoods?"

She nodded. "The Kings of the Forest said they would help me. They had one condition, though."

"What was that?"

"They're sentient beings, Silas. And centuries old. They want the humans to stop cutting them down."

"That's easy enough. I'll ask Petras to make it a law at the next Summoning."

She smiled. "Thank you."

Her lovely face warmed his heart. "You should smile more often. You have a beautiful smile."

She shot him an annoyed look. "We need to pack this crown in something."

"And your eyes are so damned beautiful."

"I suppose we could use this cloth." She set the queen's crown in the middle of the velvet square, then tied the tasseled corners at the top.

"You're so good with your hands."

Her mouth twitched. "Are you trying to sway me with a flood of flattery?"

"Ah. You're really clever, too."

She scoffed. "Would you stop, please?"

"Such polite manners."

"Stop!" She punched him in the shoulder.

"Your right jab is excellent."

She laughed. "What am I going to do with you?"

Love me. He pulled her into his arms. "We could start with a kiss."

"Silas." Her smile faded away as her eyes searched his. "We can't. You must know that."

"I don't care what people think. I'm not giving you up."

She stepped away from him and busied herself putting the rings back into the bag. "I need to take these and the crown to the Kings of the Forest. I assume you'll want to send some guards with me."

"You only need me."

She glanced at him. "You'll go with me then?"

"Yes." He would go to the ends of Aerthlan for her.

Chapter Twenty-Three

After changing into her now-dry breeches and shirt, Gwennore rushed to the courtyard, where Silas had readied two horses. The queen's crown was hidden in a plain canvas sack and tied to the saddle of his horse.

She noticed that he was now wearing leather gloves. And he'd added a sword and leather scabbard to his belt. "Are you expecting trouble?"

"Not really. It's just a precaution, since we're traveling with the crown. Are you ready?"

"Yes." She started to mount, and he grabbed her hips to give her a boost. When his hand lingered too long on her backside, she swatted at him.

With a grin, he strode toward his horse.

The rascal. She'd been so tempted to kiss him in the crown room when he'd pulled her into his arms. He was becoming increasingly hard to resist.

He swung easily into his saddle. "Let's go."

They set off at a slow pace, side by side, as they headed north toward the lake.

The sky was a brilliant blue, the air cool and crisp. Gwennore took a deep breath, enjoying the scent of pine and cedar. How she loved being outdoors in this country! And it felt especially good to be here with Silas.

When they reached the clearing, she studied the cabin as they rode past it. Should she ask him if he had recently dressed there? Should she ask if it was a place to provide clothes for dragon shifters?

He cleared his throat. "What do you think of Norveshka?"

Was he trying to distract her? She noticed he was avoiding even looking at the cabin. "I think you keep too many secrets."

His hands tightened on his reins. "Sometimes secrets can keep a person safe."

Was that a warning? She huffed. Maybe safety was overrated. But then she remembered how Romak had been murdered and the queen was being poisoned. Draven Castle was definitely not a safe place. She was already under attack with the malicious gossip going around. "I think you have too many rude and useless people at court."

"That is true."

She glanced at the sack containing the crown. "I think the Norveshki people place too much importance on jewels."

He nodded. "True."

She glanced at his hands. She'd never seen him wear a ring or any sort of jewelry. His uniform was always made of the same cloth as the ones worn by the other soldiers. For a man with a great deal of power, he was still down to earth and humble. He felt no need to flaunt his strength, and that made him seem even stronger. Even more appealing.

How could she ever leave him?

She shook herself mentally. *Stay focused on business.*

"I think the war with Woodwyn is unnecessary and a sad waste of lives."

"True. Those are things we need to change." He looked at her. "Anything else?"

When he said *we*, did that mean he was including her? "Does my opinion actually count?"

"Of course." He gave her an exasperated look. "Do you still not know how much I value your insight?"

Her heart warmed in her chest. From the beginning, he had always thought highly of her.

"Is there anything good about my country?" he asked wryly.

She smiled. "I've made some wonderful new friends."

"That's good."

She looked at the sweetly scented forest with its undergrowth of green ferns and wildflowers. Boulders lay here and there, colored green and gold with spongy moss and lichen. In the distance, snow gleamed on the mountain peaks. Nearby, the Norva River was making a roaring sound as it tumbled over the falls into the canyon. The falls that had almost swept her to her death.

"I think the land can be frightening. But at the same time, wonderfully soothing." She sighed. "It's the most beautiful countryside I've ever seen. It draws me to it. I don't know why."

His eyes narrowed. "Does it feel like your homeland?"

Yes. She shrugged. "It's fairly obvious that I come from Woodwyn."

He remained quiet and thoughtful as they rode into the green pasture next to the lake. Nearby, the giant redwoods stretched into the sky.

Gwennore winced. In order to communicate with the Kings of the Forest, she would have to drop the shield around her mind. Silas wouldn't be able to hear what the trees were telling her, but he would hear all of her thoughts.

She'd have to be careful not to let him know how much she'd fallen for him.

She dismounted before he could help her and strode toward the giant trees as she stripped away the shield. *Greetings, Kings of the Forest.*

It is the Elf.

She has returned.

I've brought the heir to the throne with me, Gwennore explained, glancing at Silas, who was tethering the two horses to the low branch of a pine tree. *He will make sure a law is passed, prohibiting men from cutting down any more of your kind.*

The trees swayed gently, even though there was no wind. Gwennore tilted her head back to watch the tops of the trees move in unison. Was this their way of celebrating?

Silas joined her, the canvas bag slung over a shoulder. His mouth fell open as he watched the slow-motion dance. "I've never seen anything like that before. They must be happy."

Thank you. Many voices echoed in her mind.

You're welcome. She retrieved the small pouch containing the rings from her pocket, along with a pair of gloves. *I believe you have heard of the curse that plagues the Norveshki royal family.*

Yes. The Ancient Ones placed a curse on the three sons of the first king, Magnus.

That was five hundred years ago, another tree said. *At the end of the Great Dragon War.*

So there were two sets of dragons fighting each other? Gwennore asked, her gaze drifting toward Silas, who gave her a wary look.

Yes, one of the Kings replied. *The new dragons rebelled against the Ancient Ones. In those days, the sky was filled with fire and the stench of death.*

The younger ones were victorious, another King added. *The Ancient Ones are no more.*

"Are you going to test the rings?" Silas motioned to the pouch in her hands.

Trying to change the subject, she thought as she knelt and slipped on her gloves. She emptied the sack onto the ground. *I suspect these three rings are poisonous. Is there a way you can verify that?*

Yes.

The ground beneath her shook.

Silas dropped the sack containing the crown on the ground as he crouched beside her. "What's happening?"

"I'm not sure." She gasped when the ground close by suddenly heaved up a foot, making a small mound.

The ground split, and the tentacle-like ends of a root emerged, uncurling as if it were a hand opening wide.

Silas sat back. "What the hell?"

Give us the rings.

She placed the three rings on what looked like gnarled wooden fingers.

"Fascinating," Silas whispered.

You are correct. This is poison.

Gwennore quickly removed the rings. *Are you all right? It didn't hurt you?*

We are not easily harmed.

We have been here for centuries.

And we will be here when you have long turned to dust.

Gwennore dropped the rings back into the pouch. *Is it the metal that is poisonous?*

It is lead. You should bury it in a cave.

We will. Thank you. Gwennore repeated what she'd learned to Silas, since he was unable to hear the trees.

"If the queen held food in her hands, like bread, she could have actually consumed some of the lead over time."

Silas removed the crown from its canvas bag. "Can they test this?"

We believe the queen's crown might also be poisonous, Gwennore mentally told the Kings.

A thick root emerged from the ground, and once it was exposed to the air, the end started to roll, curling back onto itself until it formed a large wooden knob the size of a person's head.

Silas placed the crown on top.

You are correct. This is poison.

More lead. And some mercury.

Someone is poisoning your queen.

Gwennore removed the crown and told Silas, "This is poison. It should never be worn again."

With a sigh, Silas glanced up to the tops of the redwoods. "I don't suppose they could be lying."

"I don't think so. They have nothing to gain by helping us stay alive. We're nothing more than a short-lived nuisance to them." She handed him the crown. "Is there lead in the king's crown, too?"

"Yes." He dropped the crown and the pouch of rings back into the sack. "I'll have to explain all of this to my brother, but I'm not sure he'll believe me."

"Why not?"

"He may be reluctant to see the Ancient Ones as villains."

"But if they knew the crowns were poisonous . . ."

"I'm sure they did. They were experts at stones and minerals." He tied the drawstrings on the sack, then rose to his feet. "The original agreement was that they would let Magnus be king as long as he was their puppet and his seven sons worked like slaves in the mines."

Gwennore stood as she stuffed her gloves back into her pocket. "I heard a bit of that story. Only three of the brothers survived."

With a snort, Silas motioned to the sack containing the poisoned crown. "I don't think the Ancient Ones intended any of them to survive."

He slung the sack over his shoulder as he strode toward the tethered horses. "Will you give my thanks to the redwoods for their help?"

"Of course." She turned toward the grove of trees. *Thank you so much.*

The wild ones are approaching.

They have you surrounded.

What? She spun around. "Silas!"

He came to an abrupt halt, automatically dropping the crown and grabbing the hilt of his sword. Several dozen trolls stepped into the clearing and raised their spears.

After a quick glance around, Silas lifted his hands and told them something.

Gwennore fought a surge of panic as she edged toward him. "You—you know their language?"

"A little." He turned slowly, watching the trolls. "I told them we've come in peace."

"Then why are they still pointing their spears at us? What do they want with us?"

The trolls advanced a step, then another, their circle growing tighter.

She grabbed Silas's sleeve. "We need to go."

"If they meant us harm, they would have already thrown their spears."

"That's not very reassuring. We need to get out of here!" *Puff!*

Silas stiffened, and she felt the muscles in his arm grow tense.

Puff. A chill ran down Gwennore's spine. He wasn't answering.

Silas grabbed her by the shoulders. "You don't need him. I will protect you."

"He won't come, will he?" Her eyes burned. "He can't come, because he's already here."

Silas hissed in a breath as a flash of gold shot through his eyes. "Don't say it." He pressed a finger against her mouth. "Don't even think it. Put your shield up now."

She turned away, her eyes filling with tears as she placed one mental brick after another, cutting herself off from him and anyone else who might hear her thoughts.

"I'm sorry," he whispered.

A tear rolled down her cheek. "Why didn't you tell me? I asked you over and over to be honest with me."

He leaned close to whisper in her ear. "Rule number four for dating a dragon: Never tell his secrets."

She pushed him away. "Who said we were dating?"

"Then why are you crying?"

She brushed her tears away. "You should have told me. You should have trusted me."

He glanced over at the trolls. "I'll explain later, but for now, we have a bigger problem."

She noticed that the trolls were watching her curiously and exchanging guilty looks. Perhaps they thought they were the cause of her tears.

While Silas talked to them, she dried her face and squared her shoulders. She'd deal with him and Puff later.

There is no Puff. A sense of grief hit her hard, then she berated herself. Puff wasn't gone. He was Silas.

But it would never be the same. The Puff she knew was gone.

"They want us to come with them," Silas said as he leaned over to grab the canvas sack.

He took her by the elbow, but she pulled away and walked silently beside him.

The trolls led them down a path through the forest. She counted six in front. Behind them, there were a dozen more. On either side, a few trolls were weaving through the trees. Her heart thudded. There was no way to escape.

"Don't worry," Silas murmured. "They said they only want to show us something."

"A boiling pot over a fire?" she muttered.

Silas winced, then leaned close to whisper, "They're not cannibals. Watch what you say. They understand more Norveshki than they let on."

She clenched and released her hands, trying to remain calm. But her mind kept racing with all the horror stories she remembered from *Torushki's Bedtime Tales of a Mountain Troll*.

"They're not a violent people," Silas whispered.

"They have spears."

"For hunting. They're excellent hunters."

"Are we excellent prey?"

He snorted. "They know who I am. They won't dare harm me for fear of retaliation."

"Are they holding you for ransom? Or maybe they saw the crown and they want it?"

Silas shook his head. "They have a longtime hatred of gold and jewels. They live off the land and are very much in tune with it." He glanced at her. "They referred to you as the Healer. I think it's you they're interested in."

She swallowed hard. If there was an injured troll, she couldn't do much without any medicinal herbs. Would that make them angry? "Who are they? Where do they come from?"

"I'll explain later."

She scoffed. "I'll add it to the ever-growing list."

He sighed. "I understand you're a little angry."

"A little?"

"Gwen." He stopped and told hold of her shoulders. "What do you think happens to people who figure out the state's most guarded secret?"

She tried to pull away, but he tightened his grip.

His eyes flared a molten gold. "They are never allowed to leave the country."

Her mouth dropped open.

He closed his eyes briefly with a pained expression. When he looked at her again, his eyes were green once more. "I know how much you want to go home to your sisters. I know how eager you are to leave me behind."

The trolls behind them yelled something, and Silas replied as he released her.

"They want us to keep moving." He motioned for her to walk.

Her mind swirled as she fell into step beside him. So he had kept the secret in order to protect her. He'd wanted her to have the freedom to leave if she wished. And she would lose that freedom if anyone learned that she knew the big secret. "You won't tell anyone that I know?"

He shook his head. "I know you want to leave."

"I would never tell anyone your secret."

"I know."

He did trust her. Her heart swelled. He had been the one to save her from falling to her death. He had saved her from going over the waterfall. He'd always been there for her.

Puff's voice that she loved so much had always been his voice. His sense of honor was the same as Puff's. His sense of humor the same. His courage and gentleness.

"I accept your apology." She touched his hand.

He enveloped her hand in his. "Thank you."

"No, thank you. You've rescued me twice."

"Three times if you include the dungeon." His mouth twitched as he laced his fingers with hers. "But who's counting?"

She smiled. As they walked, she became increasingly aware of their linked hands. Goddesses help her, she *was* dating a dragon. But she could never tell anyone what Silas truly was. Rule number four played through her mind. Never tell a dragon's secrets.

The trolls in front looked back and told Silas something.

"What is it?" she asked. "What do they want?"

"We're about to find out." Silas pointed at the clearing ahead of them. "That's their village."

Chapter Twenty-Four

❦

"Thank you." Gwennore smiled at the young female troll who was handing her a wooden bowl filled with a golden liquid. "What is this?" she whispered to Silas.

"It's a mead they make from honey," Silas whispered back. "They only drink it for special occasions."

"Aren't we lucky?" She took a sniff, and her eyes watered from the alcoholic fumes.

"If you don't drink it, you'll hurt their feelings."

He smiled as he accepted a bowl from the young woman, then said a few words. Thanking her, Gwennore assumed.

After arriving in the troll village, she and Silas had been invited to sit on two pillows of embroidered felt in front of the chieftain's tent. The other villagers were sitting on plain linen pillows, so she and Silas had been given the best the trolls had to offer.

The village consisted of tents of brightly colored felt, erected in a large circle. For now, all the villagers were sitting in a smaller circle, watching her curiously.

Once everyone had a bowl of mead, they lifted their bowls in the air and shouted a cheer. Silas did the same, motioning with his free hand for Gwennore to follow suit.

The trolls gulped down their mead, then slammed their empty bowls onto the ground.

"Bottoms up," Silas murmured, then downed his bowl.

Gwennore took a sip and nearly choked as the mead went down like liquid fire. Holy goddesses, this was the strongest alcohol she'd ever tasted.

Silas slammed his empty bowl down, and the trolls cheered. Then they turned to Gwennore with expectant looks.

She took a big gulp and, with her eyes watering, she forced a smile. "Yummy!"

The trolls chuckled, then talked excitedly to one another.

"They like you." Silas's smile turned into a grimace. "And they're wondering if they could persuade you to marry the chieftain's son."

"What?" She gave Silas an incredulous look.

"Over my dead body," he ground out through a smile of clenched teeth.

Her mouth twitched. "Are you worried?"

"Should I be?" His eyes narrowed when she pretended to think it over.

The young woman brought them two more bowls, and Gwennore sighed with relief when she saw they contained some sort of soup.

She tasted it and was pleasantly surprised. "This is excellent. Thank you!"

The young woman grinned.

Soon everyone was eating and chatting happily. Gwennore glanced around, admiring how colorful the tents were. The clothes worn by the troll women were equally colorful, with beautifully embroidered caps and belts.

She leaned close to Silas and whispered, "When I saw them before, they were dressed in dirty rags. But now, they seem well-dressed."

"When the men hunt, they try to blend in with nature," he whispered back. "They probably consider this a special occasion, so they're wearing their best clothes."

"Do they always live in tents? Are they nomadic?"

He nodded. "They travel far to the north in the summer, following the great herds of elk and caribou."

When everyone finished eating, a young man approached Gwennore and bowed. She spotted the bandage wrapped around his leg and realized this was the troll she'd treated in the river.

"Can you ask if his wound is healing?" Gwennore asked Silas, and he talked to the young man for a moment.

"He says he's fine and he's made a gift to show you his gratitude," Silas grumbled as the young man handed her a parcel wrapped in leather.

"Oh. Thank you!" She opened it to find a piece of wood carved into the likeness of a horse. "This is amazing." She lifted it up to admire it. "Goodness, you're so talented!"

With a blush, the young man replied, then all the trolls chuckled as he ran back to his pillow.

"What did he say?" she asked Silas.

Silas clenched his fists, then relaxed them. "He claims to have other talents as well."

"Other . . . ?"

"He's the chieftain's son," Silas muttered.

"You mean the one they want—"

"Don't say it. Don't even think about it."

She grinned as she ran her fingers over the smooth wooden horse. "I have to admit, the trolls are not at all what I expected them to be."

He gave her a wary look. "You're not planning to run off with them, are you?"

"Well, they do seem very friendly. Why did Torushki make them out to be such monsters?"

"That was four hundred years ago. Things were different back then. Whenever the trolls had an infant who died, they would steal a Norveshki baby to replace it. Thankfully, they stopped doing that about two hundred years ago."

Gwennore snorted. "Now the Norveshki are doing it."

Silas winced. "I'm trying to put a stop to it."

She glanced around and noticed there weren't many children in the village. "They must have suffered from the plague here."

"Everyone has suffered from the plague. We've lost about a fourth of our population, mostly children and the elderly. The adults who survived are infertile, so it's very difficult to increase our population."

"Did you have the plague when you were young?"

"Are you worried I might be infertile?" He leaned close. "We could put it to the test."

She shoved him back.

"Rejected again," he muttered.

The trolls stood and motioned for them to follow.

Silas rose to his feet. "At last, we'll find out what they want."

They were taken to a pen that was surrounded on four sides with a tightly boarded fence. A man set a covered cage in the pen and whisked the cover off.

Gwennore winced. Inside the cage was a large rat. It was frantic, gnarling at the wooden slats of the cage and throwing itself from one side to the other in a frenzy to escape. "What's wrong with it?"

An older woman talked to Silas for a while, then he turned to Gwennore. "This woman is their healer. She says she has spent the last twenty years studying the plague, and this is how it begins." He pointed at the rat.

A man leaned over the fence and used a hooked spear to lift one side of the cage. The rat immediately escaped from its cage and ran across the pen, where it slammed against the boards. Then it darted to the other side to crash into the fence there.

"The plague causes the rats to go mad?" Gwennore asked.

Silas listened to the troll healer explain, then told Gwennore, "The plague changes the rat's behavior, making it frantic and aggressive. It will bite humans, passing the plague on to them, or it will attack animals that it would normally run away from."

Two troll men lowered a larger covered cage into the pen. When they whisked the cover off, Gwennore was shocked to see a wildcat inside. The typical Norveshki wildcat was no bigger than a lamb, but they were known to be ferocious little hunters. The second the wildcat saw the rat it reacted, baring its teeth and hissing. The cat's spotted fur bristled as it arched its back.

The rat would have been safe if it had stayed across the pen, for the wildcat was still in a cage. But the rat dashed straight for the cat, squeezing between the slats so it could attack.

With a screech, the cat retaliated.

Gwennore had a quick and horrifying glimpse of gnashing teeth and ripping claws from both animals before she looked away. But she could still hear the awful sounds.

Silas wrapped an arm around her, pulling her close to his chest. "You don't have to watch to know what will happen. The rat will die. The cat will win, but also lose, for now it will be infected with the plague."

Gwennore shuddered as one of the trolls used a spear to kill the wildcat. "They could have just told me."

"They wanted us to see how it happens." Silas listened to the healer, then explained. "Once the wildcat is infected, it becomes more aggressive and attacks animals much larger than its usual prey. Instead of rabbits and mice, it goes after deer or elk, biting as many as possible before it's tromped to death by the herd. Then people eat the infected deer and elk."

"And that's how they get the plague," Gwennore concluded.

Silas nodded. "And the healer says it spreads easily among humans. Handling food, physical contact. That's all it takes."

The healer approached Gwennore and bowed. When she spoke, there were tears in her eyes.

"She says she has done all she can to figure out the plague, but she has never been able to heal it. She's begging you to find a cure, so you can save her people."

Gwennore swallowed hard. "I'm not sure I can." She looked over all the villagers, who were watching her with hope in their eyes.

"I may have saved you three times." Silas took her hand. "But you could save an entire country."

Tears crowded her eyes as she faced the villagers. "I will do my best."

Silas glanced at Gwennore as she rode her horse beside him. She'd been quiet since they'd left the troll village. They'd found their still-tethered horses happily munching on grass close to the giant redwoods. After putting her wooden horse in the canvas sack with the crown, he'd tied the sack to his horse's saddle. Gwen had been so preoccupied that she hadn't even noticed when he'd let his hand linger on her bottom too long as he'd helped her onto her horse.

She must be worried about finding a cure for the plague, he thought. "If you need any help in collecting plants or distributing tonics, I have an army at your disposal."

She gave him a distracted look. "Thank you."

"We've made some important progress today." He motioned to the sack containing the crown. "We know what has been poisoning the kings and queens."

She nodded. "And we know that the tainted rings made Queen Freya's condition much worse. Did you find out who gave those rings to the king?"

Fafnir. "I'll talk to my brother about it."

Gwen sighed. "Unfortunately, knowing the truth isn't going to help the queen recover. And knowing how the plague spreads to humans doesn't really tell me how to cure it."

"I believe you can do it."

Her smile was strained. "I appreciate that, but I still think I'm in over my head. I'd like to ask Sister Colleen and the court physicians in Eberon and Tourin for their advice."

"All right." Silas thought it over. It would take well over a week for messengers to make the trip. "How about we send Brody to gather information for you?"

"Oh." This time her smile was more relaxed. "That's an excellent idea. Thank you."

"I have to prove myself useful or you might decide to elope with your troll admirer."

She snorted. "Can you tell me about them now?"

He scanned the forests to make sure they were alone. "I didn't want to tell their story where they could hear it. They don't like to be reminded of their past."

"Why not?"

"Over a thousand years ago, the Ancient Ones took over the land of Norveshka because they wanted the gold and jewels that could be mined here. They terrorized the people into submission by breathing fire and burning any person or village who objected to their rule. They used the Norveshki people to tend livestock, and then they took most of the cattle and sheep to feed themselves, leaving the people to go hungry."

Gwen shook her head. "They sound awful."

"They were. They chose the smaller Norveshki to work in the mines for them, for they thought those with a shorter stature would be able to work better in the tunnels. Basically, they used them as slaves. For hundreds of years, the trolls were bred to become shorter and shorter. They spent their lives in caves, hardly ever seeing sunlight. It caused their eyes to grow larger. In their isolation, even their language became different."

"How terrible." Gwen tilted her head, thinking. "You said earlier that they have a longtime hatred of gold and jewels. Is that because of the mining they were forced to do?"

Silas nodded. "It reminds them of the centuries that they were enslaved. They won't step foot in a cave now. They don't even want to enter a castle or a house, for they view it as a form of entrapment. They need to be free now to roam as they please."

"How did they get free from the Ancient Ones?"

"Toward the end of the Great Dragon War, the Ancient Ones were losing, dying off. The trolls saw their chance to rebel and turned on the Ancient Ones, helping the rest of the Norveshki people take over the country. But having a common cause wasn't enough to reunite the trolls with their Norveshki cousins. They have never sworn allegiance to the Norveshki kings."

Gwen narrowed her eyes. "They don't feel that they can trust you?"

Silas sighed. "I think they must feel that we abandoned them for all those centuries that they were enslaved. They resented the Norveshki for being able to live in the sunlight. And their culture developed differently than ours.

We're not entirely comfortable around each other, but I think it's getting better. I want it to get better."

Gwen nodded. "I think they're willing to reach out now."

"I hope so. But I can understand why they don't trust us. After all, we have . . . dragons, and the trolls hate dragons with a passion. That's one reason why we keep the nature of our dragons secret. There are some who would want to kill us."

"So the trolls don't know that you're . . . ?"

He shook his head. "Outside of the Three Cursed Clans, very few people know."

"So all the dragons come from the Three Cursed Clans?"

"Only a few men from the Cursed Clans. There aren't that many of us. Only about a dozen." Silas winced. "That's a secret, too, by the way. We've always wanted the neighboring countries to think we have hundreds. It generally keeps anyone from attacking us."

"Except for Woodwyn."

He shrugged. "We don't know why they keep attacking."

"I don't know, either." She smiled. "But I'm glad that you're being honest with me now."

His hands tightened on the reins. He still hadn't told her she was half elf and, he suspected, half Norveshki.

Her eyes narrowed. "Is there something else?"

He snorted. She was so damned perceptive. "I don't know yet. When I find out, I'll let you know."

She frowned at him. "I still have some questions. For instance, when Eviana was kidnapped, Puff was against it and rescued me—"

"You mean I rescued you."

"Yes, but who was the dragon who kidnapped Eviana?"

Silas hesitated.

Gwen stiffened suddenly with a gasp. "You called him brother. Was it the king?"

Silas winced. "That's another secret."

She drew in a deep breath. "Now I see why it's been hard for you to stop the kidnappings."

He motioned to the cabin that was coming into view. "Let's rest there for a few minutes, so we can talk. Once we get back to the castle, we won't be able to discuss these things."

"All right." She dismounted before he could help her and strode into the cabin.

He followed her inside and shut the door.

She wandered about the room. "I have a few more questions. How can dragon shifting even be possible? Were you able to shift as a baby, or did it begin when you were older? Dimitri and Aleksi, are they dragons, too?"

"They are." Silas nodded. "That was Dimitri watching over us when we took the barge to Vorushka."

"I see." She leaned against a wall, folding her arms across her chest. "When my mind was open, you were able to hear all my thoughts. But when you're Puff, I only hear what you want me to hear. Why is that?"

"It's a matter of degree. As children, we learn to close our minds off. Then, around the age of thirteen, when we start shifting into dragons, we learn to open our minds only enough to communicate with each other."

She sighed. "If I had been able to hear your thoughts, I would have figured it out so much sooner. Instead, I was left wondering for days. Could he really be Puff? How can such a thing be possible? Sometimes I thought I was just imagining it."

He stepped toward her. "How did you figure it out?"

She shrugged. "There were things that bothered me from the start. Your voice was similar to Puff's. And sometimes you said the exact same words."

"I did?"

She nodded. "And every now and then, your eyes would take on a hint of gold."

He winced. "That only happens when I'm too strongly affected by emotions. Usually no one notices. Well, normally, I'm in complete control, so it doesn't happen."

Her face grew pale. "It kept happening with me."

"Yes." He took another step toward her.

She turned to look out the window. "When I did the reading on you, I could tell you had an extra-large heart. Then later, you said dragons were the same way."

"Yes." He moved closer. "That's rule number two. Because of our hearts, we can love more fiercely. But we can also feel more pain."

She glanced back, and her eyes met his for a few tense seconds before she walked over to the table. "I came across this cabin a few days ago, and I found these uniforms here." She unfolded two leather breastplates. "This one has two stars like the one Aleksi wears, and this one has three stars like Dimitri's uniform."

Silas joined her at the table. "We get dressed here before going to the castle."

"That's what I figured. There was a breastplate here with four stars, and one of the stars was tarnished, like this." She touched the star on his chest. "The afternoon after Puff rescued me, you came to my bedchamber, wearing this same breastplate. And that's when I . . . I was too shocked to believe it, though."

"The afternoon when I kissed you?"

She nodded. "I had just seen Puff breathe fire at the trolls, so I was afraid." Her gaze lifted to his face. "I wasn't sure if it was safe to kiss you."

"But you did." He touched her cheek. "Rule number five: Beware of kissing a dragon. He won't burn you, but he might make you melt."

She blinked. "Melt?"

"Yes." He leaned in for a kiss.

"Like a stick of butter?"

He paused. "I didn't mean it literally."

"Oh, that's a relief." She stepped back, her eyes twinkling with humor. "I rather like being in solid form."

"Gwen—"

"Do you just make these rules up as we go? Or are they official rules that are written down somewhere? Are there rules for dating a troll, too?"

He flinched. "You want to date that troll?"

"No." She grinned. "I was just wondering where these rules come from. How many are there?"

"I don't know. As many as it takes to win your heart."

"Ha!" She pointed at him. "You are making them up as you go."

He gave her an exasperated look. "Does it matter?"

"Well, I think that last one needs some revision. It was just too cheesy."

"What?"

"The rules should be more simple, don't you think? For instance, rule number five can simply be, It's safe to kiss a dragon."

"If you agree it's safe, why are we wasting time discussing it?" He pulled her into his arms.

"Wait." She planted her hands on his chest.

"What?"

"I—I know we're attracted to each other, but that doesn't mean we should—"

"Why not?" He cupped a hand around her neck.

"Because a relationship with me will only cause you trouble. I care enough about you not to hurt you—"

"You are hurting me! Every time you reject me." He stopped himself from saying more. If she knew the pain was real, she might feel burdened or obligated, and he didn't want that. He wanted her to come to him freely. "Gwen, I don't care what others are saying. My only concern is you. Can you accept me for who I am? Both man and dragon?"

Her eyes glimmered with tears. *Puff?*

She'd dropped her shield. He lowered his enough to respond. *Yes, it's me.*

She closed her eyes briefly. *I've always loved your voice.*

I want to love you. I want to— He snapped his shield back in place.

She blinked. "I can't hear you anymore."

"You don't want to hear my thoughts right now."

She snorted. "Why not?"

"You might be shocked."

Her mouth twitched. "Try me."

"I want to kiss you."

"Hardly shocking."

"Whenever you wear a man's shirt like this, I want to unbutton it, so I can see your breasts. Then I want to touch them. And taste them until I make you moan."

Her eyes widened.

"And whenever you wear breeches like this, I want to grab on to you like this." He planted his hands on her rump and with a squeeze, pulled her hard against his swollen groin.

She gasped.

"I'm thinking about removing your clothes. And I'm wondering how sturdy that table is."

"The table?" She glanced at it. "What does that have to—" She stopped when he nuzzled her neck.

"Shall I tell you more?" He kissed a path up to her ear and whispered, "Or would you like me to show you?"

Her fingers dug into his shoulders. "Silas."

"Yes."

"Show me."

He rested a hand against her cheek, turning her head till her lips met his. A sweet, nibbling kiss that didn't last long before his passion erupted. Soon he was ravaging her mouth with a deep, desperate, and demanding kiss.

She didn't shy away, but threw herself into the whirlwind of passion, delving her hands into his hair and entwining her tongue with his.

When he cupped her bottom to lift her off her feet, she wrapped her legs around him. Still kissing her, he carried her to the table and set her down.

"Oh." She glanced down at the table. "This is what you meant—" She stopped with a gasp when he unfastened the top button of her shirt.

"Shall I continue?"

She hesitated, then nodded. As he swiftly unbuttoned her shirt, he noticed there was a white camisole underneath, edged with lace and decorated with tiny pearl buttons. So feminine. His fingers trembled, fumbling with the delicate buttons.

Finally. He swept the camisole away to reveal her breasts. So soft against his fingertips. The pink nipples pebbled, the tips hardened. And his groin tightened.

"Gwen," he whispered as he lowered his head.

She let out a deliciously sweet moan when he drew her nipple into his mouth. He suckled a moment, then flicked his tongue against the hardened tip. Now the sound she made was more like a whimper.

Was she wet? Was she ready for him? He returned to her mouth to ravish her lips once again. By the Light, he wanted her now. He squeezed her thigh, then smoothed his hand up to her hip.

"Gwen." He leaned back to look at her.

Her lips were rosy and swollen, her lovely lavender-blue eyes dazed with desire.

"I want to touch you." He slipped his hand between her thighs.

She stiffened with shock, but when he pressed gently against her, she closed her eyes with a groan.

Yes. As he reached for the buttons of her breeches, he heard a thundering noise like a racing horse. His heart, no doubt.

His hands grew still as a horse whinnied. Dammit. That wasn't him.

Footsteps sounded on the porch outside. Then a loud pounding on the door.

Gwennore gasped.

"Don't come in!" He lifted Gwen off the table.

"Silas!" Dimitri yelled. "I need to talk to you."

"Dammit to hell," Silas growled.

Gwen's hands shook as she refastened her clothes.

"Wait here." He adjusted his too-tight breeches and strode toward the door.

This had better be important. Hell, even if it was important, he might still clobber Dimitri.

Chapter Twenty-Five

❧

While Gwennore fumbled with her buttons, she eased up close to the shut door to hear what was going on outside.

"Aleksi captured the priest right before he crossed the border to Woodwyn," Dimitri said.

"Woodwyn?" Silas sounded surprised. "Romak was spying for an elf?"

"We don't know. Aleksi took the priest to the army camp. He thought you might want to talk to him."

"I'll leave right away." Silas's voice grew too quiet for Gwennore to hear.

She quickly checked her clothes to make sure everything was in place. Her hands were still shaking, her heart still pounding. Goddesses help her, she'd completely lost herself in a moment of passion.

What had come over her? She'd always been the calm and rational one among her sisters. But then, she'd never met a man like Silas.

Obviously, she had no control whatsoever when it came to him. She glanced at the table, recalling all the liberties he had taken. All the liberties she'd allowed him to take. And she'd known the man a total of five days?

Could she trust a passion as sudden and explosive as this?

She took a deep breath and made sure she had erected a strong mental shield. It would be too embarrassing for anyone to hear her thoughts now.

Feigning a calmness she didn't feel, she opened the door and sauntered outside. "Hello, Dimitri." She hoped he wouldn't notice the blush warming her face.

Thankfully, he barely gave her a nod as he tied the reins of Silas's horse to the back of his saddle.

"Gwen, I have some business to take care of." Silas led her to her horse. "Dimitri will take you back to the castle." He leaned close to whisper in her ear. "I hate to leave you now, but I'll see you later. Don't work too hard. Get some rest."

"I'll be fine," she murmured as she slipped a foot into a stirrup. "Be careful."

"I will." Silas hoisted her up onto her horse, and she noticed that he refrained himself from touching her more than necessary. He gave her horse a light slap on the rump to get it moving.

As she rode off with Dimitri, she glanced over her shoulder and spotted Silas slipping back inside the cabin. Was he planning to undress so he could shift into Puff?

So much had happened today that her thoughts were swirling. Her suspicion had turned out to be true. Silas could shift into a dragon. Dimitri, Aleksi, and King Petras could, too. But their true nature was kept secret.

The dragons were not only hated by the trolls, but feared and hated by people in the neighboring countries. If the news ever leaked that the dragons were men, there would be assassins who would try to kill them while they were in their more vulnerable human form.

She would have to be careful not to let anyone know

that she knew the truth. Silas was trusting her to keep the secret, and she didn't want to let him down. Besides, if any of the dragons found out that she knew, she wouldn't be allowed to leave the country. She would never be able to return to her sisters.

Her heart clenched in her chest. Did she even want to leave now? How could she leave Silas? But how could she abandon her sisters? She'd lived with them for twenty-one years. How could she leave them for a man she'd known for five days?

But Luciana and Brigitta had fallen for men quickly, too, and they were very happy now. Silas had warned her that if they became lovers, he would insist on marriage. Good goddesses, she'd almost become his lover today!

She shook herself mentally. She had too many other things to worry about, like keeping the queen alive and curing the plague. For now, she needed to focus on work. And she had better act as if she were completely ignorant about the dragons.

She glanced at Dimitri, who was riding beside her with Silas's horse in tow.

She cleared her throat. "How will Silas get around? Shouldn't we have left him his horse?"

Dimitri looked taken aback for a moment, then waved a dismissive hand. "He'll be fine. It's a short walk to the castle. Besides, he wanted me to return the crown as soon as possible."

"I see." A shadow fell over them, and she peered up at the sky. "Oh, look!" She pointed as Silas flew over them in dragon form. "Is that Puff?"

Dimitri glanced up. "Could be."

Gwennore waved at the dragon. "It's good to see him. I haven't seen him in a few days." There, that should convince Dimitri she was still in the dark. She spotted another movement in the sky. An eagle, and it was flying straight for them. Brody?

"Why did you and Silas take the crown into the forest?" Dimitri asked. "He didn't have time to explain, but he said you could."

She nodded, grateful to have something to take her mind off her relationship with Silas. When she started describing how the giant redwoods had helped, Dimitri held up a hand to stop her.

"You're really communicating with them?"

"Yes, they said only a few elves can do it." As she continued with the story, the eagle swooped down and landed on the saddle of Silas's horse.

"Hi, Brody." Gwennore smiled at him, and he gave her a small squawk.

Dimitri snorted. "Isn't he a little obvious with his spying?"

"I'm sure he's just curious." Gwennore finished her story about the crowns and tainted jewelry. "So all the madness and suffering that was attributed to the so-called curse was actually caused by a poisonous metal."

"Do you think the Ancient Ones knew they were poisoning us?" Dimitri asked.

Gwennore nodded. "We believe so. But the good news is once we get rid of all the poisonous jewelry, the curse will be gone."

"But what about the plague? Isn't that part of the curse?"

Gwennore explained everything that had happened in the troll village. "People expect me to find a cure, but I'm not really sure how to go about it. Brody, could you go to Luciana and Brigitta and find out if their royal physicians have any advice for me? I need all the help I can get."

Brody gave a squawk, then took off.

"Thank you!" Gwennore called after him.

"I guess he has his uses." Dimitri watched the eagle flying south.

"Definitely," Gwennore agreed. "I don't know what we would do without Brody."

For the rest of the trip, Dimitri was silent. Gwennore wondered if he was thinking about Annika. With the curse gone, there would no longer be a reason for him to avoid her.

Unfortunately her relationship with Silas was not that easy to resolve.

The sun was setting by the time Silas landed at a cabin close to the army camp. While getting dressed in the cabin, he sent a mental message to Aleksi that he had arrived.

Aleksi met him on the outskirts of the camp and led him toward the tent where the priest was being held.

"Has he said anything?" Silas asked as he returned salutes of soldiers they passed by.

"No, but I haven't actually questioned him yet. We've left him alone since this morning, so he should be feeling anxious by now. Oh, he had a pouch of gold on him, and this." Aleksi handed him a rolled-up piece of paper.

Silas unrolled it. The message was written in Elfish. "Damn." There was no one here who could read it. Maybe Gwennore could. He glanced at the setting sun. It was too late to fly back tonight. He slipped the note into a pocket inside his breastplate.

So the priest hadn't planned to report to Lord Morris after all, but to an elf? And since the Chameleon had killed Romak to keep him from talking, did that mean the Chameleon was also working with an elf? Maybe the Chameleon was an elf. No one knew what he really looked like.

"Here we are." Aleksi stopped next to a tent surrounded by half a dozen armed soldiers.

Silas lifted the flap to look inside. A lit lantern, hung from a hook on the tent frame overhead, cast a golden glow on the priest. He was a thin, elderly man, slumped in a chair with his hands tied behind him.

"I'll try the nice approach," Silas whispered to Aleksi. "Lend me a knife and bring a tray of food."

"All right." Aleksi handed him a dagger, then strode toward the galley tent while Silas jabbed the dagger under his belt.

"Good evening, Father." He stepped inside the tent, lowering the flap. "My apologies for keeping you waiting."

The priest straightened in his chair, giving Silas a wary look.

As Silas approached, he suddenly whisked out the dagger. The priest flinched.

"Such a shame, keeping a servant of the Light tied up like this." Silas stepped behind the priest and sliced through the ropes.

With a relieved sigh, the priest massaged his shoulders. "Bless you, my son."

"It's the least I can do." Silas tucked the dagger under his belt. "I was raised to respect those who serve the Light."

"Bless you." The priest pressed his hands together and bowed his head. "May the Light shine upon you always."

Silas sat in the chair on the other side of the table. "You have an Eberoni accent. May I ask why you are traveling in my country?"

"I am but a humble priest, ministering to those who follow the one true god. The Norveshki are also among the Enlightened, so it is my duty to serve them as well."

"I see." Silas noted that the priest's sun pendant was made of gold, and the chain it was hanging from was also pure gold. Not exactly humble. "And how, may I ask, were you serving my people? Did you heal the sick or feed the hungry? Perhaps you were giving alms to the poor with the gold you were carrying?"

The priest's eyes darted nervously toward the flap. "I am but a humble servant of the Light."

"I understand. Why were you going to Woodwyn?"

"The elves are also Enlightened. It is my duty to serve all—"

"You were seen bribing Lord Romak for information and paying him to assassinate me." Silas noted the priest's hands suddenly clench. "You must be surprised to see me still alive."

"I am but a humble priest. I do not know of this lord you mention."

"I see. Then you needn't be concerned that he was arrested as a spy. Or that he was stabbed to death in his jail cell."

The priest grabbed hold of his sun pendant.

Silas leaned forward, resting his elbows on the table. "The Chameleon sneaked into the dungeon, disguised as one of my soldiers, and murdered Romak so he couldn't talk."

The priest's face grew pale as his hand clenched tighter around the sun pendant.

"I wonder what will happen once the Chameleon learns that you've been captured?" Silas sat back. "An interesting dilemma, isn't it? If I left you tied to that chair and called off all the guards, do you think you would survive the night?"

The priest gulped, then flinched when the flap swung open.

Aleksi strode inside with a tray holding a bowl of soup, a hunk of bread, and a cup of water.

Silas leaned forward and whispered, "What if he's the Chameleon? He might have poisoned the soup."

Aleksi gave him a wry look as he dropped the tray on the table.

Silas narrowed his eyes. "I don't think I've seen this soldier before."

Aleksi bit his lip to keep from smiling and quickly left.

"I bet you're hungry." Silas looked over the food. "Would you feel better, Father, if I tasted it for you?"

The priest nodded.

Silas tore off a piece of bread. "You know who Lady Gwennore's parents are, don't you?"

The priest shrugged.

"I heard she was a princess. But a half-breed. I'm surprised the elves want her back."

"She is but a pawn."

Silas tensed inside. A pawn? He would never let her go to Woodwyn. "Then we'll just have to keep her here. After all, she's half Norveshki."

The priest's eyes widened, but he remained silent.

"Her father, Lord Tolenko—does he want her back?" Silas continued his bluff.

The priest smirked. "You don't know everything. Lord Tolenko is dead."

Silas paused for a moment, then slowly ate the piece of bread. So Dimitri's uncle had died in Woodwyn. But not before fathering Gwennore with an elfin princess. "Good news, Father. The bread is safe."

The priest broke off a piece.

"You know, we've been watching you ever since you entered the country. After you talked to Romak, I assumed you were headed to Eberon to report to Lord Morris. But it looks like you were planning on meeting an elf." Silas retrieved the rolled-up note from his pocket.

The priest's hand shook, and his piece of bread tumbled onto the table.

"So is the Chameleon allied with the elves?" Silas

slipped the note back into his pocket. "I wonder what I'll learn once I have this note translated."

The priest grabbed on to the golden sun pendant.

"Are you worried you'll be in trouble?" Silas motioned to the bowl of soup. "You haven't eaten. You should enjoy one last meal before the Chameleon tracks you down, don't you think?"

"You cannot defeat him," the priest whispered.

"Maybe you should question why you serve a master who murders his minions once they're captured."

The priest lifted his chin. "It is an honor to serve my masters. They will bring enlightenment to the entire world."

"They? Who are they? How many?"

The priest gulped. "You won't get anything else from me. I will serve the Light, even in death!" He twisted the bottom half of his sun pendant off and lifted it to his mouth.

"No!" Silas lunged across the table to grab the man's hand. As they struggled, a white poisonous powder was scattered across the table and the tray of food clattered onto the ground.

Suddenly the priest ripped the knife from Silas's belt. He scrambled back. "You will never defeat the Circle of Five. They will conquer the world!"

"Who are the— No!" Silas jumped toward the priest as the man sliced the knife across his own throat.

Blood gushed out, splattering Silas on the face and chest as he caught the falling priest.

"No!" Silas knelt beside the priest, pressing his hands on the bloody gash. "Who are the—" He stopped when he saw the priest's eyes glaze over.

Aleksi ran into the tent. "What's—" He stopped with a jerk at the sight of the dead priest and Silas covered with blood. "Damn. That was the nice approach?"

Chapter Twenty-Six

❧

The next morning, on Garneday, Gwennore was eager to begin her work. Even though she had yet to receive any advice from other physicians, she and Annika both agreed they would need more verna leaves.

After eating breakfast in the workroom, they hurried to Karlan's office to see if Silas had returned. Gwennore hadn't heard any noises coming from his dressing room, so she suspected he was still gone.

When they spotted Dimitri inside the office, Annika halted outside the door and Gwennore dragged her inside.

"Do you know when the general is returning?" Gwennore asked, and Karlan shook his head. When Dimitri turned his back to them to look out the window, she was tempted to kick him in the rear. "The general promised he would help us collect all the materials we need. Since he isn't here, I expect his second in command to honor that promise."

Dimitri glanced back at her with a wary look. "What do you need?"

"Verna leaves, to start with. We've depleted the supply here at the castle. Is there another place nearby that has a large garden?"

Dimitri shifted his weight. "My family has a manor house not too far from here. There's a garden there."

"Excellent." Gwennore smiled, grabbing on to Annika's arm when she tried to slip out the door. "When do we leave?"

Dimitri tugged at his shirt collar. "You're both going?"

"Of course," Gwennore told him. "You'll need us to identify the correct plants. And please bring as many men as you can spare."

"All right." Dimitri strode toward the door. "Be in the courtyard in five minutes."

As he headed down the hallway, Annika groaned. "I can't believe you're dragging me into this."

Gwennore gave her a wry look. "It's a sacrifice you'll have to make for your country."

Annika snorted. "As if I didn't know you're playing matchmaker."

Gwennore grinned. "Come on. Let's get ready to go."

Once Silas learned that the Eberoni king and queen were still encamped across the border, close to Vorushka, he decided to ask them if they knew anything about the Circle of Five. So, after breakfast, he and Aleksi rode the short distance to Vorushka and tethered their horses on the north end of the bridge spanning the Vorus River.

"Wait here." He left Aleksi and strode across the bridge to where four Eberoni soldiers were standing guard. He handed them his sword belt as he addressed them in the Eberoni language, "Please inform King Leo and Queen Luciana that General Dravenko would like a word with them."

One soldier dashed toward the far end of the camp, where a large tent was topped with a pennant in the royal colors of Eberon, red and black. A second soldier motioned for Silas to follow him.

Halfway across the camp, Silas entered a clearing where he spotted Eviana, two little boys, and a young woman scampering about, laughing. She had to be the youngest of Gwennore's adopted sisters.

Sorcha was standing across the clearing, covering her eyes with her hands as she called out in a loud voice, "I can hear you, but I can't see. I hear the buzz of a bumble bee."

Silas recognized it as the poem that was recited during the game of hide and seek. He smiled and waved Eviana to come over.

The little girl ran toward him. "You came back!"

"Yes, I did," he responded in Eberoni as he made a bow. "How have you been, Princess?"

She giggled. "Can I hide behind you?"

"It would be my honor." He noticed the young woman signaling the two little boys to crouch behind a nearby barrel.

"Who are they?" Silas whispered.

"Ewic and Weyn."

She had to mean her twin brother, Eric, and Reynfrid, the son of Ulfrid of Tourin. "Is King Ulfrid here?"

Eviana shook her head. "He had to go home. But Bwigitta is still here."

The soldier nearby cleared his throat and gave Silas a disapproving look. Silas smiled to himself. The soldier must think he was using the little girl for information.

"I can hear you, but I can't see," Sorcha called out. "I hear you hiding behind a tree."

Eviana put a chubby finger up to her mouth. "We have to be quiet," she whispered loudly. "Or Sowcha will hear us."

The young woman approached him. "Ye're General Dravenko?"

"Yes." He blinked with surprise as his senses went on alert. She was a shifter.

"Maeve, you'd better hide!" Eviana whispered. "Sowcha's almost done!"

"This is important," Maeve told her, then gave Silas a stern look. "Where is Gwennore? Why didn't ye bring her with you?"

"Oh, that's wight." Eviana stuck out her bottom lip. "I want Gwennie back. I miss her."

"She misses you, too," Silas told the little girl. "She misses all of you, but she's very busy right now."

"I can hear you, but I can't see," Sorcha yelled. "I'm going to find you. One, two, three!" She lowered her hands as she spun around. Her eyes widened at the sight of Silas.

He lifted a hand in greeting as he smiled. "It's good to see you again."

She gave him an annoyed look as she strode toward him. "Ye came back without Gwennore."

With a huff, Maeve planted her hands on her hips. "That's what I've been saying."

"Me, too!" Eviana put her fists on her hips, mimicking Maeve.

"Lady Gwennore is busy finding a cure for the plague that threatens our country every summer," Silas explained. "We're very grateful for her help."

Maeve nodded. "We heard. Brody was just here and he told us about it."

"I see." Silas figured the shifter was gathering medical advice for Gwennore.

The little boys wandered up to them.

"What happened to our game?" Eric asked, frowning at Silas for interrupting the fun.

"We'll play in a minute." Sorcha reached out to tousle the boy's hair. "And ye need to mind yer manners."

The sapphire ring on Sorcha's hand glittered in the

morning sun, catching Silas's attention. At first, he felt a spurt of joy that she was wearing the ring he'd given her that had belonged to her mother. But then a sudden, ominous thought jumped into his mind.

He grabbed her hand and yanked the ring off.

"What are ye doing?" She stepped back, pulling her hand from his grasp.

"I need to check something." He held the ring up to peer closely at the metal setting. As far as he could tell it was pure silver. "I think it's safe, but to be sure, you might have the physician here examine it."

"What on Aerthlan . . . ?" Sorcha accepted the ring back.

"Lady Gwennore has discovered that the crowns and some of the jewelry owned by the Norveshki royal family were made with a poisonous metal. I would hate to find out that I'd given you something dangerous."

Sorcha gave the ring a dubious look. "I thought this belonged to my mother."

"Our mother was the late queen," Silas said quietly.

Sorcha's mouth fell open, and the ring tumbled from her hand.

Maeve snatched up the ring as it hit the ground. "Then yer father was the king? Ye're a . . . Sorcha's a princess?"

Silas nodded. Sorcha was still dumbfounded, staring at him blankly. "You're third in line to the throne."

Eviana jumped up and down. "Sowcha's a pwincess!"

Maeve laughed.

Sorcha came to with a jerk, then swatted Silas on the shoulder. "Now ye tell me?"

With a grin, Maeve pulled her back. "Now, that's not very princesslike. Ye'll have to behave from now on."

Sorcha scoffed. "Says who?" She glared at Silas. "Any more surprises?"

She'd probably be surprised if she learned that her brothers were dragons. Silas lowered his mental shield. *Can you hear me, Sorcha?*

Sorcha gave him an exasperated look. "Ye're not answering. Ye must be hiding something."

He snapped his shield back in place. She wasn't able to hear him. As far as he knew, Gwen was the only female who could hear the dragons. "I apologize for not telling you earlier. I wasn't sure if you had any interest in Norveshka. You seem quite content to live here with your sisters."

She lifted her chin. "That's true."

Silas nodded. "Even so, I hope you can visit us sometime in the future. You have an older brother, Petras, who would love to see you."

Sorcha's eyes widened. "The king?"

"Yes. And you have a cousin, Annika. She's helping Gwennore right now, and they've become good friends. She would love to see you, too."

"Can I come?" Eviana asked. "You have lots of nice toys."

"I want to go, too!" Eric insisted.

Silas rested a hand on each twin's shoulder. "I would love for you to visit, but that would be your parents' decision."

"Me, too?" Reynfrid asked, gazing up at him with turquoise eyes.

"General Dravenko?" a deep voice called, and Silas glanced up to see Leo approaching.

Leo's gaze dropped to Silas's hands resting on his children's shoulders.

Silas stepped back, dropping his arms to the side. Damn. It must be true. Because of his lightning power, Leo was afraid to touch his own children. There was no mistaking that flash of pained regret in the man's eyes.

"Papa!" Eviana called to him, and Leo gave her a smile and a wink.

Silas bowed his head. "Your Majesty. If you could spare a moment . . ."

"Of course." Leo motioned with a gloved hand. "Luciana and Brigitta are coming."

Silas glanced over his shoulder to see the two queens walking toward them. Luciana had a small clay crock in her hands.

"General!" Brigitta smiled. "It's good to see you."

"Brody was just here," Luciana said as she approached. "He had a few questions for our physician. Here." She handed Silas the crock.

"What is this?" He lifted the top off to see a red powder inside. The scent was strong, making his eyes water.

"It's a spice made from a hot pepper that grows in southern Eberon," Luciana explained. "The royal physician recommended it, so Brigitta and I went to the galley to see if we had any here. I'm afraid this is all we have right now, but I can have more delivered from Ebton Palace. It might take a few days."

"Thank you." Silas put the top back on. "We'll gladly take whatever you can send to Lady Gwennore."

"Please tell her we miss her," Brigitta said. "But we know she's doing something important."

Luciana nodded. "The plague affects our countries, too, so we're happy to assist her in any way we can."

Silas bowed his head. "I appreciate that, Your Majesties."

"Guess what?" Eviana sidled up to her mother. "Sowcha's a pwincess!"

Luciana's eyes widened as she looked at Sorcha. "Really?"

Sorcha shrugged and waved a hand at Silas. "That's what he says."

"Then you're a prince?" Brigitta asked Silas.

He sighed. "I prefer being a general."

Leo crossed his arms, studying Silas. "You're the heir to the throne?"

"For now. My brother, Petras, could still have children." Silas didn't want to admit how unlikely that was.

Leo motioned toward his tent. "Let's have a talk."

Silas followed him, along with Luciana and Brigitta.

"Is Gwennore all right?" Luciana asked.

The memory of her moaning and melting in his arms flashed through Silas's mind. "She . . . she's a bit nervous about whether she can succeed."

Luciana sighed. "That sounds like Gwennie. She doesn't always realize her own worth."

"But she's the most clever woman I know," Brigitta declared. "If anyone can cure the plague, it's her."

Silas nodded. "I believe she can do it, too."

A guard lifted the flap to the large tent, and Leo motioned for them to enter. "Did Brody tell you about the envoy from Woodwyn?"

"Yes." Silas entered the tent with the two queens. "I've discovered the identity of Lady Gwennore's father."

"Really?" Brigitta asked. "Who is he?"

"He was a Norveshki nobleman," Silas replied. "I would tell you more, but I think Lady Gwennore should hear it first."

"You said *was*." Luciana moved to the table and filled four cups with wine. "Has he passed away?"

"Yes." Silas set the clay crock on the table.

Leo sat on one side of the table and motioned for Silas to sit across from him. Brigitta distributed the cups of wine, then took the chair next to him. Luciana sat close to her husband and smiled at him when he squeezed her hand.

Happily married, Silas thought with a pang in his heart. He missed Gwen.

"Brody said the Chameleon has shown up in your country," Leo said. "He murdered a spy in your dungeon."

"Yes." Silas nodded. "That's why I wanted to speak to you."

"You think the Chameleon plans to steal the Norveshki throne?" Luciana asked.

Brigitta shuddered. "When I think how close I came to marrying that monster . . ."

"Did you ever see his real face?" Silas asked.

Brigitta shook her head. "As far as I know, he can masquerade as any person or animal. And he's vicious. He's killed several people in Tourin and Eberon."

"The spy he murdered was a royal secretary named Lord Romak," Silas explained. "One of my men spotted Romak receiving gold from an Eberoni priest. So at first, I suspected Romak was being paid by Lord Morris."

Leo nodded. "That would make sense. Morris has a network of priests all over the mainland, spying for him."

Silas took a sip of wine. "But when the Chameleon murdered Romak, I thought Romak and the priest had to be working for him. I had the priest followed to see where he would go. We stopped him as he was crossing the border into Woodwyn."

"Woodwyn?" Luciana exchanged a surprised look with her husband.

"I questioned the priest last night," Silas continued. "He confirmed my theory about Gwennore's father. And he said we would never defeat the Chameleon."

Leo sat back. "It sounds like he is working for the Chameleon. But why was he going to Woodwyn?"

Brigitta gasped. "Could the Chameleon be an elf?"

"That possibility has occurred to me," Silas admitted.

"He has many secrets." With a grimace, Brigitta shuddered. "I could tell whenever he touched me."

"Did the priest say anything else?" Leo asked.

"Not much." Silas winced. "I was trying to frighten him into talking by telling him that the Chameleon would murder him because he'd been captured. The priest tried to poison himself, and when I stopped him, he grabbed my dagger and slit his own throat."

Luciana and Brigitta sat back with shocked expressions.

Leo frowned. "That makes him sound like one of Morris's priests. I've dealt with a few of them, myself. They're fanatics. Once they're caught, they always try to kill themselves."

"Before he died, the priest said something strange," Silas admitted. "He said the Circle of Five would conquer the world."

Leo's eyes narrowed. "Circle of Five?"

"Yes." Silas eyed him carefully. "I was wondering if you knew anything."

Leo shook his head. "I've never heard of it."

"Neither have I," Brigitta said.

"Does this mean there are five people who want to rule the world?" Luciana asked.

"The priest was carrying this on him." Silas removed the rolled-up note from his pocket. "It's in Elfish. I'll ask Lady Gwennore to translate it when—"

"I can do it." Luciana extended her hand across the table, and Silas placed the note in her palm. She unrolled the note and read it. "It says, *'Princess Gwennore is at Draven Castle. Shall we capture her and deliver her to you?'*"

"Damn," Silas breathed. Gwen was in danger. "The priest referred to her as a pawn."

"We have to protect her," Luciana declared. "Can you send her back here?"

Leo shook his head. "Transporting her a long distance would make it easier for her to be captured."

"I'll protect her," Silas insisted. "You have my word. I won't let any harm come to her."

Luciana and Brigitta exchanged a look.

"Are you taking responsibility for her?" Luciana asked.

"I would like to, yes." Silas shifted in his chair. "If Gwen will accept me."

"Gwen?" Brigitta asked. Her gaze drifted over his uniform. "Green and brown."

Luciana's eyes narrowed. "Exactly."

Exactly what? Silas was confused. He motioned to the note in Luciana's hand. "Is there more? Does it say who wants to capture Gwen?"

She read some more. "It says, *'Plan for taking throne in jeopardy due to return of heir. Will assassinate him soon.'* It's signed with an *'R.'* For 'Romak,' I assume." She looked up at Silas. "Did he try to kill you?"

Silas shrugged. "Obviously, things didn't go the way he planned. Is there anything else?"

She turned the paper over, inspecting both sides. "There's a sun drawn at the bottom here. Hardly surprising, since the priests are avid worshippers of the Light."

Silas took the note to study the drawing. It did appear to be a sun with five rays radiating from a circle. "Damn, it's more than a sun." He pointed at it. "Five rays. Circle of Five."

"Five people," Leo murmured.

Luciana sighed. "I suppose one is the Chameleon."

"And the second one could be Lord Morris," Leo said.

"The third one could be an elf from Woodwyn," Silas suggested. "The one who wants to capture Gwennore and use her as a pawn."

"That still leaves two." Brigitta sat back, shaking her head. "Somehow, I always thought the Chameleon was a loner."

Leo flexed his gloved hands. "He's doing the dirty

work for the group, because he can move among us un-detected."

Silas swallowed hard. "These villains, whoever they may be, would be easier to defeat if they were loners. But they've formed a league. A secret league."

Leo nodded slowly. "They've joined forces. That will make them harder to defeat."

Silas looked around the table. "We need to join forces, too."

Brigitta nodded. "You can count on Rupert and me."

"Good." Silas reached a hand toward Leo. "Are you with me?"

Leo hesitated. "There's a chance, even with my glove, that I might hurt you."

"I know." Silas kept his hand extended. "I'll trust you."

Leo shook his hand, and when nothing happened, he smiled. "We'll be stronger together."

Chapter Twenty-Seven

❧

"You expect me to believe something a tree said?" Petras gave Silas an incredulous look.

"They call themselves the Kings of the Forest," Silas explained. "They've been here for centuries."

"And Woodwyn has been our enemy for centuries," Petras argued. "Why are you believing everything that elfin woman tells you?"

Silas sighed. After returning to Draven Castle, he'd gone straight to the royal office to tell his brother about the tainted crowns and jewelry. "All right, then. Forget about the redwoods and look at this logically. Every queen of Norveshka who survived childbirth eventually went mad. The kings didn't fare much better. What one thing have all the kings and queens had in common?"

"The curse."

"The crowns!" Silas gritted his teeth. "Just have some new crowns made. What do you have to lose?"

"Five hundred years of tradition." Petras scowled at him. "We should send that elfin woman back to Eberon. Freya is feeling better now. She was able to walk to the Great Hall for dinner."

"She's better because Margosha has been giving her a

tonic that Lady Gwennore made for her. And right now, Gwen is trying to find a cure for the plague so our people can start having children again. She's working tirelessly on our behalf. She deserves our respect."

Petras wandered over to the fireplace and gazed at the smoldering coals. "Fafnir told me not to trust her."

Silas groaned inwardly. "Fafnir is the one who gave you the tainted rings."

"The elf is lying!" Petras clenched his fists. "Fafnir would never hurt us."

"He's one of the Ancient Ones, who treated our people like slaves and gave our first king poisonous crowns."

"No!" Petras tossed a log onto the coals, then breathed a gust of fire to set the log ablaze. He spun around to face Silas. "Fafnir was never like the others. When King Magnus begged the Ancient Ones to save the brothers who were dying, the dragons refused. It was Fafnir who came forward to save them. He gave them his own blood, a piece of his own heart—"

"I know the story," Silas interrupted. "But when the three surviving brothers attacked the Ancient Ones, Fafnir didn't take their side. He fought on the side of the Ancient Ones and set the curse on us. Why would you trust him now?"

Petras lifted his chin. "He said he feels responsible for us. He's the one who made us the way we are."

"And he's the one who cursed us."

"That means he's the only one who can undo it!" Petras's eyes gleamed in the firelight. "He says he can help us take over the world. We are the only dragons left. It is our rightful place to rule over those who are less than us."

Silas's heart sank. "We're not like the Ancient Ones, Petras. We're human. Don't forget that."

"Fafnir can help us conquer the rest of the mainland. And he asks for very little in return."

Silas narrowed his eyes. "What exactly does he want?"

"Once we take over Tourin and oust the king, he wants the queen delivered to him."

Brigitta? "Why would an Ancient One want a human female?" Once again, Silas suspected that the dragon who claimed to be Fafnir wasn't actually an Ancient One. If he was a dragon shifter, it would make more sense for him to want a woman. But why Brigitta? How would Fafnir even know her?

A memory came to his mind from the meeting that morning. Brigitta had shuddered. *When I think how close I came to marrying that monster . . .*

Holy Light. Could Fafnir be the Chameleon?

It was close to midnight by the time Silas finished updating Dimitri and Karlan. The news seemed even more ominous as candlelight cast flickering shadows across Karlan's office.

"Circle of Five," Karlan murmured as he leaned back in his chair and gazed at the ceiling.

Dimitri paced about the room. "So the Five could be the Chameleon, Lord Morris, the elf who wants Lady Gwennore, and two unknowns?"

Silas took a seat. "That's what I'm thinking."

Karlan frowned at the ceiling. "If they get their way and take over the world, they'll eventually turn on each other. I can't see five people ruling together peacefully."

Silas nodded. "Especially if they're a bunch of assholes."

Dimitri snorted. "That's a given."

"They're probably using each other for now," Silas said. "Just like Fafnir is trying to use my brother."

Dimitri continued to pace. "This so-called Fafnir wants to use our army and dragons to take over Eberon, Tourin, and Woodwyn?"

"Yes," Silas agreed. "If Fafnir is the Chameleon, like I suspect, he'll wait till Petras has control of those three countries. Then he'll kill him and take his place."

Dimitri sat in the chair beside him. "We should go to the Sacred Well and find this Fafnir."

"I tried that the other day. He goes into hiding if anyone other than Petras comes."

The room grew silent as the three men considered the options before them.

Finally, Silas rose to his feet. "So, what happened here today?"

Dimitri waved a dismissive hand. "Not much. I took Lady Gwennore and Annika to my family's estate so they could raid the garden of some special leaf they wanted. They took it all to the workroom. I haven't seen them since."

"Karlan, could you send someone to bring Lady Gwennore here?" Silas asked. "I need to talk to her."

"She may not be awake," Karlan grumbled as he strode out the door.

Dimitri yawned as he rose to his feet. "I'm off to bed."

"No, stay." Silas motioned for him to sit back down.

Dimitri remained standing. "Why?"

Silas perched on the edge of Karlan's desk. "You'll find out soon enough."

Dimitri huffed, then sat back down.

Silas fiddled with the clay crock he'd brought back from his meeting with Leo and Luciana. He'd worried that he might spill the contents if he tried holding it while flying, so he'd stayed in human form the rest of the day, taking a barge up the Norva River, then riding his horse the rest of the way to Draven Castle. He'd left the crock on Karlan's desk while he'd gone to talk to his brother.

"What is that?" Dimitri asked.

"A spice made from a hot pepper," Silas explained.

"The Eberoni royal physician thinks it could be helpful in curing the plague."

"You think we can really be rid of the curse?"

Silas snorted. "There never was a curse. Just poisoned crowns and some sick rats that like to bite."

Dimitri was silent for a while.

Silas nudged him with a foot. "How long are you going to keep my cousin waiting?"

Dimitri shifted in his chair. "Even without a curse, she could die in childbirth."

"We could die every time we go into battle. You can't stop living because of fear."

Dimitri arched a brow. "Calling me a coward?"

Silas scoffed. "I wouldn't do that to my best friend."

"Good. Then I won't question why you were alone in the cabin with a certain lady, and when she came out, her shirt was buttoned wrong."

Silas winced. "Since when are you so observant?"

Dimitri gave him a wry look. "If you want her to be treated with respect, you should try it yourself."

"I do respect her."

A knock sounded, then the door cracked open and Gwen peered inside. "You wanted to see me?"

"Yes." Silas rushed over to her. "Come in."

She hesitated in the hallway. "It's late. I was about to go to bed."

He leaned close to whisper, "Is that an invitation?"

She shoved him back, causing the door to swing open wide. She stiffened with surprise when she saw Dimitri. "Oh." Her cheeks turned pink. "Good evening. I didn't realize you were here."

Dimitri sighed. "I have no idea why I'm here."

"Come sit down." Silas motioned to the chair next to Dimitri, and Gwen took a seat.

"All right." Silas paced across the room. What was the

best way to break this news? "When we arrested Lord Romak, he tried to bargain for his life by claiming he knew the identity of Lady Gwennore's parents."

She sat back. "How would he know that?"

"I'm not sure, but he was murdered before I could find out." Silas circled around the desk. "Then Brody told me about an envoy from Woodwyn who visited King Leo. The envoy was insisting on taking you back to Woodwyn. After spying on him, Brody learned that you're actually a princess."

"What?" Gwen rose to her feet. Her surprised expression quickly turned to anger. "Why didn't Brody tell me? How dare he discuss this with you and not me!"

Silas winced. This wasn't going well. "He was concerned for your safety."

With a huff, she planted her hands on her hips. "I can take care of myself!"

"Gwen, hear me out."

With a groan of frustration, she sat back down. "Continue."

"The envoy spoke of you with disdain, so Brody feared that the elves would never treat you well—"

"As if I'm being treated well here," she muttered.

Silas winced. "There are people here who care about you. And if I hear anyone say anything bad about you, I'm going to clobber him. Dimitri will, too."

Dimitri looked taken aback for a second, then mumbled, "Right."

"Now back to the envoy." Silas perched on the edge of the desk. "He called you a half-breed."

Gwen stiffened with surprise. "What?"

Silas nodded. "It's true. You're only half elf."

She gave him an incredulous look. "How?"

Dimitri studied her a moment. "I always thought her ears were smaller than the usual elf."

She shrugged with an exasperated expression. "I wouldn't know. I've never met another elf."

"Most people outside of Woodwyn have never met an elf," Silas said. "They're the most reclusive people on Aerthlan."

"If I'm only half elf, then what is the other half?" Gwen asked.

"I had a theory about it, but I didn't want to tell you until I was sure," Silas admitted. "Last night, I asked the priest we captured, and he confirmed it."

Gwen made the sign of the moons with her hands in her lap. "Who are my parents then?"

"All I know about your mother is that she's an elfin princess. Your father was Norveshki."

Gwen's mouth fell open, and Dimitri sat up.

"Your father died in Woodwyn," Silas continued. "I don't know why or how. But he was Norveshki. That's why you feel at home here. It's in your blood. And that's why you can hear the dragons. You inherited it from your father."

Dimitri looked at her, then Silas. "Her father was . . . ?"

"Your uncle." Silas nodded. "Lord Tolenko."

Dimitri dragged in a deep breath, then looked at Gwen again. "She belongs to one of the Three Cursed Clans. My clan."

"I'm Norveshki?" Gwen asked.

"Yes," Silas told her. "You're the daughter of a dragon shifter."

Dimitri stiffened. "Dammit. Why are you—" He glanced at Gwennore and his eyes narrowed. "You already know about us?"

She nodded. "I figured it out, but I won't tell anyone. You can trust me."

"I trust her," Silas said, giving her a smile. "And as a member of the one of the Three Cursed Clans, she has the right to know."

Dimitri winced. "But she's also part elf, and the elves want her back."

"The priest said she was nothing but a pawn to them." Silas removed the rolled-up note from his pocket and handed it to Gwen. "This was the message the priest was taking to someone in Woodwyn. When I visited Leo and Luciana this morning, she translated it for me."

"You saw them?" Gwen unrolled the note and read it, her face growing pale.

"As you can see, you are in danger." Silas took the note back and slipped it into his pocket.

She gave him a worried look. "You're in danger, too."

He leaned over to take her hand. "I can keep you safe here. Leo and Luciana agreed that it's safer for you to stay here. If you travel, you'll become an easier target."

She remained silent.

"I don't want you going to Woodwyn when they consider you a political pawn," Silas continued. "You belong in Norveshka just as much as you do in Woodwyn."

"You're my cousin," Dimitri whispered.

"Right. You have family here. And friends." Silas squeezed her hand. "You have me."

Dimitri suddenly rose to his feet and headed for the door. "Silas, we need to talk." He opened the door and strode into the hallway.

What the hell? Silas released Gwen's hand. "I'll be right back."

He stepped outside, shutting the door behind him. "What's the—" He stiffened with surprise when Dimitri grabbed his shirt collar.

"What are your intentions toward my cousin?" Dimitri demanded.

"What?"

"Since my father's death last year, I am the head of the

Tolenko clan." Dimitri slammed him against the wall. "So I ask you again. What are your intentions?"

Silas scoffed. "What happened to being best friends?"

Dimitri twisted the collar in his fist.

"All right, Papa Bear." Silas lifted his hands in surrender. "Relax. I've already told Gwen that I want to marry."

Dimitri's eyes widened. "You did?"

"Yes. Unlike you, I'm not afraid of the damned curse."

The door cracked open and Gwen peeked outside. "What's going on? I heard something hit the wall. It sounded like a cannonball."

Silas winced. He wasn't that hardheaded.

Dimitri released Silas's collar and smoothed out his shirt. "Just a friendly discussion."

Silas snorted. "Right. Between best friends."

Dimitri gave him a wry look. "I'll marry your cousin when you marry mine."

"Deal."

Gwen frowned at them. "Surely you're not discussing Annika or myself without our knowledge. We will be deciding our own futures. Thank you." She turned her back on them and strode down the hallway.

"I—I'm not done talking," Silas called after her.

"As the leader of our clan, I'm responsible for you," Dimitri yelled.

She ignored them both and passed through the doorway into the courtyard.

"Damn," Dimitri muttered.

Silas sighed. "This business of marriage might be more difficult than we thought."

Chapter Twenty-Eight

❧

Gwennore slept late the next morning after tossing and turning most of the night. She was a princess? Half Norveshki? Dimitri was her cousin? She'd met his mother at the manor house and had really liked her. Now she realized the woman was her aunt.

No wonder Gwennore had felt a connection to the land here. And a connection to the dragons. She had family here. She was a member of the Tolenko clan and the daughter of a shape-shifting dragon.

But what about the elfin part of her? Why had she been sent away as a babe? Had they considered her unworthy since she was a half-breed? If she was a princess, then her mother must have been from the royal family and fallen in love with Lord Tolenko. Had it been a secret affair, or had the two lovers married? How had her father died? Had he been murdered for fathering a child with an elfin princess?

And why did someone in Woodwyn want her captured and taken back to use as a pawn?

Silas wanted her to stay here. Even Leo and Luciana thought she was safer here.

But what did she want?

Her thoughts kept returning to the passionate moment

in the cabin. Could she trust her heart to Silas? Her immediate reply was *yes*. Did she love the countryside and her new friends? *Yes*. Could the Norveshki people accept her as Silas's wife and future queen? *No*.

Her heart clenched with regret, and then a spurt of anger. If she cured the plague she might be accepted, but why did she always feel a need to prove herself?

While eating breakfast with Margosha and Annika in the workroom, she told them what she'd learned about her parents. They were delighted she was half Norveshki and insisted she remain here with her new family and friends.

The verna leaves they had picked the day before had dried enough that they set to work, tearing them into tiny pieces. As the pile grew on the table, they chatted about what was happening around the castle.

"Dimitri asked me to have dinner with him tonight in the Great Hall," Annika announced, her cheeks flushed with excitement.

"Oh, that's wonderful!" Margosha smiled. "Do you have a pretty gown you can wear? I could loan you one."

While the two women discussed what Annika should wear for her date with Dimitri, Gwennore's mind wandered back to the conversation she'd overheard between Dimitri and Silas. Were the two men in some sort of race now to prove their honorable intentions?

"When I attended the queen this morning, she was feeling much better," Margosha said. "She insisted on getting dressed, so she could take a walk in the garden."

"That's excellent news!" Annika grinned. "I think the verna tea is working."

"It looks that way." Gwennore glanced at her greenish fingertips. They were becoming stained from two days of handling verna leaves.

Margosha sighed. "But because it's Opalday, Her Majesty wanted her opal ring back."

"Oh, dear." Annika winced. "Did you tell her it was poison?"

Margosha shook her head. "I didn't want to frighten or agitate her, so I told her we were still cleaning her jewelry."

"That was wise," Gwennore told her. "I don't think the queen is healthy enough to handle any stress right now."

"Olenka told me that everyone is saying you're a witch," Annika muttered. "And you're brewing secret tonics up here in your lair."

Margosha snorted. "One of the ladies-in-waiting asked me if you could make her a love potion."

Gwennore sighed. Could the Norveshki people accept her? As a witch perhaps, but not as a queen.

A knock sounded at the door, then Silas peered inside.

The rascal. Making deals with Dimitri as if marriage was their decision alone. Gwennore ignored him and scooped some shredded verna leaves into a large stone mortar.

"Silas!" Margosha waved him over. "Come in."

He strolled toward them. "I thought I would check to see how you're doing."

Just the sound of his voice made Gwennore's skin tingle.

"We're working," Annika told him, then nudged Gwennore with her elbow.

She glanced up and discovered that Silas was watching her closely. With a quick movement, she grabbed the pestle and slammed it into the mortar.

The sound startled Annika, and she leaned close to whisper, "Careful. You could break it."

Margosha cleared her throat, then smiled at Silas. "As you can see, we're preparing the verna leaves. What is that you're carrying?"

He set a small clay crock on the table. "I had planned

to give this to Lady Gwennore last night, but she left before I was finished with our conversation."

The pestle made a grinding noise as Gwennore pressed it down and twisted it.

Annika lifted the lid on the crock and peered inside. "Holy Light, this stuff is strong." Her eyes watered as she closed the lid.

"It's a spice made from a hot pepper that grows in southern Eberon," Silas explained. "It's what the Eberoni royal physician recommended. This was all that Luciana had on hand at their camp, but she said she would have more delivered from Ebton Palace. I'll go back to Vorushka tomorrow to pick it up."

"Thank you." Margosha slid the crock across the table to Gwennore. "What do you think?"

She opened the lid and took a sniff. *Holy goddesses.* "It certainly seems powerful enough to wipe out a disease."

Annika nodded. "I'm thinking a little bit will go a long way."

Gwennore glanced at the ground-up verna leaves in her mortar. "We could make a tonic of verna leaves and this spice, but it might be too hot for people to swallow."

"We could dilute it," Annika suggested. "Or mix it with honey to sweeten the taste. I've always found honey to be beneficial."

Gwennore tilted her head as she considered. Honey. She turned to Silas. "Wasn't the drink the trolls made based on honey?"

"You're talking to me again?"

She gave him a wry look.

His eyebrows lifted, but he held his gaze steady on her. "Yes, their mead is made with honey."

"You're thinking about using it?" Margosha asked Gwennore.

She nodded. "If we dilute it with water, I think it would make an excellent base for a medicinal tonic. It would have enough sweetness to offset the heat of the pepper spice."

Annika grinned. "And if it makes people drunk, it will be very popular!"

"Could you buy some mead from the trolls?" Gwennore asked Silas.

"They won't accept gold or jewels in payment, but I could barter with some chickens and maybe a goat."

Her heart raced at the way he was watching her so intently. She cleared her throat. "I'm sure they'll cooperate once they know we'll be using it to cure the plague."

He nodded. "I'll bring you a barrel by tonight."

She gave him a hesitant smile. "Thank you."

"Then we can have dinner together."

Her heart squeezed. Memories of their passionate moment in the cabin flashed through her mind. Rule number five had been: *Beware of kissing a dragon. He won't burn you, but he might make you melt.* Holy goddesses, she felt like she was melting now just from the sound of his voice and the hungry way he was looking at her.

But she was afraid to give in. Afraid she would jeopardize his future. Afraid she would never be accepted. And still peeved that he and Dimitri thought they could decide a woman's future without consulting her.

She motioned to the pile of shredded verna leaves on the table. "I have to grind all this up. And it's only the first batch." She pointed at the stacks of leaves piled up on other tables. "As you can see, I'm going to be busy all day."

"We need to talk," he said quietly.

"I'm listening." She went back to work, adding more shredded leaves to the mortar.

"In private," he added.

Annika nudged Gwennore with her elbow.

She heaved a sigh and shot Silas an annoyed look. "What is it?"

"You want to hear it now?" he asked drily, and she nodded. "Fine. Last night, I tried to sneak into your bedchamber so we could have hours of wild and passionate lovemaking, hot enough to burn the sheets off your bed. But I couldn't because Dimitri had bunked down in front of my dressing room door with a sword. The idiot thinks he has to protect your honor."

Annika covered her mouth as she choked on a laugh.

Margosha sat back with a scandalized look.

Gwennore's face grew hot. The rascal. She didn't know whether to be mortified or excited. *Excited.* "Please convey my gratitude to my cousin."

A flash of gold shot through Silas's eyes. "I understand." He turned and left the room.

Her heart clenched as she fought an urge to run after him and fling her arms around him.

"What's going on with you two?" Annika asked.

Gwennore blinked back tears. There was no point in denying it. She was hopelessly in love. Silas was everything she'd ever wanted. He believed in her. Trusted her. Loved her. He was the right man for her.

But she couldn't get over this niggling fear that she wasn't the right woman for him.

That evening, some soldiers arrived at the workroom with a barrel of mead. Gwennore told herself she wasn't disappointed when Silas didn't deliver it himself. But then Annika excused herself so she could have dinner with Dimitri. And Margosha left so she could attend the queen in the Great Hall and taste all of Her Majesty's food.

Gwennore was left alone in the workroom with her hands sore from grinding leaves all day. *Fool*, she chided herself. She could be having dinner with Silas.

She rushed back to her bedchamber and Nissa helped her into a lavender gown that matched her eyes. Her heart pounding, she dashed off to the Great Hall. When she entered, she noticed that dinner had already begun. Courtiers were eating and drinking at the different tables, busily chatting and laughing.

On the far side of the room, on the dais, the royal family was having dinner. King Petras sat on a jewel-encrusted chair in the middle with his queen to his left and his younger brother to his right. Silas looked glumly at the plate of food in front of him.

Would he be happy to see her? Gwennore started to cross the room. As courtiers noticed her, they stopped talking. Stopped eating.

She swallowed hard. Where on Aerthlan could she sit? The table where she'd sat before was close to the dais, but Dimitri was there with Annika. She didn't want to interfere with their date.

She slowed at a stop, suddenly afraid she'd made an enormous mistake. A hush fell over the room, as all the courtiers stared at her.

Silas glanced up and grinned when he spotted her. His chair made a scratching noise as he pushed it back. He jumped off the dais and strode toward her.

The whispers began.

She's bewitched him.

She must have slipped him a love potion.

We can't have an elfin witch for our next queen!

It was happening again. Gwennore fought the urge to run away like she'd always done at Ebton Palace whenever she'd overheard the ugly remarks. She clenched her fists. *Don't let them know how much they hurt you.*

Silas stopped in front of her and bowed. "As heir to the Norveshki throne, I would like to welcome Lady Gwennore back to her homeland."

Gasps sounded around the room.

Homeland?

This isn't her home.

"Twenty-two years ago, Lord Tolenko traveled to Woodwyn as our official envoy. There he met an elfin princess and fathered a child with her, Lady Gwennore." Silas motioned to her. "This lovely lady is both an elfin princess and a Norveshki noblewoman. And she is working tirelessly to cure the plague that has caused us so much suffering. She deserves our respect and admiration."

Gwennore blinked back tears and held her head high. The king and queen were still regarding her with suspicious glares, and a flurry of whispers floated all around her as the courtiers devoured this latest morsel of juicy gossip.

Silas extended a hand to her.

She placed her hand in his, and he led her over to Dimitri's table. As she sat next to Annika, her friend squeezed her hand.

"I'm glad you came," Annika whispered.

Silas took the seat across from her, next to Dimitri, and motioned for a servant to bring them food.

Annika leaned close to whisper in her ear, "You just rescued your cousin. I was about to jump his bones."

Gwennore whispered back, "If you jump his bones, I'll jump Silas's."

"Deal."

Silas narrowed his eyes. "Are you two making plans without us?"

Gwennore gave him a sweet smile. "Now you know how it feels."

The next day was Rubeday, and when Gwennore saw the ladies all dressed in shades of red and burgundy, she was reminded of her first day at Draven Castle. A full week had passed, and she'd gone from being an outsider to being a Norveshki noblewoman.

That afternoon, Gwennore and Annika were in the workroom, grinding up the last of the verna leaves, when Silas came in, loaded down with two large canvas sacks.

Gwennore rose to her feet. "I didn't expect you back this soon."

"What did you bring us?" Annika asked.

He set the sacks on a worktable and loosened the drawstring on the first bag to reveal the reddish-orange powder inside. "This is the hot pepper that Luciana promised you. It came from Ebton Palace."

Gwennore peered inside. As powerful as the spice was, they planned to use only a few spoonfuls for each batch of tonic. "This will last us a long time. Thank you."

Silas opened the second bag. "I was surprised to see this." He pulled out a bulbous brown root. "According to King Ulfrid, this is from the ginka plant."

"You saw Rupert?" Gwennore used the name her sister Brigitta always used for her husband.

"Yes. Brody made it to Tourin last night and told the king and royal physician what you were doing here. The physician recommended this root, so Rupert gathered up all he could find. This morning, he took this sack to a barge on the Norva River, then he used his wind power to whoosh upstream really fast. On the way, he stopped and picked up the spice coming from Ebton Palace. So thanks to his wind power, these sacks arrived in Vorushka before noon."

Annika's eyes widened. "That sounds amazing. I wish I could have seen him wielding his power."

"We could have used him on the barge that took us upriver," Silas muttered. "It would have been faster for me to fly, but I didn't want to try carrying two sacks."

"No, you might have dropped one," Annika said.

Gwennore stiffened. "What?" She glanced at Annika and then Silas. "She knows you're a dragon?"

He shrugged. "Everyone in the Three Cursed Clans is allowed to know."

Annika nodded. "And that includes you."

Gwennore snorted. "I never thought I would be happy to belong to a cursed clan."

Annika laughed.

Gwennore smiled at Silas. "Thank you for bringing this stuff to us."

He smiled back. "Anytime."

"And it was very sweet of Rupert to get these sacks to Vorushka so quickly," Gwennore added.

Silas nodded. "I think he was happy to have a reason to see his wife and son again. They were still at the camp."

"Brigitta stayed there?" Gwennore asked.

"All your sisters are there. They're worried about you. I don't think it's safe for you make the trip to see them, so I invited them all here. They're considering it."

Gwennore's heart filled with warmth. "I would love to show them how beautiful this country is."

Annika picked up a ginka root and studied it. "I don't think I've ever seen this before."

"I have," Gwennore replied. "Sister Colleen used it for multiple illnesses at the convent, but mainly for curing stomachaches." She pulled one out of the bag. "I've been concerned that the hot pepper might upset some people's stomachs, but if we include this in the tonic, I think it will offset any ill effects from the spice."

"Excellent!" Annika emptied the sack, making a pile of ginka roots.

"We'll have to slice them, then grind them into a mash," Gwennore said as she reached for a knife.

"Need some help?" Silas pulled a dagger from his boot. After an hour they had sliced and chopped the entire pile of ginka root. As the sun moved toward the horizon, it shone brightly through the westward-facing windows. The room became hot, so Gwennore opened the windows wider.

A large bird flew past. An eagle.

"Brody?" She stepped aside as the bird shot through the window and flopped onto the floor.

"Brody!" Gwennore dashed over to look at him. The eagle lay on its side, breathing heavily. "He must be exhausted."

"I'll bring some food!" Annika rushed out the door.

Silas picked up the folded stack of clothes Brody had left beside his pallet where he'd slept in dog form. "Here. You need these?" He set the clothes beside the eagle.

"I'll step outside." Gwennore waited in the hallway till she heard Silas call her back inside.

Brody was now in human form, sitting on the floor wearing a pair of breeches. He winced as he slipped on the shirt. "My arms are sore."

Silas sat on the floor beside him. "You flew all the way from Tourin?"

Brody collapsed back on the floor, his shirt unbuttoned. "All the way from the Isle of Mist."

"The Isle of Mist?" Gwennore sat next to him. "Why on Aerthlan did you go there?"

"The Seer has some medical knowledge. And he's—"

"You saw the Seer?" Silas asked.

Brody nodded his head. "He's lived for a—"

"How do you know the Seer?" Gwennore asked. "I didn't think anyone ever saw him."

"Of course people see him," Brody muttered. "He gets supplies every now and then from the Isle of Moon. That's how his prophecies get spread."

Gwennore's mouth fell open. She'd lived on the Isle of

Moon most of her life, and she'd never known this. "How come I never heard about that?"

"The sailors are sworn to secrecy." Brody sat up. "Can I finish my story now? The Seer has lived a really long time, almost a hundred years, so I thought I would ask him what his secret is for living such a long and healthy life."

Gwennore leaned forward. "What did he say?"

"Garlic." Brody buttoned his shirt. "Lots of garlic. He recommends you include some in your tonic."

"I see." Gwennore glanced at Silas. "Do you know where we can get a big supply of garlic?"

"I'll check into it," Silas said, then glanced at Brody. "What do you know of the Seer? What is he like?"

With an exhausted sigh, Brody fell back onto the floor. "He has bad breath."

Chapter Twenty-Nine

❧❧❧

Over the next two days, Silas helped Gwen as much as he could. He was worried about her safety, but with all the errands he had to do, he wasn't able to stay by her side. He took some relief in the knowledge that Brody was spending most of his time as her guard dog.

On the first day, Sapphirday, Silas located a supply of garlic and brought it to Draven Castle. He enlisted a few servants to help peel and chop all the garlic. Unfortunately, the kitchen staff was already swamped with work, preparing for the grand feast that would signal the opening of the Summoning.

His next mission was to collect bottles and clay jars so they could store and distribute the tonic Gwen was making. So that afternoon, he flew to the army camp, shifted and dressed, then rode into Vorushka with Aleksi and a troop of soldiers. There, they bought all the small containers they could find. Then they transported them by barge and wagon back to Draven Castle, arriving late that night.

He was glad to have the troop of soldiers with him. The Summoning would begin soon, and that meant a great deal of visitors would be arriving. Gwen's would-be captor or even the Chameleon might use the event to sneak into the castle.

As busy as Silas was, he was only able to see Gwen a few minutes at a time. She was equally busy, and he worried that she was working herself too hard. But she was determined to have the first batch of tonic ready to hand out at the Summoning, when so many of the Norveshki people would be gathered together.

Gwen convinced them that they should promote the medicine as a fertility tonic. That way, more people would be willing to take it.

By the second day, Ametheday, Gwen and her friends were bottling the tonic. Silas was busy seeing to the security of the castle as the crowds of people started to arrive. Nobles were given rooms in the castle, while commoners either found rooms in the inns in Dreshka or pitched tents along the river.

Preparations for the Summoning began in earnest. At dawn, the kitchen began roasting huge slabs of meat for the opening feast. Servants constructed a dais at the northern side of the courtyard and set two jewel-encrusted thrones on top. Benches were placed in rows to fill the rest of the courtyard with a wide aisle down the middle, leading from the dais to the southern gate.

More servants set up a long line of tables in the Great Hall. These were covered with red velvet tablecloths. The feast would take up every inch of the tables. Nobles would be allowed to go down the buffet table first, then they would eat at the other tables in the Great Hall. After the commoners had their turn, they would eat while sitting on the benches in the courtyard.

As more and more people waited for the feast to begin, the nobles gathered in the courtyard, while the commoners waited outside the southern gate. Silas preferred to watch everyone from the roof of the castle. He was able to walk along all four wings of the castle, observing everything that was happening both outside the castle and in the courtyard.

As the sun set, horns blared to signal the beginning of the opening feast. The commoners gave a cheer and eagerly waited for the southern gate to open and allow them inside. Meanwhile, the nobles hurried into the Great Hall so they could have their pick of the buffet table. The king and queen would already be there with their own table filled with dishes just for them.

Silas was supposed to eat at the royal table, but he remained on the roof, carefully watching the crowd for anyone who appeared suspicious. He spotted Brody in dog form, weaving through the crowd to make sure the Chameleon wasn't sneaking in.

As the sun set, torches were lit and placed around the courtyard. Silas spotted Margosha and some servants passing out bottles of Gwen's tonic to the commoners. No doubt, more tonic was being distributed inside the Great Hall. Some soldiers had already distributed the tonic in Dreshka, and tomorrow, as the Summoning officially began, Aleksi was planning to take several cases to Vorushka.

Gwen had warned him that it might take a few months before they saw any results from the tonic. For now, Silas hoped she would finally have some time for him. The best way for him to protect her would be to marry her. But he needed time alone with her so he could court her and win her heart.

Gwennore woke up early on Diamonday to prepare the bottles that would go to Vorushka. Annika and Margosha both came to help, and in a few hours, they were done.

Annika alerted one of the soldiers standing guard at the door, and he dashed off to find Aleksi.

"I'm so glad we're finished," Gwennore said as she checked the cases to make sure the bottles were packed well with sheep's wool to keep them from breaking. "I've been curious about the Summoning. When does it start?"

"Usually about noon," Margosha said as she sat back in a chair and stretched her legs.

Annika peered into the barrel of mead. "There's hardly any left. We'll need another barrel."

Gwennore nodded. They had used only a spoonful of mead for each bottle, but they'd filled more than five hundred bottles, so they were running low on all their supplies.

"Do you think the tonic will actually work?" Margosha asked. "I'd hate to think we did all this labor in vain."

Gwennore took a seat and massaged her sore shoulders. "In theory it should work. We included several ingredients that are known to kill disease. If the infertility problems are caused by a small amount of plague still lingering in each person, and the tonic kills that plague, then their infertility should fade away."

Annika sighed. "If it doesn't work, our country could eventually die."

Margosha winced. "Don't say that."

Annika sat at the table across from Gwennore. "I suppose the few fertile women like you and me will have to have a dozen children."

"What?" Gwennore gave her an incredulous look.

Annika grinned. "It will be our patriotic duty."

Gwennore picked up a clove of garlic off the table and threw it at her.

"The tonic will work." Margosha nodded, as if trying to convince herself. "It has to work."

Aleksi entered with half a dozen soldiers. "Is the tonic ready?"

"Yes." Gwennore showed him the three cases. "Be careful transporting them. Oh, and tell the people in Vorushka that they mustn't drink the entire bottle at once. They should take only a sip every day, so it should last them about a week. In that time, we hope to have more ready."

"All right." Aleksi ordered two men to pick up each case.

Gwennore followed them out the door. "And can you ask the people to return the empty bottles? We're going to run out soon."

"I'll arrange something with the town mayor," Aleksi said as his men carried the cases down the stairs. "Don't worry. We can handle this. You should get some rest. Silas thinks you've been working too hard."

"Where is he?"

"Up on the roof with Dimitri, watching over everything." Aleksi waved as he started down the steps. "See you later!"

"Thank you!" Gwennore called after him. As Aleksi charged down the stairs, he passed by Brody on his way up.

"Brody." Gwennore smiled at him. It wasn't often she saw him in human form. "What have you been up to?"

"I was going through the crowd, seeing if I could catch the scent of the Chameleon, but he doesn't seem to be here." He walked with Gwennore back into the workroom and greeted Annika and Margosha.

Annika passed him what was left over from their breakfast. "Has the Summoning begun yet? It's almost noon."

Brody shook his head with his mouth full of bread. "The king and queen haven't shown up yet."

"Really?" Margosha frowned. "I hope the queen is all right. She seemed a bit tired this morning when I saw her."

"She stayed up late last night at the feast," Annika said.

"Let's make some verna tea in case she needs it." Gwennore added more wood to the fireplace so they could heat the kettle of water.

Just as the water started to boil, Olenka dashed into the room. "Do you have any more of that tea?"

"We're making some," Gwennore told her. "Is the queen not well?"

"She's a little weak, but she's insisting on going to the Summoning. The king thought some of this tea would help." Olenka winced. "They're both intending to wear their crowns."

"Oh, no," Gwennore groaned.

"Here, let me have the tea." Margosha set the teapot on a wooden tray. "I'll take this to her and try to convince her not to wear the crown."

"Good luck," Annika told her as she and Olenka hurried from the room.

"Let's go to the courtyard," Annika suggested. "I want to see what happens."

Gwennore nodded. "I'm curious, too."

"I'll take you," Brody offered. He gulped down a cup of water. "But stay right next to me. Silas is worried about someone trying to kidnap you."

Annika snorted and rested her hand on the dagger at her belt. "They'll have to get through me first."

Several hours passed, and Gwennore was soon bored as she waited on a wooden bench in the courtyard. Brody had run out of his allotted time to remain human, so he'd gone to Karlan's office to shift back into a dog. He was now curled up at her feet, napping.

She glanced up at the roof. Dimitri and Silas were up

there, making the rounds. Every now and then, she caught a glimpse of him and waved. He always waved back.

The crowd grew restless, and some ventured into the Great Hall for a bite to eat, while others wandered out the gate to see the garden. Some lay down on the benches to take a nap. Most of the nobles retired to their rooms.

Late in the afternoon, Margosha and Olenka found Gwennore and told her that the queen had recovered enough to get dressed. The Summoning would begin soon.

Horns blared, and the crowd rushed to find their places on the benches. Nobles hurried into the courtyard to take their seats close to the dais.

After a few minutes, the horns blared again, and the king and queen exited through the double doors of the southern wing and stepped into the courtyard. They paused as the crowd gave them a cheer.

Gwennore groaned as she noted the crowns on their heads. King Petras strode down the aisle toward the dais, but the queen was stopped by numerous commoners who wanted to give her bouquets of flowers. Soon, she had more flowers than she could hold, so Margosha and Olenka took them from her.

Gwennore stepped closer as she noticed the glazed look in the queen's eyes. Was she about to faint? "Your Majesty, you should lie down."

Freya glanced at her with unfocused eyes. "Who—who are you to tell me what to do?"

"I'm a healer, remember? I've been making the tea that's been helping you."

Freya frowned at her. "You're the elfin witch who took my baby away."

"Please, Your Majesty. Go back to your room so you can rest. That crown is too heavy—"

"You want my crown, don't you?" Freya screeched. "You've bewitched Silas, so you can be the next queen!"

"Your Majesty, you must remain calm." Margosha tried to ease her back, but the queen shoved her away, then turned toward Gwennore with a frantic look.

"It's all your fault," Freya hissed. "You've been poisoning me, haven't you? You want me dead!"

"No, Your—" Gwennore gasped when the queen seized her by the arms and shook her.

Brody growled at the queen, then bit her skirt to try to drag her away.

"Stop!" King Petras ran toward them with Karlan right behind him.

Gwennore grabbed the queen's wrists, and her gift immediately activated. Racing pulse, irregular, lurching heartbeat. "Your Majesty! We need to get you to your—"

"No!" the queen screamed, then suddenly fell to her knees, a hand pressed to her chest.

Screams and shouts rang out as the crowd pressed closer to see what was happening. Brody growled and snapped at people to keep them back, while Margosha and Annika yelled at them to give the queen some room.

As Freya collapsed, her crown fell off, and Gwennore caught the queen's head to keep her from banging it on the stone pavement.

"Your Majesty." Gwennore's mind raced, trying to think of some kind of medicine that might help.

Suddenly, a convulsion racked the queen's body, and Gwennore felt a spurt of panic. No, this couldn't be happening. The queen went limp, her eyes glazing over as her head turned to the side.

"No." Gwennore gave the queen a shake. "Your Majesty!"

King Petras shoved her aside. "What have you done?"

He knelt beside his wife. "Freya!" He shook her, but there was no response.

Tears burned Gwennore's eyes. "She—she's gone."

"No!" Petras lifted the queen into his arms and rocked her. "No, no! She's going to be fine."

Murmurs spread through the crowd, then wails grew in volume as people realized their queen was dead.

Gwennore turned away, her heart sinking. Each time the king cried his wife's name, she could feel his pain as sharp as a stab from a knife. She'd failed. She'd failed to keep the queen alive.

Karlan stepped close to her and whispered, "Go back to your workroom now."

She gave him a dazed look.

"Go!" he hissed.

She stepped back, suddenly realizing that the crowd was pointing at her.

Dimitri dashed up to her. "Let's go."

"Wait!" King Petras rose to his feet, his eyes flaring gold as he focused on Gwennore. "You. You murdered my wife."

The crowd began to chant, "Kill her! Kill her!"

"Arrest her!" Petras shouted.

As guards started toward her, Dimitri gave her a shove. "Run out the gate! Silas will get you."

Gwennore hesitated only a second as she saw Dimitri and Karlan holding back the soldiers. She turned and dashed toward the southern gate while Annika pushed back the encroaching crowd and Brody snapped and growled at them

Tears ran down Gwennore's cheeks. So many people wanted her dead! She dropped her mental shield as she darted through the gate and into the garden. *Puff! Silas! I'm coming.*

She looked back. Soldiers were streaming through the

gate. A spear landed close by, thudding into the ground. Her heart lurched and in a panic, she ran through the garden, then skidded to a halt at the cliff that overlooked the river and town of Dreshka.

She glanced back. The soldiers were coming.

A screech sounded overhead. *Puff.* He launched from the castle roof, shooting a gust of fire to keep the soldiers from advancing.

She reached her arms up, and he swooped down, catching her and pulling her to his chest. *Puff.* She wrapped her arms around his forelegs as more tears ran down her cheeks.

His mighty wings beat the air as he lifted higher and higher into the air.

Silas. I was so afraid.

He angled his head back to look at her with his golden eyes. *Don't worry. I have you.*

Chapter Thirty

❦

Gwennore closed her eyes and let the wind whooshing past them dry the tears on her face. *You're safe now*, she told herself over and over to combat the memory of a bloodthirsty crowd chanting, "Kill her! Kill her!"

Gwen. Silas's soothing voice entered her mind. *Don't think about them. They don't know you. They didn't know the queen was ill or that the king and queen have been going mad.*

"The queen is dead," Gwen whispered.

I know. I saw it from the rooftop.

"I was panicking. I wanted to help her, but there was nothing I could do."

I know, sweetheart. I panicked, too, when I saw what was happening. After I sent Dimitri to you, I thought I had better shift, so I started tearing off my clothes.

On the rooftop? What a shame she had missed it.

I heard that.

She swatted his leg.

Did you just hit me? After I rescued you?

With a smile, she hugged his leg. He'd said the same thing the first time he'd rescued her. "How many times have you saved me now? Four? Five?"

I lost count. He made a huffing noise that sounded like a chuckle when she swatted him again.

"I suppose I should thank you."

I suppose you should.

Her smile widened as they repeated more lines from the first time they'd met. Where was he taking her? She glanced at the setting sun. They had to be headed north-west.

I have a cabin on a mountain not far from the Tourinian border. You'll be safe there.

Her smile faded. Did it matter that she was half Nor-veshki? Or that this country felt like home? How could she remain here when people wanted to kill her?

Gwen, don't give up on us. The people who attend the Summoning fit into two categories. They came there to complain, or they came because they're bored and look-ing for something to gossip about. They represent a small portion of the population. Most of the Norveshki are friendly, hardworking folk who would never judge you unfairly. They'll be grateful for everything you've done. And they'll give you all the respect that you deserve.

Could she believe that? She wanted to. As she glanced down at the green hills and sparkling blue lakes, her heart ached with a yearning to call this place home. And as she leaned her cheek against Puff's soft leathery skin, she longed to call him her dragon. Her first and only love.

His forelegs gave her a squeeze.

He must have heard her. Her cheeks grew warm with embarrassment. It hardly seemed fair that he could hear all her thoughts when she heard only what he wanted to tell her.

She gasped as a sudden jumble of thoughts raced through her mind, so crowded with her own thoughts, she could hardly keep herself separate. And even more power-ful was the sudden surge of emotion that swept over her like a flood. Love. Anxiety. Determination. Love. Desire. Frustration. Love. A longing so great, it made her heart ache. Pain.

Silas. He'd opened his mind completely, and most of his thoughts and feelings were focused on her. With a shock, she realized the pain he felt was real. He hadn't been joking about rule number two and a dragon's extra-large heart.

Just as suddenly he shut the mental door, and she felt an immediate sense of relief. There had been too much in her mind all at once.

Gwen, now you know how I feel.

Tears came to her eyes. He loved her. He loved her something fierce. Her heart filled with so much love and longing for him, she thought it might burst. "Silas."

Snookums.

She snorted. The rascal. She nestled against him and watched the lovely scenery go by. He swooped along a valley with high mountains on each side. Wind whistled off the snowcapped peaks, but she remained warm against his chest. "I love flying with you."

Rule number six, he told her with his deep voice. *If you fall in love with a dragon, don't be afraid to fly. He can take you higher.*

She smiled to herself. Higher. With Silas, she definitely felt as if she was flying higher. She was becoming the best that she could be.

As they flew into the sunset, the blue sky was painted with shades of pink, yellow, and orange. And down below, there were different shades of green. They were surrounded by color, and Gwennore was suddenly struck by how lovely the world was. The death of the queen and her narrow escape faded away, leaving her with a feeling of peace.

We're almost there.

They were approaching a wide expanse of glittering ice that reflected the rays of the setting sun.

"What is that?"

A glacier. My cabin is nearby. His wings beat the air, lifting them higher to the mountain on the north side of river of ice.

She spotted a rocky cliff, then a stretch of green pasture. A log cabin sat by itself, its roof covered with grass.

Silas swooshed down and released her onto the grass. It was cool against the palms of her hands as she pushed herself to her feet.

He landed neatly, then folded his wings as he turned slowly to face her. The last rays of the sun made his scales gleam green and purple.

She smiled at him. "You make a very handsome dragon."

His golden eyes glimmered as he stalked toward her. *Thank you.*

When she reached up, he lowered his head so she could touch his face.

Come, I want to show you something. He walked toward the edge of the cliff, then settled on the grass.

She followed him. "What is it?"

Patience. It will come.

She sat next to him. Darkness fell around them, and the air grew chilly. The wind picked up, whisking down the glacier, and she shivered.

Cold? He unfolded his left wing and draped it over her to block the wind.

With a smile, she snuggled up close to his warm body. "What are we waiting for?"

Look and listen.

She glanced up and as the sky grew dark, millions of

bright stars filled the sky. "It's beautiful." The twin moons looked closer than they had ever been before. She reached up a hand. "I feel like I could almost touch them."

An odd, hauntingly beautiful sound filled the air.

"What is that?" she whispered.

It's the music of the glacier.

She peered over the cliff at the river of ice that gleamed under the light of the two moons. "How?"

In the summer, some of the glacier melts and the water bores holes through the ice, forming pipes. When the wind blows through the pipes, the glacier makes music.

She listened for a while. "It's amazing."

I will always love you, Gwennore, whether we're flooded with rain or shining as brilliant as the stars.

She smiled. "That's lovely. Thank you."

My love for you will burn like an eternal flame deep in my chest.

She stifled a laugh. That sounded like a bad case of heartburn.

I heard that. A puff of smoke shot from his nostrils as he huffed. *You think it's easy to confess how much I love you? You give it a try.*

Should she? He could already hear her thoughts. Did he need her to say the words out loud? "All right. My love for you will last longer than the Kings of the Forest."

He made a rumbling sound in his chest that sounded almost like a purr. *My love for you is like this massive glacier.*

Her mouth twitched. "Icy cold?"

Let me finish. My love is mighty and enduring, powerful enough to wear down any mountain in our way.

"I like that."

And if anything bad tries to bore holes into our love, I'll do like the glacier and use them to make music.

She laughed. "Now you're getting cheesy again."

You love it.

"I do." She leaned against his chest, wiping away a tear of joy. "I can honestly say this is the happiest moment in my entire life."

It's about to get even better.

"How?"

Look up.

As she glanced up, a greenish ribbon of light wavered in the night sky. Mesmerized, she watched as glowing lights of green and purple floated in waves across the sky. "I've never seen anything so beautiful."

This is the life I want to share with you.

"Oh, Silas." She watched until her eyes burned with exhaustion and the music of the glacier lulled her into a sleepy state. As she sagged against Silas's wing, he shifted into human form and caught her before she could fall onto the ground.

She was barely aware of being carried into the cabin. When he set her on a bed, she rolled sleepily onto her side. He removed her slippers. She blinked as she felt him loosening the laces on the back of her gown.

"Silas?" The cabin was too dark for her to see.

"It's all right." He pulled a quilt up to her shoulders. "Get some sleep."

The bed jostled as he stood. She heard him rummaging about, so she turned over to find out what he was doing. Apparently, with his dragon eyes, he was able to see.

Her heart lurched when a burst of fire shot into the fireplace, igniting the logs. As the flames brightened the room, she realized the fire had come from Silas. He was crouched in front of the hearth, naked.

"You started the fire?" she whispered.

He glanced at her. "I didn't want you to get cold."

She swallowed hard as he rose to his feet and turned

away from her. The firelight caused flickering light and shadows to play along his broad back and firm buttocks.

"Get some sleep." He walked to the door and opened it.

The bedsheets rustled as she sat up. "You're leaving?"

He paused, halfway through the door. "You've been through a frightening ordeal, and I know you're tired from working so hard. You probably want to be left alone."

"Won't you be cold outside?"

"I can shift to stay warm." He stepped outside and closed the door with a creak.

Gwennore's heart pounded. She was wide awake now. In a bed large enough for two. How could she leave him outside all night?

She placed her bare feet on the floor and stood. What was she thinking? If she invited him in, they would end up . . .

Did she dare? She spotted a wine bottle on a table across the room and pulled out the cork to take a sip. Could she do this? If she committed herself to Silas, would she endure a life of scorn from the people around her? Or would they learn to accept her? Would they eventually honor and respect her like Silas?

Why was she even thinking about that? She loved Silas. He loved her. Why would she let anything stop her from living the life that she wanted?

She wanted to love Silas. She wanted to love this beautiful country. And most of all, she wanted to love herself.

She was worthy of being loved.

Tears came to her eyes as she realized this was the culmination of her eleven-day adventure. She had learned to trust in herself. She would love Silas, marry him, and someday, she would become the queen of Norveshka.

Her hands trembled as she removed her gown, then lay it across the back of a chair. Wearing nothing but her shift, she opened the door.

The creaking sound made Silas turn his head to the side.

He stopped halfway to the cliff, his naked body gleaming under the light of the two moons.

"You shouldn't spend the night outside in the cold," she said softly.

His hands balled into fists. "Gwen, you don't know how much I want you. If I go inside—"

"I do know." She'd felt it when he'd opened his mind. "I've decided I want to fly. I heard you can take me higher."

He turned slowly, his swollen groin coming into view. "You want me?"

Yes. She stepped back and with one swift move, she pulled her shift over her head. Before it could hit the floor, the door slammed, and Silas was pulling her into his arms.

His mouth covered hers with a devouring kiss that only left her hungry for more. The feel of his bare skin against hers was both glorious and torturous, for even while she loved it, she was instantly greedy for more.

Thank the goddesses, he seemed determined to give her more. After ravaging her mouth, he was kissing her face, her eyes, her neck. His hands caressed her shoulders, smoothed down her back, then cupped her rump to pull her tighter against him.

She gasped, arching her back as his swollen manhood pressed into her lower belly. He seemed so large. How would she ever—her thoughts scattered when he latched on to her breast.

Oh, could anything feel better than this? She moaned as he teased her nipple and flicked his tongue against the hardened tip. His whiskers rubbed against her tender skin, making her itch for more. She tangled her hands into his thick black hair and kissed the top of his head.

He glanced up at her, his eyes gleaming gold in the firelight.

"My dragon," she whispered.

"I want to set you on fire." He paused, the corner of his mouth curling up. "Before you start referring to yourself as a stick of butter, I should add that I didn't mean that literally."

With a smile, she rested a hand on his cheek. "I know. I trust you."

He kissed her brow. "Rule number seven: Once you ignite the flame in a dragon's heart, it will never burn out."

"I like that."

He took her hand and kissed her knuckles. "You have my heart."

"You have mine, too."

He placed her hand on the hard shaft of his manhood, and when she gasped, he lifted his eyebrows with an innocent look.

The rascal. "That's not your heart."

His mouth twitched. "This is me, desperately wanting you."

Her mouth fell open as she felt him growing even harder. And yet the skin was so soft. "Is it all right to touch you like this?"

"Of course." His eyes glittered as he rubbed her hand up and down his shaft. "Sweetheart, I plan to touch you everywhere. Are you ready?"

Her thighs squeezed together as a hot needy feeling gathered between her legs. "Yes."

He swooped her up and deposited her on the bed. Her skin tingled as he looked her over. "Where shall I start?"

When his gaze focused on the dark curls hiding her womanhood, she felt another rush of heat. And an overwhelming, aching desire to open her legs for him.

He sat next to her and placed a finger on her lips. She kissed him, and with a smile, he slipped his finger into her mouth. "Make it wet," he whispered.

The aching need between her legs grew more intense. She ran her tongue around his finger, then he dragged his wet finger down her neck to one of her breasts. He teased the hardened tip, then crossed to the other breast.

She gripped the sheet in her fists as her breathing become more labored. "Silas."

"Yes." He leaned over and suckled her breast.

With a moan, she latched on to his head, digging her fingers into his hair. "I want you."

He lifted his head, looking at her with his gleaming dragon eyes. "You want me touch you?"

She nodded, but his hand was already smoothing across her belly. His fingers reached the curls and she moaned. Could anything feel better than this?

"Your hair is dark like your eyebrows." He rubbed against her gently. "So beautiful."

She nearly cried when he removed his hand. Was he stopping?

He scooted down the bed and gave her toes a quick tug before planting a kiss on each ankle. He smoothed his hands up her legs, then kissed her thighs.

She couldn't bear it anymore. With a sigh, she opened her legs. He tilted his head to look at her private parts.

"You're wet," he whispered. "I can see the moisture gleaming on your pink skin, calling me in."

More heat rushed to her womanly core. "Please." She wasn't sure what she needed so badly, but she was starting to feel frantic.

She cried out when he touched her. His fingers explored, caressed, and stroked her, growing slick with her need. She gripped the sheets in her fists, dug her heels into the bed, and pressed against him. Could anything feel better than this?

When he slipped a finger inside her, her heart lurched. In and out, he dragged the finger, and a whirlwind of sensation swept her up, setting her nerves on fire. She was melting.

"Silas." She panted, unable to catch her breath.

Suddenly he grasped her thighs, spreading them wide as he dipped his head.

She cried out when his mouth came in contact with her wet and swollen core. His tongue dragged over her, then teased an extra-sensitive part that caused her to jerk in response.

He suckled her. The whirlwind swept her up. She was swirling. Spinning. Flying. He was taking her higher.

She hovered for a few delicious seconds, then crashed and shattered, her thoughts and senses completely scattered till all she knew was a sweet throbbing that radiated from her core and sizzled throughout her entire body.

"Gwen?"

She slowly became aware that he was talking to her.

His mouth twitched. "You're back."

Her cheeks grew warm as she suddenly felt a bit embarrassed. "I didn't know it could be like that."

"We're not done, actually."

"No?"

"No. We were just warming up."

"But I already melted."

He gave her an exasperated look. "You can melt again."

"I can't imagine it feeling any better than—"

"It can. Trust me." He settled between her legs.

She gasped when he fondled her with his fingers. Holy goddesses, it still felt so good. She closed her eyes, enjoying the feel of his fingers rubbing against her.

Suddenly his hard shaft pressed against her, and her eyes flew open.

"What—" She winced as he pushed farther in. This wasn't feeling better. She noted with alarm the intense, strained look on his face. "Silas, if you're not enjoying it, you should stop."

He gave her an incredulous look. "I am enjoying it."

"You don't look like—" She cried out when he plunged into her. "Ow." She swatted his shoulder. "That hurt."

He gripped her tightly, his breath warming her shoulder.

"Are you all right?" she whispered.

"Trying to control myself. You feel so good." He kissed her neck. "I'm sorry I hurt you. Are you still in pain?"

"It's a little better." She rubbed her thigh against him. "You had such a fierce look on your face that I thought you were in pain."

He raised himself on his elbows. "I'm trying to control my more beastly urges so I don't hurt you."

"Beastly urges?"

He nodded. "As a man, I know it's your first time, and I should be careful. But the dragon inside me wants to pound into you all night long until you're left breathless, ragged, and completely, totally undone."

She rested a hand on his cheek. "I'm in love with both the man and the dragon."

His eyes gleamed gold. "Then you will have us both." He pulled out a bit, then eased back into her.

After a few slow and gentle thrusts she was ready for more. Ready for the dragon. She wrapped her legs around him, remembering rule number one. *When a dragon takes you for a ride, hold on tight and never let go.*

Silas might have wanted to pound into Gwennore all night, but he'd waited too long. It took all his control to make sure she climaxed before he exploded with the most powerful climax he'd ever experienced.

With a groan, he fell beside her.

Mine. He gathered her in his arms. She was his, and he would never let her go.

"I love you," he whispered, his eyes flickering shut.

"I love you, too."

He smiled as sleep stole over him. His last thought was a hope that he hadn't hurt her.

When the sun shone through a window, he woke to discover they were under the quilt. Sometime in the night, Gwen must have covered them up.

He propped himself up on an elbow and lifted the quilt so he could feast his eyes on her beautiful body.

Her eyes flickered open, her lovely lavender-blue eyes, and he smiled at her.

"Good morning, snookums."

She smiled back, a light blush coloring her cheeks. "Is there a privy around here?"

He nodded. "The forest."

She snorted. "Is there anything to eat?"

He nodded. "You."

"What?"

With a growl, he nuzzled her neck. She squirmed, giggling.

"Stop." She pushed him back with a laugh. "I really need to relieve myself."

He climbed out of bed. "I'll take you outside."

"Naked?"

He grinned. "There's no one around for miles. Come on."

While she relieved herself behind some bushes, he watered a tree.

"Done?" He grabbed her hand and led her farther along the cliff.

"Where are we going?" She shivered as a cool breeze swept past them. "Shouldn't we get dressed?"

"First, we have to bathe." He showed her a pool

of water enclosed in a rock basin, fed by a trickling waterfall.

"Oh, it's lovely." Kneeling down, she dangled her fingers in the water. "Good heavens, it's freezing!"

"Not for long." He eased her back. "Wait here." He took a deep breath and accessed the dragon fire deep inside him. With a whoosh, he blew fire across the surface of the water. After a few minutes, he tested the water and it had warmed enough for them bathe.

He eased into the deepest part of the pool, where the water reached his chest. "Come on."

She slipped in beside him. "Oh, it feels wonderful!" She dunked down so the water came up to her chin, then tilted her head back to rinse out her hair.

He sank underwater, then grabbed her around the waist. As he straightened, he lifted her into the air. She squealed as he spun around, then he let her slip down his body till he could draw her nipple into his mouth.

"Silas." Her fingers delved into his wet hair. "I thought we were going to bathe."

"We are." He grabbed onto her rump to support her. "Wrap your legs around me."

When she did, her womanly parts pressed against his swollen cock. She was probably too sore for intercourse, he thought, but there were other things they could do.

He stroked her gently. "Does that feel all right?"

With a moan, her head fell back. "Silas, I think I'm in heaven."

"Then you'll marry me?"

She gave him a wry look. "You're proposing now?"

"Yes." He rubbed the extra-sensitive nubbin at the top of her sweet folds, and her eyes glazed over. "As you can see, I'll be a very attentive husband."

She moaned.

"Was that a yes?"

"More," she whispered, pressing herself against his hand.

He stroked and fondled her, enjoying the different expressions that flitted across her face as she neared her climax, then shattered in his arms.

As her breathing returned to normal, he nuzzled her neck. "Are you going to answer my question?"

"Hmm." She smoothed a hand down his chest. "There's something I need to know first."

He grew tense. "What?"

"Is there a way for me to be equally attentive?" She curled a hand around his swollen cock.

He hissed in a breath. "Yes, actually."

She gently rubbed her hand up and down the shaft. "Can you tell me how?"

"You're doing quite well—" He gritted his teeth. "Does this mean you'll marry me?"

She gave him a squeeze. "I'm not hurting you, am I?"

"No. You still haven't answered—oh, hell." He grabbed her hand and guided her into a more aggressive approach. "You can use your mouth, too. Licking. Sucking."

"Yes."

"Excellent." He lifted himself onto the rocky ledge at the edge of the pool so his cock was exposed. "Go ahead."

Her eyes widened as she looked at his erection.

"Gwen?"

She leaned over to kiss his cock. "I said yes."

"Huh?"

Her eyes twinkled with humor. "Yes, I'll marry you."

"Yes!" He jumped into the water and pulled her into an embrace. As her sweet body pressed against him, he stiffened, then with a shout, he climaxed.

She held on to him until he grew calm once more.

"Gwen." He patted her rump. "You naughty girl. You paid me back."

She grinned. "We are well matched, aren't we?"

He kissed her brow. "I'm not sure what will happen when we go back. But we need to stand strong and face it together."

She nodded. "Together."

Chapter Thirty-One

❧

Silas contacted Dimitri as he drew near to Draven Castle. *We're returning. Is it safe for Gwennore?*

Yes. The king rescinded the warrant for her arrest. We'll meet you in Karlan's office.

Did you hear that? Silas asked Gwen, who was cradled in his forelegs.

"Yes."

Silas could hear her thoughts, so he knew she was relieved, but still worried about the crowd who had demanded her death. *Everything will be fine. We'll announce our betrothal—*

"I think we should wait till after the queen's funeral."

All right. He swooped down to the grassy clearing by the cabin. *You should close off your mind now.*

After they landed, he dressed in the cabin while she erected her mental shield. Then they walked toward the castle, hand in hand.

In the hallway outside Karlan's office, Margosha, Annika, and Olenka were waiting with the dog Brody. He gave a yelp as he trotted toward them.

"Gwen!" Annika ran toward her, followed by the other ladies. "Thank the Light! We were so worried about you."

"I'm fine." Gwen smiled as she encompassed in a group hug. When Brody barked, she gave him a hug, too.

Silas cleared this throat. "I'm feeling fine, too, in case anyone is wondering."

Annika laughed. "That's good. Thank you for rescuing Gwen."

Margosha patted Gwen's shoulder. "There's no need for you to fret. The king has changed his mind—"

"You mean we changed it for him," Olenka boasted. "I told His Majesty that my dear friend would never harm anyone."

Gwen's eyes widened. "You stood up for me?"

"We all did," Karlan said from the open doorway of his office.

Dimitri stepped into the hallway. "I wasn't going to let my cousin be falsely arrested."

Gwen's eyes glimmered with tears as she looked over her friends. "Thank you."

Silas took her hand. "Soon everyone in the country will love you." He leaned close. "But you're mine first."

She beamed at him. "I've always wished for a place where I could be loved for who I am."

Dimitri cleared his throat. "We need to talk. Now."

When Brody trotted into the office, Dimitri glanced inside. "Shit. Don't come in now. He's shifting."

"I have a spare uniform I can give him," Karlan muttered as he went inside.

"Is something wrong?" Silas asked.

"Yes." Dimitri glanced inside once more. "We can go in now."

After Silas and Gwen went inside, the other ladies tried to follow them.

Dimitri lifted a hand to stop them. "Official business."

"But I'm on your side," Olenka protested.

"Lady Olenka," Silas said. "Gwen and I haven't eaten

since yesterday. Would you mind bringing us some food?"

"We would be delighted." Margosha dragged Olenka off.

Annika stayed put, glaring at Dimitri.

He stared back.

She stepped close, lifting her chin. "Are you letting me in?"

Dimitri frowned at her. "I assume you're referring to the office."

She huffed. "What if I mean you?"

He clenched his fists. "We'll discuss that later."

"Why?" She scowled at him. "Haven't I waited long enough?"

Silas cleared his throat. "We're not announcing it publicly till after Her Majesty's funeral, but Gwen and I are getting married."

Annika squealed and dashed into the office to give Gwen a hug. "That's wonderful! I'm so happy for you."

Gwen laughed. "After I'm married, you'll be my cousin. And Sorcha will be a real sister."

Silas gave Dimitri a smirk.

He tugged at his collar, then followed them inside and closed the door.

Gwen and Annika sat in the chairs in front of Karlan's desk, while Silas leaned over, propping his elbows on the back of Gwen's chair. Brody was behind the desk, now wearing breeches and buttoning a shirt.

"My thanks to everyone for convincing the king to rescind his order," Silas began. "How is His Majesty?"

With a sigh, Karlan sat behind his desk. "He's distraught. Not eating. Not sleeping. Not leaving the queen's side."

"The queen's body is in her bedchamber," Dimitri added as he leaned against a wall. "The priest wants to move her to the chapel so her body can lie in state before the funeral, but the king doesn't seem to even hear him."

Annika nodded. "It's very sad. When we went there to defend Gwennore, he broke into tears and said there had been enough death." She gave Gwen a worried look. "That's when he withdrew the order. He seems very confused right now, so I can't tell if he's entirely convinced of your innocence. He did believe that the tea we made was helping."

"I see," Gwen said.

"That was last night." Dimitri frowned. "This morning, when I checked on him, he was babbling nonsense."

Silas straightened. "What was he saying?"

"He kept repeating the story about how Fafnir had saved the lives of our ancestors by giving them a piece of his dragon heart. Now the king thinks Fafnir should be able to do the same for his late wife."

Silas sighed. His brother was becoming more delusional.

"A dragon gave away a part of his heart?" Gwen asked.

"That was five hundred years ago, when the mine collapsed on the seven brothers," Silas explained. "When the bodies were extracted from the mountain, King Magnus discovered the youngest five had survived. Barely. He begged the Ancient Ones to save his sons, but the dragons refused. Then one dragon, Fafnir, agreed. He gave the brothers his blood and a piece of his heart."

Gwen twisted in her chair to look at him. "And that is how you became dragon shifters?"

Silas nodded. "It was a great shock to their bodies, and two of the brothers died. Only the youngest three survived, and they soon learned that they were dragon shifters. Their sons and grandsons were also born with the ability."

"They didn't see any point in remaining slaves to the

Ancient Ones," Dimitri continued the story. "So they rebelled."

"That was the Great Dragon War," Annika added. "When the Ancient Ones were dying off, they put a curse on the three clans."

"But Fafnir is still alive?" Brody asked. "After five hundred years?"

Silas sighed. "I'm not convinced it is Fafnir. He's living in secret at the Sacred Well and only appears to the king. At first, I was worried my brother was delusional, because I went to the Sacred Well and no one was there. But then I learned that it was Fafnir who gave my brother the poisoned rings for Queen Freya."

Karlan frowned. "So Fafnir is real."

Silas shrugged. "Any rogue dragon shifter could claim to be an Ancient One. Whoever this Fafnir is, he's been trying to manipulate my brother into invading Woodwyn and declaring war on Eberon and Tourin."

Karlan exchanged a look with Dimitri. "That sounds like what His Majesty was talking about this morning. He thinks Fafnir will revive his wife if he attacks Tourin and takes their queen."

"Brigitta?" Brody looked alarmed. "Why her?"

"I heard something similar," Silas admitted. "I thought it strange that a dragon would be interested in a human female. And that's when it occurred to me that this dragon could actually be—"

"The Chameleon." Brody's eyes lit up. "When the bastard was in Tourin, he wanted Brigitta for himself."

Gwen winced. "Holy goddesses, he still wants her."

"What is this Sacred Well?" Brody asked Silas. "Did you notice anything odd when you went there?"

"It's a cave with a boiling-hot spring. The stream that runs from the spring is hot enough to kill a human, but not a dragon. So it was the place where the Ancient Ones would gather. Other than the large cavern, there are a few tunnels and rooms. I found a pallet and some clothes." Silas thought back. "A rat ran past me."

Brody nodded. "That could have been him. If I go with you, I'll be able to detect his scent."

"All right," Silas agreed. "It won't take long for us to fly there."

"What will you do if you find him?" Gwen asked.

Brody's fists clenched. "He's escaped me twice. I'm not letting him get away again."

"I'll roast him with dragon fire," Silas said.

Dimitri shook his head. "If he's a dragon, he'll be impervious to fire."

"But he might be the Chameleon," Brody argued. "If he is, then he's only taking on a dragon form. He won't automatically have all the powers that come with it."

"You don't think he can breathe fire?" Silas asked.

Brody shrugged. "I doubt it. I know I wouldn't be able to. Just because I can look and fly like an eagle, it doesn't mean I can lay an egg. Does this Sacred Well have any weapons we can use?"

Silas shook his head. "No. It's considered a holy place."

"We should ride there," Dimitri suggested as he pushed off from the wall. "Then we can bring weapons with us."

"I'll see to the horses." Karlan dashed out the door.

Margosha and Olenka brought in trays of food.

Silas handed Gwen a loaf of bread, then took one for himself.

"I want to go, too," Annika said.

"Go where?" Olenka asked as she filled cups with wine.

"You're not going," Dimitri muttered.

Annika turned to him. "I'm a soldier, too."

"I'm not putting you at risk," Dimitri growled.

"That should be my decision," Annika insisted.

"Do you think I could live if anything happened to you?" Dimitri shouted. When Annika's mouth fell open, he grabbed her arm and dragged her into the hallway.

A thud sounded against the wall.

Olenka slapped a hand over her mouth to keep from giggling.

Silas peered out the doorway and spotted his best friend and cousin locked in a passionate kiss. With a grin, he shut the door. "We'll leave them alone for a moment."

Gwen smiled as she buttered her bread.

"Are you going somewhere dangerous?" Margosha asked as she passed him a cup of wine.

"Maybe." Silas downed the cup.

"Where is this Sacred Well?" Brody asked. When Silas shot him an annoyed look, he shrugged. "You said it was a holy place. It's not a secret, is it?"

"It can be dangerous," Margosha said. "The dragons are protected from the hot spring with their scales, but a person would be burned to death."

Silas nodded. "That's why only Dimitri, Brody, and myself will go."

Gwen gave him a worried look. "Be careful."

Silas smiled at her. "Nothing will keep me from coming back to you."

After seeing Silas off, Gwennore was too worried to follow his suggestion that she take a nap. Annika seemed just as worried, so Gwennore offered to keep her company in the workroom.

The group of women took the trays of food upstairs and sat around a worktable, eating and speculating on who the Chameleon could really be.

"Maybe he's not even human!" Olenka announced.

Annika snorted. "What would he be then? A fish?"

Gwennore sipped some wine. "He seems to be fluent in several languages."

Margosha nodded. "And if he's masquerading as Fafnir, then he knows about our history and culture."

The door opened and Aleksi sauntered inside. "Good afternoon."

Gwennore smiled at him. "You're back."

He nodded. "Just now." He wandered over to the table and helped himself to a hunk of cheese. "Your tonic has become very popular in Vorushka. Lots of people want to try it."

"That's good news." Gwennore filled a wooden cup with wine and handed to Aleksi. "Did Karlan tell you what was happening?"

"Yes," Aleksi grumbled. "I can't believe they left without me."

Annika snorted. "I feel the same way."

Aleksi downed the cup of wine, then slammed it on the table. "I'm tempted to go there myself."

"I'll go with you," Annika offered.

Suddenly the door burst open and King Petras stumbled into the room, his eyes wild and unfocused.

Everyone jumped to their feet so they could curtsy or bow. "Your Majesty," they all murmured.

Petras looked around for a moment as if he wasn't sure where he was, then his gaze fell on Gwennore. "You."

She bowed her head. "Your Majesty, I am so terribly sorry for your loss—"

"Then do something!" He stalked toward her. "You're a healer, aren't you? You can bring her back!"

Gwennore swallowed hard. "Your Majesty, it grieves me to say this, but Her Majesty has—"

"She's not dead!" Petras screamed. "She's just sleeping." He motioned toward the hearth. "You can cook up some sort of concoction. Hurry!"

"Your Majesty, there's nothing—" Gwennore stopped when the king fell to his knees. Her heart ached at the raw despair on his face.

"I'll give you anything," Petras whispered. "You can marry my brother. You can be the next queen."

Tears burned her eyes. "I'm so sorry, but there's nothing I can do."

He hefted himself to his feet. "Then I'll have to do whatever Fafnir tells me to do. I'll have to go to him."

"Your Majesty." Aleksi stepped toward him. "This isn't a good time to go there."

"Why not?" Petras looked around the room, his gaze growing more frantic. "Silas. Where is Silas?"

Gwennore winced.

"Where is he?" Petras shouted.

Olenka bowed her head. "He went to the Sacred Well, Your Majesty."

"No!" Petras backed toward the door. "No, he'll chase Fafnir away!" He ran outside.

Aleksi leaned into the hallway, then glanced back at them. "His Majesty is headed up the stairs. I'm going to follow him."

"I'm going, too!" Annika dashed off with Aleksi.

Gwennore hesitated. Was Petras headed to the roof so he could shift and fly to the Sacred Well? If so, he might arrive before Silas, Dimitri, and Brody. She chased after Aleksi and Annika.

"Be careful!" Margosha called after her.

Gwennore darted up the stairs. When she reached the roof, she saw a dragon taking off. Petras.

"I'll go after him." Aleksi unfastened his sword belt and dropped it. As he unbuttoned his shirt, Annika turned her back to him and put on his belt.

"I'll go with you," she said. "And bring your weapon."

"I need to go, too." Gwennore picked up Aleksi's discarded breeches. When she glanced up, a dragon was waiting impatiently beside them.

"Come on!" Annika climbed onto his shoulders and pulled Gwennore up in front of her. "Grab on to his neck."

Gwennore held on tight as Aleksi ran down the rooftop, then launched. His wings beat the air, and they lifted higher and higher, headed north.

She lowered her mental shield. *Thank you, Aleksi.*

He made a huffing noise. *Silas is going to be pissed.*

Then why are you doing this? she asked him mentally.

I don't like being left out. When we get there, take cover and stay safe, or the general will have my hide.

I understand. Gwennore put her shield back up, so Aleksi wouldn't know how afraid she was that something terrible was about to happen.

Chapter Thirty-Two

❧

What the hell? Silas pulled his horse to a stop when he spotted Gwen and Annika at the entrance to the Sacred Well.

Beside him, Dimitri muttered a curse. Brody looked worried as he slipped into the woods to undress and shift.

Silas jumped off his horse and ran toward the women. "What the hell are you—" He stopped when Gwen put a finger to her lips.

"Not so loud," she whispered. "I heard there's a huge opening at the top of the cavern. If you keep screaming, they might—"

"I'm not screaming," he growled.

"How the hell did you get here?" Dimitri demanded, glaring at Annika.

"Aleksi brought us," Annika replied, then lifted a hand when his eyes flared gold. "Don't get mad at him. We insisted on coming. And he insisted we wait out here."

"We wanted to warn you that His Majesty is here." Gwen patted Brody's head as he sat beside her in dog form. "The king went into a panic when he found out that you were headed here. He shifted—"

"Petras is inside?" Silas motioned to the cave. "Where is Aleksi?"

"The king and Fafnir are in the main cavern," Annika explained. "Aleksi's inside a little way, spying on them. And you won't believe it! He thinks the dragon really is Fafnir. He saw it speaking out loud just like the Ancient Ones could do."

Silas considered this new piece of information. While it was true that the dragon shifters could only communicate mentally with one another, the Ancient Ones had actually been able to speak. "So it's not a dragon shifter." He glanced at Brody. "Could it still be the Chameleon? Would he be able to talk in dragon form?"

The dog hesitated, then gave them a sheepish look. "Maybe."

Silas stiffened with surprise. He'd expected the dog to nod or shake his head.

With a gasp, Gwen fell to her knees. "Brody? You can talk?"

"Holy Light," Annika whispered. "That looked so strange."

"Brody." Gwen touched the shaggy ruff of fur around his neck. "I've known you for years. Why have you never said anything?"

"Not easy," he rasped. "Impossible when I'm a bird."

Silas scoffed. "A talking dog."

Brody gave him an annoyed look, then motioned with his snout toward the cave entrance. "We should go."

"Do you smell the Chameleon?" Silas asked and Brody nodded.

"My sisters will be shocked," Gwen whispered. "Especially Maeve."

"Don't tell her," Brody growled. "Let's go." He trotted into the cave.

As Dimitri started to follow the dog, Silas stopped him. "I want you to shift and stand guard at the opening on top. If the Chameleon tries to escape that way, roast him. Since he's not really a dragon, we should be able to burn him."

"Got it." Dimitri unbuckled his sword belt and handed it to Annika. "Use it if you need to, but stay out of trouble." He rushed into the woods, tearing off clothes as he climbed the hill to the top of the cave.

Annika paused for only a moment, then followed him, and Dimitri's curse filtered down the hillside.

"Stay here," Silas warned Gwen as he handed her a dagger from his boot. "I'll send Aleksi to help you guard this entrance. If you see anything run outside, like a rat, it could be the Chameleon trying to escape. You'll have to kill it."

She nodded, her face pale. "I understand. Be careful."

"You, too." He touched her face, then hurried down the tunnel, his dragon eyes adjusting quickly to the dark.

He found Aleksi, dressed only in breeches and a sword belt, hovering close to the main cavern. "Go," he whispered. "I want you to guard the entrance. And keep Gwen safe."

Aleksi reluctantly backed toward the entrance.

Silas inched forward till he was at the edge of the cavernous room. Brody was hunched down, peering around a rock.

"I told you to trust no one but me," a raspy voice carried toward them.

Silas peeked around the rock wall to see inside. Steam and the stench of rotten eggs rose from the bubbling cauldron of the Sacred Well in the middle of the main room. The boiling-hot stream bisected the room as it made its way down the tunnel and out the main entrance. On the far side of the stream, he spotted a dragon and his brother.

Petras had shifted to human form, and he was kneeling in front of the dragon.

"Forgive me, I beg you!" Petras cried as he prostrated his naked body on the ground. "I'll do whatever you say if you'll just save my wife!"

"You have failed me," the dragon grumbled. "You should have attacked Tourin by now. You should have brought me their queen!"

Silas unsheathed his sword as he stepped into the room. "Why would a dragon want a human female?"

The dragon whipped around to glare at him.

Petras jumped to his feet. "Silas! Get out of here. You'll ruin everything. Fafnir's going to help me!"

"He's not Fafnir." Silas edged toward the Sacred Well. Once he made it around the boiling cauldron to the other side, he could protect his brother and attack the dragon. "He's only pretending to—"

"He's Fafnir!" Petras cried.

"I told you we couldn't trust your brother," the dragon hissed.

"He is Fafnir!" Petras yelled at Silas. "He has to be." Tears glimmered in his eyes. "It's the only way I can save Freya."

The dragon lowered its neck, angling its head toward Petras. "I will save her if you kill him."

Petras flinched.

"Kill him," the dragon hissed. "Breathe your fire on him."

"You do it!" Silas lifted his arms to side. "If you're truly Fafnir, prove it. Roast me!"

"Silas, no!" Petras started to run toward him, but the dragon knocked the king down with a swipe of its wing, then pinned him.

"He's mine," the dragon hissed.

"Release him!" Silas circled the Sacred Well and aimed a stream of fire at the dragon, forcing him back.

Petras scrambled away.

"You see, Petras?" Silas helped his brother to his feet. "He's not a dragon. He retreats from fire and he can't breathe it."

"Not a dragon?" Petras stared at the false Fafnir with a confused look.

Brody emerged from behind the rock, growling as he approached the stream.

The dragon reared up, baring its teeth. "You again. I'll kill you this time."

Brody shifted into a large wildcat and leaped across the stream. As he charged toward the Chameleon, the dragon also shifted into a wildcat.

The two beasts leaped at each other, meeting in mid-air with swiping claws and gnashing teeth. They hit the ground, rolling.

"What?" Petras stumbled. "He—he's a cat now?"

Silas steadied him. "He's a Chameleon—"

"He tricked me!" Petras trembled as horrified rage swept over his face. "The bastard tricked me!" He ran toward the fighting cats, shooting fire at them.

"No!" Silas pulled him back, but it was too late.

The cats howled in pain as their fur caught fire. They rolled on the ground, forgetting their battle as they desperately tried to snuff out the flames. One stopped, breathing heavily as it lay on its side, while the other rose slowly to its feet.

Which one was Brody?

The one limping toward them shifted into Brody in his human form.

Silas hesitated. Was it Brody or was the Chameleon tricking them? He pointed his sword at him. "Identify yourself."

"That one has to be the Chameleon!" Petras pointed at the second wildcat and ran toward it. "I'll kill him myself."

As he passed by Brody, he was seized in a fierce grip. "I should have never relied on a fool like you." The false Brody shifted into a likeness of Petras. "I should have killed you and taken your place months ago."

Petras grew pale.

Silas aimed his sword at the Chameleon. "Release him."

The Chameleon moved the real Petras in front of him, an arm crooked around his neck. "You can't breathe fire on me without roasting your brother first."

Silas watched, helpless, as the Chameleon backed away, dragging his brother. If he mentally called for help from Dimitri or Aleksi, would the Chameleon kill his brother? He played for time while he tried to figure out what to do. "Why didn't you replace the king months ago?"

"I was already controlling him, along with Romak." The Chameleon sneered. "And I was waiting for his damned wife to die. I thought she would know if I took his place."

"You—you wanted Freya to die?" Petras whispered.

"Of course." The Chameleon snorted. "I kept giving you poisoned rings for her, but the bitch was taking forever to keel over."

"No!" Petras struggled, but the Chameleon shifted one of his hands into a giant bear paw with sharp claws that dug into the king's neck.

"Stop!" Silas stepped forward,

The Chameleon gave him an annoyed look. "Why couldn't you do as the king ordered you? You were supposed to invade Tourin for me and get Brigitta. You were supposed to die in battle, dammit, but you kept surviving. I'll just have to kill you now. Along with this worthless king." He shoved Petras into the boiling stream.

Petras's scream echoed throughout the cavern as Silas ran toward him.

"No!" Silas grabbed a flailing hand and hauled his brother out of the stream. Most of Petras's body was a hideous red, all the skin burned away. "Shift! If you shift, maybe you can—"

Dammit to hell! His brother would never survive this. Silas grabbed his sword and leaped toward the Chameleon, but the false Petras shifted into an eagle and flew toward the opening.

"Dimitri!" Silas shouted, and a stream of fire shot down, engulfing the eagle in flames.

With a shriek, the bird fell to the ground.

Good riddance. Silas turned his attention back to his brother. "Petras." He knelt beside him. "Can you shift?"

A rattling sound came from Petras's chest as he struggled to breathe.

Aleksi and Gwen ran into the cavern.

"We heard screaming," Gwen cried as they rounded the Sacred Well to join him.

"Your Majesty!" Aleksi fell onto his knees by Petras.

"Can you help him?" Silas asked Gwen.

She turned pale with a horrified look as her gaze ran over the king's burned body. "I—I don't think . . . I'm sorry, but . . ." Her eyes glimmered with tears. "Silas, he doesn't have any skin left except for that one hand."

Silas clung to Petras's hand as his heart clenched in his chest. There was nothing he could do to help his brother.

Gwen touched his shoulder. "Silas, I'm sorry."

I should have protected him better. I should have . . .

"Petras," Silas whispered, wishing he could at least take away some of the pain.

A moan sounded across the cavern as Brody shifted

back into human form. He lay on his side, one of his legs red with welts.

"Brody!" Gwen ran toward him.

He winced. "I'll be all right."

Dimitri, dressed only in half-buttoned breeches, ran into the cavern with Annika. "Did I hit him? Did I—" He halted with a jerk when he saw the king. "Your Majesty."

Annika gasped and covered her mouth.

Dimitri approached slowly. "How . . . ?"

"The Chameleon pushed him into the stream." Silas motioned toward the burned eagle lying in a smoldering heap on the ground. "You hit him good."

Suddenly a burst of flames erupted from the eagle, and a huge bird with glimmering green and purple feathers rose from a pile of ashes.

"No!" Brody struggled to stand.

Silas ran at the bird, swinging his sword and shooting fire. With a screech, the bird shot through the opening above them.

Dammit. Silas debated shifting into a dragon to follow the Chameleon, but he hated to leave his dying brother. "Aleksi, Dimitri, go after him. Roast him!"

Brody lifted a hand to stop them. "It's no use. You can't kill him with fire. He figured out how to shift into a phoenix. He'll keep rising from the ashes."

"You mean we can't kill him?" Dimitri demanded.

Brody winced, obviously still in pain. "Not with fire, but we should be able to stab him to death. If we can ever catch the damned bastard."

"Silas," Petras moaned.

Silas knelt beside him, taking hold of his uninjured hand. "I'm here. We'll take you back to the castle."

"I—I want to be with Freya."

"Don't say that!" Silas squeezed his brother's hand. "You have to fight this, Petras. You're still the king."

"You'll be a better king than I ever was," Petras whispered. "I failed—"

"Stop it," Silas growled. "I'm going to shift and carry you back. I'll take care of you." His brother's eyes flickered shut and his hand went limp. "Petras? Petras!"

Annika covered her face as a sob escaped.

"Petras!" Silas yelled, grabbing his brother's face. "Don't do this! Don't leave me!"

Dimitri and Aleksi knelt, bowing their heads. "Your Majesty."

Were they referring to him? Silas shook his head. "No! I don't want to hear it."

Gwen sat beside him, wrapping her arms around him. "I'm so sorry."

Silas fell back onto his rump. No, this wasn't how it was supposed to happen. The Chameleon was still alive, and his brother was dead? "No."

"I'm so sorry," Gwen repeated with tears streaming down her face.

He pulled her into his arms and glanced at his friends and family. They were watching him sadly, waiting for him to take charge. Dammit.

Slowly, he hefted himself to his feet. "Dimitri, please shift and take the late king's body back to the chapel at Draven Castle. A closed casket for him and his queen. Make arrangements with the priest to bury them tomorrow."

"Yes, Your Majesty," Dimitri murmured.

"Aleksi, shift and take Brody back," Silas ordered. "Take Annika with you, so she can treat his wounds."

"Yes, Your Majesty," Aleksi and Annika replied.

"I could treat him," Gwen suggested.

"Annika knows how to do it." Silas took Gwen's hand. "You and I will ride back together. I need that time to . . .

adjust. By the time we arrive at the castle, I'll be ready to assume my duties."

With a last tearful glance at his brother, Silas led Gwen through the tunnel to the entrance. Grief struck him hard, causing a jabbing pain in his heart. He doubled over, pressing a hand to his chest.

Dammit to hell. Tears burned his eyes. He was a failure. He'd failed to kill the Chameleon. He'd failed to save his brother and the queen.

"Silas." She leaned over to look at his face. "Are you in pain?"

"Gwen." He slowly straightened. A tear rolled down his cheek. "I failed."

"Don't say that." She cradled his face with her hands. "The Chameleon wanted to take over Norveshka and use its army and dragons to destroy the rest of the mainland. He was planning to take over the entire world."

Silas nodded. "Along with the Circle of Five."

"We stopped them," Gwen insisted. "This has to be a huge setback for them."

She was making a good point. He wiped his face dry, then continued toward the entrance of the cave.

As they stepped outside into the bright sunlight, Silas spotted Dimitri and Aleksi in dragon form, flying out of the opening at the top of the cavern. His brother's body was on its way back to Draven Castle.

"Come on." He led Gwen toward the horses.

"Are you feeling better now?"

"My heart is still hurting." He pulled her into his arms. "Can my beloved healer take care of that?"

She held him tight. "There may be a scar left for years to come, but you will feel better. It will take time and a lot of love."

"I do love you, Gwen. I love you so much."

"I know." She touched his face and looked up at him, her beautiful lavender-blue eyes glimmering with love and tears. "I will love you through good times and bad. Whether we're soaked with rain or reaching for the stars."

He took a deep breath. "We're going to be king and queen from now on. Will you be all right with that?"

She nodded. "We can do it. As long as we're together."

He kissed her brow. "Together."

Epilogue

A cheer rang through the courtyard as Gwennore exited the chapel with her newly wedded husband. She and Silas had ended up having their wedding and coronation all at once in order to assure the Norveshki people that life would continue as usual.

Better than usual, Gwennore thought. For Silas had already arranged for a truce with Woodwyn and signed peace treaties with the royal houses of Eberon and Tourin. Those treaties had been easy to manage since the kings and queens of Eberon and Tourin were currently at Draven Castle for the wedding and coronation.

When the courtiers had realized the connections that Gwennore had, in addition to being an elfin princess, they had started singing her praises. They still considered her a witch, but a good one, who was going to bring fertility back to their country and save them all.

Gwennore glanced back and grinned at her bridesmaids—Sorcha, Annika, Maeve, and Olenka. Eviana had served as a flower girl, while Eric and Reynfrid had carried in the newly crafted crowns.

The troll chieftain had come with a few from his tribe, and they'd brought several barrels of mead.

Gwennore slanted an admiring glance at her husband, gorgeous as always in the green-and-brown uniform he still insisted on wearing. The crown on his head was much like hers—a simple circlet of gold with one emerald in front. The jewels from the old crowns had been used to help the poor and buy supplies to make more tonic.

As Silas took her hand to lead her up the stairs to a balcony where they could address the crowd, he leaned close to whisper, "Rule number eight: There is only one mate for a dragon, and he will love her forever."

She smiled. "That's a good one."

"It's true. My heart is yours."

"I'll take excellent care of your extra-large heart." She squeezed his hand. "But we're married now. I think you can stop inventing rules for dating."

"You're right." His green eyes glittered with humor. "Now I plan to come up with Eight Simple Positions for Making Love."

She laughed. The rascal. "Eight?"

"We can do it. We just have to stay positive."

"I believe you."

He grinned. "I'm thinking we can do four tonight."

The next morning, Gwennore met her sisters and Annika for breakfast in Luciana's sitting room. It gladdened her heart to see how close Sorcha was becoming to her cousin and her brother. She knew it was helping Silas to have his sister here.

Annika snorted when Gwennore sat at the table. "I'm surprised you're awake this early."

"Really," Sorcha agreed. "We thought you would be asleep all day."

Gwennore shook her head, smiling. Now she had two outspoken redheads who enjoyed pestering her.

"Don't mind them," Maeve said as she slipped the dog Brody a slice of bacon. One of Brody's back legs had been slathered with ointment and wrapped in gauze for a week, but it was much better now. "We're really happy for you."

"And so proud of you," Luciana added.

Brigitta shuddered. "I hate it that the Chameleon managed to escape."

With a whimper, Brody slunk under a chair.

"Look what you did." Maeve gave Brigitta a sour look. "You hurt Julia's feelings."

"Julia?" Annika looked at Brody and laughed.

He flopped down, covering his ears with his paws.

Gwennore gave him a wry look. How shocked her sisters would be if they knew he could talk!

"I hear you're getting married soon?" Luciana asked Annika.

With a grin, she nodded. "Next week." She elbowed her cousin Sorcha. "Your turn is next."

Sorcha shrugged. "Not interested."

Gwennore scoffed. She knew Sorcha had wanted to meet someone special for years now.

"Let's see what the Telling Stones will say!" Maeve ran to a trunk and pulled out a linen bag.

"No, no." Sorcha waved her hands. "I don't want to know my future."

"What are you afraid of?" Maeve emptied the stones into a wooden bowl. "Everything turned out wonderfully well for Luciana, Brigitta, and Gwennore. I'm sure it will be the same for you."

Annika fingered the colored and numbered stones. "You use these to predict the future?"

"Luciana does," Sorcha grumbled. "She's right so often that it's downright scary."

"It sounds exciting!" Annika pushed the bowl toward her cousin. "Do it."

Sorcha glared at her. "You do it."

"I already know my future." Annika shoved the bowl toward Luciana. "Will you pick them then?"

Luciana gave Sorcha a questioning look.

"What the hell," Sorcha growled. "Go ahead."

Luciana closed her eyes as she reached into the bowl and grabbed a few stones. She opened her hand, and everyone leaned forward to see the pebbles nestled in her palm.

Lavender, white, and five.

"What do they mean?" Annika asked.

Luciana studied them, her face drawing into a frown.

"Dammit," Sorcha grumbled. "I knew it. It's going to be bad news."

"It's not bad!" Maeve insisted. "It's obvious. In five days Sorcha will meet a tall and handsome stranger."

"That's what the five stands for?" Annika asked.

Maeve shrugged. "Or it could mean he'll have five fingers on each hand and five toes on each foot."

Sorcha snorted. "That really narrows the playing field."

Brigitta laughed. "Maybe it means you'll curse at him in five different ways."

Sorcha nodded. "Now, that one I can believe."

Gwennore swallowed hard. What if it referred to the Circle of Five?

"What does the lavender and white mean?" Annika asked.

"He'll be wearing a pretty lavender shirt," Maeve said. "And lavender breeches."

"And he'll be eighty years old with snowy-white hair," Brigitta added.

Gwennore eyed the stones with an uneasy feeling. Was no one realizing that an elfin man might have white-blond hair and lavender eyes? When she lifted her gaze, she found Luciana staring at her. At her own white-blond hair and lavender-blue eyes.

Luciana set the stones down. "I'm sorry. I'm not seeing anything."

Gwennore suspected she was, but didn't want to frighten anyone. She touched Sorcha's arm. "I'm sure your future will be everything you ever hoped it would be."

Sorcha turned toward her, smiling. "We're real sisters now that you married my brother."

Gwennore nodded, smiling back. "Are you going to live here now?"

Sorcha glanced at their oldest sister, Luciana. "I'm not sure."

"You're Norveshki," Annika insisted. "You should live here with Gwennore and me."

"I suppose," Sorcha said. "But I'll miss my other sisters."

Gwennore nodded. "I know what you mean. I'm going to miss everyone so much."

Brigitta sighed. "It's the price we pay for being queens."

Luciana smiled. "We'll visit one another often. And remember, it's always good to be queen."